Julia James lives in Engl
peaceful verdant countrys
of Cornwall. She also love
so rich in myth and history, with its sunbaked
landscapes and olive groves, ancient ruins and
azure seas. 'The perfect setting for romance!' she
says. 'Rivalled only by the lush tropical heat of
the Caribbean—palms swaying by a silver sand
beach lapped by turquoise water… What more
could lovers want?'

Millie Adams is the very dramatic pseudonym of
New York Times bestselling author Maisey Yates.
Happiest surrounded by yarn, her family and the
small woodland creatures she calls pets, she lives
in a small house on the edge of the woods, which
allows her to escape in the way she loves best—
in the pages of a book. She loves intense alpha
heroes and the women who dare to go toe-to-toe
with them.

Also by Julia James

Contracted as the Italian's Bride
The Heir She Kept from the Billionaire
Greek's Temporary Cinderella
Vows of Revenge
Accidental One-Night Baby

Also by Millie Adams

Italian's Christmas Acquisition
His Highness's Diamond Decree

The Diamond Club collection

Greek's Forbidden Temptation

Work Wives to Billionaires' Wives collection

Billionaire's Bride Bargain

Discover more at millsandboon.co.uk.

LOVE TO HATE HIM

JULIA JAMES

MILLIE ADAMS

MILLS & BOON

All rights reserved including the right of reproduction in whole or in part in any form. This edition is published by arrangement with Harlequin Enterprises ULC.

This is a work of fiction. Names, characters, places, locations and incidents are purely fictional and bear no relationship to any real life individuals, living or dead, or to any actual places, business establishments, locations, events or incidents. Any resemblance is entirely coincidental.

Without limiting the author's and publisher's exclusive rights, any unauthorized use of this publication to train generative artificial intelligence (AI) technologies is expressly prohibited. HarperCollins also exercise their rights under Article 4(3) of the Digital Single Market Directive 2019/790 and expressly reserve this publication from the text and data mining exception.

® and TM are trademarks owned and used by the trademark owner and/or its licensee. Trademarks marked with ® are registered with the United Kingdom Patent Office and/or the Office for Harmonisation in the Internal Market and in other countries.

First published in Great Britain 2025
by Mills & Boon, an imprint of HarperCollins*Publishers* Ltd,
1 London Bridge Street, London, SE1 9GF

www.harpercollins.co.uk

HarperCollins*Publishers*, Macken House, 39/40 Mayor Street Upper, Dublin 1, D01 C9W8, Ireland

Love to Hate Him © 2025 Harlequin Enterprises ULC

Marriage Made in Hate © 2025 Julia James

After-Hours Heir © 2025 Millie Adams

ISBN: 978-0-263-34470-7

07/25

This book contains FSC™ certified paper
and other controlled sources to ensure responsible forest management.

For more information visit www.harpercollins.co.uk/green.

Printed and Bound in the UK using 100% Renewable Electricity
at CPI Group (UK) Ltd, Croydon, CR0 4YY

MARRIAGE MADE IN HATE

JULIA JAMES

MILLS & BOON

To all those affected by cancer—
and to the day when every patient is curable.

May that not be long.

CHAPTER ONE

BIANCA AWOKE, FISTS CLENCHED, seething with fury. Damn, she'd had that dream again—the one that came in several variations but always, always, *always* ended the same way. The slash of a hand through the air. Curt, impatient words reaching her.

'It's over, Bianca. Over! Accept it.'

And Luca walking away from her...

She lay there, heart rate still elevated, staring up at the ceiling, willing the dream, the memory, to ebb.

Accept it? Her mouth thinned bitterly in the dim early-morning light. She'd had to accept it. His rejection of her, finishing their affair, had been absolute. He'd left her, left London, left the UK. Gone back to his own life in Italy.

She felt it come again. Her anger at his brusque dismissal—the reason he'd given for it.

'We come from very different worlds,' he'd said.

And he hadn't just meant that she was English and he was Italian. Far more than nationality had divided them. Far more. He'd gone back to his oh-so-aristocratic life in Italy, done with amusing himself with the likes of her...

Bianca Mason, born in the East End, raised on a council estate, a barmaid pulling pints.

Not good enough for him.

Except for sex, of course...

The words and all the searing memories that came with them were in her head before she could stop them.

A single glance from his dark, gold-flecked eyes had been able to melt her like honey...

Oh, God, I wanted him so much—so much...

She'd been helpless to resist and hadn't wanted to. Had wanted only to grab hold of him, her own desire blazing from her, matching his, urgently, hungrily stripping the clothes from him, whipping off his silk tie, slipping the buttons on his pristine white shirt, shedding the jacket of his designer business suit. Hooking one leg around his, hands roaming wildly over the smooth, hard wall of his chest as she pressed her hips against his, feeling and glorying in his blatant arousal for her.

They'd hardly made it to the bedroom in his swanky City apartment, with him peeling down her off-the-shoulder top, hitching up her micro skirt to divest her of her skimpy lacy underwear, pulling her down with him on the waiting bed, his mouth finding hers, her lush, long hair cascading over her shoulders as their hunger for each other mounted and mounted...

With a stifled cry, and a strength she'd had to learn to apply to herself, she forced her mind away. She'd had six years to learn how to do it. Six long years to not think about those searing three months with Luca, when she'd blown all her long-schooled caution about men to the winds and fallen totally, helplessly for him. Weaving about him a longing that had possessed her, consumed her—until the brutal day when it had all come crashing down around her.

'It's over, Bianca. Over! Accept it.'

And when she hadn't—couldn't—he'd spelt out brutally, callously, the reason why she had to.

In words she had never forgotten. Never could forget. Never would forget.

They'd changed her life.

Deliberately, she checked the time. Her alarm had not yet gone off, but she might as well get up anyway. Better than lying there remembering what it was so toxic to remember.

Remembering Luca.

She threw back her duvet, padded to the tiny bathroom opening off her narrow bedroom. The whole flat was tiny—half the top floor of one of a terrace of Edwardian houses converted into flats—but it suited her, and she was grateful for it. She could afford the rent—just—on her new salary, and it was only a short bus ride from work. This outer suburb on the western fringes of London, pleasant and leafy, might only be less than twenty miles from the East End as the crow flew, but it was a world away from where she'd grown up.

But then, so was her life now.

I've left it behind—totally. And that includes everything that ever happened there. And that, above all, means the toxic poison that was my time with Luca.

She stepped into the shower cubicle, turning on the water. As it sluiced down over her head it washed away the last shards of the dream that had come unbidden, unwanted, and the memories it brought with it. Washed them away, down into the fetid sewers of the past.

Luca took the chair the hospital consultant was offering him across his desk. Tension was rigid in his spine.

'What is the prognosis?' he asked.

He knew he sounded curt, even though he did not wish to.

The consultant oncologist looked at him. He was used to giving bad news, but practice never made it easier.

'The primary tumour has been surgically removed, but the cancer has spread to other organs. That means, unfortunately, that it is terminal. I am sorry to have to tell you this.'

His eyes rested on Luca.

Luca's face and voice remained expressionless. 'Is there any treatment possible?'

The consultant nodded. 'Once he has recovered sufficiently from surgery there are drugs he can take which will, if effective, prolong his life.'

Luca's hands clenched at his sides. 'How long?' he asked bluntly.

'It is impossible to say with certainty. The drugs are not successful with all patients.' He paused. 'We are talking months of holding the cancer at bay. Perhaps six. More should not be hoped for. After that, it will be a question of palliative care to make him comfortable.'

'I see.' It was Luca who paused now. Then, 'Thank you for telling me. I needed to understand the situation. When will he be fit enough to leave hospital?'

'He will need nursing care at home,' the oncologist warned him.

Luca nodded. 'That will be taken care of. He will be well looked after. He will be glad to be home again,' he said, finding it suddenly difficult to speak. He got to his feet. 'Thank you for all you are doing for him. It is appreciated.'

He turned, taking his leave. He felt cold in the pit of his stomach. Facing the grim, unwelcome truth.

Matteo was dying.

With relief, Bianca sank back into the taxi taking them to the station.

'There,' said Andrew, her boss, getting in beside her. 'That wasn't too bad, was it?' He smiled at her. 'You handled it fine—well done. It's never easy giving your first presentation.'

'I hope I didn't sound too nervous.'

'You settled into it,' Andrew said reassuringly. 'You're doing well, Bianca.'

He bestowed an approving smile upon her.

She answered it with a grateful one. She'd worked hard—only she knew how hard it had been—but she'd achieved what once she would have thought impossible...out of the question for someone like her.

But I'm not that person any longer.

She'd left that person behind—and everything else that she had once wanted so, so much. This was her life now, made out of the ashes of her old one, and Luca D'Alabruschi, with all his fancy ancestry and oh-so-aristocratic blue blood, who'd once amused himself by slumming it with her, could go screw himself...

Her old crudity went with the thought. Giving her a stab of satisfaction. Casting Luca into the oblivion he deserved. Where he could stay and rot.

Luca's sleek, low-slung supercar crunched over the gravelled carriage sweep, coming to a halt outside the Villa Fiarante. The house was surrounded by pointed cedars, with sunlight glancing off the rows of pedimented windows all along its imposing frontage. It was a familiar sight to him—almost a second home. His father had been in the Diplomatic Service, mostly posted abroad, and in his parents' absence their good friend and Luca's godfather, Matteo, and his late wife, Luisa, had been their surrogates—a relationship that had intensified when Luca's parents had been tragically killed in an air crash three years ago.

Now Matteo Fiarante was the closest person in the world

to him. Luca would do anything for him—anything and everything—out of long, long loyalty. Today was the first time he had visited since Matteo had been discharged after his surgery ten days ago. How would he find him?

He felt concern bite—a concern he expressed to Matteo's long-serving butler, Giuseppe, who opened the door to him.

'How is he?' Luca asked, without preamble.

'Bearing up, I would venture to say,' replied Giuseppe carefully. 'He will be cheered by your visit, if you will permit me to say so.'

'Thank you—that is encouraging.' Luca paused. Then, 'We must take care of him—all of us,' he said.

Giuseppe nodded. 'Indeed.' He inclined his head.

Luca smiled with the familiarity of one who had run tame here all his life. Giuseppe was dedicated to Matteo, and Luca knew he could trust him implicitly.

'Don't announce me,' he said. 'I'll go straight in.'

He did, seeing immediately that Matteo was seated in his familiar place in the library, in a leather armchair, with a rug over his knees and a marquetry table at his side bearing a newspaper, a number of books and a jug of water and a glass. Luca let his eyes sweep over him. Illness was visible in the lines around his mouth, in his thin cheeks, but Matteo's expression lightened immediately.

'Luca, my boy! I thought I heard that monstrous car of yours!'

Luca laughed. 'A dead giveaway, I know,' he said, coming forward, taking the outstretched hand, then settling himself down in the armchair facing Matteo's.

Giuseppe entered with a tray of coffee, and when he had departed Luca poured Matteo and himself a cup. Then he looked at Matteo.

'Now,' he said, striving to keep his voice light, 'tell me how you are.'

Matteo met his eyes full on. 'You know how I am, Luca. As do I. I am dying. But as the poet says...' his eyes rested on the younger man '... I am dying "with a little patience". Enough patience,' he said, 'to put my affairs in order. It is time that happened—more than time.'

He glanced at the clock on the mantel, a gilded and ornate nineteenth-century antique. Ticking the seconds away. The hours. The remainder of Matteo's life.

'More than time,' he said again.

Bianca, just getting home from work, opened the main front door of the house she lived in, glancing at the mail rack. Normally the only contents for her were mailshots or any official communications that still came by post. The envelope she lifted out now seemed to be neither. The address was handwritten in flowing copperplate, the envelope embossed.

She headed upstairs with the bag of groceries she'd picked up on her way from the bus stop. Once inside her own flat, she slit the envelope open, drawing out the thick, folded sheet of paper inside and flattening it out. She frowned. It seemed to be from a firm of solicitors. As her eyes moved down the typewritten contents, her frown deepened.

What on earth—?

Nonplussed, she lifted her eyes, staring out of the small window in her kitchenette. What possible reason could a posh firm of London lawyers have for asking her to get in touch with them? Still nonplussed, she fetched her phone from her handbag, which she had deposited on the table in the living room.

Five minutes later she still had no explanation—only an appointment to call at their offices the next day. As to why...

No possible reason came to her.

Luca was back on the autostrada, heading for Rome. It was more than a two-hour drive away, and he had a dinner engagement. He'd spent the previous night at his own home, seeing to the various matters that arose at the extensive estate he'd inherited. As well as the ancestral *palazzo*, it came with several farms, vineyards and woodlands, plus various local enterprises from wineries to timber yards. He employed a highly competent estate manager—inherited from his father who, as a far-flung diplomat, had not himself been able to take on hands-on management—and Luca, too, pursuing his banking career in Rome, was more than happy to confine his own role to that simply of overseer.

Not that he did not look forward to one day basing himself at the *palazzo*...making it a family home once more.

When he married.

Because of course he would marry—at some point.

He was an only child—an only son—and he must look to the future. Cousins were all very well, but they were remote and distant. No, he must marry himself and generate the next generation. The next Visconte.

Though aristocratic titles in Republican Italy were not official, in his circles they were still used socially. And even though he did not emphasise his own, it meant something to him. Not everyone understood that.

He felt his mind dragged back, as if a hook had caught at it, skewing his thoughts.

An image hovered.

Flaming Titian hair, emerald-green eyes set in a face that had taken his breath away. A *bella figura* that combined slim hips and slender waist with pleasingly generous breasts. Breasts that had peaked even more pleasingly beneath his palms as he'd freed them from the confines of the low-cut, clinging outfit she'd donned that evening simply to give him the pleasure of removing it from her.

His pleasure—and hers. Because she had matched him. As hungry for him as he had been for her. As eager for him to strip her down as she was to strip him likewise. She'd been open in her desire for him, revelling in it, wanting everything he was only too happy to bestow upon her. Wanting everything about him. Wanting too much—

No, best not go there.

He slewed his mind away, thought back to his visit to Matteo.

His words came back to Luca.

'I must make the most of the time I have left to me. You understand that, don't you, my boy? With my dear Luisa gone before me, she will not mind.'

He frowned. He hadn't known what Matteo was talking about, but it hadn't taken long in Matteo's company for him to understand that it was not just his body that was being assailed by the cancer. It was assailing his mind as well. Or more likely, he acknowledged, it was the strong drugs he was on. He was coherent, yes, but he was not the old Matteo. He was...frailer. In mind as well as body.

Troubled, saddened, he drove on. He would visit again soon. His eyes shadowed. After all, he too must make the most of this limited and fast-passing time he had with Matteo. For it would not last.

Bianca, smartly dressed as she always was these days, had taken the afternoon off work and now sat in front of a wide, leather tooled desk in a panelled room in a handsome brick terraced Georgian house in the Inns of Court. The offices of the firm of solicitors who had so mysteriously contacted her.

The elderly solicitor—a senior partner, or so she'd been given to understand—looked across at her, steepling his fingers.

'Tell me, Miss Mason, how much do you know about your father's family?'

Bianca stared.

'My *father*?'

She took a breath and looked the solicitor squarely in the eye. Her old life—the one she'd walked away from because it had been as toxic as the man who'd been the cause of her walking away—was colliding with her new one.

'I don't even know who he was,' she said. 'My mother died when I was very young and I was raised by my aunt, who never talked of such matters.'

That was not strictly true. Her aunt—her mother's sour, unmarried half-sister—had never flinched from informing Bianca that she should count herself lucky she wasn't in a care home, that she was nothing but a burden, and that her mother had slept around since she was a teenager. Bianca hadn't believed her, because some of the neighbours who remembered her mother—who had known her before she had been fatally knocked down by a car—had told her that, yes, the boys had always been keen on her, because she'd been so pretty, with her fair hair and blue eyes, but she should not believe what her aunt said about her because she was bitter and jealous.

'And she's collecting your childcare benefits—don't you forget that, lovey!' they'd added.

Bianca was pretty sure that without that her aunt would have put into care without a qualm. As it was, her childhood had not been a walk in the park. She had been endlessly criticised by her carping aunt, endlessly complained about, endlessly warned that she'd come to no good, like her mother...

Maybe that's why I grew up so rebellious, not bothering with school, always wanting something better for myself than a council flat on a run-down estate in the East End.

Had that been what had made her so eager to snap up what Luca had offered her?

Oh, she'd been hit on by males since she was a teenager—but she was as picky as she was choosy, and no way was she going to give her aunt any opportunity to repeat her slurs on her mother about herself. But when Luca had walked into that upmarket bar in Canary Wharf full of Hooray Henries, looking tall, cool, drop-dead gorgeous and totally lethal, every other man in the world had simply...disappeared.

The solicitor's voice cut across her memories. Memories that did her no good...

'Your mother was Shona Mason?' he put to her.

He added the dates of her birth and death. Not a long span of time, Bianca thought sadly. Not even thirty...

She nodded.

The solicitor consulted the papers on his desk.

'Then I have something to tell you that may be of interest to you,' he said.

Bianca looked at him. 'What is it?' she asked.

The solicitor told her.

CHAPTER TWO

THE PLANE WAS coming in to land. Bianca's gaze went out through the porthole to the approaching land. Italy. A country she'd never been to. Never been invited to. Not by Luca. She felt the familiar lick of acid on her skin. It had come to her repeatedly since she'd walked, dazed and disbelieving, out of the solicitor's office three days ago. Two worlds were colliding. The world she'd made for herself, taking six years to do it. And the world she'd come from.

Or thought she had come from.

Because what that elderly, dry-as-dust solicitor had told her was so far beyond belief that she still did not believe it—dared not believe it. But it was because of what he'd told her that she was sitting on this plane, having asked for impromptu leave from work.

Given the circumstances, Andrew had been completely supportive.

'Of course you must go. It's quite extraordinary!'

That was one word for it. Bianca had another one. One that made her heart beat faster and made her wish the plane would move onward faster.

Miraculous. That was the word in Bianca's head.

After all these years...

Luca replaced the phone on his desk in his office. Matteo wanted him to go for dinner in two days' time. He had been quite insistent. He had also asked him to arrive in black tie.

Luca had assented—of course he had. But he was concerned that Matteo would be tiring himself by inviting guests. Several business trips, taking in Geneva, Frankfurt and Brussels, had kept Luca from visiting for nearly three weeks, but now he could be sure he would be based indefinitely in Rome. If Matteo should take a turn for the worse he did not want to be out of the country.

He was keeping his diary here in Rome flexible too. Though his social life was full, there was currently no particular female in his life, and as Matteo was his priority right now he intended to keep it that way. Usually, given his bachelor status, plus his title, his wealth and—he knew without vanity—looks that women found pleasing, he could take his pick. That was certainly what he'd enjoyed doing when he was younger. And not just in Italy. He had self-indulgently romanced many of the all too eager females he'd encountered in his stints working abroad. Enjoyable interludes, never intended to last. As those he romanced had all understood.

All except one—

He sheered his mind away. No point remembering that hot-as-hell time with Bianca. He could ponder with hindsight whether it had been wise to allow himself to indulge in a searing affair with someone who came from so very different a world from him. Yet that fateful evening when, after a business meeting in Canary Wharf, he'd been taken for a drink at a nearby bar, his eyes had gone to the female mixing cocktails and he'd not been able to drag them away.

Titian-hair piled high on her head, striking looks, full lips… And eyes that he had seen, when they'd clashed with his, were a brilliant emerald-green.

She'd frozen, tilted vodka bottle in hand, and their eyes had locked. Message sent—and received. He'd moved in on her, knowing that this stunning flame-haired beauty had spiked in him an instant desire that demanded only one course of action.

To make her his—consumingly, totally his.

She'd come to him effortlessly, and he had the honesty to admit that he'd enjoyed the fact that she was so different from his normal fare—and not just because of her very different background. She played no games, and was totally upfront that she wanted him as much as he wanted her, that her desire and passion matched his. He'd been taken aback, he acknowledged with honesty, to find he was her first lover, but she'd told him that she'd been saving herself for a guy who was really worth it.

With hindsight, maybe that should have been a warning sign that she would not see their affair in the same way he had seen it... As something to be indulged in, enjoyed, that would then come to a natural end. That she might want... more.

More than just an affair. Something more permanent.

But his stint in London had ended, and so had his time with her.

He'd hoped she'd accept it gracefully.

She hadn't.

When he'd said he was leaving London, and that their time together had run its course, she'd clung to him. Titian head thrown back, arms tightening around his neck, she had told him that she had nothing to keep her in London, that she was free to come with him anywhere he went, anywhere at all...

He'd had to peel her off him. Say what he'd said to her...

'It's over, Bianca. Over! Accept it.'

Memory flashed in his head. Her face as he'd set it out for her. Said what it had been necessary for him to say, loath though he had been to be so harsh. But she had brought it on herself.

Her expression had been impossible to read. And then, as he'd finished, she had simply looked at him, mouth set tight, with a narrow band of colour across her sculpted cheekbones that contrasted with the icy pallor of her skin. A mask had come down over her long-lashed eyes. She'd said nothing—not a word. Had just stood there.

He'd nodded, walked away. Leaving her. Going back to his own life, to Italy, putting her into the past. Leaving her there. Where she must stay. There was no other place for her.

Right now his only focus was Matteo. Being there for him while he was still there for Luca to see him...

Bianca was walking in the villa's gardens. They were peaceful and secluded, though too formal for her own personal taste, with paved pathways, sculpted topiary, stone ponds and benches. She would need to go in soon. Matteo liked a pre-prandial *aperitivo*, and she looked forward to that special time with him. He wasn't always well enough to come downstairs. He had his good days, and days that were not so good...

Her eyes shadowed. She had been granted so much, and yet it was coming at a price. Sadness filled her, and she felt a clutching at her heart. He had made her so welcome, embraced her into his life...just as he was preparing to take his leave of it.

But she would not think such sad thoughts. That time ahead would come—it must—but for now, for this wonderful time, she would not let it spoil what she had been granted. Granted so miraculously.

Her boss, Andrew, was being wonderfully supportive. She was on an indefinite leave of absence, although she was using her spare time—when Matteo was resting—to work remotely, keeping in touch with what was going on back home.

Home? The word hovered in her head. Matteo had said this was her home now. Had pressed her hand and told her she must not think of leaving. She had given her assent willingly, whole-heartedly, and he had been reassured. As for what would happen after…?

Well, that was for then. This was for now. A special time in her life, and one for which she gave such thanks.

She wended her way back to the villa. She wanted to change—Matteo liked to see her looking nice, and she obliged him willingly. He had already insisted on sending her out in his car, chauffeur-driven, to the main town in the area, to avail herself of the fashionable shops there. To please him she had acquiesced in that too. It had seemed ungracious not to. Ungracious not to enjoy this luxurious, leisurely life here at the Villa Fiarante.

Memory rippled through her. Though she had never wanted Luca to buy her things, she had, all the same, enjoyed to the hilt the deluxe life he led. And in the time she'd been with him she'd led that life too—eating at fancy restaurants, drinking fine wines that she'd barely appreciated but enjoyed all the same, taking taxis everywhere, having the best seats in the theatre when he took her to shows.

Oh, she'd lived the high life with him all right.

But it had been borrowed from him—nothing more than that.

And now…

She walked inside the palatial villa, its resplendent rooms and décor cared for by staff—led by the stately Giuseppe—

like a well-oiled machine. She never had to lift a finger. Matteo took it for granted, of course, but then this was his world, his birthright.

Disbelief shimmered through her. To think she'd grown up on a shabby council estate in the East End of London when all along—

No, best not to dwell on that. It was too sad to think of why that had come to be. Far too sad. But thanks to Matteo that sadness had found if not a happy ending—not when he was taking his leave of life—but a lining that was richly silver indeed.

He might never have found me and I might never have known that any of this existed. Never have known Matteo.

Her mood lightened and she ran up the grand sweeping staircase to her room. It was as large as her flat—if not larger—and beautifully appointed. It took her little time to get ready, changing out of cotton trousers and tee shirt—part of her own casual wardrobe—and exchanging them for a knee-length dress in pale blue. It looked deceptively simple, but the price tag had been hefty, and she had bought it only because she'd known Matteo would like to see her in it.

He did, too, when she went into the library a short time later. He was in his usual leather chair, dressed formally, but his top shirt button was undone, and he looked comfortable and relaxed. His colour, so often very pale, looked better too, and Bianca was glad of it.

She stooped to drop a kiss on his thin cheek. 'How are you this evening?' she asked, taking a seat opposite him.

'All the better for seeing you,' he said.

His English was accented, and memory struck her, as it always did. Luca's accent when he spoke English had been to die for. Even the most unromantic statements in the world could sound sensuous and beguiling…

She pulled her thoughts away. Giuseppe was approaching in his customary stately manner, bestowing upon her the Campari and soda she liked to have as an *aperitivo*, while Matteo indulged in a well-watered-down martini. Alcohol was not forbidden to him, but it was allowed in very modest amounts only.

He made a face at the overly diluted *aperitivo*. Then he brightened. 'My dear, we are to have a visitor tomorrow.'

Bianca's expression changed. Became one of concern.

'Won't it tire you?' she asked.

She hoped she did not sound too fussing, because she knew Matteo did not like to be fussed over, but all the same she felt anxious for him.

'I will be fine,' he replied, with a touch of impatience. 'I have promised Giuseppe—and my dratted nurse—that I will not stir all day tomorrow until the evening. He is coming for dinner, you see, our visitor, and will stay the night as well.' His expression brightened again. 'It is someone I particularly want you to meet,' he said.

'Who is it?' Bianca asked.

She was still not sure about visitors. She had become very protective of Matteo, and she knew that she and his nurse and Giuseppe, and indeed all the staff, conspired to fuss over him without him realising it. Sometimes he co-operated, sometimes not. Sometimes it was up to her to persuade him, smilingly, that his wheelchair was not his enemy, and that using it from time to time would enable him to take a turn in the gardens.

In the cooler hours, she pushed him along the paved paths while he told her tales from the past. She drew him out, wanting to hear all she could, thirsty for it like someone who had been in a desert all her life…

A smile was playing about his mouth now, and his eyes were bright, less sunken into his thin face.

'He is my godson,' Matteo told her.

'Oh?' said Bianca, looking across at him. He seemed to be expecting her to say something more, so she went on. 'Does he have to come far?'

Matteo shook his head. 'He lives less than an hour away, though his work keeps him in Rome. And he is often abroad, travelling for business, too.'

'What does he do?' Bianca asked, more out of politeness than interest.

'Finance,' her uncle replied. He said it carelessly, as though it was of little interest to him. 'It is very international.' He waved a hand dismissively.

For a fleeting, unpleasant second, memory pierced her. Luca had worked in international finance. It had brought him to London—and taken him away again.

She pushed the memory aside. Any memories of him were strictly forbidden. Even here in Italy.

Especially here in Italy…

She sought distraction in another question. 'Is he bringing his wife?' she asked, merely out of politeness.

'Oh, he is not married,' Matteo replied. 'He is too popular with the ladies for that!'

Bianca caught the indulgent note in his voice, and the note of fondness too.

'He is very close to me,' Matteo went on, his voice warm and affectionate. 'And he would fuss over me as much as you and the whole pack of you do if I were to let him!' he added with some asperity. 'In a way…' his voice softened '…he is almost like the son I never had, for my dearest Luisa and I were not blessed with children—'

He broke off, took another sip from his glass, made another face.

Then he brightened again. 'I look forward to you meeting him,' he said.

Bianca gave an uncertain smile.

Matteo was continuing. 'We shall have something of a dinner party tomorrow evening! Giuseppe will see to it all. All you need to do, my dear, is dress for the occasion! How very beautiful you will look!'

Bianca occupied herself with her Campari and soda. This godson of Matteo's, who was so popular with the ladies and almost like a son to him... What would he make of her presence here? Arriving like this out of nowhere? She gave a mental shake of her head. It was no concern of hers. Matteo could make the explanations if he felt they were warranted. She would just go with the flow. If this unknown godson held his godfather in high regard, then surely he would welcome her presence here?

Giuseppe was entering the room again, announcing dinner.

Carefully, trying not to fuss, Bianca offered her arm to help Matteo to his feet. He took it, leaning on her slightly, but she suspected that was more to show affection than for support. Slowly, they made their way into the dining room.

The godson was not mentioned again, and Bianca was glad of it. Tonight she would have Matteo to herself.

Sadness plucked at her. Anticipatory grief, at knowing that this precious time was limited. So cruelly limited. She must make the very most of it, and be what comfort she could while she could...

Once again Luca was speeding north-east from Rome, heading for the Villa Fiarante to dine with Matteo.

Giuseppe, when he'd interrogated him, had assured him

no other guests would be present. Why that meant he had to wear evening dress, Luca didn't know. He knew only that Matteo had stipulated it, so he was complying. He would stay the night too, and then put in a couple of days catching up with matters at his own home before returning to Rome.

As he pulled up in front of the villa, some time later, the evening had already gathered. Stars were pricking out in the sky, the air was cooler. The villa was lit up, and Luca's mind went back to earlier times, when Matteo and Luisa had been so fond of entertaining. Then, only a little time before his own parents had been killed, Luisa had succumbed to the heart disease that had taken her so soon. And now Matteo would be following her.

They had never had children—Matteo's only sorrow, for their marriage had been very happy. Children would have been an added blessing.

But I'll stand right with you, Matteo! I may not be your son, but I am the next best thing, and I will stand by you till the end. And whatever it is you want, if it is in my power, I shall do it.

Including, right now, having dinner with him this evening.

Giuseppe was already opening the door and he stepped lightly inside, making his usual low-voiced enquiry as to how his godfather was.

'The *signor* is in good spirits,' Giuseppe assured him. 'And awaiting you with impatience.'

He led the way forward, throwing open a set of double doors. Not to the library, Matteo's usual haunt, but a room on the other side of the wide hall—the formal *saloni*.

Luca half smiled to himself. Matteo was doing this evening in style.

He walked through, ready to greet his godfather.

Instead, he stopped dead. Totally and completely dead. The smile of greeting on his face vanished.

Bianca was sitting—perching, more accurately—on a silk-upholstered chair. It was one of a trio set by the ornate carved marble fireplace, which had a tapestry screen in front of it at this time of the year. She had seen the *saloni* before, when Giuseppe had shown her around the villa, shortly after her arrival, but she had only glanced inside, taking in a room that was clearly too grand for everyday use.

Landscape paintings hung on the walls, the furniture was all silk upholstered, mirrors were gilded, and occasional tables were inlaid with mother of pearl. The floor was covered with Persian carpets. It was a room for grand entertaining. She and Matteo were lost in it.

He was looking well, though, she thought. Very smart in his dinner jacket. His cheeks were less sunken, his eyes brighter. Clearly the impending visit of his godson was cheering him.

She had only just come down from her room for Maria, the maid she usually dismissed with a courteous smile, had insisted on helping her dress and pinning up her hair carefully. She had helped, too, with the jewellery she had carried into the bedroom, depositing its case on the dressing table.

'The *signor* asks that you wear it this evening,' Maria had said.

And to please Matteo, Bianca had. They were beautiful pieces—a pearl collar, matching pearl bracelets and drop pearl earrings. They went superbly with the dress she was wearing—another horribly expensive number from the upmarket boutique in the nearby town, but one she knew Matteo would like.

Memory had flitted through her head as she'd let Maria

slip it over her head. Unwelcome memory. The dress she wore tonight was a world away from the clothes she'd worn when she had glammed up for Luca. Then, she'd always gone for glitz, and maxing out her sex appeal. Luca had liked it—liked it a lot. Making it clear all evening that he could not wait to get her back to his apartment, and strip it all off her—

No! She'd sliced down the guillotine, cut off memories that were as pointless as they were poisoned. She would not think of Luca.

But now, as she sat so elegantly perched on the chair beside Matteo, after the powerful engine note of what was presumably Matteo's godson's flash car had been silenced, she heard the low, indistinguishable murmur of voices out in the hall, and the doors to the *saloni* were thrown open by Giuseppe in grand fashion. And with the freezing of the blood in her veins Bianca realised, her eyes going to who it was that Giuseppe was ushering in, that memories were not all that remained of Luca.

He had just walked into the room.

Luca.

Matteo's godson…

CHAPTER THREE

Luca walked forward. He had no choice. His legs were as stiff as wood, but he forced them forward. His mind was in meltdown, blanking everything.

From somewhere infinitely far away he heard Matteo speak.

'Luca, my boy! Welcome, welcome! You have come, and I rejoice. Rejoice because now I have the two people dearest to me in the world here with me! I am longing for you to meet.'

His godfather turned his head to the woman beside him. His voice was doting.

'My dear, here he is! My godson, Luca. Luca, come and make the acquaintance of my very dearest treasure, Bianca.'

Though he was still encased in ice, Luca moved to Matteo, said his name in greeting. And then—because he must, because he had no choice but to do so—he turned to the woman at Matteo's side.

'Bianca.'

It had been six years since he had said her name out loud. He has last said it when he was dismissing her from his life. Telling her that their time together had finished, their affair was done with.

'It's over, Bianca. Over! Accept it.'

And now her name came from his throat again.

She gave the very slightest inclination of her head—no other movement. He might have given a savage laugh had he not been frozen in shock—she was as frozen as he was.

His eyes locked to hers. He had recognised her in an instant, but in truth he should never have known who she was. She could not have looked more different from the way she'd looked all those years ago in London.

He had taken in her entire appearance in the single moment it had taken for him to recognise her. Her elegantly styled knee-length dress was indigo, with a gracefully draped neckline. Its three-quarter sleeves showed off a pearl bracelet on each slender wrist, bracelets that matched the pearl choker around her neck and the single drop pearl earrings at her lobes, revealed by the low, full chignon into which her Titian hair had been drawn at the nape of her neck, and set with pearl combs.

As he took her in, out of nowhere a sudden rage speared him. He recognised that pearl set—it had been Matteo's wife's. Luca had seen Luisa wear it dozens of times while she was alive.

Now Bianca, a barmaid out of the East End of London, was wearing it...

In the aftermath of the shock that had iced through him, a question seared.

What the *hell* was Bianca doing here, in his godfather's house, wearing Luisa's jewellery?

The answer that came—the only possible answer—raced through him in a silent inner snarl.

There could be only one explanation—horrific and appalling as it was...

A voice sounded nearby, dragging him back. It was Giuseppe, deferentially asking him what *aperitivo* he might like. Still in shock—more than shock...worse than shock—

Luca tersely made his usual request, and then Matteo was speaking again, the warmth in his voice deepening.

'It is so very, very good to have you here, my dear boy. I have been impatient for this day!'

Luca dragged his eyes back to his godfather, and he made himself make some kind of mechanical reply.

'Yes, so very impatient!' Matteo went on, his tired face animated. 'And here you are at last!'

It was impossible to think of what to say, and Luca could only be grimly grateful that Giuseppe was now hovering at his elbow, his *aperitivo* on the upheld silver tray. He took it gratefully, wanting the shot of alcohol.

There was something else he wanted as well—badly. He wanted to seize in a vise-like grip the arms of his godfather's 'dearest treasure'—the words twisted in his head viciously—and drag her bodily from the room. And then find out what the *hell* was going on!

But he couldn't—not right now. All he could do was stand stiffly, raise his martini glass to his lips and feel the alcohol hit his system as he swallowed.

Matteo was talking again, his face less animated now, but with an expression on it that made Luca's teeth grind. 'Doting' was definitely the word for it—and it was directed at his benighted 'dearest treasure'…

'It is like a miracle,' his godfather was saying, his voice fond. 'Just when my spirits were sinking beyond all hope, thanks to this wretched illness of mine, I have been rewarded beyond measure—and certainly beyond my deserving.'

His eyes lifted to Luca, and with a start Luca saw moisture in them.

'It is a gift I never hoped for—and yet it has been given to me. To lighten my days before they are taken from me.'

He gave a slightly crooked, poignant smile, his eyes going back to his 'dearest treasure'. He extended his hand to her and Luca had to watch her take it and hold it tenderly, while trying to stop his teeth grinding yet more at the nauseating sight. It filled him with a black, cold fury he knew he had, for the moment, to conceal. Until he could get her to himself...wreak his fury on her...

Matteo was still speaking, that mawkish note in his voice. Luca steeled himself and listened to what his obviously besotted godfather trotted out next.

'My dearest treasure—come to lighten this dark time of my life! With whom I can spend these last months more happily than I dared to believe or hope! Upon whom I can lavish the wealth I must leave behind...'

Nausea rose in him, and bitter, angry bile. Was *this* what Matteo had meant when he'd said he wanted to make the most of the time that was left to him? Taking up with a woman young enough to be his daughter? Lavishing his dead wife's jewels on her?

Because what other possible explanation could there be for Bianca's presence here? As sordid as it was, what else could it be?

He felt the nausea of his revulsion mix with the deadly anger of his outrage—and mix with something more, too, that he refused to acknowledge, let alone allow. All he could allow was a vicious channelling of his reaction to seeing what he was seeing, and coming up with an explanation for it.

And why should it be Bianca ensconced here? *Bianca!* How had she achieved it? How had she spent the last six years, and then ended up battening on to Matteo, getting him to spend his money on her, dress her in designer clothes, shower his dead wife's jewellery on her? He did not know how—but he did know the 'why' of it. Bitterly and savagely.

Because I gave her a taste for it. Showed her how she could acquire it.

Nausea bit again. Not just at the sight of Matteo's doting expression and his dead wife's jewellery adorning the woman holding his hand, but at something more. Something that repulsed him. To think Bianca had stooped to become what she now so obviously was...

Something deeper still pounded at him, feeding his savage fury.

Bianca was holding another man's hand.

He pushed it from him. It was he who had severed their connection and ended their time together—he who had walked away from her. So why should he care whose hand she held now so long as it wasn't his dying godfather's? *That* was the only cause of his reaction to finding her here.

Yet as his eyes locked to hers he felt not just revulsion at the reason why she was here, but also something he could not stop himself reacting to. She was not looking at him. Her gaze was fixed on Matteo, her face in profile to Luca.

He felt words fill his head, force themselves upon him. Force admission.

She's even more stunning, more fantastically beautiful, than I remember her...

It was dragged from him unwillingly, unwanted. Dragged into his consciousness though he wished the words to perdition. Yet how could he deny it? He could feel a war within himself. Rage and contempt. And something far more basic. Far more dangerous.

Whatever she has become—however sordid—how can I deny the beauty she possesses?

Beauty that once, in a very different style—flamboyant and flaunting—had beguiled him. All those years ago. Beauty that had now matured, become styled with an elegance and grace that he had never previously associated her with.

It caught at him even more powerfully. Infusing the shock still riveting him, the outrage still possessing him, the fury still blackening his eyes, with something quite different...

His godfather was speaking again, and Luca forced himself to listen, to drag his eyes, his consciousness, from where they rested on Bianca's perfect sculpted profile. The lamplight caught the opalescence of the pearls at her ears, the combs in her glorious hair, the graceful line of her throat...

Dimly, his godfather's words penetrated.

'My boy, forgive me... You must excuse me. I must be absent for a few moments. My dratted nurse is wanting to administer my evening medications, take my pulse and blood pressure. It must be done, but it will not take too long. But I will not subject you to witnessing it.'

He patted Bianca's hand, and Luca saw her slip it from Matteo's.

'Take Bianca out on to the terrace—take the air awhile. Then, when all my nurse's ministrations are complete, we shall go in to dine and the evening can begin.'

He smiled, both at Luca and at his 'dearest treasure', who was now getting to her feet. Was she doing so reluctantly? Well she might...

Luca's thoughts were dark. As black as pitch. But Matteo's suggestion could not have been better timed. Giuseppe was entering the *saloni* and the young man Paolo, Matteo's nurse, in his neat white uniform, was following him with a tray of medicines and a blood pressure kit.

Bianca was already stepping towards the French windows that led out on to the terrace. Her spine was as stiff as a poker, and tension radiated from her with every high-heeled step she took.

Grimly, Luca went after her.

His expression, now that Matteo could not see it, was as savage as his thoughts.

Bianca stalked past Luca on legs that were as heavy as iron, gaining the terrace through the French windows. The cooler night air hit her and she shivered. Surely it was that air, and that alone, that drew such a response from her?

Out on the terrace, she turned. Disbelief was still drowning her.

Matteo's godson was Luca.

It was like a nightmare—one impossible to cope with, impossible to believe. Shock was still blanking her thoughts.

How can this be happening? How?

But her appalled question was as useless as the hammering of her heart, each blow a pain assailing her. She knew she had to say something—anything. She opened her mouth to speak, to take the initiative, to take control. But she never got the chance.

Luca's hand whipped out, fastened around her lower arm, steely like a vise. He took a half-step towards her, and in the low light of the terrace, illuminated only by the lights of the *saloni* behind him and the dim starlight, she saw his face was stark. The frozen expressionless mask that had settled over him when his eyes had first gone to her, seated by Matteo, had vanished. In its place—

In its place was fury. Cold, dark, condemning.

When he spoke his voice was the same.

'I don't give a damn what you're doing here,' he bit out, his hand like a vise still, his breath rasping in his throat. 'Because you'll be leaving first thing in the morning. Come up with any reason you like—but you'll be gone. I'll drive you to the airport myself.'

Bianca's face contorted and she tried to pull her arm free.

His grip lessened not a jot.

'Let me *go*!' she ground out. 'If you think I'm leaving tomorrow—forget it! And *I* don't *"give a damn"*...' she echoed his words deliberately '...whether that embarrasses you or not!'

He stared at her, his eyes like pits. His hand around her arm jerked.

'*Embarrasses* me?' he shot back. 'What the hell's that got to do with it? All I care about is getting your grasping claws out of Matteo!'

He took a step back suddenly, releasing her. The place where his fingers had pressed burned like a brand on her, even through the material of her sleeve. His expression had changed. That black anger had been replaced by something that chilled her even more.

Revulsion. Disgust. Contempt.

'How low have you sunk?' His voice was twisted. 'To batten on to a dying man—'

Bianca's face worked. 'I'm here because he *wants* me here! How could I refuse him—*how*?'

Now it was Luca savagely echoing her. '*How* could you *refuse* to accept what he's so obviously, besottedly lavishing upon you?' His hand reached out again, flicked at the pearl collar around her neck, then dropped away. 'He's draped you in his dead wife's jewels...'

The disgust in his voice was matched only by his anger.

Bianca felt herself flush. 'I didn't know—he just said they were family heirlooms. He never said...never said they were Luisa's.'

'Don't give me that! And don't even say her name!' His

eyes narrowed to slits. 'Or is that your ambition? Not just to batten onto him while you can, for what you can get out of him, but to aim for the ultimate prize? To get him to marry you? A deathbed marriage?'

A gasp broke from her. Shock ripped across her face.

'Are you *insane*?' she said. Her voice was hollow.

A sound from behind them broke the moment. The French windows were being opened, and a discreet cough came from Giuseppe.

'Dinner is served,' he said in Italian.

Numbly, with shock still ripping through her, Bianca stepped past Luca, past Giuseppe. In the *saloni*, Matteo was on his feet, the nurse disappeared.

Matteo's face was wreathed in smiles.

'All done,' he said. 'And now, finally, we can enjoy the evening.'

His eyes went from Bianca, to Luca, and back again, apparently pleased at what he saw.

Luca had stepped through behind Bianca, and she could feel him like a demonic presence beside her—for what else could he be?

But words failed her—thoughts failed her. All she could feel was that tearing shock still ripping right through her. Shock upon shock. Shock at seeing Luca walk into the *saloni*—walk back into her life. Shock twisting inside her nauseatingly at what he'd just thrown at her, what he thought she was doing here.

Desperately she strove to hide her reaction, school her expression. Matteo was walking towards them, carefully but steadily.

'So,' he said, his eyes bright upon them both as he came up to them, taking their hands in his as she stood stock still beside Luca, who was as still as she was. 'You have been making a start on getting to know each other? That is good—very good. For of all things, my dear Luca,' he went on, looking directly at his godson, 'I most of all want you to come to know, and to value as I do, my very dear Bianca. My dearest treasure...the blessing bestowed upon me by heaven in this my time of trial.'

Matteo's smile deepened, and his hold on her hand tightened, though hers was quite immobile still.

Emotion filled his voice as he spoke again.

'Bianca... My brother's long-lost daughter—my most precious, dearest niece.'

Luca heard the words but they did not compute, nor make sense in any way at all.

'Non credo...'

He saw a wry expression cross Matteo's face.

'Nor did I believe it, at first,' he concurred.

He let go both their hands, turning away, gesturing as he did so towards the double doors that led through to the dining room.

'I will explain over dinner how it came to be, for I cannot believe there is not the hand of Providence in it. At the very time when my spirits were brought as low as a man's can be, after receiving my own death sentence, the good Lord saw fit to lighten my final months.'

Luca could hear the emotion thick in Matteo's voice. His godfather was speaking Italian, with emphasis and insistence. The depth of his emotion almost echoed Luca's own—but his had an utterly different cause.

Disbelief—incredulity. Dismay.

Dismay that this long-lost niece, of whose existence Luca had never heard, should be Bianca.

Bianca, raised on an East London council estate, is Mat-

teo's niece? How can she be? It is impossible...surely impossible!

'That is quite remarkable,' he heard himself say, keeping his voice studiedly level with an effort as they went through into the dining room, took their places.

Giuseppe and one of the manservants went into the rituals of serving dinner—pouring water, then wine, and then serving the *primo*. Only when they had withdrawn could Luca bring himself to look at the woman sitting opposite him.

She was not looking at him, nor at anyone. Her eyes were cast down and she was looking at her plate of artistically arranged scallops, lapped by a saffron sauce with *herbes garnis* and slivers of artichoke, apparently transfixed by the artistry of its presentation. Luca was glad of it. He needed to be able to look at her—look in her direction in a way that as far as his godfather was concerned would seem normal for the situation Matteo assumed this to be.

When it was nothing like that in the least.

Because how could it be? How could there be anything 'normal' in what was happening?

He felt emotion threaten to spike up from the depths into which he'd ruthlessly crushed it. But Matteo was speaking, lifting his wine glass.

'I wish, this evening, to drink to both of you,' he announced. His voice was warm, and Luca could hear the note of satisfaction in it... The note of relief. Of achievement. 'And I wish,' he went on, 'to drink to what this means to me.'

His smile went from one of them to the other and back again. Mechanically Luca reached for his glass of wine, seeing Bianca do the same.

Then Matteo spoke again, tilting his glass slightly to each of them.

'To you, Luca, who has been so important a part of my life for so long. And to someone who, by the hand of Providence, has been granted to me in my hour of need. To my brother's child—Bianca.'

Luca's eyes went to her again as he took a mouthful of wine.

Can she really be Matteo's niece?

It seemed too extraordinary for it to be true. Yet that was better, surely, than the conclusion he'd jumped to on seeing her here. Relief speared in him. Relief that Matteo, in his illness, had not succumbed to anything sordid. And nor had Bianca.

He went on letting his eyes rest on her as she took a careful sip from her own glass in response to Matteo's imprecation to taste the wine. Two images collided in his mind. Bianca—then. Bianca—now.

So different, Bianca then. When he had known her she had been wearing tight-sheathed, low-cut outfits, designed to reveal her plentiful physical attractions. Her face had been fully made up, with sculpted cheekbones, deep-shadowed eyes, her eyelashes heavy with mascara, her lips lush and rich. Her glorious hair had been sleek and curved around her shoulders. She'd worn gold-coloured faux gem earrings, necklaces and bracelets. She had been packaged and presented to him for desire and seduction...for the pleasures to come once she was in his arms, in his bed...

Bianca now—his godfather's niece—was at home in his home in her beautifully cut, long-sleeved, elegantly draped designer number, with her hair drawn back into a low-set chignon, the soft glow of pearls around her throat and at the lobes of her ears, her make-up minimal for the evening's formality. Elegant, sophisticated, soignée...

So very, very different...

Only her beauty is the same...

But he must not think of that. Must not think of anything, right now, except getting through this ordeal. He must not look at her any more than social necessity required. Must behave as though he'd never set eyes on her before.

She did not meet his gaze, lowering her glass again and making a start on her *primo*.

His godfather looked at him. 'You must be wondering how it came to be,' he started. 'How Providence bestowed so precious a gift upon me. I will explain.'

He took another mouthful of his wine before continuing.

'When one receives news such as mine, one is advised to put one's affairs in order…'

His voice was edged a little. Luca could hear it, and he understood the reason for it,

'To make everything…tidy,' Matteo went on. 'For our families and for ourselves. When I came home from hospital, this I proceeded to do. All the usual things—my will, my finances and so on. But there were also more personal matters. Painful things I have shut away for many years.'

His expression changed.

'You may not be aware, Luca, that I had a brother—Tomaso. As boys we were very close, but as young men someone came into our lives. Luisa.'

He paused.

'We both fell in love with her, but it was me she loved. It…drove Tomaso away. He could not face seeing me marry the woman he loved. He took himself off, went to England. I let him be, married Luisa, got on with my life.'

He reached for his wine again, drank once more, as if in need of it.

'I did not hear from him again—until news of his fatal car crash in France was brought to me by the police. I was named as his next of kin in his passport. He had been heading back to Italy. His effects were sent to me—his suitcase—but I could not bear to open it. Recently, knowing how little time is left to me, I did. And I found, inside, what I had no idea was in there.'

He drew a breath—a difficult one—and his voice was strained as he went on.

'I found, inside the cover of a book, to keep it smooth, his marriage certificate to Bianca's mother. He was a newlywed, returning to Italy to prepare a home for her, his bride—but she never even knew he had been killed. She must have thought that she had been abandoned, left to raise their child alone. A child I did not even know existed until I set London lawyers to find out what they could about the marriage I had never even knew he'd made. And they found Bianca...'

Now, finally, his voice softened.

'The niece I never knew I had. My lost brother's daughter.'

Luca could see the emotion visible in Matteo's face, and for a moment it seemed his godfather would not speak again. But then he did, and his voice was warm and cherishing.

'And here she is...my dearest, dearest Bianca,' he said.

His smile went to her, encompassing and embracing, and Luca saw her take Matteo's hand and gently squeeze it.

'And here I shall stay,' she said.

She said it to Matteo, and the voice in which she spoke was as warm as his. Unlike the glance that suddenly, for a fraction of a second, she shot across the table at Luca. Icy and defiant.

He realised his godfather was speaking again, and made himself pay attention.

'So, there you have it, my boy,' he said heavily. 'How I wish with all my heart that I had known of Bianca's existence earlier, so that she might have grown up here. But at least I have found her now, even if our time together must be brief.'

Sadness was in his voice again. Then he rallied.

'I shall make the very most of that time,' he declared, sounding resolute. 'And when I am gone I shall know that my brother's daughter is well provided for. She will have her father's portion, which so wrongly came to me, and she will be my heir as well.'

Luca frowned. Why was Matteo telling him this? Yes, he knew he was to be his godfather's executor when the time came, but he had never had expectations of any legacy himself. Bianca was welcome to it.

It would make her a very wealthy woman. A world away from the Bianca he had known.

It was impossible to associate the Bianca he had known in London with the woman now revealed to be his godfather's niece. The dissonance was too great. Too unbelievable.

With difficulty, he made himself speak.

'I am glad for you Matteo, that you have found your brother's daughter.' He could not bring himself to look across the table at Bianca, so he did not. 'Thank you for telling me.'

Agitation suddenly possessed his godfather. 'I have more to say, Luca! More that you must hear! And Bianca must hear too!'

And as he spoke on, for a third time that evening, Luca froze.

Bianca was torn. Torn at least in two and probably into a lot more.

Part of her had a heart filling up with almost tearful emotion as she heard her uncle tell the sad, sad story that he had told her the day after her arrival in Italy, with mutual tears and so much emotion, of the father she had never known.

But another part of her was steely—out of necessity. Stark, pitiless necessity. Because she was holding her nerve against the man sitting opposite her.

Luca—walking out of the toxic past.

Her mouth tightened momentarily. At least it had given her a stab of vicious pleasure to see his expression as his eyes had alighted on her when he'd come into the *saloni*. His shock, and the appalled, disbelieving look on his face had matched her own. And then, after his vile accusations out on the terrace just now, she had got her own back when Matteo had made his bombshell announcement about who she was.

Oh, that had given her satisfaction indeed!

He could *choke* on what he'd suspected her of! Just *choke* on it!

And as for Luca—*Luca!*—turning out to be her uncle's precious godson… Well, he could choke on that too! She didn't give a damn…could not care less.

It's nothing to do with me—nothing.

Oh, she would never tell her uncle why she hated his precious godson. Would never give a hint of it, or of the fact that she'd known him—to her cost!—six years ago, when he'd enjoyed himself slumming it with her until he'd been recalled to his aristocratic life out here in Italy, far too posh for the likes of her! No, that could stay buried in the past—the only place it was fit for.

In the here and now, if she must, she'd bring herself to be civil to Luca—if only barely so—in Matteo's presence. But that was all. Besides, Matteo had said he worked in Rome, travelled abroad a lot on business. That, surely, would keep him away?

And he'll want to stay away, anyway. He won't want to come here...see me. I'm the last person he'd want to see. To have anything at all to do with.

He'd made that clear six years ago. Brutally clear.

No, Luca had walked out of her life six years ago and he could stay out. Apart from occasional visits to Matteo, while her uncle still lived, there would be no reason for her and Luca to have anything to do with each other. None.

He's Matteo's godson and I'm his niece—end of. No other connection.

She turned her attention back to what her uncle had started to say. And as she heard him out she could only stare in disbelief.

More than disbelief.

Horror.

Luca stilled. He surely could not be hearing what Matteo was saying now, his expression troubled, his voice agitated.

'Bianca will be my heir, but I fear for her! Alone and unprotected as she will be. Jackals will circle—those who see in her a target...someone to exploit. Wanting the wealth she will possess. Oh, I fear for her when I am no longer here!'

Anxiety was rising in Matteo's voice and Luca saw him clutch at Bianca's hand again, saw the expression on her face turn to concern.

'Which is why, my dear boy, my dear Luca, the godson I trust implicitly, completely, I make this heartfelt, impassioned request to you. To *you*. That *you* will protect my niece...guard her...keep her safe from the circling jackals who will see in her a vulnerable, beautiful woman and think...dare!...to beguile her...tempt her—'

He broke off, his face contorting. Then he found words again.

'I beg you…implore you, Luca…to protect Bianca in the one sure and certain way that she can be protected, kept safe from such jackals!'

He took another breath, a laboured one. He was becoming more agitated, and Luca's alarm was growing. But then his alarm changed to something quite different…

'It is why I asked you here this evening!' Matteo got out. 'My time is short, Luca…so short! But if I knew for certain that you would protect Bianca then I can leave this world, so dangerous to her, with peace of mind…peace of heart.' His expression changed, calmed. 'Knowing that you will be her protector in the most absolute way possible.'

His eyes burned into Luca's.

'As Bianca's husband,' he said.

CHAPTER FOUR

BIANCA HEARD THE words but could not believe she had. They had come out of nowhere, and brought a shock so great it had frozen her solid. All she could do was stare at her uncle. Completely silenced.

Then she heard another voice speak. Luca's.

'Matteo—'

Dimly, Bianca could hear the difficulty with which he was speaking, and as he continued, not faltering but laboured, her eyes went to him. He, too, had shock written hard across his face. Every feature stark.

'That is an…unexpected suggestion.'

She saw him take a breath, as if air was urgently needed, then heard him forcing himself on. Forcing his voice into a lighter pitch. And as she heard his words, she understood why.

'Marriage is a big step,' he said.

She heard an injection of what she perceived to be twisted humour in his tone, and she understood why, and what he was doing.

'Perhaps—'

But Matteo's voice cut across his. 'It's the only way,' he said. 'Marriage!'

Bianca heard the urgency in her uncle's voice, the fear. Impulsively, she spoke, pressing the thin fingers of his hand still holding hers.

'Zio Matteo...' She, too, tried to make her voice light, yet warm and sympathetic as well. 'This is...well...quite a surprise—'

She found herself glancing across the table at Luca. His expression was still frozen, and he was not looking at her but at Matteo. A mask had come down over his face—she could see it.

'You must give us time...' she went on, addressing Matteo, taking a breath herself, knowing she needed to. 'You must give us time to...'

Her uncle's eyes filled with anguish. 'There *is* no time! Oh, my dear child, how else can I make sure you are safe when I am gone? I must know...*know*...that Luca will take my place and keep you safe.'

Luca's voice came again, and it sounded as if he'd found something to attach himself to. 'Matteo, if you want me to be a trustee for Bianca, then of course—'

Had she heard something in his voice as he said her name? Something that had nothing to do with the excruciating absurdity of the moment? It didn't matter whether she had or not, because her uncle was cutting across him again. This time his free hand slashed angrily.

'*No!* It is not enough, Luca! Only marriage will keep her truly safe—permanently safe!'

His eyes flashed from Luca, to Bianca, and back again, and Bianca felt her hand squeezed tightly, almost to the point of making her flinch with the pressure.

'Why do you object? Why do you make difficulties?' asked Matteo. 'It is so clear—so obvious—the only solution! The *ideal* solution! Both of you are so dear to me! And marriage will make you dear to each other!'

The anguish, the urgency and the desperation in his voice was not lost to her—how could it be? And she saw his features contort. But even though she saw it, she could not feel it. Instead, a hollowness was filling her. There was a gaping gash inside her, slashed open by knives that had never lost their sharpness, sheathed though she had tried to keep them down the years.

She heard Luca speaking yet again, and now his voice was not *faux* light, *faux* humorous, but soothing, emollient. Placatory.

'Matteo—you have sprung this on us. Be reasonable and let us have time to…to assimilate what you have said. It is a lot to take in…'

She could see that Matteo was going to speak again, his face working painfully. But Luca was holding up a hand. Not admonishingly, or warningly, but sympathetically.

'I have heard what you have said, but Bianca and I—'

Again, she heard the gritted reticence with which he said her name, linking it to himself, and she knew why. Because it made those knives slashing out that hollow gash inside her slash yet again.

'We need to…talk it through.' And now the deliberate lightness was back in Luca's voice. 'Surely you can grant us that?'

He took another breath, shorter this time, and Bianca saw him reach for his glass of wine. His eyes, though, were watching Matteo, and hers went to him as well. He was not looking well at all. His colour was high, the agitation he had expressed was visible, and she could see the pulse at his thin neck throb.

With some difficulty she slipped her hand from his clasping grip, but did not remove it. Instead, she placed it—comfortingly, she hoped—on top of his where it lay on the polished mahogany surface of the table.

'Dear Uncle,' she said, making her voice warm and affectionate, ignoring the rapid beating of her heart, the gash inside her. 'Luca is right.'

It cost her to say his name, let alone to say he was right, but she knew it was necessary, at this appalling moment, to do so.

'And what we need to do now is have our dinner. I know Giuseppe will have arranged something wonderful for this special occasion, and it would be ungracious of us to spoil it! So, let us finish this delicious *primo*—you see how adept I am becoming to the Italian way of dining?—and then Giuseppe can show us the next culinary masterpiece that has been prepared for us.'

It was her turn now to infuse deliberate lightness into her voice, warming it with a smile. She gave her uncle's hand another gentle pat, knowing she was trying to humour him, trying to find a way, however clumsy and obvious, to extricate herself from this hideous situation.

For a moment Matteo's expression remained agitated, his face still working. Then, abruptly, he seemed to subside, as if the last of his energy had left him...been exhausted. The unnatural high colour faded from his thin cheeks and Bianca felt relief washing through her. She found her free hand reaching for her wine glass, and realised that while she'd been speaking Luca had taken a draught from his own. She knew exactly why, for she now did just the same. Slowly, she felt her heart rate ease and the knives stop slashing inside her. They had no place. Not here, not now—not ever.

Replacing her wine glass, she picked up her fork again, taking the last few mouthfuls of the delicious saffron-bathed scallops, making a murmur of appreciation. She saw Luca resume eating as well, and to her even greater relief saw her uncle, jerkily but resignedly, pick up his own fork. Though he still looked gaunt and drawn and ill, his colour was less alarming, his breathing steadier. His agitation had not done him any good.

Nor me either...

The understatement bit at her, but she crushed it down. She could not afford to yield to her own reaction—not now, not yet—for she had to think of her uncle, not herself.

And Luca?

Almost—*almost*—a savage laugh broke from her, but she silenced it. At least for now.

Her gaze slid across the table to his face. The expressionless mask was still in place, but the lines scored around his mouth told her what she already knew.

Bitterly.

How he got through the rest of the meal Luca hardly knew. Knew only that it was endless, and that all it achieved was to tighten the knot of anger inside him that was demanding to be let loose.

But not yet.

Now he required every last gram of self-control to get through the interminable meal, to make painstakingly courteous conversation with his godfather who, thankfully, seemed to have calmed down after the dangerous agitation he had displayed as he'd dropped his ludicrous bombshell.

Luca frowned. Just *his* bombshell? His darkling glance speared across the wide table. She was sitting there, cool as milk, her words smooth as butter, talking to Matteo calmly about whatever it was their conversation concerned. Luca could barely pay conscious attention to it. She was saying something about the history of the house, of this part of Italy, and Matteo was more animated now, engaging with the subject, holding forth. Luca noted that he was eating— not heartily, but steadily. Drinking too.

Giuseppe and the manservant came in to clear away the plates, bestow upon them the *secondo*—a herb and truffle-filled porchetta—and pour a rich Barolo red wine.

No more mention was made of Matteo's ludicrous, outrageous proposition—a proposition that had Bianca's fingerprints all over it.

Cold anger bit into Luca. Because of course it was her idea—it was totally, screamingly obvious. Six years ago she had wanted to keep him in her life, keep herself in his. Did she really think she could achieve that now?

He would have laughed—except that only anger filled him. Furious and savage.

Bianca kissed her uncle gently on his sunken cheek, bidding him goodnight. Giuseppe was hovering, and out in the hall Bianca could see her uncle's nurse waiting as well.

'*Buone notte...*' She smiled, stepping back. 'I dare not detain you any longer, or Giuseppe will take me to task.'

'Yes, yes...' her uncle said testily.

Bianca knew that it was exhaustion that had made him so.

He had given out so much during the evening, and his meagre energy levels were completely drained. He did not look well, his colour fluctuating.

Luca stepped forward, and instinctively Bianca eased away further.

Luca stretched out his hand to his godfather. 'I, too, will bid you goodnight, Matteo. I wish you a good rest, and promise we will regroup in the morning—but not too early! That wine Giuseppe served was strong!'

He shook his godfather's hand briefly, then crossed to the door, opening it more widely. All but ushering his godfather out into the hall.

'Goodnight, my boy,' Matteo said, then paused on the

threshold, turning back to Luca. His expression changed. Became anxious again...agitated. 'And you will—?'

Luca did not let him finish. 'Yes,' he said firmly.

Then he nodded at Giuseppe and closed the double doors to the *saloni*, where they had taken coffee after dinner. As the doors clicked shut, and her uncle was left with the faithful Giuseppe and the diligent Paolo to be escorted to his bedroom and the rest and sleep he so obviously needed, Bianca turned away. Absently, to give herself something to do, she placed the used coffee cups and the two liqueur glasses she and Luca had used on the silver tray. Matteo had abstained, and she was glad of it. The wine had been quite enough for him, given his illness and his cocktail of medications.

A voice behind her spoke. Deep, authoritative, and edged like a blade.

'We need to talk,' said Luca. 'Now.'

Luca strode to the French windows, throwing one of them open wide. He wanted fresh air, and he wanted privacy. He had things to say, and he did not wish them to be interrupted by staff clearing away the coffee cups, or asking if there was anything else he needed.

All he needed was Bianca—to himself. And to let rip with what had been burning inside him since his godfather had dropped that second bombshell.

He could feel his fury now, knifing at him to get out, black in his head as he flicked the light switch by the French windows and lit the external wall lamps. They threw a pool of light on to the wide, paved terrace, almost turning it into a stage.

He paused by the open window pointedly. Leashing his self-control with icy intent. He saw her stiffen. For a moment he thought she was going to try and cut and run...trot out some verbiage about being tired and wishing to retire. Not that he would let her.

But then her head went back and he saw her shoulders straighten. Without a word she marched past him, out into the pool of soft light beyond, and then turned. He stepped after her, closing the French windows. She stood, illuminated as if on a stage, her beauty displayed, and Luca felt something go through him that he instantly sought to repress. Extinguish.

He'd done so six years ago—he would do so again. And again and again and again.

For however long it takes!

His expression was tight, as he moved forward. Close, but not too close.

His eyes lasered her.

'You do realise,' he said, and each word was bitten out from him as he finally unleashed the self-control he'd been exerting, 'that all the idiocy Matteo spouted will not happen? Whatever fond hopes you may have been harbouring.'

His voice was withering. Scathing and scornful. He saw her expression change—saw her flinch, almost. Though it was gone so swiftly he thought he had only imagined it. Then hardness filled her face.

'Any "fond hopes"—believe me—are entirely my uncle's!' Her voice was as withering as his. As scathing and as scornful.

A short, harsh laugh broke from him. 'Oh, don't even try and pretend otherwise! This insane proposition is your idea! The moment you realised that I was Matteo's godson you saw your chance! Your chance to get what you didn't get six years ago. Marriage! That's what you were after! But I wouldn't play ball! I walked away from you. And now you see a chance of bringing me to heel the way you couldn't back then! Well, I've got news for you, Bianca—I didn't want you then, and I don't want you now either!'

As he threw this tirade at her he saw her face tighten into stark immobility. The fact that it threw her features into relief, accentuating her beauty, he refused...*refused*... to acknowledge. He refused to acknowledge anything—any damn thing at all—except his need to let rip at her.

He let rip some more. He needed to. Emotion was knifing inside him, and it had to come out or it would cut him to the quick. Do him serious damage. The emotion was anger— of course it was. That was the only emotion the situation warranted. The only one he would permit.

The shock he'd felt all evening was finally being let loose.

Bianca...reappearing out of the past with a completely new identity.

But still the same agenda. Wanting more of me than I want of her.

And now, after six years, she thought she'd found a way to get it. A despicable way.

Contempt twisted in his voice now. 'How could you make use of Matteo the way you have? Manipulate him into wanting what he announced at dinner! A dying man—and you make use of him to try and get me to marry you! It's contemptible!'

He saw her expression change, and the starkness of her features gave way—contorting. Convulsing.

'Contemptible?' she shot back, fury naked in her voice. 'I'll tell you what is *contemptible*!' Her voice was a hiss, like a snake. 'Your vanity! Your incredible, overweening vanity! You think—you actually think!—that I want to marry you? My God, I wouldn't marry you if you came served on a silver salver with an apple in your mouth, you conceited pig!

You are the *last* man on God's earth that I would ever, *ever* marry! For *any* reason whatsoever! *Any* reason! Even…' She drew a breath, narrow and constricted. 'Even for the sake of my poor uncle!'

Her eyes flashed suddenly—furiously—like emerald fire. Luca felt their power…armoured himself against their force. Her attack on him he thrust aside—her accusation was predictable and irrelevant. As was what she threw at him now.

'I am *appalled* to discover that *you* are my uncle's precious godson!'

'Make that two of us!' he threw back grimly. 'I am appalled to see *you* here—'

'That was the only upside to this evening!' she spat. 'That sweet, sweet moment when your vile assumption about my presence here was shot down in flames! When Matteo told you I was his niece!' Her words were vicious beneath the saccharine.

'Sweeter still,' he snarled back at her, 'was the moment when he said he wanted us to marry!'

She threw her head back. '"Sweet" is not the word! I love my uncle very much—and I am so incredibly glad and grateful we have discovered each other's existence. I'm devastated—horribly devastated—and heartbroken that our time together must be so short. But even loving him there are sacrifices I will not make for him—and marrying you is top of the list! You were a conceited pig six years ago, Luca—and you're a conceited pig still!'

She surged past him, aiming for the French windows.

Blind rage was in him. Rage for what she had manipulated her poor dying uncle into wanting. Rage for her trying to deny it. Rage at her daring to try to turn the tables on *him*, accuse *him*, when it was *she* who was the cause of all this fiasco!

And his rage that went even deeper than that—became something quite other than rage...

His hand lashed out. Fastened around her wrist. Stopped her in her tracks.

Bianca felt his hand close around her wrist over the pearl bracelet in a vise-like grip. Rage became outrage.

'Let me *go*!'

She tried to yank herself free, but he'd stepped up to her. Close.

Too close.

His closeness filled her consciousness. Suddenly, out of nowhere, the cool night air felt hot—stiflingly hot. She couldn't breathe. All evening she'd been burningly, punishingly conscious of Luca. Who'd suddenly appeared out of nowhere...out of a past she'd thought dead and buried. She'd thrown away the shovel with which she had doggedly, determinedly and desperately buried it, and yet suddenly, like the demon king in a pantomime, he had just...appeared.

Framed in the entrance to the *saloni*.

Walking into her life again. Invading it.

All through the whole nightmare evening she'd been forced to be hideously aware of him, feeling his fury and his outrage at her very presence. And then what had her poor, benighted, hapless uncle said and done? Dear God Almighty...

She'd known from the moment she'd heard Matteo make his unbelievable announcement that a showdown with Luca would be coming. That it had to come. That was why she'd walked out here on to the terrace, at his insistence, knowing she had to make it clear—coruscatingly, irrefutably clear—that whatever her poor, deluded, pitiful...*dying*...uncle had said, she wanted to stamp it out instantly and totally.

And now to have Luca *dare* to accuse her of having persuaded Matteo to dream up the idea! Laying it at *her* door! As if...as if...she had fed the notion to her uncle!

As if I actually wanted Matteo to say what he did!

Luca was blaming *her*...accusing *her*...sneering at *her*...

Despising her...

Like he had six years ago.

Rage contorted inside her—rage and another emotion, just as strong, that she crushed down as she had always crushed it down. She had had to learn to crush it down, for six long, brutal years.

And crushed down it would stay—whatever it cost her.

However close to her he stepped. Imposing his presence on her.

She could sense his body—the scent of his aftershave, his skin, the heat of his breath on her, the dark, killing flare of his eyes...

She had to pull free. She had to.

Desperation fuelled her.

'I said let me *go*!'

She yanked again—but the vise of his fingers only tightened. His body was looming against hers, blotting out the light from the wall lamp, silhouetting his profile.

'This is *assault*!' she ground out, eyes flashing with fury—fury at him for seizing her...fury at herself for not being able to free herself. Fury that was safer than any other emotion.

And then something changed in him. A sudden tension. In heels she was tall, but she had never been taller than him...never even as tall. Nor was she now. Her face was lifted to his, rage and outrage warring in her flashing eyes, the gritted steel of her jaw.

'Assault?'

He threw the word back at her. And as he did so she saw the sudden tension in him abruptly ceasing. Changing.

His grip around her wrist was ceasing. Changing.

Easing.

Softening...

'Assault?' he said again.

And now his voice had changed too. There was no scathing fury in it. There was a different note...one that suddenly, out of nowhere, changed her own coruscating fury into something quite different.

Her eyes were wide, filled with horror. Her whole body was filled with horror. With a drumming in her veins Bianca realised his fingers were no longer pressing on her wrist at all. They were softly, lethally, caressing it. Helplessness drowned her. The world seemed to fade away...

And then the instinctive, atavistic alarm lacing through her became overlaid with something different again. Something she needed to fight against. Something she needed to deny...suppress...escape...

She heard him speak...heard it through the drumming that was in her ears now, like a rush of blood. Her heart was suddenly thudding like a hammer in her chest. He had stepped closer to her as he spoke, filling her vision, looming over her. She was staring up at him now—knew she was staring, fixed on him, magnetised, unable to drag her helpless, hopeless gaze away. Just as she was unable to drag her wrist free of the soft, lethal stroking of his fingertips across the delicate skin of her inner wrist, beneath the lustrous pearls of the bracelet. It was making her feel as if her entire being were concentrated there, in the nerve-endings under his circling touch, and was melting...melting...

Faintness weakened her...

'Assault, Bianca?' His voice was as soft as his touch. His breath as soft. 'Is this assault?'

His eyes were pouring into hers, possessing hers. She wanted to pull away, to use every muscle in her body to do so, to get free...

But she did not. Could not.

She saw his other hand lift, felt the tips of his fingers drift across her cheek like a drift of snow...snow that wasn't cold, not cold at all, but melting...dissolving... Slowly...infinitely slowly.

She felt her eyelids dip with the sensation of it...so light was his touch, so leisurely.

'Assault, Bianca?'

She heard his voice again, as caressing as his touch at her wrist, her face. But the gaze pouring into hers was mocking...

'And this?' he said.

His breath was warm on her, infused with the subtle potency of the almond liqueur he had taken with his coffee.

'Is this assault too?'

And then his lips were grazing hers...

Her mouth was silk...softest, softest silk...

Memory filled him as his senses were filled with her, infusing him, fusing the past—so long past—to now...this moment *now*...

The night cocooned him, the soft light from the wall lamps cast its glow around him, and the murmur of the cicadas was all about as his fingers moved to curve around the nape of her neck, holding her to him as his mouth moved softly... lightly...possessively...on hers.

She did not fight him. He felt...heard...the soft sigh that came from her. She was yielding her mouth to his...quiescent...pliant...

All that he wanted.

How long the kiss lasted he did not know. Time had stopped. Collapsed upon itself. How long had it been since he had last tasted her mouth with his? That final morning, after making love to her? The day he'd left London, his posting finished, his return to Rome required?

More than required—desired.

Because if he hadn't gone back to Rome—if he hadn't thrown at her what he'd had to throw at her... If he hadn't ended it the way he had...

Their kiss now...sensual, arousing, sating...was dragging him back. Back into the past he'd walked away from. And it was telling him exactly...*exactly*...why he'd had to walk away from her.

Instinctively, he felt himself draw her pliant, yielding body against his, and all the while his mouth was deepening the kiss, seductively, languorously, tasting and taking, taking and tasting. He could feel the soft swell of her breasts against his chest, feel them engorge, feel their hips meet... feel himself engorge...

Arousal deepened as his fingers speared into her hair. He could feel his hunger build. Desire mount...

It was madness. In some small, remote part of his brain he knew it was madness.

But it was impossible to draw back...impossible to let her go. All he wanted was to feel her breasts peaking against his, feel the arousing frottage of her arousal, the low moan in her throat as their mouths met and mated...

Her hips were straining against his, fuelling his own arousal, feeding this madness...

He wanted more...so much more...

The years between them vanished, as if they had never been, and he yielded to the madness possessing him.

Until—

The violence of her wrenching herself away from him made his hand fall from her nape, loosened by force his hold on her wrist. And then she took a razored breath, her hand flashing up, descending again with force to catch his cheek.

The blow was sharp, stinging. Her words a vehement hiss as she reared away from him.

'That *is* assault!'

Her voice was breathless, panting. She surged past him, gaining the French windows, yanking them open. She turned. Her eyes were pinpricks of black fury.

'Don't *ever* touch me again! *Ever!*'

Then she was gone.

Luca's hand lifted absently to his stinging cheek, feeling the impact of her slap. She had not held back. But his mind was not on that.

It was on the madness that had just possessed him. The insane, impossible madness...

After six long years...to have Bianca in his arms again...

He should never have allowed it. Never indulged—

CHAPTER FIVE

SOMEONE WAS KNOCKING on her bedroom door. Blearily, Bianca woke from a sleep that had not come until the dawn, and had then brought no rest with it. Only dreams—hot and humid and worse than any nightmare. Worse by far than the nightmares that always ended with Luca pulling himself away from her, his harsh, callous, 'It's over, Bianca. *Over!*' echoing cruelly down the years.

But when she woke to consciousness now it was to a reality that was worse than any dream, any nightmare.

Her face contorted as the memory of what had happened out there on the terrace rushed back into her head.

Oh, dear God—had she really let it happen? Let Luca just help himself to her? Let him kiss her, crush her to him, as he had? Oh, dear God, she *had* let him! Hadn't protested. Hadn't prevented him at all! She had kissed him back, opening her mouth to his hungrily, aroused, pressing herself against him, feeling what it did to her body—to his...

She had felt herself respond to him, want more...

Want everything...

No! She sheared her mind away. She couldn't bear to think of it—couldn't bear to remember it.

Shame and humiliation flushed through her.

How could I let him do it? How could I?

Her mortification was absolute.

Memory leapt from the past, scalding in her head. That

last morning with Luca, when he'd told her he was going back to Rome and she'd flung herself at him, clinging to him, desperate not to lose him, desperate to get him to take him with her...keep her in his life.

And he'd put her from him. Said what he had said to her. And she had stood there and taken it. Let him say it.

Just like last night, she had let him do what he had done...

Her face contorted again.

She hated herself—hated him. Herself more...

The knocking on the door became louder, finally piercing her burning, scalding consciousness. Confused, she called out for the person to come in, pushing herself up on the pillows.

It was Maria, looking, sounding agitated.

'*Mi dispiace, signorina.* I am sorry for disturbing you. But the doctor has been summoned for the *signor*.'

Bianca's bleariness vanished. So did the tormenting memories of last night.

'What's happened?' she demanded, fear sharpening her voice.

'The *signor* has not spent a good night,' Maria said. 'His nurse is concerned, and the doctor is attending.'

'I'll get up at once,' Bianca said, alarm spearing in her. 'Thank you for telling me. I shall be there as soon as possible—please let them know.'

Dismissed, Maria hurried off, and Bianca plunged into the en suite bathroom. Emerging after the sketchiest of showers, she dressed hurriedly and left her bedroom.

Oh, dear God, hadn't last night been enough—and now this?

She saw Giuseppe hovering anxiously outside her uncle's room.

'What is happening?' she asked fearfully, her heart beating faster with alarm.

'The doctor is with your uncle now, *signorina*. Please, do not be too alarmed. His nurse would have summoned an ambulance, had it been a crisis, but as it is he wants the doctor to give his opinion and administer whatever help might be required.'

Another voice, deep and sharp, sounded from the far end of the spacious landing.

'What's going on?'

Bianca turned. Luca was striding towards them. Freshly shaven, hair still damp from showering, casually dressed in chinos and an open-necked shirt, he still looked just as devastating as he'd looked last night in his tuxedo. She gulped silently. For one hideous second she could not tear her eyes away as he approached. And suddenly it was not alarm that was making her heart beat faster—not alarm at all.

She made herself speak. Focus on what was important. Her uncle—only her uncle.

Not Luca! Not him—he's not important at all! He's not, not, not! So ignore him! Ignore the way he makes you feel... react. Just ignore it!

'The doctor is with my uncle...' Fear stabbed in her voice.

Giuseppe started to talk to Luca, deferential as always, and in Italian, but Bianca could hear the reassuring note in his voice.

Luca nodded, moved to enter Matteo's bedroom. It opened before he could do so and the doctor emerged—familiar to Bianca from his weekly check-ups on her uncle. His expression was grave, but he had his bag with him, as though he were ready to depart, which surely, Bianca thought, must be a good sign?

His eyes went straight to her. 'If I might have a word?'

'*Certo,*' she said immediately.

The doctor closed the bedroom door behind him, looking uncertainly at the presence of both Giuseppe and Luca. But Bianca didn't want to exclude Giuseppe—despite his reassuring words, she knew he would be anxious. And Luca might as well hear too.

'How is my uncle?' she asked, knowing her heart rate was up.

Carefully, the doctor explained. The previous evening—including, he said disapprovingly, Matteo indulging in too much wine—had exerted a strain upon his patient that was been inadvisable. It had taken a toll that was cause for concern, but not for acute alarm. Hospitalisation would not be necessary, providing his patient was afforded complete bedrest and absolute peace and quiet.

'His mind is very agitated, and that is not good—not good at all.'

The doctor was stern as he spoke.

'You must remember that the drugs your uncle is on have powerful side effects, not all benign. In the circumstances, I have administered a mild sedative and increased the level of his medication to keep him stable. But he must suffer no more anxiety. That is essential. Absolutely essential! You must understand that.'

He paused, his lips pursing.

'However, despite my urging to him the importance of complete rest, he has insisted that yourself, *signorina*, and the Visconte...' he gave a slight nod towards Luca '...must attend him now. With great reluctance I have agreed. But...' he held up a warning hand '... I have done so only because he became increasingly anxious until I conceded.'

His stern glance encompassed them both.

'I cannot emphasise enough that he must not be agitated. He must be agreed with...he must be deferred to. He *must* be kept calm! I know I do not need to speak of co-morbidities and the burden his cancer places upon his heart and vital functions, but I do not wish a crisis to develop—'

He broke off, then opened the bedroom door again.

'I shall stay until he has seen you, and then give one final check before taking my leave.' He looked at Bianca. 'If you please...?' he said, clearly indicating that she should go in.

She did, but heaviness was dragging her every step.

And it was a weight caused not only by fear for uncle. For a cause far, far worse. For what he wanted of her.

Behind her, she heard Luca's tread at her heels as he followed her in.

'You realise that we have no choice.'

Luca's voice was coming from a long way away.

Bianca didn't answer. She couldn't.

There was a stone in her throat. Her lungs. Concrete, hard set, in her stomach. She didn't look at Luca. She couldn't do that either. She couldn't do anything. She was completely numb.

They were in Matteo's library. Bianca stared blankly at the serried rows of shelving lining the walls. Matteo's ornate desk was at one end of the room, the cluster of sofas and armchairs where he liked to sit nearby. Her hand was closed over the back of one of the chairs as if for support. Support she needed.

'I won't do it.'

Her words were terse, her mouth set.

She heard Luca give a rasp from where he stood by the fireplace, one arm pressed on the mantel. Did he need support too? she thought sourly, forcing her gaze to go to him. His expression was grim—but then so was hers.

'We don't have a choice,' he repeated, his voice as grim as his expression.

'I said no.' Something flashed in her eyes like black fire.

'I said no last night and I say no now. I will say no while there is breath in my body—'

'And when there is no breath in Matteo's body?'

He cut across her—brutal and ruthless. She flinched, but only inwardly. She hardened again. Luca was good at being brutal and ruthless. She should know.

He told me—brutally and ruthlessly—that I wasn't good enough for the likes of him.

The irony of it was not lost on her and, sour though it was, she could taste it in her mouth.

But he was prepared to strike that low—stoop that low now. And low it would be as he bit out, 'Don't think that I would do it otherwise.' His voice was harsh. 'But you heard the doctor—heard Matteo when we went into him. How... obsessed he is. He's beyond reason.'

She still wouldn't answer him. Mouth set like steel.

Another rasp broke from him, and he threw up his hands angrily. 'For God's sake, all that is required is that we go through the motions! Let him think we've played into this... this fairy tale...this fantasy he's become obsessed by!'

She turned away, unable to bear looking at him. Unable to bear the stone in her throat, her lungs. It was stopping her breathing, the concrete set hard in her stomach. She felt her hands clench.

That morning Matteo had looked like a death's head. Whatever kind of collapse he'd had, it had brought him closer to death than she had ever yet seen him. His voice had barely been a whisper, and his hand had been skin and bone as it had clutched hers. Fear had stabbed at her—and it stabbed again now.

'Bianca?'

Luca's voice was still harsh. Still brutal and ruthless. But she didn't have to think of him. He wasn't worth a single thought unless it was to damn him to hell, where she'd damned him six years ago. And then again, with black, bleak fury, she had damned him to hell last night. All she had to think of was Matteo—her uncle—who had found her, brought her here, welcomed her into the home that might have been hers all along. Who had given her his love, freely and instantly, and who now was dying...

She heard words form inside her, forced away the stone in her throat, her lungs. Gritted her clenched teeth.

'I'll do it—for him,' she said.

Acid burned in her mouth.

Luca was in the pool in the villa's gardens, relentlessly ploughing up and down in a strong, tireless freestyle, his thoughts turbid as he chewed up the lengths. He needed the exertion—needed something, anything, to release what was inside him.

Dio, had he really done what he had? Let himself be manoeuvred into this? Let Matteo believe his deluded fantasy was actually real?

Should he really have gone along with his godfather's obsession—driven, he knew, by his impending mortality?

Well, it was too late to think otherwise. He and Bianca had gone up to Matteo's bedroom, told him the 'good news'—Luca's mouth twisted unconsciously—and the change in Matteo's countenance had been dramatic. The fearful, fretful, stricken anxiousness had vanished. His face had lit up and his weak, thin hand had reached out to wring Luca's in delight.

The end of the pool neared, and Luca executed a rapid tumble turn before resuming his ploughing through the water. It was too late to regret what he'd done. All he could do now was face up to it, endure it for as long as it took—and make sure Bianca did as well.

Bianca...

Of all the women Matteo wants me to marry, it has to be Bianca...

Some cosmic jester—one of the old pagan gods, no doubt, with a warped sense of humour—had conjured her up out of the past he'd left behind, walked rapidly and ruthlessly away from, and dumped her back in front of him. Forced him into this distasteful farce.

But it was a farce he was stuck with now.

An old saying—bitter and cynical—intruded into his head. *No good deed goes unpunished.*

His good deed was taking pity on his godfather at this drastic hour of his failing life.

His punishment—well, that came with a name, a face, a body...and a whole heap of memories he could do without right now.

Especially the memory of that clinch out on the terrace last night. Por Dio, was I mad...insane to do that?

It was the only explanation. She'd goaded him, repudiated him, scorned him, and it had infuriated him...inflamed him. He'd acted on impulse—on something that had flared in him. Something that he hadn't been able to stop, hadn't wanted to stop...

He'd wanted to indulge instead.

So he had. He had indulged. Indulged very pleasurably. Finding her mouth with his...drawing her soft, pliant body against his...letting the contact arouse him...arouse her...

No! He pulled his mind away, increased the pace of his strokes to a punishing degree, refusing to let himself remember how it had felt to have Bianca pressed close against him, the feel of her peaked breasts against his chest, the feel of her soft, silken mouth opening to his, the hardening of his own body as she'd aroused it with hers...

He had wanted her—wanted her totally, consumingly, urgently...

He reached the end of the pool again, dived down to execute another tumble turn, twisting and propelling himself against the wall of the pool to force himself forward again, surfacing to take a gulp of air. Air that might suffocate the memory he must not allow. Cold water all around him that might quench the desire he must never allow himself to feel for her again.

Because if he did—

No! His negation came again. For Matteo's sake, and that alone, he'd agreed to pander to the desperate fantasy of a dying man. But that was *all* he'd agreed to. From now on, whatever it took, what had happened last night must never happen again.

His time with Bianca was over—six long years over. He would keep it that way.

There was no question of her uncle being anywhere near well enough to leave his room that evening. Which meant, Bianca thought bleakly, she was going to have to face dining alone with Luca. She wished she could take the cowardly way out and ask for a simple supper tray to be brought to her bedroom, but then her spine stiffened. She wasn't going to hide or run from Luca. She wouldn't give him that satisfaction.

Instead, she'd do the complete opposite.

With an expression on her face that she did not like, but which was impossible to remove, she sat down at the antique dressing table and started on her make-up. War paint—that was what it was going to be. Giving herself courage and taunting Luca at the same time.

Her eyes darkened. Once upon a time—a long, long time ago, when she was a different person altogether—she'd have put on as much make-up as she could, wanting to look a total knock-out. Wanting Luca to take one look at her and instantly sweep her off to bed...

Her mouth thinned. Now she was a little more subtle about it. Her touch lighter...but just as provocative...

'Yeah? Well, you can want, sunshine, but you ain't touchin'!'

The echo of her old, rough, ungrammatical speech pattern was raucous in her head, and she welcomed it. It reminded her of the image he'd had of her—had looked down on her for.

As she had so bitterly, painfully discovered.

She dropped the lipstick back onto an embossed silver vanity tray, reaching for her perfume. It wasn't the one he'd have been familiar with before—that had been overpowering, as she now realised, one of those cheap, knock-off copies of expensive names. This was a whole lot classier—the real thing and a lot more sophisticated. A quick spritz either side of her throat and on her wrists and she was done.

She got to her feet, looking at her reflection.

Tonight she'd thrown together an ensemble of jade-green evening trousers in a soft, silky material, worn with low-heeled sandals and a top in a lighter shade of green, made of similar silky material, with elbow-length sleeves. A jade pendent and matching bracelet—both her own, not gifts from her uncle—were her only jewellery. Her hair was loosely confined with a pale green scarf looped at the back of her neck.

For one long second she went on looking at her reflection. She could feel her heart thudding her chest. She was going to have to face Luca again, on her own, and somehow come to terms with what they'd done. Work out just what this insane decision to let her uncle think they really were going along with his dying dream was going to involve.

Her expression hardened again. Well, one thing it was *not* going to involve was any repetition of what had happened out on the terrace. She was never…*ever*…going to let Luca pull a stunt like that on her again.

For a moment—hot, humid and disastrous—she was there again. Feeling that complete paralysis of her will, of her body, as his mouth had lowered to hers, as her body had pressed against his, as he had swept her back into the past—

She rasped an indrawn breath, breaking the moment. Last night had been a warning—a warning she would heed from now on. She wasn't letting the past come back.

Deliberately, as she strode to the door, braced herself to go downstairs to face him, she replayed his parting words to her.

'It's over, Bianca. Over! Accept it.'

She would keep it that way.

'Thank you.'

Luca's nod towards Giuseppe was both a thank-you and a dismissal, and the butler inclined his own head in stately acknowledgement and withdrew, along with the rest of the staff, leaving Luca to face Bianca across the dining table.

She'd murmured a thank-you too, as their plates had been placed in front of them and the vegetables served, their wine glasses topped up. But she had said not another word. Not a word to himself, either, since entering the dining room and taking her place opposite his. The place at the head of the table—Matteo's—was conspicuously empty.

Luca lifted his knife and fork, made a start on his food. Across the table Bianca was doing likewise. Her face was a study. As for the rest of her…

Yet again, as she had last night, she looked nothing like the way she'd used to look in London. There—back then—

she'd dressed revealingly, provocatively, flauntingly. That had been her image then—and for what he'd wanted of her it had worked. Appealed.

But it hadn't been an appeal that would last.

Not beyond the affair he'd indulged in.

His eyes rested on her now, in an understated jade-green ensemble that offset her Titian hair, which had been styled with casual elegance. Her make-up was minimal. She looked so very different from how he remembered her.

She held a very different appeal...

But she was still as stunningly beautiful...

No. The guillotine sliced down. He took another forkful of his lamb, took a breath. Made himself address the only subject that had any relevance to them now.

'We're going to have to discuss how we handle this ludicrous situation.' He kept his voice matter of fact.

Bianca looked up. 'What do you mean?' she asked shortly. 'What situation?'

'The *situation*,' Luca said with sardonic emphasis, ignoring the flare in the green eyes levelled on him, 'in which Matteo thinks we're engaged to be married.' His voice tightened. 'We will have to put on some kind of show for him.'

He saw colour stain her cheeks, but then it was gone.

'No, we won't,' she rebuffed. 'All you have to do,' she told him tersely, 'is clear off. Go back to Rome. Better still, take yourself off on some business trip—New York, China... The further the better!'

Luca frowned. 'You think it's that simple?'

'Of course it is! My poor uncle isn't going to think anything of it. And I'll keep up the farce this end until—'

She broke off. Reached for her wine glass and took a gulp, set it back defiantly on the table. Then she lifted her chin and looked straight at him.

'I don't want you around, Luca. This whole thing is a nightmare. I've agreed to this hideous lie simply for my uncle's sake...so that he can die happy.'

'And you think I haven't done so for exactly the same reason?' he retorted, not hiding the blade in his voice.

He saw her face darken. 'You don't need to tell me that! I know your opinion of me—you made it crystal-clear six years ago! I was dirt beneath your feet. Good enough for sex, but nothing else.'

'Don't speak like that!' His remonstrance was harsh.

Anger flashed in her eyes, emerald-hard. 'Why not? It's only the truth.' Her voice twisted. 'And even if I was ever stupid enough to think otherwise, you damn well showed me again last night! Thinking you could just help yourself to me!'

Luca's expression steeled. 'Last night was a mistake—'

'Too damn right it was! The whole damn time I spent with you six years ago was a mistake! I was just too blind, too besotted, to see what you really thought of me! To realise you'd just gone slumming it with me!'

It was Luca's turn to reach for his wine. As he set the glass back she resumed eating, a set look back on her face, her movements jerky.

'It wasn't like that,' he began stiffly.

Her head flew up, eyes flashing again, turning them into green fire.

'Don't give me that! It was *exactly* like that! You said I was a common-as-muck, pig-ignorant, low-class nobody, dragged up in the East End of London—'

'I *never* said that!' Anger was open in Luca's voice now.

She cast a vicious smile at him. 'Oh, no, of course you didn't! You said,' she went on savagely, 'that we came from "very different worlds", that we'd had "a good time" together, but now it was over. You were going back to your ancestral palace and I would go back to being a barmaid pulling pints. Believe me, I didn't need a translation—I got the message!'

Luca's mouth compressed. He didn't want to be reminded of how their affair had ended. How difficult she'd made it for him. How brutal he'd had to be.

He picked up his knife and fork again, attacking his lamb with displaced ferocity. He could do without her riling him—he really could do without it.

'The past is gone, Bianca,' he said repressively. 'It's the present we have to deal with. Matteo will want more than he got this morning—he'll want to go on indulging in his fantasy. He won't be confined to bed indefinitely. The moment he feels strong enough he'll be downstairs, wanting evidence.'

The green fire in her eyes was extinguished. 'Evidence?' Bianca's voice was blank.

'Of course evidence. For a start, he'll want to see my ring on your finger. Which means we'll have to go and get one.'

For a moment his thoughts went to the antique emerald and pearl betrothal ring that fiancées in his family had worn for generations. But no, he'd done enough for Matteo.

'We can go tomorrow,' he said. 'Pavenza has decent enough jewellers—we'll find something there.'

'*You* can go,' she corrected.

He shook his head. 'No dice. You'll come too.'

She looked across at him. 'I said no.'

'And I said yes.' He took a forkful of his food. 'Bianca, Matteo will expect it. He'll expect us to spend time with each other. He said as much to me this morning. You probably didn't get the gist of it when he spoke to me in Italian, but he acknowledged that as we don't know each other, he wants us to spend time together. Yes, of course it's absurd—this whole sad, pitiful fantasy of his is absurd, and makes no sense except inside his head. But we've committed to it, Bianca. We have to see it through now. For Matteo's sake.'

Without realising it, he had altered his tone.

Something changed in her face. Slowly, reluctantly, she nodded. As if it were costing her dear...

But it was costing him too. Her vicious denunciation just now was still ringing in his ears. He had to silence it. Silence the past with the present.

He pressed on. 'Don't fight me on this. We have to put on a show. The show he wants to see—expects to see. Hopes to see. We can do it if we set aside our...our differences.'

A corner of her mouth pulled. A humourless twist. 'That's more ironic than you know,' she said. 'Or maybe it isn't? Six years ago our "differences" were impossible to set aside...'

Her words were pointed.

He gave an impatient shrug. 'Don't keep bringing up the past. It's over, like I said.'

'Oh, yes, you definitely said! Quite a few times! Every time more brutal!' The green fire was back in her eyes.

Luca threw up a peremptory hand. 'Let it go, Bianca. It's not relevant to the current situation.'

It was a putdown. He knew it and he didn't care. He didn't want her throwing their final parting back in his face the whole damn time.

What the hell else was I expecting? We had an affair—it was good, then it ended. It was our differences that made us appeal to each other—and our differences that made anything other than a fling impossible to contemplate.

And if he'd ever thought differently about their differences...?

He pushed the question aside. He hadn't gone to London

to find a wife…to come home with a bride-to-be. He'd been there to work, to put in his time in the City, build his career and enjoy what London offered. And enjoy it he had. And so had Bianca. Right up until the messy end he'd assumed Bianca knew the score. It wasn't his problem that she hadn't.

He let his hand fall. It was the present he had to deal with now—not the past.

'Like I say…' He dropped his admonishing tone. 'We have to get through this somehow. And it seems to me that the least worst way is to behave as though we are what Matteo thinks we are—complete strangers to each other. So, let's do that. Behave like we're strangers. No past, no recriminations. Just Matteo's niece and his godson, thrown together in this pitiful situation and trying to grant a dying man his dying wish, however absurd that wish is against any standard of reality. A sad, hopeless fantasy he's clinging to as he makes his untimely farewell to life. Let's have the…the compassion to do that. For him. Because we care about him.'

He paused minutely, never taking his eyes from her. Her eyes were on him, unreadable, her face closed.

'I guess I'm calling for a truce, Bianca. Just so we can deal with what we have to deal with now.' He took a breath, eyes still on her. 'Well? Will you agree?'

She didn't say anything, but something changed in her face, went out of it—as if, maybe, she was letting something go. Reluctantly. Warily.

For a moment she did not speak. Then, 'All right,' she said, her voice low. She did not meet his eyes.

Luca reached for his wine. Relief was going through him—or something was. Something he was glad of.

Though he did not know why.

CHAPTER SIX

Luca nosed his car through the gate controlling access to her uncle's villa and turned on to the cypress-lined road that led between fields and vineyards towards Pavenza. Bianca sat beside him in the passenger seat of the low-slung car, tension in every line of her body. Was she really doing this? Setting out with Luca to get an engagement ring to convince her poor uncle that, yes, despite the entire absurdity of it all, his godson was going to marry his long-lost niece and make some kind of fairy tale happy-ever-after so Matteo could die in peace?

It seemed she was.

Bizarre was one word for it—though a lot of others crowded into her beleaguered mind. She sought to quiet them…silence them. There was only one way to get through this ordeal—this exquisitely painful ordeal—and that was by trying not to think about it. Trying not to feel anything. Trying not to remember anything. That was the only way she was coping.

That—and trying not to look at Luca.

It helped that both of them were wearing sunglasses against the glare of the day. What didn't help—and she couldn't deny it—was how Luca wearing a pair of designer sunglasses made him look. Which was—

She gave a silent gulp, feeling her head twisting without her volition, under an impulse so strong she could not quell it.

Drop-dead incredible—gorgeous—fabulous.

The litany of words could not do the impact justice.

Sexy as hell...

That was the only description that did. The description that had leapt in her head the very first moment she'd laid eyes on him, leaning casually against the bar, eyes on her. It had kicked inside her, and she had felt her eyes lock to his. Knowing she'd never, ever, seen a man who could stop her dead in her tracks like that.

But that was then—this was now. She forced her gaze back on to the road. Had he noticed her looking at him? She hoped to God not—that was the last thing she could cope with.

She'd got through the rest of dinner last night by clamping a rigid control over herself as they'd laboured through a conversation that focussed on Matteo's illness and his course of treatment, what its limitations and side-effects were, and how they could be best managed and minimised. She'd told Luca that his oncologist had mentioned a clinical trial, designed to stimulate an immunological response to attack the secondary tumours, which might, if it proved successful, offer a prolonging of life the current drugs could not. However, Matteo would need to be strong to be included in such a trial, and that was the problem. Another collapse like yesterday's would rule him out.

She stared bleakly through the windscreen at the passing countryside. That was another reason for doing what she was doing now.

Keeping Matteo happy.

Whatever it cost her.

'This way.'

Luca moved to take Bianca's arm to guide her, then let his hand drop. With any other female he would not have hesitated in making such a casual, courteous gesture, but Bianca was not any other female. A jaundiced twist tightened his mouth. How the pagan god of malign humour must be laughing, having thrown together two people at daggers drawn with each other.

He frowned. *Did* he have a dagger drawn against Bianca? Why should he? If her vitriolic protestation was genuine—and she wasn't after any kind of renewal of their former relationship, let alone wanting to exploit what Matteo yearned for—then no, he didn't.

No, the only drawn dagger was Bianca's. She was still, it seemed, six years on, holding a grudge for his ending his affair with her. Well, that was her problem, not his. He had other things to cope with.

Like this insane way of placating his godfather.

Starting with the charade of supplying Bianca with an engagement ring.

The twist of his mouth deepened. She should like that—an engagement ring. If he'd offered her one six years ago she'd have bitten his hand off to get it on her finger…

He pulled his mind away again from thoughts that were pointless and irrelevant. The past was gone. It was this absurd, pitiful present he had to deal with now.

The streets of the ancient town were busy and crowded. It was still holiday season, and Pavenza was an established destination for art and history lovers, and those just wanting to hang out in pavement cafés and shop in the plentiful and upmarket boutiques. He was heading for the latter right now, with a particular jeweller in mind. It was small, but prestigious, specialising in antique jewellery and modern interpretations thereof.

Bianca wasn't saying anything as they walked along the pavement, across the main piazza and into a narrow, cobbled street. She'd said the minimum ever since they'd set out. He'd breakfasted on the terrace, in the fresh morning air, but the table had been set only for one. Bianca, he'd been informed, was taking breakfast in her room. He had been glad of it—it minimised the amount of time they had to spend together.

After breakfast, Giuseppe had informed him that his godfather would like to see him, and so, dutifully, he'd attended the bedside. He hadn't been sure whether to be glad or dismayed that Matteo was looking distinctly better than he had yesterday—glad that he was, but dismayed that, as his godfather had made rapidly clear, the reason was the 'good news' Luca and Bianca had given him.

Luca realised he'd been hoping, somehow, that Matteo would have resurfaced realising just how insane his fantasy was, and absolving Luca of fulfilling it. Instead, he'd been eager to discuss it. Luca's heart had sunk even more when he'd seen how overjoyed he was to hear that Luca was intending to take Bianca to Pavenza to choose an engagement ring. All he'd been able to achieve was saying, pointedly, that Bianca had told him she'd prefer a new purchase—not the traditional D'Alabruschi betrothal ring.

The family heirloom was out of the question. Bianca would have to make do with today's acquisition.

They arrived outside the jeweller's, nestled between a Milanese fashion designer's boutique and an expensive leather goods shop. Politely, Luca held the door open for her, following her in. The interior was dim after the bright sunshine, and automatically he slid off his sunglasses. Bianca was doing likewise. The proprietor looked up from examining a gemstone with a loupe under a desk lamp, greeting them courteously and awaiting their pleasure.

'We should like to look at rings,' Luca opened without preamble.

'Certo,' came the immediate reply. Followed by enquiries as to whether they'd prefer antique or modern style, and which stones.

Luca turned to Bianca. 'What do you prefer?' he asked, switching to English.

'Does it matter?' she returned indifferently. 'You might as well choose something you like, since it will be yours when this is all over. Get something you can resell.'

She hadn't spoken loudly, but Luca assumed the jeweller spoke English to accommodate his tourist trade.

'Let's stay in role, shall we?' he murmured, tight-lipped. More loudly, he went on, 'Emeralds for your eyes, *mia cara*?' His voice was caressing.

Even as he spoke, memory snapped in his head. Bianca had met him one evening at the restaurant he'd usually taken her to, just around the corner from his apartment. She had been sporting huge, dangling clip-on crystal earrings in a vivid green.

She'd flicked them with a crimson nail extension. 'Like them?' She'd grinned. 'Under a fiver in Brick Lane Market!'

She'd been pleased by the acquisition, and he'd had to allow that they looked stunning on her, with her lush auburn hair. But then, everything about Bianca was stunning...

He pulled his thoughts away from his irrelevant memories, instructing the jeweller to show then some modern designs incorporating emeralds. Absently he visualised the family betrothal ring with its emerald and pearls. Then he pulled his thoughts away from that too. It was as irrelevant as the memory of those garish crystal clip-ons.

The jeweller extracted a tray from a cabinet behind the

illuminated desk. One row held emeralds, in various settings and designs.

Bianca stepped forward, looking down at them. 'How about that one?' She indicated one that had the smallest gemstone.

'Oh, I think I can run to something a little more suitable,' Luca murmured. He cast a rapid eye over the rings, selecting a design he didn't care for, with a large cabochon cut stone.

'No—too flash. And these are all too modern.' Bianca looked at the jeweller. 'I think you said you stock some antique rings?' she asked.

'Of course...of course,' came the immediate reply, and the offending modern tray was whisked away to be replaced by another.

'Oh, but these are beautiful!'

There was a warmth in Bianca's voice Luca had only heard before when she was thanking Giuseppe or her uncle's staff, or talking to Matteo.

She reached forward, letting her fingertip trace over the rings, pausing at one that had, of all things, Luca realised, an emerald nestled in a circle of pearls.

'May I try?' she asked the jeweller. She was holding out her hand. 'Will it fit, do you think?'

'I believe so, *signorina*,' the jeweller informed her. He extracted the ring, but instead of sliding it over her extended finger himself, he handed it to Luca. 'You may perhaps prefer ?' He paused for a moment, then added, his tone both deferential, and curious, 'So very similar...if you will permit me to say so?'

As he spoke, Luca did not miss the rapid, flickering glance at Luca's own outstretched hand, and the signet ring he wore, its distinctive crest clearly visible. He cursed him for it. Damn—he would have preferred not to announce his identity.

'Forgive me, Signor Visconte, but my father once had the privilege of resetting one of the pearls in the D'Alabruschi betrothal ring. I was only a boy, but I remember the ring vividly—an incomparable piece.' He cleared his throat carefully. 'But, of course, for everyday wear perhaps something more as the *signorina* has selected…?'

'Precisely so,' said Luca, his voice clipped.

He was aware that Bianca was looking at him, and that she had stiffened. Visibly tensed. As he, perforce, grazed her hand in sliding the ring onto her finger, it seemed to jerk minutely.

The ring fitted perfectly, and the jeweller said as much.

Bianca dropped her gaze to look at it. For a moment that was all she did. And then she spoke. Her voice was as clipped as Luca's had been. But in it was a sardonic note he'd have needed to be deaf not to hear. And stupid not to know why.

'So it does,' she murmured. 'Who'd have thought?'

Then, with a rapid movement, she removed the ring, handing it back to the jeweller.

'It had better go in a box for now, please. I have no idea of the price, but I would not like to lose it on the street.'

The jeweller looked uncertainly between them, but Luca only nodded. As the jeweller found an appropriate case, and then proceeded to the delicate business of payment, Luca was aware that Bianca had turned away, ostensibly to look at the window display from the inside of the shop. But not before he had seen her blink rapidly. As though something were in her eye.

Payment completed, the ring secured in its dark blue velvet lined case and secreted in the inner pocket of Luca's jacket, they were politely ushered from the shop. What the jeweller was speculating, Luca didn't care—he knew only that he resented it. He'd never said the word *fidanzata*, but even so... Plus the man had guessed his identity.

Well, he would just have to rely on the man's professional discretion. After all, there must be plenty of times when the jewellery he sold was not destined for a woman who had any legitimately acknowledged place in the purchaser's life. Half his stock doubtless went to females without an engagement ring on their finger, let alone a wedding ring. Men were often all too happy to lavish their *innamoratas* with expensive jewellery.

Not that he ever did. He considered it insulting and demeaning. Nor did he consort with the kind of women who expected it.

Not even Bianca had. He'd give her credit for that.

'If you like the ring,' he heard himself saying as they headed out into the town's main piazza, 'please feel free to keep it.'

'A souvenir from this happy occasion?' Her tone was openly sarcastic. 'No, thanks—sell it and get your money back.'

'As you wish,' Luca replied repressively.

She'd put his back up again. But at least the ordeal of the farcical ritual of bestowing an engagement ring upon her had been accomplished.

It had left him feeling hungry.

He glanced at his watch. 'Let's get some lunch,' he said. There was a restaurant across the piazza he was familiar with, and it would do well enough.

She halted in her stride. 'I don't want lunch with you,' she said.

Luca halted too, turning towards her. 'Tough,' he said.

'I'm hungry, and I want to eat. If you really can't stand the thought, go shopping.'

He strode off. He was fed up with her balking at him, the hostility coming off her in wave after wave. Had he asked for this infernal situation? No, he had not. So she could damn well give up on giving him a hard time over it.

He reached the restaurant, sat himself down at a table on the wide pavement under the shading awning. A waiter glided up, handing him a menu, taking his drinks order. As he gave it, Bianca stepped through a gap in the planters separating the restaurant's seating area from the piazza and took the chair opposite him.

He threw a caustic glance at her. 'Not keen to shop?'

'Not right now,' she replied, and held out her hand to the waiter for a menu of her own, asking for *'agua minerale con gaz'*.

Luca's eyes went to her. Given the awning, she hadn't put her sunglasses back on, and nor had he. For a moment…a fraction of a second…their eyes met.

Met—and held.

Hers were the first to drop, and he was glad.

Unreasonably so.

For a longer moment he went on looking at her as she assiduously studied the menu. He felt something change in his expression. Something he was not even fully aware of. But one thing he was aware of. One thing it was impossible for him *not* to be aware of.

The fact that six years on from his having walked out on her, Bianca's incomparable beauty still reached out to him…

Bianca stared blindly at the contents of the menu, taking nothing in. All that was in her vision was that moment just now when Luca had looked at her and she at him. Their eyes meeting…

Memory flooded.

That was just how it had happened that evening at the bar, when she'd been pouring drinks for the Canary Wharf Hooray Henrys. Lifting glasses, lifting her eyes—she'd collided full on with the man waiting for his turn to be served. Waiting…and watching her.

Tall, svelte, lethal.

Looking her over. Liking what he was seeing.

Just as I did. Not just his incredible Latin looks—the sable hair and chiselled features and those dark lidded eyes resting on me—but the whole package of him. The pale grey expensive business suit that fitted like a glove across those elegant shoulders of his. That indefinable air of cosmopolitan cool that he possessed so effortlessly. That awareness… Yes, he knew perfectly well that all female eyes went to him, knew perfectly well that I would welcome his appreciation of me—and that he would welcome mine of him in return.

And return that open appreciation she had.

Handing over the drink she'd poured to the customer who'd ordered it, she had then turned her full attention on the man she wanted to pay attention to. Asking him what he'd like to drink…mixing and pouring it. Handing it to him and not minding that his fingers briefly touched hers as she slid it towards him, sending a quiver of awareness through her, quickening of her already quickened pulse. Letting him engage her in conversation—she asking what part of Europe he came from, with that giveaway accent of his, him answering and then, nodding at the name tag which all the bar staff wore on their shirts, murmuring something soft and fluid in Italian. And she'd given a laugh, saying with a half-toss of her head that her name was the only Italian thing about her...

Her thoughts slewed away. Her name had not been the only Italian thing about her after all. And it was because of that that she was sitting here now, with Luca, doing what they were doing.

Heaviness weighed her down, pressed upon her. Somehow—*somehow*—she had to cope with this.

She made her eyes focus on the menu, making her selection, closing it with a click and putting it back on the tablecloth. White linen, posh cutlery, tall-backed chairs—it was an upmarket restaurant. But then, what else would Luca patronise?

Memory came again, whether she wanted it to or not. She'd got such a kick out of being taken to all those posh places in London with him, gazing around, revelling in the expensive classiness of it all. He'd been amused. Indulgent. And she'd been open about how impressed she was by it all.

I never hid who I was from him. Never tried to be anything else. What he saw was what he got.

Except that what he'd got was not what he'd wanted—not for anything more than a fling.

I was a novelty act. That was all. And I have to accept it.

The waiter was returning with her mineral water and a glass of white wine for Luca, plus a bowl of salted almonds, olives and savoury biscotti. They gave their respective selections from the menu—they'd both gone for fish, she realised.

'You won't have wine?' Luca asked, civilly enough.

She shook her head. 'Not for lunch. I'll just fall asleep.' She drank some of her mineral water instead, feeling the fizzing bubbles effervescent in her mouth.

'Have you had much opportunity to see anything of Pavenza?' Luca was asking her.

He was still being civil, and she might as well be too. After all, how else were they to endure each other's company, minimal though she wanted that time to be. Luca had said they should behave as strangers thrown together—maybe he was right. It would be less painful.

She made an effort to reply in kind.

'I've been here a couple of times—just to shop. Matteo's chauffeur drove me. I don't dare drive in Italy, and certainly not in a town—least of all a town like this, with such narrow streets. And all those deadly scooters cutting up the cars!'

Luca gave a wry laugh. It did things to her she didn't want it to. Didn't want to be reminded of.

'Pedestrianised zones are the answer...especially in historic town centres,' he went on. 'And *zonas silencios*—you'll see the sign with the old-fashioned motor horn crossed through—are another advance. Essential, too, given the Italians' twin love of both noise and protest!'

She laughed. Almost unconsciously she felt the net of tension that had wrapped her ever since seeing Luca appear back in her life like the demon king in a pantomime lessen minutely. For Matteo's sake they should do this with the least ill grace possible. Let the past go.

Yet even as she made that resolve memory struck—not from six years ago, but from last night. That kiss...that clinch on the terrace. For a moment, hot and humid, the memory scalded her, a perilous reminder of how vulnerable she was. She steeled herself. It had been a warning to her—one she'd learn from. One Luca had better learn from too.

In her head she heard the sharp crack of her palm against his cheek. That slap had been as instinctive as it had been essential—but she must never, *never* be caught out again. Not like that...

The waiter was back with their *primo*. She'd gone for

salad leaves, and helped herself to some of the olives and biscotti to bulk it up. Luca had chosen *carpaccio*, the ultra-thin slices dark red in the shaded light.

She forked up some leaves, glancing out across the busy piazza lined with old buildings, an imposing church at its far end. 'It's very atmospheric,' she remarked. 'I can see why tourists flock here.'

'It's better in the winter, perhaps, for that very reason,' Luca commented.

'I'm not sure I'll find out.' There was a bleakness in her voice as she spoke. 'I don't think my uncle has that long.'

There was a pause as they both went on eating. Then Luca spoke again, and Bianca heard reluctance in his voice.

'What do you plan to do—afterwards?'

'Go back to the UK,' she said.

He frowned. 'Why? What is for you there?' His frown deepened. 'Or should that be *who* is there for you?'

She shook her head, then immediately regretted it. She should have let him think she had a man to go back to. It would have created another barrier between them—another safeguard for herself. Too late now, though.

'No one special?' he probed.

She set aside her fork on her now empty plate. 'What's it to you?' she countered. There was a note of belligerence in her voice.

He countered it with an acid expression. 'On one issue, Matteo was right, Bianca. After his death you'll be a wealthy woman. You'll become a target for fortune-hunters, just as he fears.'

'They won't get far. And not every man insists on marrying for money...' She smiled sweetly. 'Or cares about where you were born and who to!'

His face tightened. He pushed his empty plate away,

picked up his wine glass. 'It's the way of the world, Bianca,' he retorted.

She went on staring at him. 'It's the way of *your* world,' she said.

A heaviness seemed to be filling her. She didn't know why. Luca D'Alabruschi, *visconte* or whatever the hell he was, whatever title he ponced around with these days, was nothing to do with her any longer. He meant nothing to her—nor did she mean anything to him. She'd never meant anything to him other than a novelty bedwarmer…

So why this heaviness? It had hit her in that jeweller's shop, taking that ring off her finger. As if it could ever have any significance to her! She'd turned away, and the heaviness had hit her like a slug, making her eyes water. Or something had…

The waiter was coming again, and she was glad of it. She'd agreed they had to put the past behind them—well, she must stick to that. Not let it back in.

Their finished *primo* plates were replaced by their *secondos*. Grilled fish for her, with green beans, and for Luca fish in a piquant sauce with *parmentier* potatoes.

They made a start in silence. Maybe it was her turn to break it. There were details of their bizarre arrangement yet to be worked out.

'Are you spending the night at Matteo's again?' she asked.

Luca shook his head. 'I must get back home. I have to arrange some furlough from work. I can't be away too long. Matteo will understand. When we get back this afternoon we'll show him the ring, make it look convincing—put on the performance he needs to see to feel reassured.'

She cast him a suspicious look. 'I'll wear the ring, Luca—but that's it as far as "performance" goes! I made that clear last night.'

He threw a look at her. An old-fashioned one that she did not like. Did not like one little bit. He paused in eating, reached for his wine glass again, leant back in his chair. Let his dark, expressive eyes rest on her.

'I've never been slapped before,' he remarked ruminatively, rubbing his cheek absently with his fingers.

His signet ring glinted in the light. The family crest visible. Did his sense of entitlement come with all that aristocratic lineage? she wondered. Thinking he could help himself to anything he wanted? Any woman he wanted…

He helped himself to me, all right. And I helped myself right back!

But not any longer.

Her eyes narrowed. 'Try anything on with me again, and you'll find you'll be getting used to it!' she bit back.

He gave a laugh. She didn't like that either. Not even one little bit of a little bit.

'Maybe, Bianca, I might just change your mind on that.'

His dark eyes glinted, and she liked that even less.

He went on contemplatively, 'You know, you've become even more amazingly beautiful in the last six years.' He spoke conversationally, as though he were merely passing the time or remarking about the weather. 'And I have to concede this new look suits you.'

His eyes were resting on her in a way that made her determination to let the past go fall at the first fence. Suddenly she was all too conscious of the way her pale yellow cap-sleeved shift dress, so simple and yet so expensive, sheathed her body. It was a world away from her cheap, tight-fitting outfits six years ago—very modestly cut, with a round neck and a hemline skimming her knees.

His expression changed to a slight frown. 'There's something else different about you too,' he said. 'It's not just your fashion sense that's changed. It's your voice. I only hear accents in English with difficulty. But yours has definitely changed.'

She looked at him. 'RP—that's what you're hearing. Received Pronunciation. BBC English. Middle class.' She gave her acid smile again. 'Don't worry—I don't want to wreck your memories of me. I can still revert easily enough. I think sociologists even have a term for it when people have two different modes of discourse—one for the world, the other for at home. Probably it's only people like you who don't have any use for that, because the world is already the way you like it to be, designed for your benefit.'

She went on calmly eating her fish. She didn't care what Luca thought of her—then or now. Didn't care anything about him, period. End of.

'It's over, Bianca!'

It rang in her head again. It would always ring there. And not even this sad, pitiful charade they were embarked upon to please a dying man would change that.

Something seemed to tighten inside her chest, but she ignored it. Went on eating instead.

CHAPTER SEVEN

'Would you care to take in any of the shops while we're here?'

Luca had kept his enquiry polite. They had finished lunch and were heading back across the piazza.

Bianca shook her head. 'No, I'd like to get back to Matteo,' she said.

Luca wanted to as well. Trailing around shops with Bianca would have been a waste of his time. Few things were less enjoyable than shopping with a female.

Memory flickered. At least Bianca had never imposed that upon him. Nor had she accepted gifts from him either, now he thought about it.

He'd once bought a scarf for her—they'd gone out of London one Saturday afternoon, driving into Kent, heading for the coast, then staying overnight at a country house hotel. There had been a table in the hall with a tasteful array of upmarket knick-knacks, including some folded scarves, hand-dyed by a local artist.

He'd scooped one up, presented it to Bianca when they were up in their room. The scarf had been in shades of vivid sea-green and cobalt.

'Perfect for your Titian hair,' he'd told her lightly.

She'd looked puzzled. *'What's Titian when it's at home?'* she'd asked.

'Your hair colour—Titian was a Venetian artist in the Renaissance, famous for painting beautiful redheads,' he'd explained, seeing her looking blank.

'Oh...' she'd answered. Then she'd gone on, *'It's a beautiful scarf, Luca, but it must have been pricey—how much, so I can pay you back?'*

He'd waved a hand. *'It's a present to remember this weekend by.'*

She'd brushed his mouth with hers. *'Don't worry—I'll remember this plenty! And, Luca—don't give me stuff. I can't afford to give you anything fancy in return.'* Her kiss had deepened. *'I'm not with you for the freebies, Luca—it's your gorgeous body I want...'*

He cut the memory of how that scene had ended—It was not wise to remember. Not wise at all.

Bianca was speaking again, and he was glad of that.

'So can we just head straight back?' she was asking.

He led the way to where he'd left his car and they set off. They didn't speak on the journey, and he was glad of that as well. Only when they pulled up outside the front door of the Villa Fiarante did he turn to her.

'You'd better start wearing your ring,' he said.

He reached for the jewellery case in his jacket pocket, handed it to her. He didn't want to put the ring on her finger—let her do it herself.

Silently she flicked open the lid, staring for a moment at the ring inside. The emerald glinted in the sunlight, the pearls opalescent. Then, wordlessly, she slid it on to the third finger of her left hand. With a jerky movement she opened the car door and got out, walking indoors without looking back.

Luca went and parked, wondering why his mood had worsened suddenly. Probably because—as he'd warned her—they were going to have to go through the ordeal of presenting themselves to Matteo.

As he gained the interior, the omnipresent Giuseppe appeared. 'The *signor* is awaiting you, Signor Visconte,' he informed Luca,

'How is he?'

'Stronger, I am very glad to report. But he is obeying the doctor's orders and keeping to his bed.'

'Good.' Luca nodded, vaulting lightly up the stairs and knocking briefly on Matteo's bedroom door.

It was opened by Paolo, Matteo's nurse, and Luca could see Bianca was there already. He strolled in. His eyes went straight to Matteo. He was looking better than he had that morning before they'd set off for Pavenza, but still frail. Yet his expression was lit up—and Luca saw why. Bianca was perched on the chair by his bed, holding out her hand, displaying her ring.

Luca took his cue. 'Yes, her choice, Matteo. I did not prompt.'

'It's ideal,' enthused his godfather. 'It can be worn every day, and the original kept for special occasions.'

He reached forward, taking Luca's hand in his. Pressing it to Bianca's. Luca felt hers stiffen beneath his.

'Oh, my dear ones…' Emotion was rich in Matteo's voice. 'How happy you have made me! Now I can leave this world content.'

His eyes grew misty, and Luca could see his focus going, his concentration fading. He understood more clearly now, after what Bianca had told him over dinner the night before, how the powerful anti-cancer drugs he was on could cause brain fog and other such complications. It helped him understand why Matteo had become so unrealistically obsessed with this passionate determination to 'protect'—as he saw it—the niece he had only so recently discovered.

Luca could see his frustration, his bitterness—his deep sorrow that he would be leaving her so soon. Compassion filled him, making him glad that he had urged Bianca to go along with Matteo's sad, pitiful fantasy.

He felt his glance go sideways to Bianca, who was saying something comforting to her uncle. It was still extraordinary to think of her as Matteo's niece. Thoughts flickered in his head. What if he'd known that six years ago? What if she had known it? The questions hovered...unanswered.

Matteo's eyes cleared, refocusing on Luca, and Luca turned his gaze to him.

'Now that the engagement is official,' Matteo was saying, his voice enthusiastic, 'you must show Bianca where she will be living. Why not drive her there tomorrow?'

Blankness moved across Luca's face. Urgently, he tried to think of a reason why that was impossible.

It was Bianca who came to his rescue.

'Zio Matteo, tomorrow won't be possible. Luca has told me he must return to his office for a while.'

Matteo's face fell. 'No, no, my boy! Tell them this is a special occasion! Of course you must show your *fidenzata* her new home!' He turned to Bianca. 'The Palazzo D'Alabruschi is an architectural historic gem, my dear. You will love living there, I know.'

Bianca took Matteo's hand. 'I wouldn't dream of leaving you,' she said. 'You must not think of it. I shall continue to live here.'

'But only until you are married!'

Bianca smiled. 'Until then I shall be here with you,' she said soothingly. 'I am sure Luca's *palazzo* is beautiful, but it can wait.'

'But you must see it as soon as possible!'

Matteo was getting agitated, Luca could tell, and he intervened.

'I shall defer my return to Rome and take Bianca there tomorrow,' he said calmly.

Matteo subsided. '*Bene, bene*—then it is all decided.'

The exchange seemed to have exhausted him, and he closed his eyes. Luca could see he was sinking into sleep. Carefully, Bianca reclaimed her hand and got to her feet.

'I'll get Paolo,' she murmured, moving to the door.

Luca followed her out to the landing. Matteo's nurse slipped into the bedroom to check on his patient, and Bianca turned.

'There's no need to show me your home,' she said. 'Just tell me enough about it to give my uncle the impression that I've seen it.'

Luca gave a half-shrug. 'What is that English expression? In for a penny, in for a pound? You might as well see it for yourself. It makes no difference.'

'I have no particular interest in seeing it,' she responded tartly. 'It has no relevance for me, after all. Nothing about you, Luca, has any relevance to me other than your connection to my uncle and this deplorable, distasteful lie we've embroiled ourselves in! Even if we *have* done so for Matteo's sake.' She slid the emerald and pearl ring from her finger. 'Here—take this. It's served its purpose.'

Luca shook his head impatiently. Her tone of voice had irritated him, as had what she'd said.

'Of course you have to keep it—for the duration, at any rate. Matteo will expect it.'

She gave an annoyed sigh, but folded the ring into her hand, not replacing it on her finger.

'I'll set off now,' Luca said. Irritation still filled him. 'I'll call for you at eleven tomorrow.'

'As you wish,' she acknowledged indifferently.

Her gaze levelled on him expressionlessly. As though both simultaneously evaluating him and rejecting him. An impulse to rile her, unsettle her in that disconcerting evaluation, filled him.

Before she could realise what he intended, he helped himself to the hand that was not clutching the ring he'd bestowed upon her that morning. 'Until tomorrow then,' he murmured, raising her hand to his lips with deliberate exaggerated gallantry, pressing her fingers as he did so.

She all but snatched it back, and with a rasp in her throat turned and headed along the corridor, her pace more rapid than required. He watched her until she'd disappeared inside her own bedroom, shutting the door firmly. She had not looked back, or said anything else, but the stiff set of her shoulders told him why.

Luca's mood suddenly improved, and he strolled downstairs.

Once again, Bianca was sitting in the passenger seat of Luca's car. She vaguely recognised the distinctive logo on the long, lean bonnet—it was one of the latest supercars, she knew, and its styling matched its powerful engine with a characteristic throaty roar as Luca accelerated along the *autostrada*, effortlessly overtaking humbler vehicles.

Her mouth compressed. The car was like him. Sleek, powerful, expensive...and gorgeous to look at.

All the qualities that I fell for hook, line and sinker when I first set eyes on him. Knocking me sideways with my first glance. Making me go 'Wow!' and catch my breath, my mouth practically falling open.

Her eyes slid sideways to him as he overtook yet another vehicle. It was a guilty pleasure to look at him. She acknowledged that. Reluctantly, resentfully... But still true. She felt a stab of anguish, Oh, God, *why* did he still have this power over her?

No answer came.

The low burring of a mobile phone penetrated her troubling thoughts as he sped along the autostrada. It was hers, not his, she realised. She picked up her handbag from the footwell, getting out her phone and glancing at it.

'Excuse me,' she said, 'but I must take this.' Her voice warmed as she spoke to her caller. 'Andrew. Hi! No, this is a good time. I'm being driven. Have you had a chance yet to see what I sent you?'

Beside her, she could see Luca had stiffened. Five minutes later, when she'd hung up, he turned towards her. There was an open question in his glance. Astonishment behind it. She knew the reason for it.

'As you probably took in,' she said dryly, replacing her phone in her handbag, leaving it on her lap, 'I work at an environmental science consultancy. That was my boss, Dr Andrew Stevens, who was very understanding when I told him about my uncle's diagnosis and prognosis. I have been very kindly given an indefinite leave of absence, but I'm using my spare time, when Matteo's resting, to put in some research and collate some information from various reports, surveys and scholarly papers into specialist briefing notes for our team.'

'On environmental science?' Luca's voice was expressionless.

'On environmental science, yes,' Bianca echoed.

His gaze had, perforce, gone back to the road, but she went on speaking. Her own voice had an odd quality to it, she thought. Part defiant—part defensive.

'Luca, six years ago, when you told me that as well as being common-as-muck I was also pig-ignorant—yes, I know you never used those actual words, but believe me that was what I heard—it hit home. It *really* hit home. It made me angry, as well as hurt—and I wanted to fight back. Oh, you were gone, and I wasn't getting you back—I knew that. But I wanted… I don't know… I wanted to show you—prove you wrong! I realised I couldn't do anything about being common-as-muck, but I *could* do something about being pig-ignorant. So I did. I *did* do something about it.'

She paused a moment and he glanced at her again. Her hands were clenched over the handles of her handbag as she went on, not looking at him but out through the windscreen, dead ahead.

'I hated school. I told you as much, I remember. I thought I was too smart to need it. That I was fine not knowing all that "stupid stuff" as I thought it. But you threw a light on me that for the first time in my life I didn't like. So…' She swallowed. 'I enrolled in my local further education college…signed up for some classes. I didn't know what I wanted to study, but eco stuff was popular, so I went for that. And—amazingly—I took to it. Got really interested. I passed the exams I needed and then…'

She took another breath.

'And then I went to uni. I went as a mature student, to an east London campus, and I went and I stayed the course. A year ago I got my degree—Bachelor of Science—and then I got a job as a junior researcher at the consultancy I work for. And… Well, that's it, really. I find it fascinating, and sometimes I have a hard time remembering just how pig-ignorant I was when you knew me.'

Her voice changed.

'The thing about education is that when you start learning about one thing you realise there's a hell of lot of other interesting stuff out there. Being a student exposed me to things I'd never paid any attention to before—like cultural stuff and history, arty things.' An acid note crept into her voice now. 'It was while I was a student that I also realised that the world was a lot more welcoming if I spoke RP English. I got taken more seriously...was much more accepted. It's hypocritical, I know, but it's made it easier to progress in my career. It shouldn't, but it does.'

She paused again. Then, 'People are quick to judge—for good or ill.'

For a long moment Luca was silent. Then he spoke. 'And I was one of them, wasn't I, Bianca?'

'Yes, you were. But...' She took a breath. 'Your condemnation did me good in the end, didn't it? Without it—without you dumping me so brutally and making no bones about why I would never fit into your elite world—I doubt I'd have been angry enough...hurt enough...to do what I did. Achieve what I have. I'd probably still be pulling pints in the East End.'

She could see Luca's hands tighten on the steering wheel. When he spoke there was an edge in his voice, a self-condemning one.

'That gives me a degree of comfort I don't deserve.'

'No,' she agreed, 'you don't deserve it. But you can take the credit for doing good by me in the end.'

'I never said you were stupid, Bianca, at least allow me that.'

'Just not fit for the elite world you live in.' She knew her voice had gone back to being flat again.

He didn't answer—but then what could he have said? She'd only spoken the truth, after all, about how very different their backgrounds were.

A thought struck her, and her brow furrowed. She turned her head towards him.

'Giuseppe, the doctor and that jeweller addressed you as

"Signor Visconte"—which I assume is the Italian version of "Mr Viscount", or whatever.' She forbore from putting any sardonic tone into her voice, keeping it neutral. 'But I don't remember you using that title in England?'

'Because I wasn't a *visconte* then,' came the reply. 'My father was still alive.' He paused, overtaking yet another vehicle. 'He died three years ago. Together with my mother.'

His voice had no expression in it—but she heard emotion all the same. It took her aback.

'How...?' she faltered, and then went quiet.

'A plane crash. My father was a diplomat, and spent most of his life in other countries because of it. My mother went with him usually. They were in a light plane in South America when a storm hit, downing the plane. There were no survivors.'

'Oh, God, how awful...' She knew there was sincerity in her voice—how could there not be? 'I'm sorry,' she said quietly. 'That must have been unbearable for you. You don't even have siblings...'

She knew from her time with him in London that he was an only child, as was she. It was something they'd had in common. And now there was something else.

Having no living parents.

'It was hard,' he acknowledged. 'Matteo... Matteo was a tower of strength for me. I'd... I'd always been close to him, and to Luisa. With my parents abroad, I often spent the school holidays with them—they were very good friends of my parents. He helped me through a very bad time when my parents were killed.'

She was silent for a moment. Then, 'You are all but a son to him,' she said. 'Not just a godson.'

'Yes.'

He didn't say any more, and she respected his silence. Knowing what he'd gone through—losing his parents so traumatically, so tragically—could not but draw on her sympathy. Did it make her feel different about him? Thoughts flickered...circling, unsure, uncertain. Feeling their way...

Silence fell between them again, and Bianca went back to looking at the passing countryside, glad to let her thoughts subside. The landscape was becoming hillier, and more forested. After a while Luca turned off the autostrada onto a quieter road, leading deeper into the countryside, and then again onto a smaller road that wound around the foot of a hill, gaining elevation as it did so.

He slowed, and Bianca could see an impressive-looking ornate pair of three-metre-high gates with gilded scrolling set into high stone walls. She could see there was a lodge situated just behind the gates, and as Luca turned the car towards them someone issued from the lodge to throw open the gates.

Luca slid down his window. 'Luigi...*grazie.*'

The man beamed, and Bianca could see him glancing curiously at her. Luca said something more to him, in rapid Italian which she could not follow, and then he was closing his window, Luigi was standing away, and they were moving off down the wide, gravelled drive.

Ahead, Bianca could see their destination.

She had thought her uncle's grand villa large—but this was, indeed, a *palazzo*, much older than Matteo's opulent nineteenth-century house. Bianca could see at once why her uncle had called Luca's home an historic architectural gem. She gazed at it appreciatively, impressed. Despite its size and grandeur, it was quietly beautiful, with a charm about it that was instantly obvious. It might be a historic *palazzo*, but it was also clearly a home, too.

Strange feelings went through her as they drew up outside it on the broad white gravel carriage sweep.

Luca's home.

His natural environment.

His ancestral pile...

His very own personal stately home...

Thoughts hollowed out inside her, whether she wanted them to or not.

No wonder he thought I wouldn't fit in here.

His words to her echoed in her head.

'We come from very different worlds, Bianca...'

Totally different.

It was a disquieting thought, and one that hung uneasily in her consciousness.

She could see two heraldic beasts—mythical by the look of them—guarding the ancient-looking front entrance, and some form of hatch inset into the architrave.

Luca was cutting the engine and opening his door. As he did so, someone emerged from the *palazzo* and came around to open her door. Murmuring, *'Grazie...'* she got out, looking around her. Extensive gardens and grounds surrounded the *palazzo*, bathed in warm sunlight, and the scent of flowers was all about.

'It's very beautiful,' she heard herself say.

'Yes,' said Luca.

It was all he said.

She realised, with a glance at him, that he was tense, and immediately knew why. Her sense of disquiet grew. He hadn't wanted to bring her here—she was an interloper, an uninvited guest he was being forced to allow to be here simply for the sake of his godfather's peace of mind.

But that isn't my fault!

Protest replaced disquiet. She would not feel intimidated by Luca's ancestral pile. Yes, it might have brought home to her how glaringly true his words to her six years ago had been, but that did not mean she had to apologise for the differences between them—not then, not now.

And those differences are less—far less now.

She was the niece of his own godfather—legitimate, respectable—and she was her uncle's heir. Nor was she an East End barmaid pulling pints any longer—someone who'd never heard of Titian, or the Renaissance, or anything else that people like Luca and Matteo took for granted.

Her chin went up.

Even if I still was, so what? That doesn't make me dirt beneath his lordly feet!

Feeling more resolute, more justified, she followed Luca, stepping into a high-ceilinged marble-floored hall far grander than her uncle's, and far more graceful too. Pilasters marched along the wall, and sculptures too—busts that looked Roman—and the ceiling, when she glanced up, her eye drawn to it, was adorned with a flamboyant mural of classical gods and goddesses disporting themselves, with cherubs peeping out over *trompe l'oeil* balconies.

'One of my ancestors got a bit carried away,' Luca remarked dryly. 'His wife indulged him for this space, but you will be glad to know she restrained him elsewhere. Come and see. I'll give you the quick version of the tour, and then we can break for lunch.'

His tone was civil enough, and he seemed less tense. Bianca followed his lead.

Briskly, he showed her around the grand but gracious rooms, giving her a thumbnail commentary on what they were seeing. Despite her mixed feelings about the place Luca called home, she found its graceful, elegant beauty very appealing.

He only showed her the ground floor, ignoring the sweeping double staircase soaring upwards from the wide main hall.

'We'll have lunch in the small dining room,' he said. 'It's a breakfast room, really. My mother had it refurbished, as it had become somewhat shabby and neglected.'

He led the way to the rear of the house, to a room opening out by the sweeping double staircase.

Immediately she stepped inside, Bianca exclaimed, 'Oh, this is so beautiful!'

She gazed about pleasurably. Though far smaller than the grand reception rooms along the front façade, this room was just as elegantly proportioned, and it had an intimacy to it that gave it a charm she could not resist. The walls were hung with warm yellow silk, and there was a delicately stencilled ceiling, an exquisitely woven oval carpet in matching warm yellow, with patterning that echoed the ceiling tracery. An elegant eighteenth-century oval table sat in the centre of the room, set with silver and crystal, and a simple but beautiful floral arrangement of creamy yellow roses was held in a silver-gilt epergne.

To one side of the room French windows stood open to the gardens beyond. Instinctively, Bianca stepped through them. As at her uncle's house, a paved terrace ran along the rear façade, leading on to the level gardens, but here, because of its elevated position, there was an immediate vista— a sweeping view of the valley beyond the distant edge of the gardens, each side sheltered by the gentle rise of a forested hillside.

'They chose this site well, I think, my ancestors,' she heard Luca say, stepping out beside her. And for the first time Bianca heard warmth in his voice.

'It's absolutely beautiful,' she breathed. She gave a low laugh. 'I seem to be saying that all the time...about everything you've shown me!' She gestured with her hand. 'I love the way the gardens seem to blend into the landscape all around, as if they are part of it. It's hard to see where the grounds end and the countryside and woods begin.'

'That was the idea. The gardens were remodelled in the late eighteenth century, when the *visconte* opened up the formal baroque arrangement to accommodate the natural topography. It was deliberately done in the English style, which was much admired at the time—and not just in England.'

Bianca nodded. 'Yes, Capability Brown and Humphrey Repton and their followers.'

Luca cast her a swift look. 'Exactly,' he said.

She gave a slight smile, gazing about her at the glorious vista. 'English aristocrats at the time often came out to Italy,' she remarked musingly, 'going home with Roman and Greek trophies to ornament their own stately homes, and Italian aristocrats adopted the fashion for naturalistic landscaping. Each borrowing from the other!' She turned to Luca. 'I know that many English stately homes are littered with *faux* Roman temples in the classical style, but presumably here in Italy you can boast the real thing?'

'We can indeed,' Luca said. 'Where the gardens give way to woodland, as the hill steepens over to the west...' he indicated with his arm '...there are the remains of a very small Roman temple. It's at the site where a spring that was believed to have healing qualities emerges.' He paused. 'I'll show it to you after lunch, if you're interested.'

She smiled. 'Thank you—that would be lovely. And Matteo will probably ask if I've seen it.'

For a moment something changed in Luca's eyes, but she didn't know what. Not that she should care, of course, what he felt or thought. He was nothing to do with her any more. They were being forced into each other's unwilling company simply out of mutual compassion for Matteo—that was all.

I need to remember that.

They went back indoors. It was cooler inside—noticeably so. A manservant was there, and Luca greeted him in a familiar fashion as Bianca took the chair being held for her and Luca sat himself down too. The oval table was now adorned with a variety of platters whose delicate decoration matched the walls and carpet.

'My mother found this service hidden away and was delighted with it. She styled the room around it. The original wall coverings were too faded to save, unfortunately, but the carpet, which was originally in a bedroom, was mended where it had become worn, and the ceiling was re-stencilled. It became her favourite room in the *palazzo*.'

'I can see why,' Bianca said warmly, casting another appreciative glance around her.

It was strange to think of Luca with a mother—or a father, come to that. Or a home at all. In London he'd been a high-flying ex-pat, his apartment ultramodern and anonymous.

He was just passing through—and picking me up in passing too. Then letting me go again. I never meant anything to him...

She felt a knot start to form inside her at old, painful memories. Determinedly, she unknotted it. That was then, and this was now—and there was no connection between them. No connection between herself and Luca, either, apart from Matteo.

Luca glanced at the manservant. 'Thank you—we'll look after ourselves now,' he said, and the man took his leave.

Bianca reached for the crested silver serving spoons and helped herself to a slice of cold poached salmon, and then a liberal helping of salad. Luca poured them both a glass of white wine. Today she accepted it—she felt she needed it.

It was disquieting to see Luca here in his ancestral environment. All the silver was crested with the same device as on the gold signet ring on his finger—some mythical heraldic figure—and the two guardian stone beasts at the front door had brought home to her just how very different the world he came from was from the one she came from.

No wonder it never entered his head that I might ever be a part of it. To him it was absurd—unthinkable. An Italian aristocrat, with a centuries-old palazzo, and a girl like me off a council estate in the East End? Of course I was nothing more to him than a novelty! How could I ever have been anything else to him?

The pang that came was familiar, but the thought that came with it was not.

I wanted too much from him. More than our affair allowed me.

She started to eat. The salmon was delicious, perfectly poached, the salads fresh and light, the wine crisp and cold.

For a while they said nothing, then Luca spoke.

'You're not wearing the ring I bought you,' he said.

Was that annoyance in his voice?

Bianca looked across at him. 'Of course not. If the jeweller could tell that it looks like a miniature version of the D'Alabruschi betrothal ring, I assumed your staff here might well notice it too! That's the last thing you need. As it is, I'm just a guest you're showing your stately home to and that's all.' She paused. 'I'm sorry I chose that particular ring. Obviously I had no idea—' She broke off. Took a breath. 'You should have stopped me...bought a different one.'

'I didn't know the jeweller would recognise it, or, indeed, recognise me. And besides—'

It was Luca who broke off now. Then resumed. 'Besides, it suits you. Emeralds always will,' he added dryly. He paused again, minutely this time. 'Of course you'll be able to buy your own soon.'

'Oh, yes—going on a jewellery acquisition spree is the first thing I'll do the moment my uncle is dead and buried!' Bianca retorted sarcastically.

Luca's brows snapped together in a frown. 'I didn't mean it like that.'

She subsided. 'No, I'm sorry.' She took a breath. 'It must be...odd...for you to see me with your godfather...as his niece.'

He looked at her. 'Yes,' he said. He paused a moment, his expression changing, then added, 'But I wish you well, Bianca. I hope you know that.'

She met his eyes. 'Do you? But it doesn't really matter, does it? It's a long time since our paths crossed.' She took another breath. 'And seeing you here, in this place, surrounded by all this... I can see more clearly than I could then. Of course what I wanted was impossible—unthinkable!'

She resumed eating. The silence seemed awkward suddenly.

'I didn't mean to hurt you, Bianca.'

Her eyes flew up. He was frowning again, but there was a shadowing in his eyes she had not seen before...something in his voice she hadn't heard before.

'I said what I did about how different our worlds were, and how impossible it was for us to continue our affair, let alone anything else, because...'

He took a sharply indrawn breath, and she could see his grip on the crested silver cutlery tightening.

'Because it seemed to me better that you should hate me than miss me.'

She stared. 'I did both,' she said. Her voice was bleak.

Her hand reached for her wine glass, a jerking movement, and she took a gulp, setting it back down on the coaster— that was silver and crested too, she noticed absently.

'I loathed your guts—and I howled into my pillow every night!' Her lips compressed. 'But whilst it was *your* fault I loathed your guts, it was my fault I howled.'

She levelled her gaze at him, unflinchingly. Suddenly she was going to say what she felt she should. Seeing Luca's ancestral pile, having it brought home to her just how great the differences between them had been six years ago, was—like it or not—giving her a different perspective on why he had ended things with her. Put bluntly, it would have seemed impossible to him to continue with her once he'd left London. To him, she had been an East London girl, fit only for an affair that belonged to his posting to the City. She might have had hopes that were actually delusions—he never had.

She held her gaze steady. 'I can't blame you for dumping me, Luca. I was an idiot to fall for you, and an idiot to think there was anything more between us than there was… to want there to be more. I should have accepted what it was—that we'd had a good time together and we were nothing more than a novelty act to each other. It was my fault I didn't see that…my fault I got hurt.'

She went back to eating, not wanting to see his reaction. Her throat felt tight. For all her painful honesty in admitting he hadn't been responsible for what she'd come to want from him, she didn't want to see that bleak truth reflected in his face.

It would hurt too much.

Far, far too much.

And the fact that it would hurt at all was the most disquieting thought yet…

CHAPTER EIGHT

'So, here it is. The *palazzo*'s very own Roman ruin, as promised!'

Luca paused at the far end of the path that had brought them here.

'What you see is likely to be second century AD, but built over earlier foundations. There's nothing particularly remarkable about it from an archaeological perspective, but it's picturesque. I enjoyed clambering around here when I was a kid, and the bubbling spring was always fun, though I'm not sure it's ever healed anyone! It's mineral water—but not sulphurous, thankfully. Nor is it geothermically hot either, which again is probably just as well. There's enough restless geology in Italy for us to prefer it not too close!'

'Do you get earthquakes in this vicinity?' Bianca asked.

'Blessedly not—sometimes tremors, but we've largely been spared. It's in the mountains that they usually hit.'

'The African plate moving north and squeezing the Med. Sad to think the Med will disappear in a few million years...'

Luca looked at her. It was still disconcerting, what Bianca had told him on the way here—that she now had a graduate-level science-based job. The Bianca he'd known wouldn't have had a clue about plate tectonics, any more than eighteenth-century garden landscaping. Those kinds of subjects had never cropped up in their time together in London.

Not that he'd minded or cared—nor thought less of her for not knowing things he took for granted. Why should she? It wasn't part of her world. Nor had it meant she was stupid, either. She'd had a sharp mind, was capable of holding her own in any conversation, and she'd asked questions—from asking who Titian was to what kind of work he did in international investment banking, where he'd been in the world on business and what those places were like.

He'd enjoyed telling her, he remembered. And enjoyed, too, her regaling him with what she knew about—celebrities, films, shows in London. Her opinions had been forthright and often pungent, always entertaining.

She could make me laugh. We had a good time together.

Then he'd ended it.

Because it needed to end. It had run its course and I was leaving London. Whatever she might have wanted, I didn't.

His eyes followed her as she picked her way carefully into the ruined temple. Thoughts circled. He'd told her at lunch he hadn't intended to hurt her—but what had he known, six years ago, of emotional pain? He'd learnt since then...

His expression changed. He'd come here, to the ruined temple, that bleak time three years ago, trying to come to terms with his parents' tragic deaths. Sitting down on one of those broken walls, staring into space, feeling the pain, the cruel rawness of loss. Loss that was for ever.

That pain was there still, though muted by the passage of time—pain he knew he would feel again at Matteo's passing when it came.

Loss was always hard.

His brow furrowed, eyes still on Bianca. She'd had to lose a man she hadn't wanted to lose. And whether or not it had or hadn't been his fault that he hadn't wanted to continue their relationship, and even though he hadn't intended to hurt her by severing it, hurt her he had.

He might have claimed that he'd thought it better she should hate him than miss him, but that wouldn't have made her hurt any less. He could see that now—now that he, too, knew what loss was...

I could have been less brutal...not spelling out how impossible it was, given our differences, that there could be anything more between us. I could have let her down more gently.

He felt regret pluck at him, and knew that the man he was now, six years older, scarred by his own emotional pain, would not have been so callous, so unfeeling. But back then he'd wanted only to find a way to get away from her, whatever he had to say to do so.

His thoughts moved on. Because of Matteo, Bianca was back in his life. He deplored it, wished it not so—wished he could deny what he could not.

His eyes lingered on her. She'd paused by the little spring that poured its water into a stone basin before running off in a channel out of the temple. She was wearing the same elegant pale yellow shift dress that she'd worn the day before in Pavenza, with the same low-heeled shoes, and her hair was in the same neat pleat, make-up still minimal. The cool image suited her...enhanced her beauty.

A beauty whose effect on him he could not deny.

Oh, he knew that he'd gone into that clinch with Bianca on that first shocking night when she'd walked back into his life simply as a reaction to her scornful repulsing of him, nothing more than that. But since then—

Since then he'd been discovering more and yet more about her. How she'd remade herself by her own hardworking efforts—how his godfather had discovered her to be his unknown niece—how obviously devoted to Matteo she was. But he was being reminded of all that she had always been, too. The Bianca he had known so well—plain-speaking, honest, never putting anything on, just being herself. He was reminded of everything that had gone beyond her eye-catching looks to draw him to her. And for a moment past and present seemed to merge...old Bianca with new Bianca.

But she's the same person—the core of her always has been.

There was a maturity about her now that went with the new image, the achievements her own efforts had brought her, but that only drew him to her more.

Unease flickered within him. Uncertainty...

They were being thrown together only because they both wanted to protect Matteo. There could not be any other reason. Should not be.

And yet...

She was turning around, standing in the centre of the ruins, looking towards the *palazzo*, now bathed in sunlight, and then back to the ancient ruins and their immediate surroundings. It was very peaceful. The grass growing around and between the stones was dry and tall, winnowed by the light breeze lifting the air. A little lizard was basking on one of the sun-warmed blocks. The muted chirruping chorus of the cicadas mingled with the low gurgle of the spring splashing into the stone basin, and there was the buzz of bees, busy gathering nectar from wild flowers nearby, and the call of birds from the woods behind the ruins.

Her gaze came back to him. For a moment their eyes met and held. They were wrapped by the peace all around them. Uniting them...

'It's a beautiful place to call home,' she said quietly, her gaze sweeping around once more in slow appreciation. 'You were very fortunate to grow up here.'

Was there a trace of envy in her voice? It would not be unreasonable if so, Luca allowed. Anywhere more different from the crowded, noisy, unlovely city council estate she'd told him she'd grown up on would be hard to imagine.

'Yes,' he said, 'I was.'

There was a wealth of feeling in his statement.

She turned her face to look at him, and their eyes held each other's again. For a moment he saw those two images of Bianca blurred together, past and present. He felt emotion pluck at him—but he did not know what, or why.

Then she was speaking again.

'I can see now why it was so impossible for me to want what I wanted six years ago.'

Her gaze swept around again, then back across the wide, landscaped gardens to the *palazzo* that had been his home all his life. Elegant, gracious—privileged.

She was stepping beyond the boundary of the temple now, back on to the path. 'Hadn't we better start heading back?' she said. Her tone of voice had changed. 'I wouldn't want Matteo to get fretful.'

Luca nodded. 'Yes, you're right,' he answered her, following her lead back into the present—not the past that had ended so badly. 'But there's time to refresh ourselves before I drive back. I'll give Giuseppe a call and tell him when to expect us, so he can let your uncle know.'

He led the way along the path across the gardens, past the south-facing façade of the *palazzo*. Bianca's words echoed in his head. Could he ever have seen the Bianca of six years ago here? It was a question he did not want to ask—or answer.

But there was one he could answer—and answer immediately. It was easy to see the Bianca of now here. His eyes flickered to her. Elegant, poised, soignée—perfectly at home in a *palazzo*.

Emotion moved within him, but still he did not know what. Knew only that something, somehow, was changing inside him. Something in this day—showing Bianca his home, letting her into his life—was causing him to change.

And, although he could not give reasons for it, he was not repulsing that change.

Not repulsing it at all.

Bianca took a sip of her citrus spritzer, welcoming its chilled, tangy fizz. They were sitting outside on the wide terrace, shaded by a sail parasol, and Luca was on the phone to Giuseppe, as he'd promised.

Her mood was strange. Almost melancholy.

She hadn't wanted to come here...to see Luca's ancestral home. But now she had seen it she was glad she had. Her words to him at the temple had been sincere. Having seen how he lived—what he called home—had showed her just how hopelessly unrealistic she'd been all those years ago. And although the realisation hurt—how could it not?—it seemed, it was also draining from her some of the six long years of anger at his dismissal. The anger that had possessed her ever since. A wound was finally cleansing itself. Was that what was happening?

If it is, then I must be glad of it—welcome it.

'Let it go, Bianca,' Luca had told her.

Was that, finally, what she was doing? Was she able to do it?

But seeing Luca here, in his ancestral home, as beautiful as it was, was engendering other emotions within her. She could feel them plucking at her.

How wonderful it must be to have a place like this to call one's home.

He belongs here—I can see that, now I'm seeing him here. In London he was only passing through—but here... here he is at home.

He had grown up here, come to manhood here—then endured the horror of losing both his parents so tragically and taken his father's place as the Visconte.

And one day there will be a woman to take his mother's place here.

One day Luca would bring his bride here—the woman he'd choose to spend his life with. He would make her his *viscontessa*. He would present her with the heirloom betrothal ring that the jeweller had known all about. She would make her home here...be at home in Luca's home, loved and cherished. She would be a fortunate woman...

A pang went through her, but she pushed it away. It was nothing to do with her...

Could never be.

She drew her thoughts back from that inevitable future to the present. Till then, what would Luca do? Amuse himself with passing affairs as he had once, in London, amused himself with her?

She pulled her thoughts away again. It was not sensible to think of that. Not sensible at all. For so many reasons.

Past and present.

No, she must not go there. Neither in the past nor in the present.

Yet as she watched him talk to Giuseppe in rapid Italian that was too fast for her to follow with her primitive grasp of the language, her gaze still rested on him, unable to look away. Unwilling...

Again she felt it welling up inside her...that response to

him—the same response that had always been there, unquenchable. She was as susceptible to him as ever—as that oh-so-passionate helpless kiss that first evening had shown her…shown her so disastrously.

And her time with him yesterday in Pavenza, and today here at the *palazzo*, was only reinforcing the fact.

Wariness flickered within her like an early warning system. One she knew she must pay heed to.

Luca disconnected, dropping his phone on the table. 'Giuseppe reports that Matteo gives no cause for concern. He has had a quiet day, and Paolo is pleased with him. He looks forward to seeing you.' He smiled at her. 'I hope that reassures you?'

'Thank you, yes,' she answered, back in control of her wayward thoughts. She made her eyes meet his, keeping in hers nothing but due civility. 'And thank you, too, for showing me your home, Luca. Matteo was right to urge me to see it, even if he is only imagining the reason for it. It's so very beautiful.'

'I'm glad you think so,' Luca said in reply. 'And I am glad to have invited you here.'

A wry twist formed at her mouth. 'You didn't really *invite* me,' she said. 'It was forced upon you.'

'And I am glad that it was,' he answered. He lifted his glass to her, tilting it slightly. 'To your visit here, Bianca.'

Three was something in his eyes—something in the way he was looking at her—that quickened her pulse. It was a quickening she knew she must not allow. Six years ago she had allowed it, indulged it, and it had cost her so much. Today—seeing the reality of Luca's life, the world he came from—had finally allowed her to accept how impossible her longing to stay with him had been. It had enabled her to let go of her anger at his dismissal of her, his rejection. And now she must let go and deliberately set aside what had led to that impossible longing. Quench it as she had not six years ago.

She cast about for something anodyne to say that would break the moment. 'Did Giuseppe say whether Matteo will be up to dining downstairs? Will you have dinner with us at the villa, or return here?'

It was a neutral question, nothing more.

Luca replaced his glass on the table, his eyes going to her. There was still something in them that quickened her pulse.

'Which would you prefer?'

That should have been a neutral question too. It was not.

'To have my company—or not?'

His eyes were on her, holding hers, and suddenly Bianca felt heat beating up inside her as Luca's dark, lidded eyes rested on her with that expression in them. An expression she had once known so well...

She forced back the heat flushing her skin, stilled her quickening pulse. What was Luca doing? Why? Nothing had changed—nothing at all. They were acting out their roles for Matteo, but they were off the stage now. And even though she could not help but acknowledge that her reaction to him now was the same as it had been six years ago, and just as powerful, she had no reason to indulge—and every reason *not* to indulge.

He should not indulge either.

She had to make that clear. Because otherwise...

'Luca.' Her voice was repressive, flat, her expression closed, and she chose her words heavily, deliberately. 'We agreed that the best way to cope with this impossible situation is to behave as though we are the strangers Matteo thinks we are. Please stick to it.'

Something glinted in the depths of his eyes. Something she didn't like.

'But we are not strangers, Bianca. Not strangers at all...'

The statement hung in the air between them. She wanted to knock it aside—needed to.

His dark, lidded eyes were still resting on her. She felt her chest tightening. So she went on the attack instead.

She levelled her gaze at him, face expressionless. 'I know you're just trying to wind me up, Luca—like you did that first night at my uncle's. You didn't like my slapping you down—literally—and you don't like it that I'm angry with you. So—'

'Are you? Are you still angry with me?'

His question cut across her. Silencing her.

She swallowed, his question echoing. She looked away, her eyes going out over the vista beyond where they were sitting. Then they came back to Luca.

She answered him. Honesty infusing her voice. 'No. No, I'm not. Not any more. Because seeing you here, in this ancestral pile of yours, brings home to me just how great the differences between us are. It makes sense of what you threw at me all those years ago—however much I didn't want to hear it.'

It was Luca who was silent now, his expression changing. He reached for his glass, took another draught, set it down again.

'Those differences,' he said slowly, 'are lessening.'

His gaze rested on her and she kept looking at him, gaze unflinching. When she spoke, her voice was flat.

'That's because I'm Matteo's niece. Because I'm wearing a dress I couldn't have afforded on a month's wages pulling pints. Because now I can speak RP instead of what you'd probably call Cockney. Because now I'm a university graduate, not a barmaid. That's all, Luca. The differences between us go much deeper than that. Much deeper.'

She took another breath, a steadying one. There were things she needed to say—things it was time for her to acknowledge. Acknowledge and accept. And as she spoke she knew she was speaking to herself, not just to Luca. He needed to hear her so he could understand, as she now could, just why she had wanted to hang on to him six years ago.

She held her gaze on him and her voice was steady as she spoke. Unemotional. Painfully honest.

'Luca, when I so desperately wanted you to take me with you when you left London, to go anywhere that you went, it was because I was besotted with you. You were like no one I'd ever met before—from a different world, as you threw at me at the end. You might have thought I wanted the luxury that came with you, but it wasn't just that—it was never just that. Yes, I got a kick out of it—you know I did—but the reason I wanted to go with you was not for that.'

She stopped. Then made herself go on. Haltingly, but with an honesty she was only just recognising in herself.

'Luca, our time together meant a lot to me—more than I realised, I think. I thought it was fun and glamour and excitement and sex, and I didn't want that to end. But…' She paused, trying to put into words what she never had before. 'But I know now that what I also wanted was…was something else. I wanted,' she said, her eyes on him unflinchingly, 'someone to belong to.'

For a moment she did not say any more. Then words began to fill her head, coming out in her speaking voice.

'I'd never belonged to anyone. My father had never existed…my mother I had almost no memories of. My aunt resented me and didn't want me. No one gave a damn about me. I'm not saying this to get your pity—only for you to understand why I was so…so desperate.'

Her hand reached jerkily for her glass and she took a gulp.

Emotion was building up in her, though she was trying to keep calm, dispassionate. She set back her glass, looked straight across at him.

'But now...now I'm not desperate any longer. Because I do belong somewhere. I belong,' she told him, as if declaring it to him and to herself, 'with my father's family—with Matteo. And although I can't bear it that I shall lose him so soon, in the most important way I will never lose him, Because I will always know that he sought me out... found me and took me in. Gave me the love that I never knew growing up.'

She took a breath—a ragged one, because her throat was tightening.

'So, you see, whatever it was that I was so desperate for from you six years ago, Luca, I don't need it any more. Nor want it. It's really that simple.'

She reached for her glass, drained it, then got to her feet. A sense of relief was going through her—something more than relief.

Release.

Release from a past that had tormented her for six years.

Release from those recurring nightmares, with Luca slashing down his hand, his voice harsh. *'It's over, Bianca. Over! Accept it.'*

Well, now, finally, she did accept it. Because now—at last—she understood.

Luca was standing up. He wasn't saying anything in reply to her—but then, what was there for him to say?

He slid his phone away. His expression was strange. Withdrawn.

'I'll drive you home,' he said.

CHAPTER NINE

LUCA DID NOT speak as he drove away. There were things he wanted to think about—*needed* to think about. He needed to accept that six years ago he hadn't appreciated the pain he'd caused her, even if unintentionally, because he'd never experienced anything similar himself. His life had been sunny, pain-free—until the tragedy of losing his parents had hit him.

Her words to him on the *palazzo* terrace echoed in his head—how she'd never felt she belonged to anyone, how that had made him more important to her than just a passing affair.

She wanted someone to belong to—anyone.

Of their own volition his eyes slid to her. She was sitting quite still, hands looped in her lap, looking out through the windscreen, her face in profile. He could not read her expression. But with his rapid glance he saw there was something about it that, on impulse, made him drop his right hand from the steering wheel, reach across, press lightly on her folded hands. As if to comfort her...

Her reaction was immediate. She flinched. Pulled her hands away. She didn't say anything, but the message was clear.

Once they had shared a communal body space.

No longer.

He changed gear, accelerating and then slowing down as a curve approached. Out of nowhere he heard his own voice speaking. Where the words came from, he didn't know—he knew only that he wanted her to hear them.

'I missed you, Bianca, when I went back to Italy. I want you to know that.'

Did she turn her head to look at him? He didn't know. He was keeping his eyes on the road. It made it somehow easier for him to talk.

'There were times when I wanted to get in touch with you…maybe invite you for a holiday.'

'But you didn't.' There was no emotion in her voice as she spoke.

'No, I didn't. It didn't seem…wise.'

'Because it might have given me ideas…false hopes?' Bianca's voice was flat.

'Yes, I suppose that was it,' he said.

There was another silence. He wanted to look at her, but made himself not.

Then she was speaking again. Her voice less flat, more… weary. 'It was better that you didn't get in touch, Luca. It would only have prolonged matters. I had to do what you told me to do. Accept that our affair was over.'

He heard her draw a breath.

'And now I've finally done that,' she said. 'It's taken six years, but now it's done. Seeing you again has enabled me to do so—ironic though that is.'

He wanted to say something, though he wasn't sure what. What she'd just said jarred. 'Ironic', she'd called it. But that irony applied to him, too. Only in reverse. Seeing Bianca again had not had the same effect on him as it had on her…

She's decided she is over me finally. Whereas I—

He let his eyes go to her now. Only a rapid glance, because he was driving. But something had flared inside him—something that refuted what she'd just said to him.

I've said I want us to behave as though we are the strangers Matteo believes us to be. But even if we were it could not make me impervious to the effect she has on me! Her beauty is too great for that.

And they were not strangers—he had reminded her of that inescapable truth. They had been lovers who had burned in each other's arms, consumed in a passion that had never quite been sated.

I could have made my London posting twice as long and still not tired of her.

Only when his recall had come he had faced up to reality. A reality he'd forced upon her.

A reality that no longer exists.

His glance flicked to her yet again, and then away, leaving her image on his retinas. She had said the differences between then had lessened only because she'd turned out to be his godfather's niece, and because now she dressed accordingly and was a university graduate with a professional career. And, yes, he was glad for her that she'd found the family she'd never known and had made a career for herself—an achievement to be proud of. And, yes, six years on he did prefer her more elegant fashion style and image. But what had flared between them from the moment he'd set eyes on her was flaring once more.

For him, at least.

And for her?

She'd said he'd only kissed her that night at Matteo's to wind her up, to retaliate for her scathing denunciation of his assumption that she'd persuaded his godfather to come up with his insane idea. And that was true. But the moment their lips had touched there had been only one motivation, one reason for kissing her.

And only one reason for her kissing him back... He knew that with every male instinct in his body.

That reason had not disappeared when he had ended their affair. It was still there, in every glance at each other, every flicker of constant awareness. Yes, perhaps six years ago she had looked to him to provide the sense of belonging that she now had from her uncle, but that did not mean that what he felt whenever he looked at her she did not feel too.

If she would only let herself...

Because it's there—it's still there. And not even all her denial can deny its truth.

Not to her. Not to him. Not any longer.

Bianca was on her laptop, but her mind was not on her work. Other things were filling it. The day had brought so much—too much. How could she make sense of it? Less than three days ago she'd had no idea that Luca was about to walk back into her life, and now—now he was dominating it. Dominating her thoughts, her feelings.

Her desires.

She felt herself tense, lifting her hands from the keyboard. Restless, suddenly. Abruptly she levered herself off her bed, where she'd been propped up against the pillows, and set aside her laptop. She crossed to the window overlooking the villa's gardens. A moon was rising, casting silvered shadows over the topiary standing sentinel in the night. How different this formal garden was from the naturalistic landscape of the *palazzo*.

Luca's *palazzo*. His home...his birthplace...his birthright.

Her thoughts moved to and fro, sifting through all that

she had thought and felt that day, the day before, the night before…

So short a space of time, and yet so much had happened. So much had changed.

Her anger at Luca had dissipated…drained away. She'd let go of it. Because now she realised why she had been so desperate not to lose him. And he—he had changed too. Had acknowledged how brutal his dismissal of her had been—how he had been driven to it because she had wanted him too much, had feared losing him too much. She must accept that. And he had to accept—*had* accepted—that she was not who she had been when he'd walked out on her.

She was his own godfather's niece. Bianca Fiarante. Who one day would be a wealthy woman. She was a woman already embarked upon a demanding science-based career, earned through her own determined efforts, and now she dressed and looked and sounded perfectly eligible and perfectly entitled to be part of the elite world of wealth and ancestry that Luca had always been part of.

The world of Luca the Visconte D'Alabruschi, with his eighteenth-century *palazzo*, his land and his estates, his crested silverware and his very own personal Roman ruins—the world he had always been part of.

The world she had once been excluded from.

Yes, so much had changed since then.

But one thing had not.

Her eyes looked out over the shadowed gardens, mysterious in the moonlight, and she heard the cry of a nightbird piercing the low, nocturnal murmur of the cicadas.

One thing had not changed at all.

She shut her eyes, but on her inner eyelids was still the image imprinted there six long years ago. And three brief days could never expunge it. It would always, always be there.

Luca. Only Luca.

She thrust away from the window, a half-cry of anguish stifled inside her. Oh, what use was it that she should feel like this? What use was it that she should still be so drawn to him? Nothing could happen between them. Nothing *must* happen.

Somehow—for the remainder of this painful, conflicted time, while they were still playing out her uncle's sad, desperate fantasy—she had to stay strong. Keep Luca at bay. She shut her eyes, as if she could shut him out of her vision, out of her head. Why was he tormenting her, saying what he had said to her, that her beauty still called to him?

I must resist it—I must!

Because anything else—

She would not go there. Not in her thoughts, nor in her imaginings. And most of all not in any reality at all.

Determinedly, she sat herself down on her bed, swung her legs up, propped the laptop on her knees once more, and made herself focus on her work. Blocking out, as best she could, all that had happened since she'd looked across the *saloni* to see Luca walking out of the past...

Again, ruthlessly, she pulled her thoughts away.

Luca had left the villa after he'd dropped her off, staying only to spend a few minutes with Matteo, then heading off. She'd been relieved—especially when he'd told her, in a voice without expression, that he'd be going to Rome the next day and was unlikely to return for a fortnight. She'd only nodded as he'd bade her goodbye, watched him head downstairs, then gone in to see her uncle.

Matteo had been in high spirits, and over the dinner she'd shared with him upstairs in his room had been eager to hear all about her visit to the *palazzo*. She'd waxed lyrical, but evaded any questions or assumptions her uncle had made about what she would do when she was mistress there.

That day would never come—for all her uncle's hopeless fantasies.

For any fantasies at all...

'Luca, you sly devil! When did all this happen? You've kept it damned quiet!'

Luca looked nonplussed at his colleague, a friend from school and university, and the son of good friends of his parents and Matteo.

'Kept what quiet?' he asked.

Pietro slapped him on the shoulder. 'Your engagement!'

'My *what*?' Luca's reaction was explosive.

Pietro laughed. 'No point trying to hide it any longer! Not with your engagement party the weekend after next. Short notice—but I won't be missing it, I can tell you.'

A pool of ice formed in Luca.

'Engagement party?' His voice was still blank.

Pietro gave another laugh. 'Trying to keep it secret a bit longer, were you? No luck, my friend. The invitations have gone out!'

The moment he could get to it, Luca was on his phone. As soon as Bianca was on the line, he exploded.

'What the *hell*,' he demanded, 'is going on? An *engagement* party?'

'*What?*'

Bianca's reply was just as explosive as his had been.

'I have just been congratulated on my engagement by an old family friend who tells me he will be delighted to come to my engagement party in a fortnight,' Luca bit out grimly.

'Oh, grief...'

Bianca's voice was hollow. He heard her take a breath. 'OK, Luca, I'll try and find out what Matteo has done.'

'Matteo?' There was an edge in Luca's voice—he could hear its sharpness himself.

Bianca's, however, was even sharper. 'What are you trying to imply, Luca? That I had *any* idea about this?' Her tone hardened. 'Still indulging in your conceited vanity that I might actually *want* to marry you and let the whole world think so?'

Her derision stung. Rightly so. He should not have said that. He knew she deplored their charade as much as he did. Because that, after all, was the only way to regard it.

There is nothing between us except in Matteo's deluded longings.

Yet even as he asserted it, memory challenged. That day at his *palazzo* had drawn him and Biance closer together as they had exhumed the past to exorcise it. Get it out of the way.

But out of the way for what?

The question hung unanswered...unanswerable.

Bianca was speaking again, brisk and impersonal. 'I'll speak to Matteo and phone you back.'

She cut the call.

Slowly, Luca put his phone down. Conscious, with a sense of confusion and disquiet, that it had been good to hear Bianca's voice again...

But what has that to do with deepening this unholy charade with, of all things, an engagement party conjured out of Matteo's imagination? Dear God!

Surely there had to be a way to knock it on the head?

But when Bianca phoned back, his heart sank.

'I asked Matteo over lunch,' she said, her voice heavy. 'He said he wanted it to be a surprise for us, but he is glad we know. He says he's invited "everyone"—whatever that means…you'd know better than I—and it will be in two weeks' time. It is short notice, he admits, but Giuseppe will see to it all. All I have to do,' she went on, her voice hollow, 'is buy a beautiful gown for the evening.' She paused. 'He…he sounded so happy, Luca. I didn't have the heart to show how dismayed you and I are by it.'

He could hear the choke in her words and gave a resigned sigh. 'I can't see a good way out of it—not without hurting Matteo. All we can do is play along…for now, at least.'

He got off the line, his disquiet mounting. This whole deception was getting deeper and deeper. Now he would be parading Bianca as his fiancée—his *fidenzata*—deceiving his friends with a lie. Because what else could it be but a lie? There was nothing between Bianca and himself. Not any longer.

Yet even as he made the assertion in his mind he knew, with even more confusion and disquiet, that that, too, was a lie…

With Bianca at the heart of it.

CHAPTER TEN

BIANCA STARED AT her reflection. The evening gown she had bought in Pavenza had been Matteo's choice. He'd seen it on the website of Pavenza's most upmarket boutique and urged her to buy it. For herself, she would not have chosen it. It was strapless, silvery white, falling from a softly draped crystal-beaded bodice in silken folds to her ankles. It was exquisite—but it looked far too much like a wedding dress...

But if this was the gown Matteo had set his heart on, she could not refuse him—whatever her misgivings. She wore it now with a delicate, light-as-air chiffon shawl, woven through with silver thread, gathered over her elbows.

Her jewellery was Matteo's wife's pearl collar, once again, with the pearl bracelets on either wrist and the matching pearl and tortoiseshell combs fastening the elegant upstyle of her hair, exposing the pearl drop earrings against her throat.

On her finger gleamed the emerald and pearl ring Luca had bought her. Her eyes dropped to it. Disquiet showed in her expression. The ring was proof of the lie she was perpetuating, and now it would not just be Matteo she was lying to, but his friends as well.

The warning words of that old poem flitted in her head.
Oh, what a tangled web we weave
When first we practise to deceive...

But what else could she and Luca do now except go on with the lie? In the two weeks that had passed since Luca had told her what Matteo had done, her uncle had been revelling in anticipation for the coming party.

'I want everyone to see—to know—how happy you and Luca have made me! My friends will rejoice with me!'

Would they? Uncertainty filled her, and she lifted her gaze to look at herself again. At least she looked the part in this exquisite gown, which had cost she dared not think about how much, and wearing her aunt's jewellery—which presumably people other than Luca might well recognise.

A sudden jarring image forced itself into her head—how she had once looked, all those years ago, with her flashy fashion sense, her fake jewellery, her extravagant hairstyles, her lavish make-up. She had loved the way she looked, and Luca had enjoyed it too, but the Bianca of six years ago would never have convinced any of Matteo's friends that she was his godson's fiancée...

And now...?

She let her gaze rest on her own reflection. Now she was Matteo Fiarante's niece, wearing pearls and a designer evening gown, with Luca's betrothal ring on her finger—a miniature version, it seemed, of his family's priceless ancestral heirloom.

Now I look entirely eligible for his elite, rich and aristocratic world.

Emotion twisted inside her. What if she'd looked like this six years ago? What if she'd met Luca then, as a university student, speaking BBC English and knowing all about Titian and the Renaissance and anything else that he and all the people who would be here tonight took for granted and knew about?

Would he still have finished with me? Declared our affair over?

The questions hung in her head. It was pointless even to ask. Pointless to revisit the past. She had made her peace with it. Now, all she must do was cope with the present. Get through this evening as best she could, playing the part she and Luca had accepted. And so must he.

A tremor went through her. She had not set eyes on him since he had gone back to Rome. She had schooled herself not to think about him and to focus only on her uncle, on keeping him company, lifting his spirits, letting him enthuse about the coming party, trying the best she could to deflect him from talking about the future, when she and Luca were married…

Yet Luca had stayed in her head, a background presence, all the time. It was worst in the reaches of the night, when she would wake and unguarded thoughts would spring into her unwary consciousness. She'd see him in her mind's eye, hear him, replay his presence.

She dreaded seeing him tonight.

Tonight would be an ordeal not just because of the lie she must parade in front of her uncle's friends, but for a far more daunting reason. It would be an ordeal simply to be in Luca's company again…

Somehow, she would have to endure it.

Somehow she would need to face not just those people, but Luca. She'd heard his car with its distinctive engine note pull up some ten minutes ago, and presumed he was talking with Matteo, awaiting her descent. She knew she needed to go downstairs, that guests would be arriving. But she wanted to delay the moment just a tiny bit longer.

Steeling herself, she reached for the bottle of scent on her dressing table, spritzing lightly, covering the pearls with her hand as she did so. Then, after a swift pursing of her lips to check her lipstick, and a final glance to check her mascara had not smudged, with a determined movement she headed for her bedroom door.

Just as she did so, there was a quick knock on it. Assuming it was Maria, she called out for her to come in.

But it was not Maria who walked in.

It was Luca.

Luca stopped dead. It had been two weeks since he had last set eyes on Bianca, that day at his *palazzo*. But even if she had been out of sight, she had not been out of mind. Troublingly so. They had communicated by phone, on updates on Matteo and over the practicalities of this party Matteo was insisting on. The calls had been mutually civil…amiable, even…but every one, he knew, had ended with him feeling disquieted. Knowing that, however much he should not—for what would be the purpose of it?—he wanted to see her again.

And now he was.

And now, as his gaze rested on her, he knew exactly why he had wanted to.

For the reason that was sweeping through him now, making a mockery of all his disquiet, his confusion. Making something inside him totally clear.

Whatever had once been between him and Bianca was blazing again…making everything else irrelevant. The charade they were performing, the lie they were getting deeper and deeper into, the deception they were perpetrating. All irrelevant.

There was only one truth now.

And she was standing there and it was radiating from her.

Barely more than a metre away from him, he saw Bianca face him. He felt something clench inside him and knew exactly what it was. A slug to his solar plexus, wiping the breath momentarily from his lungs.

She looked…breathtaking. And so much more.

He was dazed with it…with the undeniable truth. It was possessing him entirely. Knowing there was only one reason for it, he heard himself murmur in Italian…words that were superlatives of superlatives…expressing his reaction to the vision he was beholding.

As for her reaction—she, too, had stopped dead. He saw the hand with his ring on her finger tighten over the gossamer shawl around her elbows. And there was something in the way she was staring at him—something he didn't bother to put a name to because he knew perfectly well what it was. Because he had seen it in her eyes a hundred times before…six years ago…

He stepped forward. Made his eyes move over her, his lashes sweeping down, appreciating every centimetre of her.

He was not hiding it from her…

Not even trying to.

Nor wanting to.

Bianca saw his reaction. It hollowed her out. His eyes were washing over her, doing things to her that swept her back six long years… Things she had spent the last two weeks wanting never to feel again, wanting to arm herself against.

But his single glance was sweeping all that away, like a surge tide demolishing a puny barrier of sand. And it was impossible—*impossible*—for all her anguished resolve since he had left the villa for her to withstand it. Weakness drenched through her, and she felt herself almost sway, disastrously aware that a pulse was throbbing in her throat, that colour was flaring across her cheeks, heat flushing in her veins like a warm, sensuous tide.

Her eyes were locked to him, standing there immaculate in his evening dress. And as she stood helpless, motionless, she knew with a dismay that it was impossible to dispel that all her defences were no more. That her resistance to what she saw now in his eyes, felt inside herself, was futile. Impossible to sustain.

From somewhere within, using some last vestige of control, she made herself speak. Made her voice sound nothing more than neutral.

'Is it time to go down?' she made herself ask, wanting only that her voice should not tremble.

It was time to take up her role as Luca's *fidenzata*—his bride-to-be, his chosen future *viscontessa*. The woman chosen to be his wife, chosen to share his life.

Emotion stabbed in her, but she refused to recognise it. Bad enough to feel what she could not deny—the helpless weakness sweeping through her under Luca's sweeping, melting gaze.

'Yes.' His answer sounded staccato. 'I am sent to summon you.'

Luca held the door open for her and she nodded, walking forward, conscious as she passed him of the scent of his aftershave...tangy, with citrus notes, and an underlying ultra-masculine undertone that caught at her senses.

She stepped out onto the broad landing, heard the sound of the band tuning up—for there would be dancing later on, out on the terrace, after a lavish buffet had been served in the dining room.

The practical organisation of the party had fallen on Giuseppe's apparently infinitely capable shoulders, and he had reassured her, with smiling enthusiasm, that such events had been frequent when her uncle's wife, the *signora*, had been alive. He had told her that the household could easily accommodate what Matteo had in mind, and how good it was to see the *signor* so happy. His smile had deepened. And for so good a reason…

There had been nothing she could say to that—any more than she could say something to her uncle. All she could do now, as she descended the stairs, Luca a pace behind her, was remain supremely conscious of his presence, of her helpless response to him.

She walked into the *saloni*, where Matteo was awaiting them. The furniture had been pushed back, to provide more room for guests to mingle, but Matteo's chair was in its customary place by the marble fireplace. He got to his feet as she walked in, just ahead of Luca. His face broke into a smile of the warmest welcome and delight.

He came to her, taking both her hands in his, his eyes glowing as they beheld her. 'Oh, my dear—how beautiful you look! I knew that gown was perfect for you!' He turned to Luca. 'Do you not agree, my boy? Our treasured Bianca could not look more exquisite! She is radiant with beauty!'

'She is indeed. Without question.'

Luca's voice had a note in it she could not recognise. Nor did she wish too. All she could wish was that this evening was over. The ordeal would be agonising.

Giuseppe appeared in the open doorway to the *saloni* and made the announcement that their guests were starting to arrive.

Matteo's face lit up again. He patted Bianca's hands, slipping his from them. 'And now,' he said, delight in his voice, 'the evening begins!'

Luca's eyes were on Bianca. She was in another man's arms. It happened to be Pietro's father, and Pietro himself was standing beside Luca, grinning as he watched them dance out on the softly lit terrace.

'He may be pushing sixty, and he may still love my mother like she was twenty, but I've got to admit he's bowled over by your Bianca! And who wouldn't be? She is, to use the vernacular, an absolute total knockout!'

Pietro cast a sly look at Luca, who was still looking at Bianca, dancing sedately with Pietro's father, smiling at him courteously and engaging him in whatever chitchat they were exchanging.

'So, how did you Bianca get together? She told me she only came out to Italy quite recently, when she learned of her uncle's diagnosis.' He shook his head. 'Bad business, that, Luca—life can be totally bloody sometimes.' Then his voice lifted again. 'But maybe if it's catalysed you and Bianca getting serious…?'

'Something like that,' Luca said tersely.

He was giving, by implication, the impression that he and Bianca went back a while, but because she was based in the UK their relationship had not shown up on his friends' radar. That was all he was prepared to say, and though he knew Pietro and everyone else in his circle wanted to know more, he was not going to oblige.

His friends could think what they liked. Whatever they came up with, it would not be the truth.

The band at the far end of the terrace was keeping to old-fashioned melodies and the number was ending. Pietro's father was bringing Bianca back to Luca and Pietro.

'I have indulged myself sufficiently,' he informed Luca, relinquishing Bianca with a flourish. 'Your *fidenzata* is beyond delightful, and has borne with me bravely, but I know there is only one man in whose arms she wishes to be!'

He took his son's arm. 'Come, Pietro, leave the lovebirds to each other.'

He drew him away, heading back to his wife, who was talking to Matteo.

For a moment Luca didn't move, and nor did Bianca.

'I'll go and see how my uncle is doing,' she said. Her voice was abrupt. 'I don't want him getting too tired.'

Luca stayed her. 'Matteo is fine—Pietro's *mamma* has been keeping an eye on him.'

He reached for Bianca's hand. All evening she had haunted him, tormented him. From the moment he had set eyes on her in her bedroom, in that gown, only one impulse had filled him. And now everything that he had felt as he drove away from the villa two weeks ago was overwhelming him.

Six years ago he had set Bianca aside.

No more.

Certainty filled him. Desire... A desire he would not deny, nor suppress, nor walk away from.

And nor will she.

He knew that—knew it with every fibre of his being. All evening he had been conscious of it...conscious of how she was conscious of *him*. Trying not to be—and failing. She was as aware of him as if she were a compass needle seeking north. His north.

Oh, she might have deliberately kept a space between them as she'd stood beside him, with Matteo on her other side, as they'd received his godfather's guests in the *saloni*, not wanting his sleeve to brush her arm, or any smile to be exchanged with him, and barely addressed him except when social necessity demanded it as they'd conversed in niceties with Matteo's invited friends. But it had been in vain. The very air between them was charged...

And here it was again, as he took her hand...took her into his arms...into the dance.

They had danced once already this evening. Matteo had insisted they open the dancing, having made a speech—brief, but emotional—telling his good friends how blessed her was that his dear godson and his dearest niece were to be married. He had implied that he'd always known of her existence, corroborating, even if unintentionally, Luca's similar implication about himself and Bianca. Then Matteo had urged them on to the dance floor and they had complied, even though Bianca had been stiff as a board. They'd kept their dance as short as possible, and the moment other couples joined them Bianca had loosed herself, left the dance floor.

But now he would not permit that. He would ignore, deliberately, the stiffening in her body as he walked her into the strains of the slow, seductive waltz that the band had struck up, with other couples doing the same.

'This isn't necessary, Luca,' she gritted, gazing fixedly over his shoulder, which she was barely touching with her hand. 'We've already done our duty dance.'

He ignored the tension in her voice. He knew the reason for it. He only slid his arm around her slender waist, resting his hand at her back. He could feel the warmth of her body through silk of her gown. His other hand tightened a fraction on hers.

'We have to put on a show, Bianca,' he said, *sotto voce*.

His voice was husky, and he knew the reason for that too. Knew, too, with a self-mockery that was wry, but mordant, that even though he wanted to draw her tight against him, to do so would be...unwise.

Instead, he gave himself to the lilting music—a familiar Italian favourite—letting his hold on her relax, his hand splay over the arch of her spine like a caress. He felt a fine subliminal tremor go through her, as if she was using the last of her strength to resist him. To resist what was happening.

And then…

He felt her resistance fade.

He felt her hand fold over his shoulder, and she drew back her head so that her eyes were looking into his. Looking—and melting…

He saw it happen…felt it happen. His eyes held hers, and hers held his, at the still point between them as they moved in the dance, impelled by the music, slowly, ineluctably, the familiar, seductive, hypnotic rhythm of the music weaving about them. It was drawing them closer to each other, their gazes entwined.

He felt his breath quicken, his body quicken…

And still they danced…

The world was disappearing. She knew it was. It was fading away, blending into the night, unseen, unnoticed, uncared about. Dissolving into an insubstantial mist.

For now there was only one reality.

Being in his arms again…

Luca's arms…

Yes, he was holding her in the formal embrace of this slow, lilting waltz, and yet it was as intimate, as close, as intense, as if they were in the privacy of their own company.

It was strange, and yet it was so familiar—as if she had danced with him like this a thousand times. But she never had. Not like this.

Being in his arms, feeling his hand splayed against her spine, warm and firm through the thin silk of her gown, feeling his other hand close around hers, her body brushing his, his brushing hers…

And gazing, gazing, gazing into his eyes...

His eyes were holding hers and it was impossible to look away...impossible...

Faintness drummed through her, and yet she had never felt so vividly, never seen the world in sharper focus. Because the world was being in Luca's arms...nothing but that...

Dimly, she was aware that the music had stopped, that she and Luca had stopped, that all the other couples had stopped too. They were moving apart, moving away, and with a sudden start she knew she must move too. She let her hand fall from his shoulder, slid her other hand from his. Felt his resistance to her withdrawal.

Heard him say her name. Soft and low...a breath...nothing more.

'Bianca...?'

Her expression flickered and she broke her eyes away from him. She had to. She must not go on just standing here like this, his hand still around her waist, gazing at him. She felt breathless, trembling.

His hand dropped away, as if with an effort, and he stepped apart from her. She saw him frown, as if confused, taken aback.

She took a breath—a steadying one. 'I... I must get a drink,' she managed to get out.

He didn't stop her, and she headed back into the dining room. One of the household staff was manning the drinks table and she hurried up to him, gulping down the glass of water he poured for her.

Oh, dear God, what had just happened?

But she knew—oh, she knew.

How could she deny it?

Impossible to do so.

Her heart rate was still elevated, and now she could feel that her cheeks were flushed, her breathing ragged. She needed to get control of herself. Needed to put that catastrophic five minutes out of her head—completely out of her head.

Replacing her empty glass with a murmured thank-you, she turned and made her way out to the terrace again. She didn't want to. All she wanted to do was bolt upstairs, gain the sanctuary of her bedroom, lock and bolt the door.

Not against Luca—against herself...

Against her greatest weakness. The weakness she could not defeat.

Wanting him again...

Luca was going through the motions. The band had packed up and gone, and Matteo's guests were leaving. It was not that long after midnight, but by general tacit agreement none of his friends wanted their host to tire. Luca could see Giuseppe hovering, and Paolo behind him, as he and Bianca stood beside Matteo in the hall, thanking everyone and bidding them goodnight.

It seemed to take for ever for the last guests to leave, and Luca understood their reluctance, knowing it might be the last time they saw Matteo. Their farewells were sympathetic, their smiles warm and their wishes warmer—for Luca and Bianca as well. She was receiving them with difficulty, Luca could tell, but he knew it would be presumed by Matteo's guests as sadness at her uncle's illness.

At last the doors were closed. Paolo was stepping forward, and Matteo was turning to Luca and Bianca, embracing them both, emotions heightened. He was looking exhausted, but content.

'I shall yield to the anxious looks Paolo is trying not to

show,' he said, lowering a goodnight kiss on Bianca's cheek. 'My dear, dear children—how happy you have made me!' He turned to Giuseppe. 'And you, faithful friend that you are—thank you! For making all this happen!'

Luca, still standing beside Bianca, watched Paolo help Matteo upstairs, one step at a time. Then he spoke to Giuseppe, thanking him in turn.

He heard Bianca's voice echo his thanks and urge that he and his staff should enjoy the surplus buffet, the remaining wines and champagnes, and go off duty, their rest well earned. Bestowing a small smile on him, she bade him goodnight, following in her uncle's wake.

Luca strolled into the dining room to fetch a half-finished bottle of champagne in its cooler, and two unused glasses.

There would be a celebration of his own to make…a celebration to share.

CHAPTER ELEVEN

BIANCA SAT AT her dressing table, gazing at her reflection. She could not make out the expression in her face. It seemed like a stranger's face to her. Her eyes were both troubled... and dazed. Her pulse seemed both quick...and slow. Her breathing shallow...and intense.

She gazed almost blindly at the woman she could see in the glass.

The quietness of the room lapped about her, dimly lit by the bedside lamp she had switched on and the lamp that sat on the dressing table, casting only a soft glow in the darkness. After the chatter of voices in lively conversation, the music from the band, the clink of crystal glasses, the silence seemed absolute. She could not even hear her own breathing.

But the click of her door catch she could hear.

She turned. It would be a maid, surely, come to help her divest herself of the beautiful silk gown and put away her jewellery. Surely only that?

But, as at the start of this long, difficult evening, when she had been nerving herself to go down and play the part her uncle had cast her in, it was not the maid.

As she had known since that moment he had taken her into his arms out on the terrace, into that dance...that slow, seductive waltz...it was Luca.

Only Luca...

Luca...

* * *

She was so beautiful. So exquisitely, incredibly beautiful. It took his breath away. For an endless moment he simply stood there, gazing at her, as she turned towards him where she sat at the dressing table.

He did not speak. There was no need to. He knew that she knew why he was here. Why this had been waiting to happen. Not just since they had danced on the terrace, but since she had come back into his life. Uninvited, unthought-of, uncalled-for—but back.

He moved towards her, closing the bedroom door behind him, absently placing the champagne and the glasses on a pier table beside the door. She did not speak, and he did not want her to. Did not want protestations or resistance...

Because there will be none. Not any more. For she wants what I want too.

And he wanted to do only what he was doing now. Reaching out his hand to find hers...drawing her to her feet.

She rose with a soft rustle of silk, her face uplifted to his.

'Bianca...'

It was all he said. All he needed to say.

His mouth lowered to hers.

How long ago it had been...how achingly long ago...since she had given herself to him. For this was a giving of herself—and a taking too. Slowly, sensuously, as his mouth softly caressed hers, his hands reached to her back. Slowly, sensuously, he eased down the long zip...eased open the catch on her strapless bra.

She stepped away, her mouth leaving his, but her eyes never moved from him as she stepped free of the gown. It was far too beautiful and precious to let fall to the floor, so she draped it over a nearby chair, adding her bra to it, slipping off her satin sandals.

Then she turned to Luca. He was gazing at her…just gazing.

'My most beautiful, exquisite Bianca…' The words were breathed from him.

He came towards her. Methodically, he started to shed his clothes. Jacket first, deposited on the dressing table stool, then his tie, his shirt. He dropped his cufflinks on the dressing table, added his shirt and tie to the stool.

She watched him, unable to tear her eyes away as his sleek, hard, so well-remembered body came into view.

Not for an instant did he take his eyes from hers. Nor did hers move from him as he revealed his body to her—as hers was revealed to him. Only when his hands went to his waist did she turn away, shy suddenly. It had been so long ago…so very long ago…

But when he came to her, resplendent in his natural state, all shyness dissolved…dissolved completely.

He drew her into his embrace, her slender body pliant against his. Gently, so gently, he kissed her. A kiss of sweet desire. Of homage. Of renewal. Carefully, so carefully, he lowered her to her bed. All that remained of her clothes was the wisp of her panties. He eased them from her slowly, sensuously. Returned to where they had been and just as slowly, as sensuously, made exploration.

He heard her give a sigh, a whisper…no more. And then he silenced her with a kiss as soft and as sensuous as his exploration…his rediscovery.

Thoughts inchoate and insubstantial formed in his mind. How right it was to yield to what had been growing between them since she had come into his life once more. What had once drawn them together was as potent as ever.

More so…

This Bianca—the Bianca of the silvered gown, so elegant, so exquisitely beautiful—was impossible not to desire. Not to claim as he was claiming now.

Softly, sensuously, he eased his hand between her silken thighs. He felt her give another sigh of pleasure, felt her hands come around the naked column of his back, her fingertips running slowly, exploringly, along the contours of his spine. Her thighs were slackening, granting him access to where he most desired to be. His lips were still caressing hers, his tongue lacing with hers. He could sense her arousal mounting, the liquid glide enticing his slow, questing exploration, revealing her response to him. And a restlessness was starting up in her—he could feel it, sense it, knew its cause.

He lifted his mouth away, gave a low, husky laugh. 'Patience, *bellissima* Bianca. Patience…'

He would not keep her waiting long, for he knew that what was happening to her was happening to him too. But self-control was absolute. This was too exquisite. He would not rush it. It was a feast…a banquet to be savoured slowly.

All the night long…

His touch at her most intimate places was unbearable…impossible to endure. He was toying with her…playing with her. She felt her thighs slacken, her legs splay. Her hands were running up and down his spine, grazing the muscled contours of his back. She wanted to reach for him, guide him to her. But he was holding himself away. She could not bear it—could not endure it.

She lifted her shoulders, wanting, aching to feel the frottage of her crested peaks brushing the hard wall of his chest.

As if it was a signal, his mouth left hers. Found another place. A moan broke from her. His lips and his tongue at her breast were unbearable—impossible to endure.

She wanted more…so much more…

I want everything. Everything that I have yearned for, longed for, for six long years. To have Luca again. To be in his arms…his embrace…

Restlessness filled her again. The arousal he was drawing from her was mounting, but she did not want it to be hers alone. She whispered his name, an imprecation—a plea.

'Luca…' she sighed. 'I want you…only you.'

He lifted his mouth from her aching coral peak. Smiled down at her. Gold glinted in the deep darkness of his eyes in the soft light from her bedside lamp.

'Then you shall have me, Bianca *bellissima*. You shall have me…'

He moved across her body, slipping his hands from her. She gave a cry of loss, for she knew her moment was very near, and she ached for his touch…

It came slowly…questing. Teasing…toying. Her hands went to his hips, to draw him fully down, but he was too strong for her. His weight was on his elbows, either side of her. His gaze poured into hers.

'How much I want you,' he said.

His voice was low, and what was in it was all she yearned to hear.

'How very, very much…'

He lowered himself down on her, coming into her waiting body, which was opening to his, fusing to his. And as their bodies fused wave after wave broke through her.

Not pleasure—nothing so mundane.

It was far more than pleasure.

Ecstasy.

Her spine arched, her head falling back, hips lifting, and still wave after wave took her far beyond mere earthly delights. To a realm where time and place did not exist. Only eternity.

She cried out. Heard her own cry. Heard his deep echoing of it. Felt him surge within her, completing their fusion, their absolute union, their coming together after so long... so unbearably long...

It was a gap in time that made her weep with the pity of it. Or something did.

For her cheeks were wet with tears.

And her heart was full with all she had not dared to desire.

There was dew on the grass, and long, narrow strips of early sun striped through the gaps in the hedging. There was the faintest chill in the dawn air. Birdsong came, nascent as the day began, and the night yielded to it. Bianca stood barefoot on the lawn, hair tumbling down her back, a thin cotton dressing gown wrapped around her. She was staring sightlessly, her expression bleak.

She had told Luca that day at his *palazzo* that the reason she had been so desperate for him six years ago was that she had yearned to belong to someone. She'd thought that now she did belong to someone—to Matteo—she was free of such desperation.

Her throat tightened, anguish filling her. She was facing the truth about herself—the truth revealed in Luca's arms. There was something she was not free of...never could be free of...

She gave a smothered cry, tightening her arms around her body as if to staunch a wound that could never be healed—not in six years, nor in sixty, or six hundred. A wound that would be there for ever.

How long she stood there she did not know. She knew only that the sun had risen, and pale morning light was filling the garden. Surely Luca would have woken now, found her gone. Would be relieved that she had gone.

Sparing him.

Surely he would go back to his own room, making it safe for her to go indoors.

She caught her breath suddenly.

What was that noise?

A moment later she knew. It was the low, distinctive throaty growl of that lean, mean beast of a driving machine that Luca had arrived in. She stood frozen, listening intently. The growl increased in volume and then, as the car set off, moving away from the house, started to recede.

Relief washed through her. And also something quite different…

Luca sat back in his first-class airline seat, closing his eyes. He was on a long-haul flight to New York, then Toronto, then Chicago, then the west coast. Two weeks out of Italy.

Matteo had been dismayed, but Luca had been adamant. It was essential he take himself out of the country. Absolutely essential.

He'd made himself text Bianca, to tell her he was off, but would return at short notice in case of any emergency with Matteo. He'd said nothing more.

Her reply had been succinct, simple.

Thank you for letting me know.

He'd made no attempt to contact her since. Nor would he.
Not after the night they'd spent together.
The mistake he'd made.

Bianca was listening to what Matteo's doctor was telling her. When he'd asked to speak to her after a routine appointment to check on his patient she had been scared—had the exertions of the party weakened her uncle further? And her uncle had been fretful when Luca had disappeared across the Atlantic, although the news had come as an abject relief to her. His absence, however brief, would give her time—essential time—to strengthen her defences. However hopeless and impossible that was.

Familiar anguish filled her—too familiar... And it took her a moment to take in what Matteo's doctor was telling her. But when she did, it was the very opposite of what she'd feared. Her face lit up. This was wonderful news—just wonderful. And although making contact with Luca was the last thing she wanted to do, this was something she must tell him.

Her spirits lifted, despite the anguish inside her.

Luca was replying to the email Bianca had sent him. This was good news—unexpected, but so welcome. Matteo, Bianca had written, had been deemed sufficiently strong to take part in the immunotherapy trial which—if it should work—would give Matteo real hope, for the first time, of a substantial extension of his life.

Luca's reply was enthusiastic—how could it not be? But having hit 'send', he paused. Steeled himself. There was another message he must send Bianca. An essential one. A personal one.

He got out his phone...started to text.

Bianca was with Matteo in the library and she saw his face had fallen.

'Must you?' he asked.

'My boss has been very good so far, and as you know, you will be in the clinic for your trial. And because it involves suppressing your immune system you will not be allowed visitors anyway. Now is the best time for me to be in London.'

Bianca's tone was placating.

'Yes, I suppose so,' Matteo conceded. 'But with me away, you and Luca could spend so much time together!'

Bianca schooled her reaction. 'I really do need to be back in London a while,' she said.

But not for the reason she'd given her uncle.

For one far more essential.

In her head were the words Luca had written to her.

Bianca, after our night together we need to talk.

She felt her heart clench. No, they did not need to talk.

More words echoed in her head. Echoed from six long, bitter, anguished years ago.

'It's over, Bianca. Over!'

She did not need to hear that again…

Luca was back on a plane again—but this time his destination was far closer. He'd returned from America to find Bianca gone. Which had filled him with one purpose only.

Staying only long enough to escort Matteo to the clinic to start his treatment trial, and to assure his fretful godfather that, yes, he was heading for London the very next day, he had booked his flight.

Determination fused within him.

Bianca could run, but she could not hide. He had things to say to her. Things she had to understand. Things he must make clear to her.

His own words to her in his brief text from America echoed in his head.

We need to talk…

Other words echoed, from much longer ago.

'It's over, Bianca! Over!'

As the plane's powerful engines fired for take-off, Luca tensed.

The two sets of words were fusing in his head.

Bianca was sitting on a tube train, heading east across the city. It was strange to be doing so. Strange to be in London at all. Alien. But it was absolutely, totally essential. And it was the only safe place for her to be.

Safe from Luca.

Emotion clenched in her.

How could she have let it happen? Let herself succumb to what she knew...*knew*...she should never have done?

To be in Luca's arms again had been heaven. But to wake in the chill of the dawn and face what she knew must await her... Ah, that had taken her to a very different place. One she had been in before...

Fiercely she called on her strength of mind, of will. She had fought this before—fought it and won. It had been a bitter, costly victory, but she had done it. She had torn Luca from her life six years ago.

And I can do it again—I must!

Six years ago she might have torn Luca from her life, but this time she knew it was going to be far more agonising.

It was not her life she had to tear Luca from.

It was her heart...

Luca checked into his Park Lane hotel. He'd made no contact yet with Bianca, but tonight he must. He would invite her to dinner here at the hotel, tomorrow. He would imply it was to discuss Matteo—surely she would agree to that?

Because I have to get her to agree. I have to speak to her!

The imperative was essential. If she didn't agree to tomorrow, he would keep pressing. What else could he do?

She has to understand about our night together. I can't afford for her to have the wrong idea about it—make assumptions—misunderstand.

Her return to the UK might have been necessary for work, as she'd told Matteo, and she was taking advantage of the time he would be spending in the clinic, incommunicado. But it might be her continuing to avoid the conversation they *must* have. To make things clear to her.

Memory was vivid in his head.

Six years ago he'd had to make things clear to her.

Now he would have to do so again.

Whether she wants to hear it or not.

CHAPTER TWELVE

SLOWLY, BIANCA WALKED into the hotel restaurant. She didn't want to be here, but Luca's text had said he needed to discuss Matteo. Heaviness weighed her down. Though she hoped with all her heart that the immunotherapy would be successful, at some point Matteo would come home—and he would expect her there, want her there.

Now the heaviness crushed her. He would want her and Luca to continue to be engaged, as he so fondly thought. But to play that role now—with all that had changed between her and Luca—would be agony.

It was an agony that pierced like a dagger as she was shown to his table, her heart leaping uncontrollably. He got to his feet, his eyes going to hers immediately. Faintness washed through her and she sat herself down, heart beating faster. The last time she'd set eyes on him had been when softly, silently...agonisingly...she'd dropped the lightest, slightest brush of her lips to his cheek as he lay sleeping by her side. Before slipping from the room to face the truth she hadn't been able to bear to face.

But she must face it now. Face Luca.

She realised, as he resumed his place and the waiter came to the table, hovering to take their drinks order and bestow menus upon them, that despite his customary svelte elegance, his perpetual air of sophisticated cool, tension was radiating from him in the set of his shoulders, the line of his jaw.

He's steeling himself to tell me what I already know he's going to tell me.

She sheared her mind away. She could not bear to hear that—not yet. Instead, as the waiter left them in peace, she asked after Matteo, and the latest update.

'He's still doing well,' Luca answered immediately.

Was he relieved not to have to tell her quite yet what he must know she would not want to hear? she wondered.

'Still upbeat,' he went on. 'He sounded cheerful when I phoned this morning.'

She gave him a flickering smile. 'That's good,' she said.

The waiter was returning with their drinks. She'd opted for a glass of white wine, and so had Luca. She felt she needed it. Her eyes kept wanting to go to him, drink him in, and her consciousness of his physical presence was overwhelming her. But she had to stay composed. Couldn't let her response to him show. For his sake. For hers.

The polite enquiry from the waiter as to their menu choices was a welcome distraction. They both opted for fish, and a memory came to her of how she had Luca had both ordered fish at the restaurant in Pavenza, that first day they'd gone there together. Buying the fake engagement ring.

A sudden spurt of courage filled her. She would be brave.

She took a mouthful of her wine to help her. Looked straight across at him. 'Luca, we have to think ahead—to when Matteo is home again. How...how are we to deal with this impossible fantasy of his? We can't... We can't just go on with it.'

For a moment—a moment that seemed to last for ever, unbearable and excruciating—he did not reply. His face was impossible to read, and yet she read it like an open book. Knew exactly what was in it.

She saw him take a breath. Heard him make his reply.
'No,' he said, 'I don't think we can.'

Luca's eyes were locked to Bianca's eyes—so green, so luminous, like the emerald in that engagement ring he'd bought her. The fake engagement ring for their fake engagement. The fake engagement that had yoked them together for the sake of her uncle, his godfather, to make him happy.

But how could they sustain it now?

Impossible.

He heard himself speak, answer again Bianca's faltering question. 'We can't. Not any more. It's impossible.'

He saw her face pale. Her tension was visible, as it had been since she'd walked up to the table. She must have been at work today, for she was wearing a charcoal pencil skirt teamed with a dove-grey blouse with a soft collar. Her make-up was minimal, her Titian hair confined into a pleat that emphasised the sculpted beauty of her face.

But he must not be distracted by her beauty, even though it was filling his senses.

He reached for his wine to break the moment, break eye contact. He took a mouthful of the crisp white Sauvignon Blanc, then set down the glass. She hadn't moved, but he could see a pulse at her throat.

He drew a breath, knowing he must speak.

'Bianca, I wanted to talk to you—that's why I've asked you here. You didn't give me the opportunity in Italy.' He held her eyes again and saw she still had not moved. Only the pulse at her throat moved, beneath the pallor of her face.

'There's something I need to tell you,' he said.

Bianca felt her lungs tightening. It was almost physically painful. So he was going to spell it out to her—even though she didn't want him to and it wasn't necessary for him to do so anyway. She knew exactly what he was going to say. Had known it since she'd stood there, all those weeks ago, on the dew-wet grass, watching the sun rise over the garden, listening to the birdsong starting to fill the air with the dawn chorus.

Quickly, she spoke. Wanting…needing…to get in first. 'No, you don't.' She took a breath, a painful one, and looked right at him. Past and present mingled and merged. 'You don't need to tell me, Luca. Not this time.'

She swallowed before making herself go on.

'Six years ago you had to spell it out to me. This time you don't. I know—' Her voice dropped. 'I know it's over.'

Memory stabbed at her of that day at his *palazzo*, when she'd made herself think about the time, one day, when Luca would take his bride there, his new *viscontessa*, and how until then he would doubtless continue his fleeting liaisons.

And I was one of them. Even that night after Matteo's party. He simply succumbed to the desire he's always felt for me…made me his again. For that one night. It would never have been for more…

Luca had stilled, his eyes meeting hers full on.

Slowly, very slowly, he spoke. '*That's* what you thought I was going to say?'

And there was blankness, complete blankness, in his voice.

Luca stared. It was all he could do. That and register that something was changing in her expression. But then things were changing inside his head…rearranging themselves.

Was *that* what she'd thought? Was that the reason she'd avoided him—refused to see him, talk to him? Refused to have any kind of meaningful contact with him since the moment she'd slipped from her bed, from his arms?

Enlightenment was dawning through him.

He leant towards her slightly. 'Is that what you thought I wanted to do to you? Warn you off?' Incredulity was in his voice.

She was staring blankly at him. 'Of course I did,' she said. 'What else? You did it before, the first time around.'

His hand reached across the table. Folded over hers resting immobile on the stem of her wine glass. Her hand was cold, but his…his was filled with the warmth that was flooding through him.

'How could you think I would not want you after our night together?' His voice was a husk. 'How is it possible that you should think so?'

Relief was filling him, moving up through his body. The tension that had been his companion since he'd woken that morning to find her gone had fled…dissipated as if it had never existed. He'd thought that she regretted what had happened.

'That night, Bianca, when I made you mine again…' He took a breath—a ragged one. '*Por Dio*, it was your avoiding me—leaving my arms…the bed—that made me think it was *you* who did not want *me*! That the night we'd spent together was nothing but a mistake! It has been a torment to me—an agony—to think that you rejected me—'

Her expression was changing—he could see it. The change was visible in her face, her eyes. Wonder was filling them…and a glow…a radiant glow. It told him everything he wanted to know. Needed to know. But she was saying it anyway, her voice a breath.

'How could you think that?' she asked. 'How could you ever think that? Oh, Luca—'

He heard the choke in her voice, felt her eyes clinging to his. All of a sudden he pushed back his chair, lifting her hand with his, tightening his fingers over hers. They were no longer cold.

He saw the waiter nearby, summoned him even as he drew Bianca to his feet. 'Will you hold our order, please?' he said to the waiter. 'We'll call for room service. Later.'

They barely made it to his room. He rushed her through the door and then swept her up into his arms. Hunger leapt in him. His mouth swooped down on hers as her arms looped about his neck, pulling him against her. He could feel his body react to hers instantly, and hunger leapt even more. He was moving with her, still kissing her, his tongue twining with hers as they tumbled down on the waiting bed. She was rolling him over, on to his back, sliding his jacket from him, loosening his tie, her mouth barely leaving his as she did so, as hungry for him as he was for her.

Then her fingers were at the buttons of his shirt, slipping them rapidly, and she was sliding her hands over his bared chest. He reared up, eager to repay the courtesy. Words were falling from him in between kisses, telling her how irresistible she was, how infinitely desirable, how his hunger for her was consuming him. She gave a laugh, uninhibited and joyous, throwing back her head as she knelt on the bed beside him and he fumbled urgently with the buttons on her blouse. He wanted to rip it from her.

She laughed again, her hands lifting to the back of her head, and a moment later her hair...her glorious Titian hair... was cascading over her shoulders. She shook it free and he seized it with his hands, drawing her mouth to his once again. Her lush breasts were straining from her bra, and he slid his hand beneath the open front of her blouse, unfastening the catch so that her breasts, coral-tipped and engorged, spilled free. A groan broke from him, and his mouth swooped.

She gave a cry of pleasure, her hands going to his head,

keeping his mouth on her. Her thighs were splayed, constrained by the tightness of her skirt, and he took instant objection to it. Lifting his mouth away, he flipped her on to her back, reaching for her zip. In seconds the restraining garment was gone, and then it was her turn to minister to him. Her hands reached for his waist, unfastening his belt...more than his belt...

His arousal was mounting, becoming unsustainable. With a groan he shucked himself free of the rest of his useless clothes as she threw aside her blouse, pushed her discarded skirt off the bed, whisked her bra away...her panties.

For a moment they paused, gazing at each other. He was ready for her...so ready...and she was ready for him. They were hungry for each other...

Memory seared in his head. Their lovemaking in that long-ago time of heady passion and desire had been eager and fervent. They had gloried in each other's bodies, fulfilled, taken to the heights that they could give each other and take for themselves, free and uninhibited.

He caught her hand now, lowered it to his groin. 'Take me,' he said. His voice was hoarse. His eyes locked to hers. 'Take me, Bianca...my most beautiful, irresistible Bianca...because I am all yours...'

She gave another laugh, glorious and joyous, and lowered her naked, eager, oh-so-ready body to his...

And passion, hot and searing, voluptuous and indulgent, consumed them both in its furnace of desire. Until they burned together in its flames.

Luca's arm was warm around her naked shoulders and Bianca lay beside him. One of his hands cradled her elbow and his other hand was across her body, pressed by hers, as if she wanted to hold him there.

For ever.

After the heady passion of their union, when she had cried out with him as their moment came, their bodies fusing and the white heat of almost unbearable pleasure searing through her, she had clung, half sobbing, to his chest. After the very last echoes and eddies of that ebbing pleasure she had rested against the exhausted thudding of his heart as slowly, oh-so-slowly, their bodies cooled and eased and slipped apart, yielding to the peace that filled her now.

Such peace...

Thoughts, drifting and easeful, glided across the surface of her mind. How wrong she had been...how wrong to fear what she had feared. If she had stayed that blissful morning after the party...if she had woken with Luca in the bright, warm light of day, not in the doubting reaches of the dawn... he would have told her then what he had told her now. That they had found each other again, their union complete.

A wash of wonder, of happiness, lifted through her as she laced her fingers with his, warm on the smooth softness of her waist. One thigh nestled against his, and she felt the fall of her hair across his strong chest as they lay beside each other, the tangled bedding strewn around them, pillows awry beneath their heads.

As if he could sense her happiness—and surely it was radiating from her like brightest sunshine—Luca lifted his head to kiss her softly, sensuously. Smiling as he did so.

'My Bianca—my beautiful *bellissima* Bianca,' he said, lifting his mouth away.

His dark, lustrous gaze was pouring into hers. She touched her fingers to his face. 'My Luca,' she answered. 'My irresistible, my very own Luca. Mine—all mine!' Her voice was as warm as his, as warm as their bodies lying together.

He laughed, softly and seductively, and held her yet closer against him. Desire would come again, she knew, but for now all she wanted was to go on lying here like this, warm against him, soft against him, close against him.

He was speaking again, his voice full of confidence and contentment. 'How right we are for each other, Bianca!' He propped himself up on his elbow, looking down at her. 'I know that till now we've only…conspired in the fantasy Matteo has woven about us, but…' He took a breath. 'Why should it be a fantasy? Hasn't it been real since the night of the party? Then we only went through the play-acting of being an engaged couple, but now—'

He broke off, his eyes still pouring into hers, alight with a flame that made her feel faint.

'Let's make it real, Bianca! Why shouldn't it be? It's what Matteo dreams of, and it's what the rest of the world assumes anyway—thanks to that party! And why wouldn't they? They saw how ideal you are for me—how could I want for more? They saw you that night…the perfect future *viscontessa*, so beautiful, so elegant, so absolutely right for me. And the daughter of my godfather's brother… Matteo's beloved niece…'

Slowly, with infinite care, Bianca drew away from him. Cold was pooling inside her. A creeping arctic, icy chill.

She lifted Luca's hand off her, slid her thigh away from his.

She looked at him looking down at her. Smiling down at her.

It was a smile that slayed her.

'But I'm not,' she said. 'I'm not Matteo's niece.'

CHAPTER THIRTEEN

LUCA HEARD HER speak but it made no sense.

He frowned. 'What do you mean?'

Her expression did not change.

'I mean I'm not Matteo's niece,' she said again.

His frown deepened. 'What are you saying?'

She stood up, not answering him, simply picking up her discarded clothes and putting them back on. He watched her, lying back, propping himself up on a couple more pillows. What the hell was going on?

'Bianca—speak to me!'

She started to button her blouse. 'I'm not Matteo's niece,' she said, and her voice was as expressionless as her face. 'For the simple reason that his brother was not my father.'

'*What?* But Matteo—'

'Matteo thought he was because his brother thought he was. And his brother thought he was my father because that was what my mother told him.'

Luca saw her take a breath, and then something finally showed in her expressionless face.

She finished doing up her blouse, slipped her feet back into her shoes.

Luca stared at her. 'You *know* this?'

He saw her swallow.

'I've known for a few days now. You see...' She hesitated, as if speaking was difficult. 'When I came back to London from Italy there was something I knew I needed to do. You know that after my mother died my aunt took me in, even though she resented me? She gave me a home when she could have handed me over to be put into care.'

She paused, then went on.

'She hasn't stayed in touch before—I send her Christmas cards, but never hear back—but now she's getting on, and she hasn't had an easy life. I wanted to do something for her. Matteo had settled some money on me, saying it was from my father's estate. Out of that I wanted to buy her a bungalow near the sea, which I knew was her dream. After all, why not? I could afford it now I'd discovered who I was. So I went to see her and I told her.'

She paused again for a moment, her expression changing again.

'And she told me I had no right to offer her anything.'

Her voice dropped.

'Because I had no right to accept anything Matteo Fiarante possessed. Because I was not his brother's daughter at all. Because...' she took another ragged breath '... my mother was already pregnant when she met Matteo's brother. She'd been "carrying on", as my aunt put it, with an Irishman who worked at a pub. A red-headed Irishman.'

She picked up her handbag from where she'd dropped it on the floor.

'That's where I get my red hair from, Luca, and my green eyes.' Her mouth twisted. 'And that's probably why I was pouring drinks in a bar when you first met me—blood will out, after all.'

She looked at him with eyes that had no expression in them—none at all.

'I won't tell Matteo. Not yet. If the treatment is successful—as I hope with all my heart it will be—then I'll tell him. He'll be able to take it then. And if it isn't successful...'

For the first time Luca could hear emotion in her voice.

'Well, then what I think I must do is go and see his lawyer on some pretext...explain the situation to him. If...if he thinks it would hurt Matteo too much to know the truth then I won't tell him. When the time comes, I'll simply refuse his legacy to me. I have no right to it, and presumably whatever Matteo was going to do with it before he knew of my existence can still be done—I'm sure the lawyer will sort it out.'

She hitched the strap of her bag onto her shoulder and took another breath, steadier this time. Her face had gone back to being expressionless.

'I want your word, Luca, that you'll go along with me on this. I may not be Matteo's niece...there may not be a drop of shared blood between us...but I've come to care for him—care about him. I can't turn that off just because I'm nothing more than a stranger to him after all. And I can't hurt him with the truth before he's strong enough to take it. And if that time doesn't come—well, he shall die in peace, in the happy belief that I'm his long-lost niece, his brother's daughter. As for his other fantasy...' She paused. 'That's all it was—all it is. I'm not your godfather's niece, not his heiress, and not suitable to be your *viscontessa*. I'm just a common-as-muck girl out of the East End of London, just like I was six years ago.'

She walked to the door. Pulled it open. Cast one last look back at him.

'Sorry about that, Luca.'

Then she was gone.

Luca stared at the closed hotel room door. Inside his chest, his heart had started to thud like a hammer pounding him into the ground.

* * *

Bianca had reached the lift. How she'd got there she didn't know. How she walked inside it and found a button to press she didn't know either. Because she couldn't see. Her vision had gone.

Everything had gone.

Luca had gone.

Lost now for ever like the fantasy he had only ever been, conjured up by the man who was not her uncle after all.

She felt the lift plummet down, leaving her stomach behind—and also an organ even more vital.

The lift stopped moving. There was the slightest pause, and then the doors were opening.

On robotic legs, she stepped out into the lobby.

Two hands fastened around her upper arms like vises.

'Where the *hell*,' demanded Luca, 'do you think you're going?'

He thrust her back into the elevator, jabbing at the control button for his floor. How he'd reached the lobby before she did, he didn't know. How he'd yanked on the barest minimum of clothing to make him even fractionally decent—just his trousers—he didn't know either.

He knew only one thing.

Bianca was trying to leave him.

He pressed her back against the wall of the car as it soared back up. She struggled against his grip, but he would have none of it. He was breaking every rule in the MeToo handbook, but he didn't give a damn. He kissed her instead, crushing her to him. Kissing her and kissing her till she was breathless, boneless, helpless...

'Don't leave me!' he said. 'Don't *ever* leave me!'

The lift was stopping, the doors sliding open. He pulled

her out, hustled her back into his room. He hadn't shut the door—there'd been no time. But once inside he kicked it shut with his bare foot, crushing her against him.

'No more leaving, Bianca! No more leaving ever! Not you—not me—not either of us! Do you understand me? *Do* you?'

He broke into Italian. It was the only language that would do. The only one that could be spoken fast enough, vehemently enough, passionately enough.

Lovingly enough.

As the torrent poured from him he cradled her face in his hands, tilting it up so she would look at him. Tears were shimmering in her eyes. With an oath he broke off, pressed passionate kisses on her eyelids, which fluttered closed.

'No tears! No crying! No weeping! And no leaving! Because why would you want to leave? *Why?* Six years it's taken us—six years!—to be back together again! To make it right between us!'

Her face contorted. Words spilled from her.

'We're only together because you thought I was someone worthy of you now! Because you thought me Matteo Fiarante's niece! But I'm not! I'm not his niece! I'm exactly the same as I was six years ago—when you said I wasn't good enough for you.'

Italian broke from him again. Crude this time, and full of expletives. But he didn't care.

'Then shame on me!' The hands cupping her face gentled, his voice too. He poured his eyes into hers. 'Bianca, six years ago I said what I should never have said. I said it because I thought you wanted too much of me—more than I wanted. But now…now I want everything. *Everything.* Everything that you are.'

He took a breath, his expression changing, his voice changing.

'As for what you've told me—yes, I'm sad. How could I not be? I am sad that you are not Matteo's niece...that he is not your uncle. Sad simply because it meant so much to you and to him. Of course I'm sad. But that's *all* I am, Bianca.'

He let his hands slip from her face, rest on her shoulders instead. Tears were still shimmering in her eyes and he wanted them gone. Wanted that haunted look in her face gone.

He wanted only one look in her face...her eyes. The one that echoed his.

'Forgive me,' he said simply, plainly, so that there could be no doubt, no misunderstanding—not ever again. 'Forgive me if I gave you cause to think it would make a difference to me. Because how could it? How could it change you for me? How could it change *me*? I am what I am, Bianca.' His eyes held hers, and then he said to her the most important thing he would ever say in his life. 'And what I am, what I will always be, is the man who loves you.'

Softly, gently and infinitely carefully, he lowered his lips to hers, in a fleeting touch whose echo would last for ever. All his life—and hers.

And as he lifted his mouth away he saw the tears in her eyes well up and spill, then pour down her cheeks.

It was all he needed to see.

She went into his arms and they came about her. She felt the bare wall of his chest against her breasts, his hands around her waist, holding her while she wept.

After a long while her tears dried, and she could cry no more. He let her straighten. As she did so, she became aware of a discreet but insistent knocking at the door. Frowningly,

Luca released her, opened the door. Two men in dark suits stood there.

'Is everything all right?' one asked.

His voice was polite, but wary too. The other one, Bianca realised, was looking past Luca at her.

'Are you all right, madam?' the second one asked her directly.

With a start, she realised who they were, why they were here, and what they were seeing. Luca wearing nothing but a pair of trousers, chest bare, feet shoeless. Herself with her face swollen with tears. They had presumably, she realised, received a report of Luca hauling her into the lift.

She gave a laugh—a shaky one. 'Thank you, yes, we're fine. I promise you. Thank you so much for your concern,' she said.

'Yes, thank you,' corroborated Luca. 'I apologise for my...alarming behaviour. You see...' he turned to address the hotel's security team '... I wanted to propose to my fiancée, but I was somewhat...precipitate.'

The first security guard looked suspicious. Confused. 'Fiancée...? Propose to her...?'

'It's a long story,' Bianca said.

'And complicated,' added Luca.

'But I'm absolutely fine,' Bianca assured the two men. 'Truly I am.'

'So you see,' said Luca, 'I'm sure you'll understand that we wish to be a little...private right now?'

Two pairs of wary eyes went from Bianca to Luca, then to Bianca again. She smiled at them reassuringly. And there must have been something in that smile to make them reassess the situation. Or perhaps it was the radiance in her face...the glow of happiness in her eyes. The look of love about her...

'Then please accept our apologies for having disturbed you,' the first one said dryly.

'Not at all,' said Luca graciously.

He shut the door, turned back to Bianca. But he did not come to her. Instead, he stayed where he was. Went down on one knee. Lifted his face to look up at her.

'Will you marry me, Bianca?' he said.

And it came from his heart. From his very being. From all that he was and ever would be.

She'd thought she had cried all her tears. Thought there were none left to shed.

She was wrong.

She was crying again, and with an oath in Italian, Luca lurched to his feet.

'Bianca!'

He knew alarm was in his voice, and a lot more. He caught her hand and kissed it. Hung on to it tightly.

'You do *want* to marry me, don't you? I mean, we can live in sin...or just go on being *fidenzato* to each other for the next hundred years...but wouldn't you *like* a wedding? Most females would, or so I'm told, and to be honest I'd probably quite enjoy one too.' His throat tightened. 'I know Matteo would. We could do it for him. Because, you see...' his voice changed, became sombre '...whatever the outcome of his treatment, and whenever you tell him about your real father, I know... I *know*, Bianca...that it will not kill his feelings for you.' And now he gave her hand a little shake of remonstrance. 'Any more than it will kill mine for you. Because it's you, Bianca, who we care about...feel for. *You* we love. You I love.'

He lifted her hand to his mouth, grazed her knuckles in the time-honoured gesture of homage.

'Say yes,' he said to her as he lowered her hand again. 'Say yes and make me the happiest of men. It's taken me six long years to deserve to be happy, but now I truly think I do. We'll take care of Matteo, you and I together, until the end comes. And when it does—whenever that should be—he will know that his fantasy, his dream…' his voice softened '…has become the truth. A truth that will last our lifetimes.'

He paused, his gaze pouring into hers. Her eyes were diamonds, with the last tears to be shed.

'Say yes, Bianca,' he said again.

Her lashes lowered, sweeping away the tears.

'Yes…' she said, her voice a whisper.

And then a cry, a broken sound, was wrenched from her.

'Oh, God, *yes*, Luca! Yes! Because I love you so, so much. I always have and I always will, and I can't ever not love, love, *love* you!'

He crushed her hand to his lips again, emotion filling him, and as he lowered it he slipped from his finger the signet ring he always wore. Slid it onto hers.

'This must do until I get you back to Italy,' he said, a crooked smile forming at his mouth.

'I left the one you bought me at Matteo's house,' she said.

He shook his head. 'Not that one. Oh, you can wear it every day, if you like, but that's not the ring you'll wear on our wedding day. Not that one at all. Only one ring will do for you then.'

She gave a wry laugh, looking pointedly at him. 'A priceless heirloom for an East End girl?'

He shook his head again. 'For the beloved of my heart,' he said.

Another cry broke from her and he swept her into his arms. Where she would stay for ever now.

Beloved of my heart.

His own words echoed through him—as he knew they would through all the years ahead.

EPILOGUE

Bianca stood poised at the top of the sweeping flight of stairs in Luca's *palazzo*, ready to descend.

Memory was vivid in her head of how she had stepped down the long staircase at her uncle's villa on the night of the party he had organised to celebrate what he had so fondly assumed was the celebration of his beloved niece's engagement to his equally beloved godson. Then, she had been wearing an evening gown, chosen by her uncle, which had dismayed her by looking far too much like a wedding gown—an item of clothing she would never wear for Luca...

Or so she had thought.

As she stood now, at the top of the staircase, a wash of wonder and of radiant happiness went through her.

For today was her wedding day.

Her wedding to Luca.

The man she loved so much.

And there, waiting at the foot of the stairs, was another man she loved too.

Matteo. Looking so well—for his pioneering treatment had worked, and he was now permitted to mingle once more, his cancer if not quite in remission, then certainly more reduced than anyone could have hoped. For now, at least. Oh, he still had to be careful, she knew. His strength was limited, and his life was still limited. But for now he had the wonderful gift not only of the present, but of a future that would surely encompass seeing her and Luca well established in their marriage.

And perhaps, too even seeing the birth of their first child. She felt hope quiver within her. She and Luca had determined that conception would be a first priority for them after their wedding.

The wedding had been organised the moment she had returned with Luca to Italy. The old proverb came into her head: *Marry in haste, repent at leisure.* But she dismissed it summarily. She and Luca had already done their repenting—six long years of it—and both regretted that their youthful affair had ended as it had. And they were marrying in haste only for Matteo's sake, not wanting to keep him waiting a moment longer than was necessary.

It was taking place here, at the *palazzo*, with the ceremony in the D'Alabruschi family chapel. The guests were the same as those who had come to the engagement party, plus Giuseppe and all the staff from the Villa Fiarante—she would not dream of being married without those stalwarts. And Nurse Paolo was coming too, even if he was also here to keep an eye on Matteo.

Bianca had invited Andrew and his wife, and several of her colleagues, who had all flown out for the occasion. She had arranged with Andrew that she would continue to work part-time, and remotely, as a researcher here in Italy—a compromise that would keep her career open for now. Perhaps one day, she hoped, when her Italian was sufficiently fluent, she might be able to work for an Italy-based environmental consultancy and forge links with Andrew's?

But that was all for later. For now, she was focussing on her wedding.

As well as her colleagues, she had invited her aunt too—but had not been surprised to receive no answer. It was a sadness to her, for her aunt was all that remained of her mother's family, but it was something that she accepted. Just as her aunt had accepted, after all, the gift of a little bungalow in the south coast seaside town where she was now living. It had been paid for by Luca, though. Not from the money Matteo had said was Tomaso's and therefore his daughter's.

Bianca's expression shadowed for a moment. She knew that she must tell Matteo what her aunt had so shockingly disclosed about her paternity, but she and Luca had agreed not to do so until they were married. After all, their marriage would take place whoever's daughter she was.

Another wash of wonder and of happiness went through her. To know, with absolute and total certainty, that Luca loved her, and could not care less what her background was, or who she was, was a reassurance beyond measure to her. He cared only that she was the woman he loved, and always would.

Yet it was a grief to her, all the same, to know that Matteo was not her uncle—that she was not his brother's daughter. Discovering her existence, as he had thought he had, had brought comfort to him at a time when there had been little to comfort him, and she grieved in advance that she would have to take that from him. For all that, though, she hoped that it would not sever their relationship. Because she knew, with a lift of her heart, that she would always feel for Matteo what she had come to feel for him, even without any link of blood between them.

And after all, she consoled herself, she would still be the wife of his beloved godson—dear to him, surely, for that reason alone.

She took a breath, filled with resolve. Dimly, she could hear the faint strains of organ music echoing along the marble floors from the chapel at the far end of the *palazzo*. It was time to go down.

Gathering her full skirts, her vision slightly blurred by the veil over her face, she started her careful descent. As she gained the final step Matteo stepped forward, arm outstretched. She slipped her hand from her satin skirts, placed it on his sleeve. She turned towards him. Smiled through the lace veiling.

'Oh, my dearest, dearest treasure...' Matteo's voice was warm and full, his eyes alight. 'How beautiful you look!'

He pressed her hand to his sleeve and she felt her ring finger heavy not with the ring Luca had bought for her that day in Pavenza, but with the huge, antique heirloom ring—the betrothal ring every D'Alabruschi bride wore on her wedding day.

Its weight was considerable, and Bianca would indeed revert to the smaller version for everyday wear, returning this one to the family vault after the wedding. But she had asked Luca to take her back to the little jeweller's in Pavenza, wearing the heirloom ring, to show it off. The jeweller had been delighted to see it again, and had examined it closely, exclaiming at the workmanship, the perfection of the stones and the setting, thanking her and Luca for the opportunity to do so.

She had been glad to do it—and she was glad now to let her eyes fill with all the warmth that was in Matteo's.

'And how well *you* look!' she said.

'How could I be otherwise on this happy, happy day? I am fulfilling my dreams!'

'And fulfilling mine, too.' She smiled.

'And Luca's,' Matteo said. 'Never have I seen a man more smitten!' He took a breath, patted her hand once more. 'And now,' he said, 'I shall take you to him. Bestow you upon him. Come.'

He started forward and Bianca went with him down the long, marbled passageway, pausing a moment at the far end, where two ushers threw open the double doors to the chapel. As they did so the music swelled, the congregation rose to its feet and there at the far end, by the altar rail, Bianca beheld the figure of the man she was to unite her life with, unite her heart with.

The man she loved.

Luca—always and only Luca.

He turned at her entrance, looking so handsome in his light grey morning dress that she thought she must die from beholding him as she walked towards him. His eyes went to hers, his face transfixed.

At his side, his best man, Pietro, murmured something to him. With a jolt, Luca stepped forward, ready to take her hand when she reached him, still looking dazed, transfixed. Skirts rustling, veil trailing behind her, she came to him. Matteo lifted her hand from his sleeve, placed it in Luca's waiting clasp. Then stood aside.

Luca's fingers were warm around hers, his gaze warmer. He stepped with her up to the altar rail, where the priest was raising his hands. The organ music died away and the congregation sat.

The priest waited a moment, holding Luca and Bianca's eyes. Then he lifted his gaze to the congregation beyond in the little chapel. His sonorous words were addressed to them all.

'Dearly beloved...'

And the wedding began.

The guests had departed. Evening darkened the sky. It was autumnal, but not cold. Luca took Bianca's hand. They would spend their wedding night here at his *palazzo*, but tomorrow they would set off on their honeymoon. It would not be a long honeymoon, for neither of them wanted to leave Matteo for long, and it would be in Italy. A touring honeymoon, with Luca driving them wherever the fancy took them. The coast, the hills, the mountains and the lakes, the historic cities, the woods and forests, the peaceful countryside... Then they would return to the *palazzo*.

They would make their home here, he and his beloved Bianca, his bride, his wife, his peerless and most beautiful *viscontessa*. A home for themselves and for Matteo too—for it had been agreed that he should move here from the Villa Fiarante to keep company with them. They would split their time between the *palazzo* and the villa, especially when Luca was required in Rome, or for brief and occasional foreign trips abroad. He had already arranged to work largely from home.

And as soon as Nature proved co-operative he and Bianca would start a family. New life to encourage Matteo... to give him yet another reason to retain his own life for as long as it was possible. He was determined upon it, Luca knew, and had been open in his avowal that he would see his godson's son.

'It might be a daughter first,' Luca had warned him smilingly.

'Another Bianca,' Matteo had approved.

And Luca would be just as approving—son, daughter, whatever they were blessed with, it would be a joy and a privilege.

Now, taking Bianca's hand, he raised it to his lips. 'Have you enjoyed our wedding day?' he asked her.

The glow in her emerald eyes gave him his answer—she had been radiant all day. And he... He had been in a daze of disbelieving happiness all day. He dropped a soft kiss on her sweet lips, keeping his touch light with effort. Soon… oh, very soon…their wedding night would begin…

But not quite yet. Matteo was coming towards them. He was looking tired, but his happy contentment was visible.

'My dear ones, the day has been long, and I know that my good Paolo is waiting in the wings for me, but before I let him claim me there is something I want to show you. I have had something delivered which I hope you will find room for. Let me show you…'

He ushered them out into the wide entrance hall, and Luca, still holding Bianca's hand, walked with him towards the small dining room—the one Luca's mother had had redecorated and that Bianca had thought so beautiful on her first visit to the *palazzo*. It had been set aside to display their wedding presents, and the oval table was groaning with them, but clearly what Matteo had in his mind was not there.

An easel had been set up to one side of the table. What was on it was covered by a silk cloth. Luca and Bianca exchanged puzzled glances.

Matteo was smiling. 'You will not have seen this,' he told them, 'for it always hung in Luisa's bedroom, which was once my mother's. I have seldom gone in there since my dearest Luisa died, but now I have braved it.' He turned to Bianca. 'I wanted to give you this.' He gestured to the easel. 'It is a portrait of my mother's mother—and it belongs here, with you.'

At his side, Luca felt Bianca tense. He knew why. And though he had agreed with her that Matteo's illusions about her should not be shattered before their wedding, perhaps they had been wrong in that decision. Perhaps the truth would have been more honest. Sparing them moments like this.

Matteo was walking forward. Lifting the corner of the cloth over the painting. Removing it with a flourish.

As he did so, an audible gasp broke from Bianca. And from Luca too.

Matteo turned back to them. 'You see?' he asked. 'You see why this portrait belongs here, with you, my dearest, dearest Bianca?' His voice softened and his eyes went back to the portrait. 'My *nonna*,' he said lovingly. 'When I was a boy she often came to stay, and one of my earliest memories is of sitting in her room with my brother as my mother brushed out her long white hair, telling me she remembered it from when she was no older than I...when her hair was exactly as it is in this portrait.'

Luca could not speak, and nor could Bianca at his side. But she was stepping forward, her hand outstretched, her fingers brushing gently, so gently, over the portrait before her. It was a woman—a beautiful woman in her prime. Matteo's grandmother...with her emerald eyes and her flaming Titian hair...

A choke came from her and she turned back, her eyes wide. Eyes that resembled Matteo's grandmother's not only in colour but in shape, as did the shape of her nose, the line of her jaw, the wave of her red, red hair...

'*La rosa rossa*—the red rose. That's what my grandmother was called...' Matteo's voice was fond. He came to Bianca, kissed her cheek. 'Your great-grandmother,' he said. 'No one knows where her red hair came from—perhaps some Venetian ancestress painted by Titian? But now...' he kissed her other cheek '...it descends to yet another generation.'

He stepped away, cast a last look at the portrait, and then looked at Bianca and Luca.

'I shall leave you now, my dearest ones, and give myself over to the ministrations of Paolo. And I leave you to each other—for tonight and for all your lives. Be blessed in your love for each other, as my beloved Luisa and I were blessed.' His voice changed, grew sad. 'Be blessed as my poor brother and your dear mother had no chance to be. But you, Bianca,' he said, and now Luca could hear not sadness in his godfather's voice, but gladness, 'my dearest niece, are their blessing. Be blessed for them...for their sakes and for your children's sake. And who knows?' His voice lightened now, and he started to walk towards the door. 'Amongst them may be another red, red rose...'

At the door he turned.

'Goodnight, my dearest ones, goodnight.'

Then he was gone.

For a long, long moment neither Luca nor Bianca could speak. Then Bianca turned to the portrait again. Still saying nothing.

So Luca spoke for her. 'You can ask for a DNA test, if you want, but it cannot tell you more than this.' He looked at her. 'She's you,' he said simply.

Wonder was filling Bianca's face—wonder and hope.

'Do you really, really think so?'

Hope was in her voice too, and in her eyes.

He took her hands, held them closely. 'What I think, beloved of my heart, is that Matteo has given you a gift he does not know the price of—a gift we shall treasure and pass on to our children, whether they be redheads or not!'

She gave a smothered cry. 'I am so glad! So incredibly, gratefully glad! Perhaps my aunt believed what she told me? I want to think that of her—that she did not speak only out of malice. But if this is true...' she glanced back at the portrait '...if this really is my great-grandmother, then I am truly Matteo's niece and he's my uncle...' Her expression changed. 'But I won't probe any further. Let it be as it is. It's enough...quite enough.'

Gratitude was in her voice, and Luca blessed her for what she had avowed.

'I think that's wise,' he said. 'Let's let it be.'

He dropped a kiss as light as a feather on her lips. Then he drew back, not relinquishing her hands.

'Speaking of children, however…'

His voice changed and he could hear the husk in it. He knew why it was there.

'I think… I really, really think, beloved of my heart, that as it is our wedding day, and we have now made our vows, consumed our lavish wedding breakfast and bade farewell to all our guests, the hour grows late. We are quite, quite alone, and it is time…' he dropped another kiss on her lips, not so light this time '…that you performed your first duty as the new Viscontessa.'

His eyes glinted wickedly.

'It is time for you to present your lordly husband with an heir. The begetting of which…' he kissed her again, not featherlight at all now, but sensuously and oh-so-arousingly '…requires that we retire to the bridal chamber and proceed, with due decorum, taking our time over it quite exquisitely, to remove this most beautiful wedding dress and my increasingly constricting monkey suit solely and exclusively for the purpose of partaking in connubial bliss—an exercise that I fully envisage will take all the night long.' He kissed her again for good measure. 'It will be dawn, beloved of my heart, before we sleep…'

He drew her towards the door. Her long skirts rustled as she came with him, brushing the marble floor. She glanced up at him, his bride, his wife, his *viscontessa*, the love of his life, the purpose of his being, his heart of hearts, and her emerald eyes were aflame with green fire.

'Sounds good to me,' she said. Her voice was wicked with anticipation and agreement. 'I can't wait!'

No more could he.

They were in perfect accord, sharing a single mind, as he crushed her hand in his and her free hand scooped up her suddenly cumbersome skirts. Their heels ringing on the marble floor, they all but ran along the hallway and up the soaring staircase into the waiting bridal chamber, where the tester bed was strewn with red rose petals and the air was perfumed with vast bouquets.

There was chilled champagne in a huge silver bowl filled with ice, crystal glasses beside it on an inlaid bouillotte table. And there were dishes of canapés, petits-fours, sun-ripe figs and peaches and truffled chocolates to ward off night starvation, together with a pot of coffee on another table nearby, keeping warm on a hot plate. Almond and pistachio biscotti were set beside the porcelain cups, and in pride of place, on a silver gilt stand, was a miniature wedding cake—an exact replica of the towering construction that had graced their lavish wedding breakfast earlier.

They ignored it all. Only one priority consumed them, and one priority alone. For the bridegroom to claim his bride and the bride her groom. A husband for a wife…a wife for a husband. A *visconte* for his *viscontessa*…a *viscontessa* for her *visconte*.

This very night, this very hour, they would begin their married life—and it would last for all their lives and for so much longer.

For Luca knew, as he took his *viscontessa*, his wife, his beloved and his bride into his enfolding arms, that for a love like theirs only eternity would do.

* * * * *

AFTER-HOURS HEIR

MILLIE ADAMS

MILLS & BOON

For Soraya, thank you for being so amazing.

CHAPTER ONE

When Sylvie Jones walked into her apartment she toed her high-heeled shoes off—thank God—then set her briefcase and swept it toward the wall with her bare foot as she took her phone out of her pocket and walked into the narrow galley kitchen.

It was almost time.

Almost.

She was angry and edgy. Work had not gone well. She could feel the board turning against her, their hostility getting more and more open by the day.

She wasn't her father.

She wanted to remind them that it was her father who had been at the helm when the ship had sunk the first time. Her father had been attempting a merger with Culver Books which had been torpedoed by RedMedia, who had flagged them for antitrust violations. They'd been "streamlining" the publisher beforehand and what had remained had been little more than spare parts. Then Culver Books had gone on to acquire Martin & Burke which had created a mammoth publishing house that had effectively eaten its competition alive, including Jones & Abbott.

Who had already been bite-sized at that point.

He'd only just begun to rebuild the publishing house when he'd died and she'd been working toward getting everything back into the black as best she could, and now she felt... something ominous looming.

Mainly, something to do with RedMedia and its tall, dark and devilish owner.

But that didn't matter right now. Safe in her little walk-in closet of an apartment, with leftover takeout in her future, it didn't matter.

It mostly didn't matter because...
Ding!

Baby: Sometimes I find schedules inconvenient.

She saw the banner on her phone screen, and her heart nearly burst through the front of her chest. It was him.

The man she knew only as Baby. The man she'd been texting with for five months. The man she was falling in love with, sight unseen.

Kid: Schedules can go to hell!!!

She laughed as she sent the text and opened up her fridge. Her phone dinged again, and she abandoned the open fridge doors.

Baby: But you'll keep yours. Tomorrow, and the next day and the next...

She sent him a middle finger emoji and began to heat up her leftovers. He was right, of course. Because she was saddled with keeping this company afloat while she basically existed as a legacy CEO even though the publishing house carried her actual name.

Baby: Did I offend you?

She scoffed at her phone.

Kid: You don't care if you offended me.

Baby: I absolutely do care, Kid.

She called him *Baby*, he called her *Kid*. A song reference that had come up when she'd first called what they were doing an illicit affair, and she'd thought it was hilarious at the time, but now it made her stomach get unbearably tight.

Kid: You care because you're afraid I won't send you sexy words later. Though to be fair, you could get an AI chatbot to sex you up.

Baby: It wouldn't be you, would it?

She bit her lip and squeezed her thighs together as she turned to the microwave—the weirdest combination of activities known to man—and got her leftovers out. Then she carried them to her couch, along with the phone, her laptop and a glass of wine and settled in for the evening.

She switched to her laptop so she could type faster.

She imagined him doing the same.

Would they ever talk on the phone? Video call? She was so reluctant to disrupt this thing they had, and she ignored the little alarm bells that went off that they hadn't.

This felt so fragile, whatever it was.

She'd found a cell phone on the street after the worst publishing event she could remember attending, and she'd been huffing out of the building, stressed and angry, when she saw a phone lying there on the wet sidewalk, all lit up.

The rain had kept the screen from locking.

She'd picked it up and had turned back toward the hotel to hand it in, and something had…stopped her.

It was a totally generic phone. The lock screen and wallpaper were default. She hadn't snooped or anything, but she had pulled up the texts, and started a new one:

This is from the girl who found your phone, hope you get it back.

She'd sent it to herself from that phone, just to see.

The next day, she'd gotten a text.

Unknown Number: This is definitely the most interesting way I've gotten a woman's number.

And so it had begun.

It was like sending words into a safe void. She told him nothing about herself, and yet she told him everything.

No identifiers, only deep philosophical discussions. And…virtual sex. Which was something no one would ever believe given Sylvie was a sad midtwenties virgin.

But on this text thread? She'd done lots of things. Scandalous things.

The "sex" was great. But so was everything else.

Kid: Sometimes I wonder if I hate my job. Do you ever wonder that?

There is no pause on his end.

Baby: No. I live it. Which isn't the same as loving it, I suppose, but it is the thing that gives me purpose.

Kid: I get that. It gives me purpose, or I guess it's like, I was born with it as my purpose and now I don't know how to live without it but some days I want to burn it to the ground and start over. Reasonable?

Baby: Arson is always reasonable.

He said nothing for a moment.

Baby: If you hate it why do it?

Kid: I don't know who I'd be without it.

Baby: You have never told me what you do, and yet I feel like I know you. Which means you don't need your job to be who you are.

That made her feel so much warmer than it should.

"I wish you were here." She said that into the silence of her apartment instead of texting it, and she was surprised to discover how quiet her apartment was. When they talked she heard his voice in her head. Or what she had decided it was. Smooth and pleasant. She imagined him in the same way. For some reason, with light brown hair and glasses, tall with a slim build. The kind of intellectual handsome like a character from an old nineties cartoon she'd watched where they searched for a lost underwater city.

Childhood crushes on cartoon characters died hard.

Instead of being maudlin, she finished her dinner and pushed her bowl to the side. Her heart fluttered and she pulled a blanket over her lap as she scrunched up and pulled her laptop close like she was a child who might get caught doing something bad.

Kid: If you were here I'd kiss you for that.

That was better than a sad, wistful *Wish you were here*.

Baby: I'd do more than kiss you.

She arched her hips up slightly, a response to restlessness between her thighs.

Baby: Or perhaps it's more about where I'd kiss you.

She let out a hard breath and laid her head back on the couch arm. He was going to kill her. She didn't know why it was like this. She didn't know why typed-out words from a man she'd never seen got her hotter than any guy she'd ever known in real life.

Her twenties had been hijacked by her family's financial issues and her dad's death, but she knew if dating had been really important to her she would have found the time, probably. She'd found the time to knit, after all.

This wasn't knitting.

Baby: First on your lips, of course. But then I would kiss your neck.

She slipped her hand between her thighs.

Baby: I would strip you naked and kiss your breasts, down your stomach, right to the center of your thighs. I wouldn't be able to get enough.

How did he know? He didn't even know if he thought she was pretty. The idea of meeting him terrified her for that reason. What if he didn't like her? What if midsized redheads with frizzy hair weren't his thing?

What if...

Baby: I'd push two fingers inside of you as I ate you.

Kid: Yes. Yes. Yes.

It had embarrassed her at first. But now she got consumed by it. By him. By all the dirty things he said to her. And she said them back.

Kid: I want you. Please.

And he told her exactly how he'd take her, in detail.

Her release came hot and fast and if anyone had been there to see how easy it was for him to get her there with a few keystrokes she'd have died. But this was her secret. Their secret.

In the aftermath, she sat there, breathing hard.

Baby: I don't do things like this.

Kid: And you think I do?

Baby: I don't know, maybe you have ten men on retainer.

Kid: Very gendered speculation, Baby.

Baby: Ten people.

Kid: Just you.

She sat there and stared at the text box. Dots appeared: he was typing again.

Baby: I'm a very powerful man, you know. That I'm sitting here typing these things out when I could simply take a woman to bed... I don't understand it.

Something about his words hit her, hard and square. Made her heart beat faster.

Kid: A very powerful man? Is that something that gets a response out of women?

Baby: Very gendered, Kid.

Kid: Women. Men. Anyone.

Baby: No, usually I do. I don't engage in months' worth of conversations only to type out fantasies I could just as easily be living.

She couldn't hear any of this in the voice she'd created for him, and she didn't understand it.
In her mind, it felt hard now. Had an edge.
She didn't fantasize about him having an edge.

Kid: In deference to your power, why don't I get on my knees and serve you?

Christos Onassis had not taken himself in hand so many times since he was a green boy. And yet he found himself chasing his release as he read the words coming in fast on his computer screen.

This was an anomaly. An atrocity.

A...

He pictured a woman he did not wish to imagine. With her wild, riotous, intrusive red hair a mess falling all around her shoulders as she knelt before him, her angry eyes looking up at him. He didn't mean to imagine it, and perhaps that was why it was so damned hot. Perhaps it was why all of this was.

Christos was denied very little in life. At least at this stage. He had wealth and power, he was tall, and had the kind of good looks that guaranteed him access to any woman's bed he wanted to be in. After a childhood of fighting for survival, all of this ease verged on boring.

He'd lost his phone after a publishing event—which he'd found mind numbing—had spent far too long locating it, and had been in a rage when he finally had. Then he'd had seen that outgoing text. Out of uncharacteristic curiosity, he'd sent another one directly to that number.

It had felt like a harmless diversion. And so had all of it, really. He hadn't expected this anonymous exchange of thoughts and ideas to turn into this. A sexual relationship that was taking place without them ever having exchanged photos.

Something that was dangerous, in his opinion, because of moments like this.

When it was so easy to imagine *her*.

Defiant, until she got to her knees before him to give him everything he wanted.

His release was hot, sudden. Powerful.

If he paused to consider the absurdity of this, he might feel shame. But he didn't find himself absurd, and he never felt shame.

It always felt so real and vivid when they talked. It was only afterward that it felt too quiet and she felt distant.

Kid: Did that work for you?

She sent that with a winking emoji. She was truly so… He didn't know what to make of it. Of them. She didn't know who he was, and that made her treat him completely differently than anyone else ever treated him.

She had no idea who he was, how rich, how tall.

Though he'd told her he was powerful. And she'd laughed at him.

Baby: It nearly killed me.

He had no reason not to be honest. It was a rare thing. To just speak to someone like this, without any investment in hiding a part of himself.

He *could* meet her.

It would ruin things.

She would know who he was. As the owner of RedMedia and one of the richest men on earth, his image was quite recognizable.

And it wasn't a very good image. Not that it made women want him less. He was dangerous, forbidden in an era when so many wanted to believe they despised the wealthy, when in truth they simply wanted to be among them.

He didn't do relationships. He didn't sleep with the same woman twice. They'd been doing this for months, and if he brought it into the physical realm she would be subject to the rules of his life, and he found he had no appetite for that at all.

Kid: You really are so powerful, Baby.

Baby: And you're a brat.

Kid: You could spank me.

He felt his body stir. He could go again. And she wasn't even here.

Baby: If I spanked you, you wouldn't be able to sit for a week. You'd have to think long and hard about how badly you wanted your job since being at your desk would be torture. Or perhaps I'd just come visit you at your job and take you, bending you over your desk.

He wondered if he was pushing it, but for some reason he felt on edge tonight with her. More than he had.

Kid: I'd be okay with that.

But as the fantasy took shape, it was clear he was imagining one woman. And one woman only. Was that who he saw every time he spoke to Kid?

Because as he typed to her, spinning out a whole new fantasy, it was impossible to deny that the woman he had bent over the desk in his mind's eye, the pale, glorious ass he was riding, belonged to the woman currently making his life a living hell.

The woman whose business he was about to take over.

The woman whose life he was about to destroy.

Sylvie Jones.

CHAPTER TWO

Sylvie was wrung-out the next morning, like she actually had spent all night having sex with a mystery man, instead of just typing steamy erotica for two in a round-robin with a stranger.

She took a sip of her coffee as she walked into the lobby of the publishing house and waved her badge in front of the elevator.

She had that meeting today and she was trying to block it out and think about Baby. It was a stupid name. She wished she knew his name.

She wished she could actually have his hands on her.

There were so many reasons not to, though. First of all, she was drowning in her job. Second of all, she was not a glossy, sleek socialite, and maybe it was weird to think he'd expect her to be.

They only knew vague things about each other. The conclusions she'd drawn about him were based on the way he came across in writing. She knew he worked a lot, like she did, so she'd drawn conclusions about him being in the corporate machine—as she was.

He didn't know who her mother was. She did. And even when her mother shouldn't be a factor in something it felt like she was right there.

Are you going to finish that whole plate?

I can get you in to see my stylist, Sylvie. You could do with a keratin treatment on your hair to manage that frizz.

You should get that hyperpigmentation treated.

She'd only been able to stare at her mother after that one. Until she'd figured out her hyperpigmentation meant… freckles.

Sylvie looked like her dad. A midsized short redhead with cheeks that got very red when they were angry, excited or overheated.

Sylvie didn't actually want to know what had ever drawn her mother to her father, so she hadn't asked. But whatever had been there once had soured, and Sylvie was never sure if her mother was critical of her looks because she reminded her mother of her former husband, or if she just thought Sylvie was unattractive.

Either way, it had done a number on her self-esteem.

And it informed how she felt about the potential for meeting her mystery man and she just…she couldn't bear it if she met him one day and the first time she saw that face it was twisted with disappointment.

Bleh.

Her heart was beating too fast. It was the eternal problem of being a somewhat anxious person who also needed a hefty dose of caffeine in the morning. She could make it so that she wasn't sleepy, but then she was a little bit overly charged-up.

And she refused to credit this feeling to anything else.

Her mind was spinning in circles. The meeting. Last night. The giddy feeling that her secret created inside of her. The reality of what was happening with work.

How disappointed her father would be if she couldn't save this. And then somehow the way that her mother was just always unimpressed. No matter what.

Around and around in her head as the elevator went to her office floor.

She walked in, and was satisfied to see that she was one of the first people there, which meant she didn't have a lot of conversations as she navigated the narrow hallways and went toward her office. The office that she knew so many people at the company didn't think she had earned.

One she sat in largely because of her father. It was true; it was also true that she had eaten, slept and breathed this publishing house from the time she was a teenager.

If not before.

She had been raised here.

She had sat in this office underneath her father's desk, listening to him talk about books, profit margins and distributors from the time she was a little girl.

Had she been given something she might not have gotten otherwise? Yes.

Some days it was really hard for her to think that she deserved it. But she didn't think there was anyone else who knew it better.

Because she hadn't just been raised in a bubble and handed the publisher. She had been raised *in* the publisher, and she had been raised *for* it. When her father had died, she was the one who helped muscle them out of the hole.

It was only now the board seemed to forget. Five years on and she wasn't seen as a wunderkind, but as a mediocre nepo baby. She could feel it.

And that was the story of her life. Always underwhelming, no matter what.

She pushed open her office door and stopped dead.

There *he* was. Standing with his back to her, broad shoulders made sharp by the severe cut of his black suit. His black hairstyle sleek and ruthless as the rest of him. With the sunlight shining across him, she was certain she could see some strands of gray there.

But they weren't flaws.

No.

Christos Onassis did not do *flaws*.

Of course, he was in her office, in her building before her. That was who he was, how he was.

She did her best not to catalog every interaction, every encounter she'd ever had with him over the last twelve plus years because there was just no reason to go over that.

And over, and over it.

She dreaded seeing his face. As if he sensed her trepidation, he turned slowly.

And then, she was looking square at her enemy. The enemy that made her whole body freeze up every time she saw him.

She remembered one time when her father had taken her to church, a rare occurrence but something that happened on occasion when he felt guilty about the manner in which he was raising her. She remembered the priest saying that Satan had been God's most beautiful angel. That he had felt he was himself godlike, deserving of worship and praise, and it was why he had fallen.

Christos Onassis, unsuitably named for Christ, seemed to her closer to Lucifer than anything else.

Beautiful. In an otherworldly way.

Arrogant. As if he, too, would boldly claim he was worthy of more praise than God himself.

His eyes were so dark they were nearly black, his brows definitive slashes across his glorious brown skin. His face was sculpted to perfection. High cheekbones, the square jaw. His lips the only thing that looked like they had the potential to soften.

And yet she had never seen that.

When he smiled, she thought of a shark. There was nothing comforting about it.

But it wasn't just his beauty that disturbed her. It was the wrenching, physical response that she'd had every time she had ever encountered him since she was seventeen years old.

The only thing that could ever come close was her text relationship with a man she had never even seen.

Usually, that cheered her. The idea that she could make a connection with a nice man, and have it be entirely separate to this nightmarish physical response she had with Christos.

But right now, with the X-rated conversation still creating need inside of her body, it was only a bad thing.

Very, very bad.

"Good morning, Miss Jones," he said, his voice dark, smooth.

He was a man known for his ruthlessness. How cold he was. He had not tried to fashion himself into something more palatable in a world where rich people were often hated for their bank balance, no matter how nice or kind they were.

He wore the mantle of villain comfortably.

He did not pander to a social media–driven world. A world where people often wanted corporations to function as a reflection of their own conscience.

His media conglomerate destroyed smaller, independent news outlets, magazines, publishers, TV channels all the time.

And he seemed to wear it with pride. Like a warrior from ancient days, his body might be painted with the blood of his enemies.

There was nothing modern about him. Nothing remotely accessible.

For a moment—a strange, searing moment—she *envied* him.

She was a young female CEO, and she needed to be *likable*. People needed to be able to connect with her, to find her relatable. Who she was mattered to people who bought books from the publisher. What she did, how palatable she might be.

Nothing he did mattered. He succeeded regardless of whether or not anyone like him, approved of him. He was a man, and he was interesting. He didn't have to be good.

She had to be good.

"I didn't expect you so early," she said.

"Well, I have other things to do."

Somehow, his early arrival to the meeting made him seem less interested, made the meeting seem insignificant. She worried if she showed up too early to a meeting she'd seem eager.

"I'm not sure what you hope to accomplish with this meeting, Mr. Onassis."

"The thing is, Miss Jones, I don't have to accomplish anything. I am here to have a look at the building. I'd like to have a conversation about the financials."

"Perhaps I don't want to have that conversation with you."

"That's just fine since I don't need to have it with you. I'm meeting with your board later."

Terror clawed at her stomach.

"The wheels are set in motion. RedMedia will be acquiring Jones & Abbott. I hope you are prepared for that."

She felt like she'd been punched in her stomach. "Why? You don't *need* it."

"I don't need it. You're correct." He moved toward her and paused at the edge of her desk and touched a clear glass paperweight. He moved it, one inch to the left. "I want it, though." He looked up at her, his eyes black holes. "And I get what I want."

Her body went rigid. "It doesn't mean anything to you," she said.

This man was an emblem of everything that had ever gone wrong in her life. His ruthless sabotaging of that merger had sent her father's health into a spiral.

He was always around, a shark cutting through the water.

It was... It was like he hated them, hated *her*: she could not understand it.

Then she looked into his eyes, and she saw something worse than hatred.

She saw nothing. Absolutely nothing.

"I'm asking you not to do this," she said. "Because I love this publishing house. Because it is my life's work. Because it belongs to my family..."

"Because your family built their empire?"

"How can you stand there and call this an empire when you're absorbing it without lifting a finger. Into your *conglomerate*."

"You misunderstand me. I don't think people ought not to have empires. But if you're going to step into the arena you must be prepared to do battle. As I am. I do not believe in taking advantage of the weak and the innocent. The Jones family is neither. You have built the company on the back of those that could be taken advantage of. There was much free labor being done, particularly in factories doing bookbinding and printing back at the founding of this place. You swallowed up smaller publishers on the way to greatness, and now your era of greatness is past. No one is innocent. If you are going to engage in such tactics, you cannot weep when they are used against you." He lifted a dark brow. "Rather you can, but I will not respect it."

"You don't respect me," she said. "Don't pretend that you could if I responded with as little emotion as you seem to have."

"Do I put on such comfortable pretense, Miss Jones, as to make you think I am pretending to care? I did not think so. Perhaps I need to stop being so soft."

There was something disquieting in his words, and it sent a skitter of electricity over her skin.

"Maybe the company wasn't founded in a perfect way," she said. "I'm quite certain it wasn't. Human beings are awful. That has nothing to do with me, and it has nothing to do with my father. You don't have to continue to act in such a ruthless manner."

"Of course I don't. I *enjoy* it. And make no mistake, I'm not a crusader. I am merely pointing out that your protestations are hollow. This is the arena. Gladiators will act accordingly."

He moved closer to her, and she felt her breath simply leave her body. She couldn't breathe, she couldn't move. He was even more glorious up close. She would love it if media photos overinflated his beauty.

If anything, the camera hated him.

He was so much more mesmerizing in person. Every line, every angle, cut to perfection.

It was a shame about his soul.

And she had no idea where it came from, but she found the strength to meet his gaze and hold it. "Then, you won't be surprised if I fight back."

"I would be disappointed if you didn't. But I would be lying if I didn't tell you I will find it quite sad. You have no weapons, Miss Jones. And I myself am a whole armory."

He straightened, and she felt like that frozen air was suddenly pulled straight from her lungs in one gust.

"What is your plan for the company?"

"The same as it ever is. I plan to keep what is profitable and make use of what might be a unique asset for me. Your foreign distribution channels are strong. Stronger than the other publisher in my stable, and I think there is benefit there."

"You want to strip it for parts."

"Not immediately. And not necessarily. I am moving quickly to complete the acquisition, but changes will not occur overnight, and you're of course welcome to negotiate the contract."

"You've excluded me from the process. The board is flinging me under the bus."

"You can still read a contract from under the bus."

"Not if I'm being squished by the tires."

His gaze was uncompromising. "You don't look damaged to me."

She hated him. Right now more than she ever had. What did he want her to do? Peel her skin back and show him every place where she'd ever been hurt? Never. She would never give him that. She wanted to beg him to leave her alone. To leave her family business alone. To stop dancing on her father's grave.

She wouldn't do that. She wouldn't let him see her break. She wouldn't let him see the things he made her feel.

"I can't threaten you," she said. "You're right. I'm fighting with sticks, and you have a sword. But what I can't respect is the fact that you seem to find that a worthy battle."

"You mistake me, Miss Jones. This is not the battle, it is not the war. The world is a war zone, and every day is a battle. And if you do not win regardless of who your opponent is, then you are nothing. And your life is nothing. I don't need you to be a worthy opponent. I need you to lose."

His words chilled her straight to the bone. "I hate you."

She hated herself for saying it. For letting him see the way he'd gotten to her. All the way down deep.

"I don't care."

He walked past her then, down the hall and into the boardroom, where he closed the door firmly behind him.

There was a meeting behind that door to decide her fate, and she wasn't invited.

All she could do was stand there while Christos Onassis took the one thing she cared about in her life and turned it into ash.

CHAPTER THREE

Kid: I think I might be having a breakdown.

Christos looked at his phone and frowned.

Baby: Why is that, Kid?

Kid: Work. It's always work, I know.

Baby: Work can be stressful.

It was a strange experience, looking down at his phone, reading these words and experiencing…empathy for the faceless woman who was typing them.

Christos was largely unfamiliar with empathy. It was a useless emotion.

Even so he found that he almost wanted to offer something like comfort to this woman. He had never experienced a feeling like that, not in his memory. It was possible he had felt such things before. But he could not readily recall.

He was the sort of man who conducted himself with ruthless precision. While he indulged the pleasures of the flesh when the need arose, he was not a libertine. He was not given to excess. He had never been one for illicit substances, but if he was pressed, he would say he imagined this was what a drug habit might feel like. There he was, in his penthouse apartment, his ruthlessly pristine apartment that had not one shred of softness, sitting on the edge of his couch, a glass of scotch to his left, his phone in his right hand, staring at it like an addict waiting for his fix.

Hiding it. Like it was wrong.

It did feel wrong. It felt like a line of cocaine.

Maybe that was why he liked it so much. Because nothing was truly forbidden.

Connection, though, that he withheld himself from, and maybe it was why it felt so intoxicating to indulge this now.

Baby: What happened?

Kid: It's nothing...

Her text paused for a while. He knew that he was skating against the edge of their rules. The rules they had about revealing too much about themselves. He wondered if she was someone with a degree of notoriety or fame. It was possible. He didn't care: all that he knew was that she prized her anonymity as much as he did, and that made this work.

But he wanted this. He wanted to do something for her. He wanted to find the right words to type out to make her feel better.

It was funny, he did not feel this compulsion at any other point throughout his day.

He thought back to Sylvie Jones's expression when he had told her that he was going to speak to the board to begin finalizing his purchase of the company.

She had been devastated. But this was business, and he couldn't understand the personal nature so many people applied to it. Businesses succeeded, and they fell. It was the natural order of things. At least, in this world where nature had been imposed upon by men, it was. In a capitalistic society, it was how the earth turned. He saw no more cause to feel emotional over a company like his consuming a smaller one than a lion eating a gazelle. And if someday he was weak enough that the same could be done to him, he was no hypocrite. All was fair in the arena.

It did not mean he wouldn't fight. But he wouldn't sit down and weep about it. People like Sylvie Jones seemed to think a family business meant something. That it was their family. Family meant nothing to Christos. He was therefore unmoved by such sentimentality.

Kid: I feel like a failure.

He looked at those words, and he could not imagine any other moment in time where he might have cared that another person felt that way.

Baby: I'm quite certain you aren't.

Kid: Are you?

Baby: Yes. I am never wrong.

Kid: LOL. I know you think that.

Baby: I know that.

Kid: Has anyone ever told you you're arrogant?

For some reason, he imagined her saying that with a smile in her voice, even though no one had ever said that to him with a smile in their voice. But she would. She would. He just knew that. For some reason.

Baby: It has been said a time or two. But, in this instance, it means that I'm right about you. And what I believe you can achieve.

Kid: You don't know me at all, and you're so confident that I can achieve what I want? You don't even know what it is.

Baby: I know that. But I

He stopped typing. He didn't know how to say the thing that he wanted to say. He had so few casual conversations with other people in his life. He tended to talk about business. And when he was with a lover they didn't speak at all. This woman he had never met was the first person he had ever found pleasure with, spoken to, connected to.

Baby: I don't think you know how unusual it is for me to have a—he had to pause again—friendship.

Kid: Is that what we are? Friends?

Baby: More of one than I've ever had.

Kid: Well, that's difficult to believe because you have been wonderful to me.

A low rumble reverberated in his chest, a sound of satisfaction that he had never heard himself make.

He wanted to give her things. To shower her with jewels. She could be anyone, he knew that. Yet another reason he was in no hurry to ever meet her face-to-face. But also mostly…what he could maintain in these moments, he would never be able to maintain in person. If she had to integrate into his life, rather than fitting snugly in his pocket, then it would fall apart and quickly. He didn't want that. He wanted it to be this. It was better to crave more than to know that he could never have more. Than to kill all the little spark that they had. He felt that, deep in his soul, he felt it.

Baby: You are a singular person. I don't have to meet you to know that. And I know that you will figure out exactly what needs to be done. I know you will.

He had never expressed confidence in another person either. But he meant it. From the bottom of his soulless being.

Kid: Thank you. We can talk about something else. How was your day?

Baby: Unremarkable. Though I would have no one else to tell about it if it was remarkable.

Kid: I'm the same. I don't really have anyone.

Baby: You have me.

He had never been there for someone. He had never been someone else's…person. Maybe his mother had loved him in that way, but he couldn't remember. Maybe he didn't want to remember. But his father…his father had seen him only as an inconvenience to be off-loaded. Short-term gain, long-term loss, it had turned out.

Christos smiled when he thought of that. It still gave

him pleasure to remember how he had rubbed it in the old man's face. How he had held it over his head. How he had made him beg.

He took pleasure in life, it was just that other people would not generally relate to those pleasures. And he had never much cared about that.

He found he cared a bit now.

Kid: You have no idea how much I appreciate that. I feel really alone. I'm missing my dad.

He could not understand that. He did not miss his father. He didn't miss his mother either. It was possible that he might have missed the void where she once was, as it was that void that had sucked him in, seen him thrown away into that life of hard labor. He just couldn't remember.

Baby: I know a great many people love their fathers.

Kid: You don't?

How did he tell her he didn't love anyone? How did he tell this woman who seemed so lovely, so nice and kind that love was a foreign concept to him?

Baby: No.

That was simpler.

Kid: I'm sorry. He must be a bastard.

He chuckled.

Baby: You have no idea.

Kid: I know. I know I don't really have an idea of you at all. But I feel like I do.

He wanted her to maintain this distant idea. This fantasy. He wanted her to believe that he was good. That he was a man who could be trusted. A man that she could lean on.

He wanted to be that for her because he knew that it wasn't true. Because he knew that it wasn't him.

He did. Truly.

Was this a role-playing fantasy?

He wasn't used to questioning himself at all. He wasn't used to examining his motives. He simply did whatever was expedient at the time. But this wasn't expedient. It made no real sense.

Indulgence.

Maybe that was the problem. He had made it thirty-eight years without an indulgence, and now he couldn't resist this one that had dropped into his lap. He didn't believe in fate. He believed that a man made his own fate.

With blood and sweat.

Tears accomplished nothing.

Baby: If you were here, I would kiss you.

He decided to move it into intimate territory. They could talk, and honestly, he enjoyed it as much as he enjoyed their more charged encounters. But sometimes moving it to sex felt more comfortable, because at least if it was sexual he could categorize it. He could make it about the physical reaction he had to her, and not the emotional one. The truth was, in the months that he had been talking to his mystery woman, he had not slept with anyone.

She had been his all-consuming focus. His night and his day.

She had been...everything.

Everything.

Kid: I wish you were here. I

The text paused for a long moment. And then...

Kid: I want to meet.

Sylvie could barely breathe. She couldn't believe that she had typed that. She didn't want to meet him. She was destroyed and crushed after today. She couldn't tell him all the things that were riding around inside of her, and she wanted to. She had this feeling that this man could be her ultimate fantasy. The port and her storm. She needed someone. So desperately. But as soon as she said it, she regretted it, because the stakes were too high. What if he didn't like her? What if he didn't...

His response came slowly, but it was definitive.

Baby: That isn't a good idea.

Kid: I know it isn't. It's just that I want you. I am so tired of writing to you and wishing that you could hold me.

She was getting emotional now. Ridiculous. Their conversations were personal and impersonal all at the same time. The sexual encounters steamy, but not...this.

They didn't talk about holding one another.

But it was what she wanted.

Baby: If we meet, we must maintain anonymity.

She paused. Her teeth clenching together.

This was a red flag. She knew it. She was insecure about her looks, and it made her want to keep this anonymous, but she had a feeling that her arrogant counterpart didn't suffer from insecurity. If he was asking for anonymity it could be for a very damning reason.

There was a question that had hovered around the edges of her mind for a long time. A concern. And she had pushed it away. He was talking about meeting and maintaining anonymity, which meant he was talking about the two of them meeting and not talking. He was talking about the two of them meeting for sex.

The very idea sent a rush of physical attraction through her.

Yes. She wanted it. She wanted him. She had never been with anybody because it had never been right. But this was right. She knew it. And yet she was also very worried that it was wrong.

Kid: Forgive me. I have to ask you this. You don't want to stay anonymous because you're married, do you? And I need you to be honest with me about that.

There was a pause. Her stomach sank all the way down almost to her toes.

Baby: Sorry. It never occurred to me that you might think I was married. I am not married. I'm the furthest thing from married. I have never even been close. My reasons for wanting to keep this anonymous are my own. But I promise you it is not because being with me could hurt someone else.

It was just the perfect answer, and she chose to believe him. Because she needed to. Honestly, a person had to have a little bit of naivety to fall in love. She was certain of that. But her real concern was that most of her naivety wasn't an intentional choice, but a fact of her lack of experience. So she was trying to be canny here. While she knew that if she told any of her casual work friends about this situation they would judge her.

But they were only casual work friends, and casual work friends were all she had. He was the closest thing to a real friend that she possessed.

But he was also…a sexual fantasy. She felt a little bit chagrined that what he wanted was the sex in person when she had been wanting… Well, she wanted the sex, she had just wanted emotion as well.

Kid: This is silly. How in the world can we meet but stay anonymous?

Baby: We will meet in the penthouse of The Luxe. The lights will be off, and we will not turn them on.

She stared at the text. She felt like he had been thinking about this for a long time because it was definitive and fast.

She didn't hate the idea. The idea of making love with him in the dark. Of finally having his hands on her body, of having half of what she wanted.

Of what she'd dreamed of.

She sat there. *Half.*

No. It wasn't half. It was an opportunity to have anonymity and closeness. It was an opportunity for their bodies to prove their compatibility before they took it any further.

It was a chance for them to maintain this fantasy, and

whatever his reasoning was, she had a feeling it was close to hers. A desire and need to make this sacred. To keep it separate.

Kid: When?

Baby: Tomorrow.

Her heart thundered hard. And she knew this was her opportunity. To say no, to say yes. She thought about it. About how tomorrow she could have his hands on her body. About how tomorrow they could be together.

She needed this. Now more than ever. She needed him.

Kid: Yes. 8 PM. Send me the room number.

Baby: I will.

Did they continue to talk now? She didn't know. Her stomach was a mass of nerves, her body on edge. She felt like she was dying, but she also felt like she was coming alive. Everything with her company was a travesty. It was painful. It was the worst it had ever been. Christos Onassis was seeing to that. He was breaking her life into pieces, and he didn't even care.

That had been the worst part of all of that. Looking into his eyes and not seeing triumph, not seeing rage, seeing nothing but the bottomless black pit that seemed to exist inside of him.

He was a man without a heart. A man without a soul.

She had never hated another human before.

She hated Christos Onassis.

And she needed something, someone, to take that pain, to

take that unending worry, anxiety and sadness, and turn it into something good. This man was the only one that had ever been able to do that, and now she was going to get to touch him.

Even if she didn't see him, it didn't matter.

They would see each other eventually, this would only be the beginning.

Everything would be fine.

They would have this night, and they would finally get to experience the reality of this thing between them, and then they could work toward the rest.

Then they wouldn't need this shield.

Yes. She was certain. She was resolved. She almost told him the truth. That she had never done this before. That she was a virgin. But she decided to keep that to herself. That, she reasoned, was one of the many gifts of anonymity. She was going to hang onto it.

Kid: Good night.

She typed it quickly because she didn't know what else to say. And as she went about her evening routine, it wasn't her work tragedy that dominated her mind.

It was the potential to take her life and make it something more than it had been. Not the business, her.

She had neglected herself all this time, and that was really what this text relationship had shown her.

It was what he had shown her.

That she needed more.

And this was the beginning of more.

She had thought that she had nothing to look forward to except dreading tomorrow.

But now? Now she was anticipating it with an eagerness that took her breath away.

CHAPTER FOUR

SYLVIE COULDN'T HELP IT. She spent the entire day watching the clock. She watched, and she waited. She met with the board. They told her that they were in the process of selling to RedMedia. She had smiled, in many ways grateful that she'd had the heads-up. Yes, it was only Christos gloating, but at least this wasn't her being blindsided. At least. It was perhaps the only consolation.

"I oppose this," she said.

"It doesn't matter if you oppose it or not," said Daniela, one of the directors when she caught Sylvie in the hall after the meeting. "This is the decision that we've made. It's the best thing for the company. It might be the only way we can ensure our survival beyond the past five years. Unless you're going to personally go online holding one of our books and doing a choreographed dance in hopes of going viral."

"I would," Sylvie responded. "Except I don't think we need to do that. I think what we need to do is to continue to focus on our editorial."

"That's naive, Sylvie," Daniela said. "You must realize that. If you love books, you should work in an industry other than publishing. This isn't about stories. It's about profit margins. And we're fighting for our lives here. We are too small to compete. If we have RedMedia behind us—"

"He isn't going to do anything to push this company specifically. He is simply going to strip it for parts."

"Even then, at least they'll be valuable parts, and we'll have a hope of getting out of this with some money in our pockets."

She wanted to scream. She wanted to rage. If all she wanted was money in her pockets she could have gone and worked at a Jamba Juice. Then at least she wouldn't be working sixteen-hour days and dealing with constant acid reflux and nightmares that disrupted her sleep. Constant feelings of failure and inadequacy.

No. She would probably still have those.

They were certainly linked with the publisher, but they weren't *only* about the publisher.

"I'm going to vote against this."

"You're welcome to," Daniela said. "But it won't make a difference. This is a largely unanimous decision. But Christos said that he was going to give you an opportunity to review the contract—"

"Christos?" Sylvie asked, crossing her arms and regarding the other woman closely. "First-name basis. Wow. Are you sure you're not just agreeing to this deal because the man in question is a handsome devil? Because the key word here is *devil*, Daniela. He is quite literally Satan."

And with that, she turned and went back to her office. She stewed, and then she turned her focus to tonight. The problem was there was nothing she could do about the Christos Onassis situation at the moment. All she could do was see to the day-to-day operations of the company while the dark storm cloud that was Lucifer hung over her as the world's most depressing threat.

She could do nothing about it. She had to stop ruminating about it. She had to stop letting it eat her from the inside out like a feral animal. A small, wretched animal with sharp snapping teeth and oily claws.

She leaned back in her chair and looked up at the ceiling.

Then she looked at the time. She had half expected him to text her, though he didn't tend to during the workday.

But they *were* meeting *tonight*. *They* were *meeting* tonight.

She should ruminate on that because she could do something about it.

She had downloaded a particularly erotic romance novel and felt a lashing of guilt for buying something from an evil online conglomerate rather than her own company, but she needed a *specific* thing. An erotic romance about anonymous sex, and she had paid particular attention to the details.

She knew about sex.

She knew the mechanics. But she had always found it easier to learn something by doing it, and therefore it wasn't like she felt entirely as if she knew what she was doing.

As soon as work was over, she left. She was prone to staying late, but she wasn't doing that today.

Yes, she needed to see to the day-to-day operations of the company, but if she was destined to lose this job, then she was going to go home and spend that time preparing herself.

She went back to her apartment, and she turned on some music, before taking her clothes off and slipping into the shower. She sadly wished that her apartment was big enough to have a bathtub. She supposed she should just be grateful that she had her own bathroom and not a shared one in the hallway.

She smoothed lightly scented lotion all over her skin. She wanted to be soft. If all he could do was touch her, then she wanted to…

Just thinking about it made her shiver.

She carefully selected a pair of underwear that was sexy, even though he wouldn't see it. He would feel that it was lace and thin. He would know that it was for him.

She bit her lip, arousal coursing through her. It was twenty-five minutes until they were supposed to meet.

Her phone lit up.

Baby: 807

It was the room number. That was all.

She checked her appearance in the mirror, which was silly, because he wasn't going to see her. But she wanted to feel beautiful.

Her hair was wild, and her makeup was as inexpertly done as it ever was. She couldn't say that she felt beautiful. She felt like herself.

But he seemed to want her.

So that had to mean something. She needed it to.

She stepped outside and decided to get in the cab that was passing, rather than fussing around with a rideshare app.

"The Luxe."

She sat back, tension spreading across her shoulders, up the back of her neck.

Her heart was pounding hard, anxiety ripping through her body, creating a sharp feeling at the center of her breastbone, making her stomach feel sick.

She was very used to anxiety.

Excitement?

Yes. Maybe it was just excitement. Something she was far less familiar with. Something she wanted more of. God. She wanted more of it. She wanted ecstasy. She wanted... She wanted to feel special. She wanted to feel wanted. She was so lonely.

She hadn't really let herself focus on how lonely she was until just this moment.

She craved another person's hands on her. It did matter

that they were meeting. It was okay that it was anonymous. She just wanted him to touch her.

She wanted him so much.

She nearly tumbled out of the cab after she paid when it pulled up to the curb, and she all but raced inside the hotel. She paused at the front desk. "I'm meant to be in room 807."

She also had no idea how that was going to work, because he must've given the hotel his name, but not hers, because he didn't have it.

The employee did not seem put off by this. "Of course. Here you are."

He handed her a key.

So he had arranged this. Perfectly.

He must be a man with money. That surprised her. She hadn't thought of him being…

She made a decent salary, but she had sacrificed quite a bit of it in the interest of trying to reinvigorate the company. It was why she lived so modestly.

Granted, she lived in New York, so modest was on a sliding scale, but she would have to think twice before throwing money down for a room like this. And after thinking twice would have to come to the conclusion that she couldn't afford it.

But the service that she had gotten, the way she hadn't been questioned…

He had left a specific set of instructions, and they had been followed.

She got into the elevator and touched her key to the panel inside. It began to take her up to the top floor.

She swallowed hard, unsure of what she would find when she got there. Except him.

You want this. You want this.

She said that to herself as she made her way out of the

elevator and down the hallway. There were very few rooms on this floor.

She touched her key to the door and pushed it open. Her mouth was dry, her heart thundering. She let the door close behind her.

"Hello?"

She walked deeper into the space, holding her hands out, trying not to fall.

"I'm here."

And suddenly, a hand reached from somewhere in the darkness and took hold of her arm. Pulled her close. "I've been waiting."

A thrill shot down her spine. His voice was deep. He was speaking in a near whisper and softening it, but she could still tell that it was a low rumble.

There was something that itched at the back of her brain, but anything that had been in her brain suddenly evaporated, because he was, very suddenly, claiming her mouth. It was real. This was real, and so was he.

He was kissing her with a heat and fire that she had never experienced before. The fumbles that she'd engaged in in college had been tepid enough that she had not been tempted to pursue anything more, but this—it was a whole inferno. And she was desperate. For everything.

It was entirely dark, and she had no idea how he navigated them through the space. Perhaps it was the magic of him having been here longer than her. His eyes were maybe accustomed to the dimness, but certainly not enough to be able to see details.

Once they were in the bedroom area, he began to kiss her again.

She wanted to talk. She wanted to say *Finally*. She wanted

to do this like they would if they were on the phone. Ask about his day while he asked about hers.

But she didn't.

Instead, she let herself get consumed by the kiss. Instead, she let herself begin to drown in it. In him.

It was magical. Beyond anything that she had ever experienced.

His large hands moved to span her waist, to grip her hips, to pull her hard against him so that she could feel the evidence of his arousal pushing against her stomach.

He did want her. She was here in the flesh, and he wanted her.

It was simply astonishing.

As was he.

He was so much taller than she had imagined. She had thought he might be three inches taller than her, not what felt like half a foot. She could feel how large he was, broad and muscular. He was solid, a great mountain of a man.

Why did this man want to remain anonymous? It didn't make any sense. But he began to kiss down the side of her neck, and any thoughts of sense fled.

Sense didn't matter. What could possibly matter more than this?

Whatever could?

She moved her hands up his body and began to unbutton his shirt. She separated the fabric slowly, breathing out as she touched his skin. She could feel chest hair, rippling muscle. She began to tremble. This was almost too much. But it was also not enough. She couldn't imagine if they were trying to do this with the lights on. The truth was, she was so attracted to him she could hardly breathe.

It was crazy that she could feel this while they couldn't even see each other. What would've happened to her if the lights were on? What would happen if he realized that she was not the specimen that he was? Because he was something else altogether. And it was soul-crushing.

Incredible.

She pushed the shirt off of his shoulders and took a tactile tour of his torso. Moving her fingertips down his pectoral muscles, his abs and back up again. He gasped when her fingertips grazed his nipples.

Her own breath became shallow, and when her fingertips met the closure on his pants, she hesitated.

"Yes," he said.

She undid them and brought the zipper down. His breath hissed through his teeth. She found herself being pressed against the wall, his hands moving over her body, her curves. Cupping her breasts, bringing his fingers down her hips and to the hemline. He pushed the fabric up, and even though he couldn't see, she felt herself getting overheated. Blushing.

He moved his hand between her thighs then, stroking her lightly over the fabric of her panties. She was wet.

She was glad.

It would've been awful if nerves or something equally unworthy had kept her from enjoying this to the absolute fullest. Because she definitely deserved to feel everything. Then he moved his fingers so that they delved beneath the fabric, and she gasped as the rough pad of his fingers made contact with her slick, sensitive skin.

She had never been touched intimately before. Nothing could've prepared her for this. Certainly not the touch of her own hand. He played her body expertly, the pad of his thumb moving over the sensitized bundle of nerves there at the apex of her thighs. He stroked her. And she cried out. The pleasure was white-hot and electric.

Incredible. Unreal.

He kissed her then, continuing to stroke her with his finger, pushing one deep inside of her as his tongue slid against hers.

And she fractured. Dissolved into a million pieces. She crested so quickly she was nearly humiliated by it.

And when she came down, she realized that her fingernails were digging into his back.

That she was calling him Baby.

Clinging to him.

Begging.

He took her clothes off. Easy. The darkness did nothing to diminish his skill.

He stripped her dress off and threw it down to the floor. He unhooked her bra with one hand. He gripped her panties and tore them away from her.

And then he picked her up and carried her to the bed, laying her at the center.

She was breathing hard, and she could hear that he was divesting himself of the rest of his own clothing. Thank God. *Thank God.*

When he joined her, it was all the heat of his skin and the strength of his body.

He was kissing her. Down her body, taking one nipple into his mouth and sucking hard. She had no idea what he would do next or where he would go.

He kissed his way down her inner thigh until his mouth met the most intimate part of her.

Then he licked her. Going deeper with his tongue, painting her with unimaginable pleasure as he ate her like she was the finest delicacy.

She was trembling, shaking. There was no way she could come again so soon after that incendiary orgasm. But she did. Crying out, bucking her hips up off the bed. He growled and gripped her hips tightly, holding her against his mouth as he pushed her further, higher than she had ever gone before. She was on the verge of telling him to stop. But she didn't want it to stop. Not ever.

She came again on a harsh cry, and he made his way up her body, pressing his mouth to hers.

Then the blunt, heavy head of him pressed against the entrance to her body, and he entered her in one smooth stroke. It didn't hurt as bad as she expected, but there was still some pain. Still, the darkness shielded her from revealing herself with her expression.

He took it as a cry of pleasure, and he began to move.

She clung to him, arched her hips in time with each and every thrust.

And when he began to lose control, she reveled in it.

He pressed his forehead against hers and growled against her mouth. "Beautiful. Perfect."

Beautiful. Perfect.

He couldn't see her, and yet he said that all the same.

He had never seen her face, and yet he called her *beautiful*.

All he could do was feel her, and he called her *perfect*.

It was perfect. He was perfect. And so was this. It was everything. Everything she had always been afraid to dream of.

He moved his hands down beneath her ass and lifted her up off the bed as he thrust hard inside of her, over and over again.

"I can't," she gasped.

"You will. Come for me."

She shook and trembled, cried out as the orgasm swept over her. And she was gratified when he met his own release, a shout of triumph on his lips as he poured himself inside of her.

And when it was over, she could only lie there, the darkness pressing in around her. She turned toward him, grabbing hold of his arm and holding onto him.

She just had sex with the man of her dreams.

They were together, in bed. And yet they weren't together. She felt like she had lost him. He said nothing. She was hungry for the sight of him, but also afraid. Something felt irrevocably changed.

She could not quite say what it was. He didn't hold her.

"You should go," he said.

"Oh, I—"

"I'll text you. But I think it's best if we don't…linger here. On this."

"Okay."

She felt absolutely disintegrated by that. She wanted to stay with him. All night. But he wanted to be finished. She had a feeling that this had done something to him emotionally, but he wasn't telling her what it was.

Maybe this was why he wanted anonymity. He was physically perfect. He had done things to her that had forever altered the way that she felt about her own body.

Perhaps his emotions were the problem.

She had been foolish enough to think that he was emotionally available because of the texting.

But there was a reason he wanted the distance.

And it wasn't the same reason that she wanted it.

She stumbled around the bedroom, collecting her clothes.

"If only I could turn a light on—"

"No," he said, his voice hard. Harsh.

And she felt that tickle again at the back of her brain. She dismissed it as she made the decision to abandon her underwear and simply put on her bra.

Her shoes, she knew, were in the other room, and she

walked out of the bedroom, searching for them with her feet. She found them and slipped them on.

And then she stood there for a long moment in the darkness. The silence.

Was this it?

He said that they would text, but she had a horrible feeling that this wasn't the beginning of something at all.

She had a feeling that it was the end.

She had been so afraid of that. So really, what was keeping her from running back in there and turning the light on?

You care too much about him. About what he wants.

It was true. This hurt. But she really did care a damn sight too much about why he was the way he was to violate what he'd asked for in some way.

So she stumbled out of the hotel room and into the hallway. Knowing that she was changed forever.

Devastated that it wasn't in the way she had hoped.

Now suddenly everything felt terrible.

Absolutely everything.

She had no idea how she was going to survive the devastation of Christos Onassis without the man that she had come to love.

But she had the feeling she was going to have to figure it out.

CHAPTER FIVE

AFTER SHE WAS GONE Christos turned the lights on and poured himself a drink. She might come back. He froze, standing there in the living area of the suite. He almost hoped that she would. For one strangling moment.

What had just happened between them had been...singular. He had never experienced anything like it before in his life, and he was not a man given to fantasy, nor was he a man who overinflated things. And yet.

He had sent her away, which was perhaps not the best move, but he had felt undone. And he had no idea what to do with that.

Years spent working in horrendous conditions had taught him to ignore his body. And long before that he had taught himself to ignore his emotions. Because they were insignificant. Because they meant nothing. Because in the grand scheme of things, feelings didn't indicate your likelihood for survival. There was instinct, yes, but worrying about whether or not you were happy did not guarantee anything. And often it could lead you in a dangerous direction.

Something was happening to him. He didn't like it.

He took a drink of the whiskey in his tumbler and stared at the resolutely closed door.

He would have to leave her behind. He had destroyed the fantasy, even though he had thought that anonymity would retain it.

Because she had affected him. In ways he could not articulate. In ways he could not understand, and if he did not understand something, he could not indulge in it.

He had been a fool. All these months he had been a fool. He could not afford this.

He had to continue on as he had begun. Conquering. Emerging victorious.

And what then?

He felt a strange, hollow sensation at the center of his chest that began to spread outward.

He didn't ask that question. Not ever. For very specific reasons.

There was no *what then?* There was only each and every day when a man put one foot in front of the other and continued to make forward motion.

It was all there was.

It was all that mattered.

He could afford to let nothing else affect him. He could afford to let nothing else inform him.

Not this existential question of what happened after.

There was no *after*. There was life and there was death.

And in life, you either won the battle, day in and day out, or you were dead.

He had decided a long time ago that when death came for him, it would be a battle. He had chosen survival.

He had watched the struggle, the inhumane conditions, the machinery, claim the lives of other teenage boys around him, working impossible hours doing dangerous tasks.

He had decided that it was some sort of weakness that led to their demise.

He would not succumb.

He had refused then, and he refused to now.

And so, he would refuse her.

He would not contact her again.

The determination made a sick feeling spread in the center of his stomach. Another wholly foreign response.

He was not used to this. Not any of it.

Another good reason to stay the course. Another good reason to end this.

That it made his hands shake to think of doing so only reinforced what he had realized earlier.

She had become an addiction.

Of course. He was too smart for something as basic as a drug or other substance to get its claws into him. He was too aware.

It was this woman. This text relationship. It came from a place he hadn't anticipated. From a place he hadn't planned.

What a fool he had been.

He supposed he should be grateful that he had been foolish at a time in his life when he could afford it.

Foolishness back when he had been a boy would have ended in his death.

No more. He was aware now. There was a vulnerability inside of him that he hadn't realized was there before. He had let her slip beneath it.

It would never happen again.

Never.

He drank down the rest of the whiskey and hoped that it would do something to get rid of the impression her hands had left on his body.

It didn't matter whether it served its purpose or not. He would never indulge himself with her again. Not ever.

He was set on his next conquest. All that mattered was that he completed the acquisition of Jones & Abbott.

It was all there was.

He put the woman out of his mind.

He would not think of her again.

CHAPTER SIX

SHE TEXTED HIM. Just one time. Two days after they met.

He didn't text her back.

Her brain spun scenarios about why this was happening.

That something happened to him on the way home from the hotel? Had he been hit by a taxi?

She was embarrassed to admit she had done a combination of Google searches trying to find out if a man had been killed in that area. Or been in some kind of horrible accident. Because the alternatives weren't...*worse* per se, but they were painful in a different way.

What if all he had wanted was to lure her into a sexual encounter?

Well. That didn't make sense. They had been texting for nearly six months. She was the one who had suggested they meet. If he had only wanted sex there was no reason for them to text that long, and he would've suggested a meetup long before.

She reminded herself that she had been in the driver's seat, and it did something to quell the heartbroken feeling that she was grappling with.

She had sensed that there was something off with him emotionally. And she felt like maybe he was imbalanced after their encounter. But because of that she thought that he might break and eventually text, but he didn't.

She had never felt this kind of heartbreak. She had experienced it in other ways. Her mother broke her heart routinely.

Her father's death had been heartbreaking.

The initial stutter and stumble of the publishing house had been heartbreaking.

This was different. This felt like constantly breathing with a jagged piece of glass embedded in her chest.

It was ridiculous. But she missed him. She had no one to talk to. And as the acquisition of the company ramped up, that became more and more difficult.

She stared at her phone so often, wishing that she was brave enough to make an overture. She just wasn't.

The first time Christos Onassis came into the office after she had been ghosted, she had nearly fallen over where she was standing. She hadn't remembered how much of an impact he made, and that was ridiculous because she had just seen him a few days earlier.

But there was something different. Or maybe it was something different in her. She hated that. But suddenly, she realized that the impact of him wasn't just based on the anxiety she was feeling about the role he was playing in this difficult season of her life, but her new understanding of what a man who looked like him could do with a body like that. She hated that she would even think that in connection with this man that she hated so much.

She distanced herself as best she could because she wasn't really being included in any of this. The contract was sent over to her, and she surrounded herself with legal representation and worked at figuring out exactly what her best options were.

One month turned into two, which turned into nearly three, and then she started to feel nauseous in the morning.

She really hadn't thought much about anything other than

the great implosions happening around her. How much she missed Baby, how much she hated Christos. How stressed out she was by everything. But when she got out of bed, ran straight to the bathroom and threw up, she had the realization that she hadn't actually had her period for way too long.

What an idiot she was. She had just been consumed by all the misery that she was dealing with, so she hadn't been tracking. She hadn't been paying attention.

She sat down on the edge of her bed and put a hand on her stomach. She didn't have time for this. She didn't have time to be sick, she didn't have time to deal with this. She had to get to work. There was literally a final meeting today with Christos. And they had to sign paperwork. And she hated him.

She rallied and finished getting ready. She couldn't look as bedraggled as she felt.

She had to get it together.

She walked out of her apartment and popped into the bodega, grabbing a pregnancy test and taking it to the counter, trying not to feel self-conscious or embarrassed as she purchased it.

The man barely looked at her; he just ran her card.

She accepted the offer of a small bag and tucked it into her larger bag. She was going to have to take the test when she had a break. And then what? Text the man who had ghosted her? Well, she would have to.

Because she had to at least give him a chance to engage with this.

She supposed.

She realized that she was oddly numb. She was going through the motions of taking care of this, but it wasn't…it wasn't penetrating. It wasn't sinking in. But there was no point making it real until she knew for sure if it was.

She could not deal with this right now. Her life was imploding.

In every way.

But they hadn't used a condom. Something she hadn't been fully conscious of until afterward.

It was just…everything had happened so fast, and she had been so aroused. So shrouded by fantasy. But she hadn't really thought that one time…

Truthfully, she had just put it all out of her mind. It had been completely hijacked by all of the work stuff, by all of the emotional upheaval that had come with it.

The potential odds of getting pregnant from one sexual encounter had not been at the forefront of her mind.

More fool her.

By the time she got to her office her hands were shaking.

Christos would be in soon.

She had about twenty minutes to deal with this.

She curled her fingers into fists, gathered herself up and went into the bathroom, locking the door securely behind her.

She took the pregnancy test out of the bag and took the plastic off the box with shaking fingers.

She opened it up, only to find a difficult foil packet ensconced the test itself.

She pierced it with a key that was down at the bottom of her bag before tearing it open.

Then she read the instructions and followed them.

And waited.

Her heart was thundering so hard she thought she might pass out.

And when one faint pink line appeared, followed by another, she felt her whole world tilt.

No.

She couldn't…

The meeting was now in ten minutes.

She picked up her phone.

It had been months since they had contacted each other, he wasn't in the scroll of texts anymore. Her phone offloaded messages after thirty days.

She picked it up, typed in *Baby*. And there he was.

She had resisted contacting him again all this time. She swallowed hard, her throat dry.

Kid: I need to meet with you. Today. No anonymity. It's an emergency.

What would he think about that? Would he question it?

There was no response. She walked out of the bathroom and went back to her office. She was sweating. She felt like screaming. Like throwing things across the room. Like having a literal breakdown because everything was coming down around her all at once. And she had to keep going.

She didn't have anyone to call for moral support. Her mother would simply laugh and give her the card for a trusted clinic. There would be no discussion. There would be no heart-to-heart. And worst of all, no place for Sylvie to try to reason out what her own feelings were.

But then, with her mother, her feelings had never mattered.

That was the example that Sylvie had for motherhood.

How was she supposed to…be a mother herself?

She looked down at her phone, right as a message popped up on the screen.

Baby: We can't meet.

Kid: We have to.

She hadn't intended to tell him that she was pregnant over text. She only had two minutes until the meeting.

Baby: There is no "have to." This is over.

Kid: Do you think that I have so little pride that I'm texting you because I want to keep sleeping with you? That isn't why, you bastard.

That had been a little bit excessive. She was angry. She had trusted this man. She had slept with him. She had given him her body, and now she was pregnant with his baby, and he was acting like the one thing that might motivate her was a desperate need for him to...love her.
If only that was her one issue. If *only*.

Kid: I'm pregnant.

There was no response.
She had to go to the meeting.
She picked her phone up and tried to collect herself as she walked into the hall.

Baby: I'm unavailable for the next hour. I can meet you after.

Kid: I'm not available for the next hour either. We can meet at Rosie's, on Sixth.

Baby: Fine. I'm near there.

That made her frown.

Kid: Okay.

Just then, the elevator doors opened, and Christos stepped out, dressed all in black.

Her anxiety wrapped its hands around her throat and forced her stomach to plummet.

She hated that he was tied up in all this. She hated him. She might hate everybody. The company was against her, her mother was against her, the one man that she had trusted seemed to be against her now, and then there was this idiot.

This fool that she had to deal with because he had decided that he was going to target Jones & Abbott. And there was no negotiating with him. The best-case scenario was that he kept her on in her position to continue the day-to-day operations uninterrupted. But that was literally all she was working for. It was no longer going to be what it had been.

It was no longer going to matter in the way that it had. It was going to be his.

Did she even want to fight to keep her job? She was going to have a baby.

She was going to potentially be a totally single mother doing this all on her own.

Well. She might not have a good example in the form of a mother, but her father had been an excellent single father. Who had done his very best to clean up whatever disarray her mother had left her in routinely when they had spent time together—times few and far between.

She knew that a parent doing it on their own could make an immense amount of difference.

So she went. And she wasn't in the mood to be nice.

Because she wasn't fighting for this job anymore.

She was fighting for herself. She was fighting for her baby.

They walked into the boardroom.

There he was. The dark and foreboding angel of hell himself. Satan's very own. Lucifer in a custom suit. The absolute worst man on earth who didn't have access to the nuclear option.

She was stalling on coming up with new titles for him so that she didn't catalog his physical features. His perfect, far too appealing physical features.

"I assume you have all the paperwork?" she asked.

"Of course," Christos said, leaning back in his chair as if this meeting were a relaxing holiday. "This is merely a formality. All the terms have been agreed to."

"That's a stretch. I have pushed some of the terms as far as they can go. And I accept that."

"Good. I'm glad to hear that you've reached a place of acceptance," he said.

"That's me. I'm the picture of perfect sanguine acceptance."

The other members of the board, her legal counsel and his walked in.

They all took their seats around the table and began the meeting, going over everything that was in the contract she had already read. The timings of different phases of the acquisition process, and the plan to keep her on in her position for guaranteed length of time, so long as she continued her work in a manner that kept the company meeting certain metrics.

It was extremely poor consolation, but it was the only consolation she was going to get. And it gave her time. Which she desperately needed. Time to figure out what she was going to do. Time to figure out what was important to her.

Because everything had changed this morning.

Whatever she had thought might happen, something different was happening now.

"I understand that this is not an ideal situation from the perspective of everyone in this room," Christos said. Totally detached as ever. His dark eyes met hers, and there was something there, but she couldn't read it. It was like staring into a well. Bottomless. Fathomless. Maybe there was something at the bottom, maybe it was dry. Who would ever know?

Who could ever know?

"But I am grateful that we have come to satisfactory terms."

She didn't think he meant that. He didn't care. If he'd had to come in and physically sword-fight everybody, he would've done that. Bloodshed would have worked for him to. And he probably would have appeared just as calm in the aftermath.

He stood, and so did she.

And the breath left her body as he crossed the room and moved toward her. He extended his hand, and because she thought he was certain she wouldn't, she extended hers and shook his.

The contact of his skin against hers was like an electric shock. She had only experienced something like it one other time. God, she despised him. How could he make her feel this way? At this moment, when everything was a disaster?

"I hope we can keep you on, Miss Jones," he said.

Then he dropped his hand and swept past her.

She grabbed her bag and walked past him. She had to go

down and meet the father of her baby now, and she didn't have time to ruminate over Christos. She didn't have time to ruminate on anything. She said nothing to him as she bustled past him and pointed toward the elevator.

It opened, and she got inside. But he followed.

She should've closed the door, but that would have been an action tantamount to pettiness, and it wasn't that she was above pettiness, she just didn't want to look quite as ruffled as she felt. That was the problem. He cared about nothing, so he was continually in a state of being unbothered.

He said nothing to her in the elevator; he reached into his pocket and took out his phone, looking at the screen.

She did the same.

She didn't have any messages.

He didn't appear to have messages either, since he didn't pause to read anything or respond.

It was almost impossible to believe she was about to be face-to-face with the man she'd had sex for the first time with. And it wasn't something she wanted to process while standing beside Christos.

She did her best not to think about it. She was on another planet.

Today could honestly go straight to hell.

It was absurd.

She walked quickly out of the elevator and out of the building. She didn't say goodbye to him. She wouldn't.

And she moved as quickly as she could down the street, toward Rosie's.

It was her favorite coffee shop, and normally she would be looking forward to a latte and a croissant. But really not at the moment. Because she felt like she was going to throw up again, and she felt like maybe it would be easier to lie down in the middle of the sidewalk and take a nap. Because truly, everything was awful.

If she could sleep through the next few hours that would be great. The next few days. Hell, maybe the next few months.

She was going to need to actually go to a doctor. Maybe she had contacted him prematurely.

No. He didn't get to be excluded from this. From the turmoil that it was causing her. From everything. If she was pregnant, then he needed to know, and now. Not so he got to make his choice, but so he had to live with the discomfort of it all alongside her. Because she deserved that.

She did.

She heard heavy footsteps near her, and she turned slightly, to see Christos moving toward the door of Rosie's at the same time she was. They both reached for the door. "Why are you following me?"

He scowled. "I'm not."

"It seems like it to me."

Really, she did not want the man that had just acquired her company to be present at this meeting. She'd already dealt with one awful meeting that he was central to. She didn't want him at this one.

"Get coffee somewhere else. Anywhere else," she said, stepping inside. But he was close behind her.

"I am meeting someone."

She stopped. And looked up at him. And suddenly, the world began to fall away. She had thought that it was crumbling before, but that had been theoretical. It was *really* crumbling now. Like everything that held her to the earth was breaking off in great chunks and leaving nothing behind. Any moment now she was going to start falling. Falling and falling. Into that well in his dark eyes, or maybe hell. Who could say?

"Who are you meeting?" she asked, her mouth suddenly dry.

"No one of any interest to you."

"Who are you meeting, Christos?"

"Why?"

"Because *I'm* meeting someone," she said, her eyes filling with tears against her will. No. That would be…outrageous.

Impossible.

Where did you find the phone, Sylvie?

Outside of the publishing event. A publishing event that Christos Onassis had been present at.

No.

Because that man could not be the man that she had carried on all those text conversations with. Because Christos didn't have a heart, and that man had a heart. He had…he had comforted her when she was at her wits' end because of Christos himself, so it couldn't be…

His eyes sharpened. "Who are *you* meeting?"

Her throat was constricted; it was nearly a whisper. "I don't know what he looks like."

And she knew satisfaction for one second. Because he looked as if his own world had done very much the same thing hers had done.

He was shocked. Which really did a lot to eliminate what her next question and accusation would have been. That he had done this to her on purpose.

He hadn't.

He hadn't known.

Brilliant tactician, Christos Onassis, genuinely had not known that he was talking to her. He hadn't known that she was the woman that he'd met for sex.

He had no idea, all through that meeting, when they were sitting across from each other, that she was pregnant with his baby.

Just as she hadn't known who she'd been speaking to, who she'd met that night.

Who the father of her baby was.

That's why you reacted to him the way that you did.

No. God. It was awful.

It was terrible.

He... She *had* known. Her body had known. That was absurd.

She had felt this rising tension every time she saw him because her body had known. She hadn't been able to put the two together because she just hated him so much. She hated him so much even now as they stood there with people moving around them, getting visibly frustrated with the fact that they were taking up so much floor space standing there motionless, staring at each other, unable to move. She hated him.

Even as the truth seemed to bloom and throbbed between them.

"Let me see your phone," he said.

"You don't need to see it." She picked it up and went back to the text screen.

Kid: I'm here.

He took out his own phone, and she saw her message pop up right there.

"This is unbelievable," she said.

He was still saying nothing.

"Aren't you going to say something? Are you going to

throw your head back and laugh and say something about how this was part of your evil plan?"

She had already accepted that it wasn't. But honestly, seeing him stunned was disconcerting. She would almost prefer to see him laugh maniacally, because then at least one of them would know what was going on. At least one of them would have some hint of a plan, whereas at the moment, neither of them had any idea what they were doing. She was an idiot. And he was an asshole. And the two of them were having a baby.

No.

That thought wrenched her apart inside. She was screaming inside. Running out the door, in her heart. But in reality she was just standing there. Staring. Unable to move.

A baby. *Christos's* baby. If she thought that he was ruthless when it came to business, how much more ruthless would he be in a situation like this?

It was incomprehensible.

"What do you drink?"

"A latte. And I usually get a croissant. But I'm not sure that I…"

He turned away from her and went up to the counter. "An espresso, please. And a latte. A croissant as well."

It was weird to watch him be civil to someone. She just wasn't used to it.

She watched his back, trying to…make some sense of this.

And when he turned to her, her heart stopped beating.

She had kissed him. That ruthless mouth had traveled all over her body. Had licked the most intimate part of her.

Those hands had touched every curve.

She had moved her hands over his chest. She had taken him inside of her.

She wished that she could feel something. Some connection, some sense of intimacy. It was too jarring to think of him as the man that she had spent all that time talking to.

And it was even more impossible to think of him as the man that she had slept with.

Except…

The aftermath. The way that he had withdrawn from her like that: *that* felt like Christos.

The way he had gone dark.

That actually made sense. As did his desire for anonymity. Because, of course, anyone would have known who he was. And for some reason, he had needed anonymity to communicate with her.

Was there another facet to this man that she had never considered?

She supposed that if there was, she of all people should have some insight into it, but she only felt more confused.

"Did you know?"

"No," she said, laughing as they went over to a table and sat.

"Not at all?"

"I had no idea. Did you?"

He looked truly appalled by the thought that he would've ever slept with her while knowing it was her. Great. Somehow, he had managed to take her deepest fear, turn it into one she hadn't even known she had, but include some of the original features. He really was a modern marvel, that man.

"I did not know."

"I thought… I thought I was coming here to meet a stranger. I thought that the hardest part about today was that I was going to have to look into an unfamiliar face and discuss the terms of…whatever is going to happen here. But it's worse. Because I've already negotiated to deal with you, and I know that I hate it. I know that I hate you."

He laughed. "What a waste of energy. Hate."

"Is it? Because I have it on good authority that you hate your father."

His face turned to stone. "Anything that I said to you in the confines of a text conversation might well have been overinflated. Did it never occur to you that I might have just wanted the sex?"

She would be tempted to think so. But the truth was, Christos could have anyone. In person or online. So it really didn't make any sense why he would've been wasting time with her, unless he had been saying something somewhat honest.

"So now what?" she said.

"Obviously a paternity test."

"Prenatal paternity tests have risks. I know because I had to look it up for a book that I helped edit."

"A risk is acceptable. Everything has risks."

"Are you kidding me?"

He shrugged. "No. Why would I be kidding?"

"Because we're talking about your child."

"Maybe."

Don't do it. Don't do it.

But she was boiling with rage. She could barely contain it. She thought that she was going to overflow. To burst.

"I was a virgin, you arrogant bastard."

He froze. And just at that moment, a woman came over with their order.

Christos didn't bother to try to smile, but she did.

The woman set the food down and then went away.

"Impossible."

"Oh, good. Now you're going to tell me about my own

vagina. I look forward to hearing all your opinions about my uterus, which I am certain is going to be in the next part of the conversation."

"I am just saying, what virgin would meet a man for anonymous sex in a hotel room?"

"One that thought she was in love with him."

She shouldn't have said that. Because she wasn't. Not now. In truth, she hadn't been, not ever since she had really accepted that he wasn't going to contact her again. So it didn't feel so awful to admit it now. Mainly because it wasn't the biggest, most awful thing hovering between them.

"You really are a fool," he said.

"I guess so. But who spent so much time talking to a fool?"

He said nothing. "This is a terrible place to have this conversation."

"It is," she agreed. "But I didn't know what else to do. I just found out this morning."

"Before the meeting?"

"Yes."

"You told me right away, even though I hadn't been in contact with you?"

"I didn't overthink it. I knew that whatever decision I made, I wanted you to suffer along with me."

He laughed, but there was no humor in it. "That is more ruthless than I tend to think you are."

"I'm feeling ruthless, to be honest."

For a second, she looked across the bistro table at him and felt completely upended. How had they just been sitting across from each other in a conference room? How had he been the man on the other side of those texts? How had it come down to this? She wasn't going to think about the fact that he was the man she had made love with. Because that was an even more difficult truth to wrap her mind around.

"This changes everything," he said.

"We don't know what it changes yet. We haven't fully processed—"

"There's nothing to process. You're pregnant with my child, and so you will marry me."

CHAPTER SEVEN

It was a cold day in hell when something surprised Christos Onassis. Which meant right now the underworld must be experiencing its first blizzard.

Because never in his life...not in his wildest...

Dreams?

He didn't even have dreams. He went to sleep and closed his eyes and saw nothing but darkness.

He had never conceived of this.

Sylvie Jones?

She was the woman, his secret. She was the one he had been carrying on an affair with. The one who had left him rocked, gutted, after their time together?

He looked at her frizzy red hair, her freckles, her ample bosom. He felt attraction to her. He had for a long time, but he had always put that down to the fact that it was human nature to crave the forbidden, and very little was forbidden to him. Lusting after a woman who so clearly hated him was of course its own sort of fantasy.

One that he welcomed.

And yet. And yet. The thought that she was the one that he had been...

She knew him.

For a moment, he felt as if his ruthlessly tailored suit had been stripped from his body. Like he was sitting there in the coffeehouse naked.

He had never worried about such a thing and had never found such a thought embarrassing in his life.

He wasn't even sure he had ever been embarrassed before.

She knew things about him. This woman that he was engaged in a business battle with knew things about him.

He'd...he'd had sex with her. And it had stripped him of his protective layer, and it had been her all along.

And suddenly, something occurred to him.

"Did you know?" he asked.

"Why are you asking me that again?"

"Because this is extraordinary, and I have a very hard time believing this wasn't orchestrated. Did. You. Know?"

"What?" She slapped the top of the table with her open palms. "What kind of question is that after you just made a marriage demand? Did *I* know about it? Of course I didn't know about it."

"It seems as if it would be a good way for you to begin to understand your enemy."

"Would it? Because I understand you less now than I ever have. Believe me, it would be a stupid plan if it was my plan. Because what did I get? What did I win? Is this my prize? This horrendous coffee date and the fact I'm carrying your fetus?"

His lip curled. "Don't say it like that."

"It *is* like that. And you think we should get married? That's ridiculous. We can't even say two words to each other. We had sex—" she looked around, obviously a little bit embarrassed that she'd said it so loudly "—and you sent me away. Like nothing that had happened before meant anything."

"It didn't," he said.

"Then, why are you asking to marry me?"

"I don't have to. When I tell you that my first offer is my kindest, I expect you to listen."

He saw fear shimmering in her eyes, and he felt a strange experience of…softness. Sympathy. He didn't like it. Why would he feel anything for her? It was like reading her texts. Looking at her when she was this distressed. Suddenly, he couldn't separate her from the woman in his phone. And he ought to. She had been misrepresenting herself. Because there was no way that Sylvie was actually that woman. Who was smart and knew exactly what to say to him. Who had reached beneath his armor and found part of him that still had feeling. No.

"What exactly does that mean?"

"I will maintain control of my child." It felt like a desperation. Like a clawing, animal need.

Because all he could think about was his own childhood. And what happened when you were in the wrong hands. What could become of you. Once his mother had been out of the picture, everything had fallen to pieces for him. Once his mother was gone, all his safety had been destroyed. And his father… Once he had been away from his father, who was a truly awful man, things had only gotten worse. No. This child would be bonded to him. Tied to him. Safe.

"We will move on to full custody from there. I think the safest way to guarantee that I have access to my child is through marriage."

"That's…archaic."

"Perhaps. But it is the easiest way for us to have default custody, and for me to have default acknowledgment. You can call it archaic all you want, but there are still realities to the physical custody of the child."

"And you're just so desperate to be a father?"

"I am desperate to make sure that my child is safe. That they are in my life. That I always know what is happening with them."

"As for now," she said, "they are a zygote."

"And are you choosing to end the pregnancy?"

She looked down at her hands. "No."

"I didn't think so."

"What makes you just assume that?"

"Because if you had already decided on that course of action, you would have been resolved. And you wouldn't have been half so terrified that you were going to have to deal with me. Because you would've already decided that you weren't."

She looked away. "It's not the right decision for me."

"If you wish to surrender custody, you can. I will assume the role of single father."

She looked horrified at that. "Absolutely not. You are not going to have full custody of this child. Because I already know what it's like to have one dysfunctional parent. You need the other one to be involved."

"Don't be so hard on yourself. I wouldn't call you *dysfunctional*."

"I didn't mean me, Christos."

He couldn't process what she was saying.

"I am not dysfunctional. I'm a billionaire."

She laughed. Like it was the funniest thing she had ever heard. "What does you being a billionaire have to do with whether or not you're functional?"

"If I am doing so well at managing my life, how could you possibly classify me as dysfunctional?"

"You do realize that there's more to life than money?"

She was maddening. If she was trying to imply that he didn't function, then she was ridiculous. And how dare she?

He'd won. When it came to matters of her company, he had beaten her decisively, and he felt that spoke to functionality fairly damned well.

He'd heard it said there was more to life than money, of course he had. Multiple times. But it had never meant anything to him. "Do you mean power?"

"Have you never seen a Christmas movie in your life?"

He stared at her. "I don't think I have."

"Friendship. Family. *Love*."

"I find that I do perfectly well without any of those things."

"And yet you're trying to muscle your way into having a family. You think that you're going to marry me. You think that I should just be content with… What do you even want with me? You want to throw me up in the attic? You know you can kidnap me without making it official."

"All I know is that in my life, when my parents were together and I had both of them, I was safe. I was well fed. I had a roof over my head. Then everything fell apart. And yes, I am logical enough to know that there are many variable factors in play. But what I want for my own child…is security. In every way."

"Yet again," she said, "you *are* a billionaire."

"Yes, which means I have resources you don't have."

"I have enough resources to take care of a baby, and as far as I can tell you don't care about anyone or anything. You lied to me in those texts. You made me think you were a decent man, and I thought I was meeting a decent man here today. But I will not be strong-armed into anything by a man who doesn't even know why he wants to be involved in his child's life."

"I know why I want to be involved."

"You gave me a reason, but I don't think it's a good one.

Nothing you've said has anything to do with how you feel, just what you're afraid of."

Her words were like a dagger in the center of his chest. "I'm not afraid of anything."

"Then, you're not afraid of me walking out," she said, standing up and turning away from him.

Desperation gripped him. An old feeling. One he didn't recognize in this new body he'd created, this warrior frame he did battle from. He didn't do desperate, he didn't beg, he didn't feel fear or vulnerability, and yet now he did, and it forced his next words from deep within him.

"I'll give you the company back," he said.

"What?"

"I'll sign Jones & Abbott back over to you. As a gift."

She didn't look pleased, which he thought was ungrateful of her. He was making her a more than generous offer in response to her childish tantrum, her threatening to leave, and she was still unhappy. "You...you have to be kidding me."

"I'll be a silent investor, and you can do whatever you want with it. Provided that you marry me."

The company wasn't as important as this. He had to be certain he had access to his child, and he would do whatever it took to make sure that happened.

He was a warrior, and battle meant having to make sacrifices, having to make quick decisions. He had made his, and he was resolved.

"You are...you're unhinged. How is that—"

"I want what I want," he said. "And I am willing to do what I need to get it. I thought that was explicitly clear."

"Months," she whispered, her voice shaking. "Months and months," her words grew in intensity, "of being terrorized by you and your intent to acquire my company, and now you're just *giving* it to me?"

"Everything has changed, Miss Jones. Or did you not notice?"

Her features softened; he was shocked by that. She suddenly looked like perhaps what he had said made sense. And he realized when he said it, how true it was. He really didn't believe in love. He didn't much care about anyone or anything. But that was why it was easy to transfer the company back to her. She didn't seem to understand that. That the brilliant thing about living the way he did was that when something else became a bigger priority, he could sacrifice the thing that had mattered previously.

She held on to so many things too tightly. While he...he pivoted easily. For that reason.

"What exactly do you envisage for a marriage?" she asked, her expression violent in a way he nearly found amusing.

He'd seen her look at him like that across boardroom tables many times.

This was different.

"I don't know that I envisage anything for marriage. It can be nothing more than printed paper, and it does not need to last the duration of the child's youth. But it is important to me that we are married when the child is born."

"I see. And as far as our relationship goes?"

He felt like there was an ice block in his chest. But that was nothing new.

"There is no need for us to engage in one. I should like you to move in with me. I believe that you should be kept close."

He didn't question himself. It was logical. Easy. Anyway, she had wanted him to be involved in this process. So he was considering himself involved.

"I see. And what you want, that's going to be the definitive answer here?"

"I have the most power of the two of us, Miss Jones. That means that I will be the one to get my way."

"You have power in the traditional sense."

"Yes. And the traditional sense is the only one that really matters."

"That isn't true. Normal people can use social media now and gain sympathy and—"

"If only you could eat sympathy. If only you could buy a house with it. But you cannot. How can you paint someone as the villain when they already did? Those kinds of campaigns only work if your opponent cares what the public thinks, and I have made a study of not caring. Better, I don't have to study it. I simply don't care."

"How?" she asked. It was an odd question and not what he had expected. Why did she care?

"It's easy. Someone's opinion of me has never been the determining factor in my survival. I have only ever been able to count on myself. Once you start caring about the opinions of others, you involve other people, and whether or not you might live or die. And I refuse to leave that fate to anyone else."

They were silent for a moment.

"What are you talking about? You are continually mentioning gladiators, battles, and life and death."

"Where do you think I came from, *agape*?"

The Greek slipped out. Unbidden. He didn't use his native tongue often. He had no remaining accent.

"I suppose I haven't given it a thought. When one is about to be eaten by a tiger, one does not wonder where the tiger was born."

He surprised himself by laughing. Because she was genuinely amusing. It reminded him of the texts she used to send.

Texts he no longer received and would not again.

That was fine. He didn't need them. If not for this he would never have contacted her again.

He had the sudden realization that wasn't true, because even if he'd never discovered it, she would have been Sylvie Jones. He would have seen her, interacted with her at the company. And what would have happened?

He had been battling some sort of attraction to her for years, separate to the texts. Would they have succumbed to their attraction even not knowing?

The idea was an intoxicating one.

And yet, he rejected it. The idea that he and Sylvie were anything like fated was a ridiculous one. He didn't believe in fate.

He believed in fighting until you had no breath left in you. That was when you got what you were owed. And only then.

"I suppose not," he said. "I wasn't born with money. I wasn't born with a family legacy to inherit. I have fought for my survival." He felt a strange hollowness at the center of his chest. He looked behind her, his gaze meeting the back wall. "Do you know, I read somewhere that human beings can die from loneliness. I thought that was fascinating. And it reinforced the decisions that I made as a youth. If you cut out the part of yourself that craves connection, you would be amazed at what you can accomplish. No matter the circumstances. It is a strength. A survival skill."

He looked back at her, and he saw concern on her face. He didn't like it. It made him feel something warm that seemed to surpass that block of ice. He didn't want to feel that.

"What do you mean...fighting for your survival?"

"You are always fighting for your survival. If you think you aren't, then you are putting yourself in danger." He shifted topics. "I will call my lawyer and make sure that the documents are not processed. That means the sale will never go through. Everything will be as it was."

Any interest or curiosity he'd seen on her face the moment before vanished, replaced by anger. "You know you're a bastard for holding this over my head."

"Perhaps. But are you not somewhat mercenary for being swayed?"

"No. It's a terrible time for me to have to figure out something new to do with my life. Maintaining the company maintains a legacy for my child."

"Your child has a father who's a billionaire."

She looked down at her hands then back up at him. "Yes. I suppose. But we'll see how long your interest lasts. And whether or not you decide—"

Fury made him interject. "I will never abandon my child. I will never leave them to fend for themselves. Never."

It was rare for him to show emotion. Or maybe it was just rare for him to feel it. But the way she looked at him, with a deep measure of skepticism, irked him. "Never," he said again.

"I don't trust you," she said. "And why should I? Why should I trust you at all?"

"I've done nothing to earn your trust. I have done nothing to earn anyone's trust," he said. "And I won't start now. I also don't give my word. Not lightly. And really, not ever. Because I do not make promises to people. But I will promise you this. My child would be cared for. Always. They will never worry about a thing. Ever."

"And what about me?"

He looked at her, and he chose to focus on the coldness in the center of his chest. "What about you?"

"I need assurance that I'm going to be taken care of. That you won't take our child away."

"I would not," he said. "Because I believe...more than one parent must be involved."

"We will sign an agreement."

"Obviously there will be a detailed prenuptial agreement."

She stared at him, and the nod she gave was almost imperceptible, but it was there. "Excellent. I will call my lawyer and have the paperwork for the acquisition stopped."

CHAPTER EIGHT

SYLVIE WALKED BACK to the office on numb legs. She was going to have to tell everyone that the acquisition was off. And that they had a very substantial injection of cash promised by Christos Onassis.

And it was inevitable that the rest of the story would come up.

She felt like she was in a haze. How was this possible? If her father were alive, she would've had the fortitude to tell Christos no. She would've been able to cope well enough to reject him. It needed to be done. Instead...

She had seen the easy way, and she had taken it.

Really? You really think the easy way is being married to Christos Onassis? It has nothing to do with the fact that you're...fascinated by him?

No. She wasn't going to acknowledge that. Because it was ridiculous.

Yes, they'd slept together. But it never would have happened if she would have known that it was Christos.

It really never would've happened if he would've known it was her.

The audacity of that man. To ask whether or not she had known. Of course she hadn't. She would never... She simply would have never.

She was still shimmering with spite when she walked

into the board room, where most of the board was still assembled.

"Great news," she said. "The acquisition is off."

Daniela looked up at her. "How?"

Sylvie opened her mouth to speak, when the door behind her opened, and she whirled around and nearly flat out into Christos.

"Because I called it off," he said.

Her shoulders bunched up around her ears. "Yes," she said. "He did."

"But don't worry. I will be investing a sizable amount of money in the future of the company."

"This doesn't make any sense," said Ben, one of the other board members.

"Luckily, it doesn't have to make sense to you," said Christos.

He turned and walked out of the boardroom, and she almost went after him, but Daniela stood up. "What's going on, Sylvie?"

"I… We… That is to say… Christos and I are having a baby. And getting married. And he agreed to give me the company as a wedding gift. Bye."

She turned on her heel and began to walk out of the office, and Daniela pursued her at a hasty clip. "And you had the gall to accuse me of sleeping with him?" she asked.

Sylvie turned around. "I didn't accuse you of sleeping with him. I was really only accusing you of finding him attractive. And I'm sorry. I'm sorry. But I am not sorry that I have maintained ownership of the company. And if I have my way, when we sell it off, if we ever do, and if it becomes hugely profitable, your pockets will not be lined because you betrayed me."

"It's business, Sylvie," Daniela said. "And generally

speaking, you can't *talk* your way out of a situation like that."

Sylvie supposed she deserved that. It wasn't how it had happened, but how would she ever explain what had *actually* happened? How was she ever going to convince anyone that what had happened was she had slept with him, not knowing who he was? Right. Like anybody was going to believe that. It was ridiculous. It was flat out ridiculous. It was what had happened, but it was ridiculous.

She was standing in the hall fuming, when the door to her office opened and Christos looked out at her. She scampered over to him and then inside. "What are you doing here?"

"I'm not finished with you. We need to establish a firm timeline."

"Why?"

"Because it is important. First, we will have a doctor's appointment. Do you prefer to have it at your house or mine?"

"I don't… Excuse me?"

"The doctor. I have found one who can see you in an hour. Do you prefer to have the appointment at your house or mine?"

She blinked. "What the hell kind of appointment is it?"

"We need to establish the viability of the pregnancy. Also, do a paternity test."

"I already told you, I'm not sure about the paternity test."

"I don't trust people. I don't take them at their word. It is not meant to offend you."

"It's the risk involved."

"There is no risk. There are noninvasive methods now. We will be able to have everything done today."

Her stomach went tight. "Wait… Everything?"

He nodded. "Yes. My lawyers have also begun work on a basic prenup—to be revised within thirty days of the marriage if both parties agree. As it stands, my assets remain mine, with agreed-upon alimony and child support should we divorce, and your assets remain yours. Including Jones & Abbott."

Her head was spinning and she didn't think sitting down would be enough. She needed to lie down. With a cold compress. In a dark room. For the next six months.

Instead she took a deep breath. "You want to get married before the baby is born?"

"Yes. I already told you I did. There is no need to have a wedding, filled with pomp and circumstance. I have no friends. And any colleagues who decided they wanted to make much of my nuptials would simply be doing so for grim purposes. No one would actually be happy for me. And anyway, I don't care for parties."

Of course it was a party that had started all this. He'd managed to go to that, hadn't he?

"You do go to them, though," she said, pointed.

He shrugged. "If I have to." Then he made a sweeping gesture, as if he were changing the subject with the wave of his hand. "If the fetus is viable, and if it turns out that it is mine, we will marry after the appointment."

"What?"

"We will marry today," he said. "There is simply no point putting it off."

Her heart was pounding so hard she thought she might actually pass out. She couldn't get a breath. "I disagree. There is... the need for things to adjust. The need for us to wrap our heads around the changes."

"There will be no changes, not after we've gotten the full picture of the situation."

"Meaning if the baby is alive and if it's yours? I can't believe how callous you're being."

"No less than you were."

She felt a twinge of guilt. "I…"

"You were trying to hurt me," he said, tilting his head to the side, an expression of wonder on his face.

She had been, she realized. She wanted him to feel lost and uncertain like she did. She wanted him to feel something over losing the relationship they'd had.

It had mattered to her.

She'd loved a man who hadn't existed. Who'd taken her virginity and then ghosted her.

She'd loved a man who had turned out to be the man she hated most in all the world, and she was still reeling with it.

That and the truth that she wanted him.

When the reality of who he was had crashed into the reality of what she'd believed, she'd felt like she'd lost her breath. She hadn't gotten it back.

He'd been shocked for mere seconds and now he was combating it by taking control. So yes, she had tried to hurt him.

It was hollow and horrible to realize it wasn't possible.

Because the emotion she felt, the fear, the grief over losing what she'd thought was a real love affair meant nothing to him.

"Should all tests come back positive we will marry. You will move into my home in New York. We will not see each other with great frequency. The house is large. You will have plenty of space, and I spend a great deal of time traveling for business."

She blinked. "Just like that. Just like that you think I should marry you and vacate my apartment and—"

"Are you attached to your apartment?"

The truth was, while it would be big enough for her and her brand-new baby, it was not suitable for a toddler or a child. Though, she doubted his penthouse was any more suited to it.

"Can you imagine raising a child where you live?" she asked.

"Not long-term. But we will discuss the best places for the child to spend more of their time."

"You're willing to plan all this out, but choosing a child-appropriate home is a bridge too far for you?"

He ignored her. "As for now, it will make the most sense for us to reside in the city."

Everything was happening so quickly, and she didn't know why she ought to be surprised. Except it was…it was impossible to marry the image that she'd had of her lover with the reality of him.

It hurt. It hurt, and even though she knew she couldn't hurt him she had to do something with the pain, the poison rising inside her now. She hated him then as much as she'd thought she'd loved him and she was very, very clear Christos and her mystery lover were one in the same. Because the betrayal felt so sharp. So real right there.

She might not be able to hurt him, but she'd swing at him anyway.

"I wish I hadn't found your phone that night. You know, what's really funny is I remember I ran into you that night. And you were an ass. Making it very plain that you were intent on acquiring the company. My father had died six months earlier, and you didn't express any sympathy. And then I found that phone, and I reached out to the person who owned it. And he responded to me. With empathy. He gave me someone to talk to. I think the worst part about finding out that it's you is knowing that none of that was real. Because *look at you*. You're made of stone. You don't have any feelings. You're…you're awful."

"Trying to hurt me again?"

But there was something in his gaze. Something different. Something that seemed to suggest he didn't feel nothing about what she had said.

"I'm not stupid enough to think that I can hurt a rock wall. If I fling myself at it, I'm only going to end up injured."

He seemed to consider that for a moment. "I'm sorry. For what it's worth. That it was me. And that it was you."

The words were strange, uncharacteristic, really.

"Why are you sorry?"

"I don't know."

She felt slightly run-over by the statement. But it didn't get any better, because after that she found herself being propelled from her office and toward the elevator.

"You know everyone thinks that I slept with you to stop the acquisition."

"Does it matter?"

"Yes. In the way that it completely compromises any integrity that I might've had." She let her head fall back against the elevator. "You know, it was you I was talking about. Whenever I texted you, and I was talking about difficulties at work."

She looked at his expression, to try and see if that affected him in any way.

"I imagine I would find that funny if…" He trailed off.

She frowned. "You would find it funny if what?"

"I don't know. If I found things funny."

"Why are you such a godawful prick?"

She was angry. And she was getting really tired of his nonsense. He was just… He expected people to just accept him as he was. Because he was Christos Onassis and he was a villain and blah-blah-blah allusions to his inner darkness.

But she didn't have to accept it.

"Does there have to be a *why* for everything?" he asked.

"I tend to assume that there is," she said.

"Why?"

"Because. Because I am desperately insecure. Because my mother is a polished socialite who thinks nothing tastes as good as being skinny feels, and who constantly victimizes me with her cutting statements about both my appearance and my value system. And that is why I didn't want to meet you in person. Then there's my father, who was the only parent really involved in raising me, and he was wonderful. He loved me. And he loved this place. And I can't separate those things out. If I want to continue to be worthy of his love, of the legacy he left me, I have to say that, don't I? And if I can't, I'm everything my mother thought I was, and nothing that my father hoped I would be. So yes. I think we all come from somewhere."

"How neat." He tugged on the cuffs of his perfectly tailored shirt. "A little narrative to explain each and every difficulty in your life. I don't know that I think the story of my life is at all relevant. Because the truth is, I watched everyone around me go through the same things that I did, and they emerged differently. Or didn't. But I can't say definitively that a specific instance shaped me into what I am."

She thought he had to be lying.

"Or rather," he continued, "I cannot say that it did so without my permission."

"Oh. Well. Of course. Even your issues didn't appear without your express written consent."

"For what it's worth," he said, "your mother is incorrect about your appearance. You are extremely attractive."

She blinked. "I am... What?"

"You're beautiful," he said.

With as much emotion in his voice as she had ever heard. Meaning none.

"I'm not sure what to say to that."

"Many people would say *thank you*."

"Many people would probably not say it to you, since there is undoubtedly some…lurking danger beneath the compliment."

"When have I ever been a *lurking* danger? I am quite in the open with it, I would think."

Well. That wasn't wrong. She resented him for that.

"I just have a hard time believing it. Given that you and I had many, many interactions over the years, and there was never an indication that you—"

"Fantasized about bending you over your desk and smacking your ass while I rode you?"

She actually lost her footing, in the elevator. Her knees sagged and gave out, and it was only because she was leaning against the wall that she didn't plummet entirely to the floor.

"Excuse me?"

"Do you really need me to restate that? Because I thought it was quite clear."

"You cannot have thought that."

He still looked so unbothered.

"I did. I couldn't decide whether I found it titillating or perplexing. Because you were involved in a business dealing, and it is not usual for me to have sexual feelings in context with business matters."

She gritted her teeth. "Oh, that's weird. I'm constantly getting aroused over staplers."

"When did I say that I saw you as a stapler?"

The weirdest thing was a small bubble of jealousy welled

up in her chest. "Did you really fantasize about…that while you were carrying on conversations in our texts?"

"So were you," he said.

"But you didn't know that."

"No. I didn't."

He said nothing else to follow up.

It was weird that she was jealous of herself. Astonishingly so. Especially since everything that had happened between them before now felt fake.

How could it be real? Because everything she knew about him led her to believe that the texting had been a game. Yes. That would make sense. That it had been a video game to him. Something he had found amusing, as he had texted words of support, filthy sentences and the kinds of sensitive reassurances that she was fairly certain had never crossed his mind before.

Too soon, the elevator reached its destination, and they were moving quickly out of the office. His car was there, waiting up against the curb.

She was having difficulty processing things.

They got into the car, and it began to drive away from the building.

"I have asked the doctor to meet us at my penthouse."

"We didn't really decide—"

"It is decided."

She swallowed hard.

She wished she didn't feel so alone. She wished that she still felt like she could text him. And in a fit of minor panic, she reached into her purse and took her phone out. Pulled up the tech stream she now knew was him.

It still said *Baby*. She kept it that way.

Kid: I'm dealing with this guy, and he's a real dick.

His phone buzzed. He took it out of his pocket and opened it, looked at the text.

"Really?"

"Really I think you're a dick? Or really I texted you?"

"I know I'm a dick."

She laughed. "Well, why shouldn't I text you? I'm used to communicating with you that way."

He looked down at his phone and began to type as she watched her screen.

Baby: Are you going to make this difficult?

She looked up at him. And she smiled. "Yes. I think I will, Christos. Because I have made far too many things in this world easy for people."

She wanted to call her mother and ask for advice. But her mother wouldn't give good advice. She wanted to do a séance and get in touch with her father's ghost. She wanted the man who had once been a source of great comfort to her to actually be real and not some specter of Christos. A variant who wasn't real.

It was like the two of them in those texts had been people existing in another timeline. In another life. She just wished that… She really did wish that she could somehow pop herself into that timeline. Where maybe that version of them was real.

Instead, she was stuck with this one.

She looked at him, at his rigid, unsmiling profile.

All too soon they were at his penthouse.

The building was like a fortress. He had a private entrance at the side, a private elevator that only worked with his fingerprint.

"What if other people need to come up without you?"

"They can use the front. And there are certain people approved to enter."

"I see. But only you get to use this fancy private door."

"Yes."

"And what about me? What about when I'm supposed to live here? Do I get to use the fancy private door?"

"I'll program your fingerprint into it."

She wrinkled her nose. "Thank you."

She didn't really mean it.

When the doors to the elevator opened, his pristine penthouse was revealed. She had never thought about where he lived. She looked around the space and took in the clean lines, all black and stainless steel everything.

"I always thought that you lived in a cave. I guess this is close enough."

"Did you think that?"

"Yes. That's where one imagines the dragon returns home to at the end of the day, isn't it?"

"A dragon?"

He nearly looked amused by that. And she did her best not to feel something in response to creating that amusement for him.

He was such a difficult man.

"Yes. That was what I thought about you the first time I met you. When I was a teenager."

He lifted his dark brows. "I don't remember meeting you then."

She blinked. "Of course you don't. Why would you? I was invisible."

"If you were a child, I can guarantee you I had no reason to notice. I'm not interested in children."

"I was sixteen."

"A child to me in many ways. I find you to be a child now."

"Excuse me?"

"I only mean that you have lived nothing of the kind of life I have."

"Maybe you want to share what you've been through?"

"I don't. But that is interesting that you thought me something quite so dangerous as a dragon, even then. I suppose that was your self-preservation instincts. Which failed you later on."

"The man I was texting with wasn't a dragon."

He looked up at her, his dark eyes blank. "But he was, silly. All along."

That made her stomach twist tight. Made her heart feel like it was being squeezed.

She felt like she was gasping for air.

Just then a different set of doors to the penthouse opened, and a medical team entered. A *whole team*. There was equipment, being rolled in on great wheels, and she was stunned by the sight.

"We're going to do a sonogram," Christos said.

"In your house."

"Of course. Why would I have my fiancée trek all the way down to a medical facility?"

"You're picking a strange thing to be chivalrous about. Considering you're literally strong-arming me into a marriage and are in general not at all courtly in any manner."

"Do not question it when I decide to show chivalry."

"I think you aren't understanding, Christos. I have agreed to this. Because it is the best thing for me. Because you're right, it is going to make things easier in some ways. Because I believe you when you say that your first offer will be the best one. And I am very aware that you could take me apart piece by piece. But you are a fool if you think I'm going to make this easy for you. If you think that I will suddenly become compliant. I have always known what you were. And you're right, except for a very brief failure within my instincts to keep me safe, I have always known that I needed to be on guard with you. It's not going to stop now, not because I'm having your baby. Not because we might get legally married."

She realized just then that there was another person not wearing scrubs or a medical-type coat standing there as well. A woman with her hair tied back, her features plain. She was holding...the Bible.

"Is this the minister?" she asked.

"Yes," she said. "I'm...on standby."

And nobody seemed to think that their conversation was out of the ordinary. Or at least, nobody cared enough about any of it to defy Christos in any way.

"We'll get set up in here," the doctor said. He was a genial man in his midforties. Soft and pleasant-looking in comparison to Christos.

Who was all granite, harsh angles and too much beauty to take in.

That was the problem. She was outraged at him. She genuinely might hate him. And she still thought he was gorgeous.

"First we have to take a cheek swab from both of you and then a blood test from Miss Jones as well."

She felt a little bit persecuted, but she knew blood tests were part of pregnancy anyway, and she looked forward to winning here. To him finding out that he was being an ass by implying she might be lying.

Maybe he would even feel guilty.

As she sat in the plush chair, got swabbed and had the

blood drawn, she looked at him. And wondered how it was possible she felt like she'd never met him before in her life.

The nurse squeezed her hand. "I'll take you into the bedroom and provide you with a gown."

Tears pressed against her eyes as she realized that Christos had never seen her in any state of undress, because when they'd slept together it had been entirely in the dark. And now this was going to be the first time that he saw her...

"I need to be entirely covered before Christos is allowed in the room," she said.

"A sonogram doesn't necessitate—"

"Then, he needs to stand somewhere where he cannot see my skin."

She waited. She waited for everyone to defer to him and defy her.

"I will stand by, please," said Christos.

The doctor looked at Christos directly. "I'm afraid I must defer to what the patient has requested."

"I am paying—"

"Regardless of pay."

The nurse held her arms steady. And she felt supported then. She could see Christos doing mental gymnastics like he was trying to figure out... Did he really not understand why she might not want him to witness it? It was hard to imagine that he was so...*naive* was the wrong word. He could never be called naive. And yet... There was something missing. In personal relationships of people. She had never noticed it in the context of business, because he was always one step ahead of everyone. But ever since he'd had to attempt to deal with her, he had been a step behind. And that really was baffling.

She was taken into the bedroom and given a gown and also a sheet. Then the nurse left the room and entered again a moment later. "He has left the room. We will get you positioned on the bed. The only part of your body that will be exposed is your stomach. But we can keep him standing by your head."

"Thank you," she said.

It meant something. Knowing that at least here she had found allies.

"I don't know what the nature of your relationship is with him," the nurse said, "but if you ever feel unsafe, it doesn't matter how powerful he is. We would try and help you."

"I don't feel unsafe," she said. "I'm just angry at him."

She knew that Christos would never hurt her. Not physically. She hoped that he didn't possess the power to hurt her emotionally.

She truly, truly did.

She lay down on the table, the ultrasound machine set up and ready to go.

The doctor put some gel on her stomach, and at that point, Christos was given permission to come back into the room.

She wondered how long it had been since anyone had told him what to do. She imagined it had been even longer since he had complied.

When the Doppler was put onto her stomach, she paid close attention to the screen. It only took a moment for a swooshing rhythmic sound to fill the room.

"There's the baby's heartbeat," said the doctor.

A hard pang hit her in the chest, made her feel hollowed-out. She didn't know what she had been more terrified of. Finding out that there was no heartbeat, or this.

That realization made her want to weep, because of course it should be easy to want the heartbeat. To want to keep the promise of this life that had come into her life when she had taken the pregnancy test. But it was also hard. She could imagine holding a baby, her baby, and it was a beautiful thought. But she was also just so afraid. Because she had all but signed her marriage license with this heartbeat. And there would be no going back.

"The test is finished," one of the other medical staffers said. "You are the father, Mr. Onassis."

Sylvie had known for a fact what the outcome would be. She found she couldn't even bring herself to react to the news.

Christos was staring at the screen with his expression like granite. Still hoping to find out that there was a chance the baby wasn't his, she supposed. How was she supposed to feel about this? How in the world could she feel simple joy?

It was impossible. When the whole situation was just so complicated. She swallowed hard.

"You are about thirteen weeks," the doctor said.

Thirteen weeks.

If the test hadn't been conclusive, surely that would have done it.

She glanced up to where Christos was standing and tried to see if there had been a change in his expression.

But he was as stoic as ever.

Perhaps it wouldn't have mattered. Maybe all that would ever matter to him was black-and-white dates.

The doctor took measurements, but admittedly, she couldn't tell what she was looking at.

Her vision was too blurry anyway.

She couldn't tell if it was tears, anger or stress.

When she was finished, she went back into the bedroom to change. She was shaking. And when she came back out, the equipment was gone, but the nurse and doctor and chaplain remained.

The nurse looked at her, with sharp eyes.

"I agreed to it," she said.

There was a marriage license, already filled out. And the prenup was there. It was brief and allowed for revision, just as he'd said.

He'd taken care of everything. How fortunate for her.

It was just all so...so cold.

She blinked. Of course he had all of this. Because, of course, he was Christos Onassis, and he could make the world turn in a different direction if he wanted to. She would spare herself the monologue.

It turned out, you didn't really have to say vows to get married. Not in the traditional sense. They had to be pronounced husband and wife by someone ordained and file the right paperwork. And they did.

It didn't feel like a marriage. It didn't feel like anything.

She was wearing the same thing she had been wearing at work. They hadn't kissed. They hadn't promised to love, honor or obey one another. They hadn't promise to stay together at all.

Marriage, she realized, really was about the emotion. The ceremony. The paperwork felt like nothing. She might as well have filed her taxes.

She nearly laughed when she looked up at him because that was actually how it felt. Like her taxes had come due in a very big way.

She was having a baby. She had married Christos Onassis.

"I'm having a moving company go to your place and pack up everything you might need. Your furniture, of course will stay behind."

"Oh. Of course. Why would I want my furniture?"

"Did you not find the suite you were just in to your liking?"

"It's very nice, I'm sure. But it has nothing to do with me."

"Perhaps you would like one on the second floor. Or the third? There are infinite rooms for you to choose from."

"Which is farthest from yours?"

"The third floor it is," he said. "You will have a bathtub in a bathroom with all glass walls. It overlooks the city below. I imagine it's quite evocative."

"You don't know?"

"I'm not given to long, scenic baths."

"Then, what's the point? What's the point of any of the excess?"

"I can have it. And so I do."

Gladiators in the arena...blah-blah-blah.

The usual Christos soliloquy.

"You know that nurse offered to rescue me."

"And you didn't take her up on it?"

"I'm here of my own free will," she said, if for nothing else than to remind herself of that, because she had felt vulnerable just moments before, and she badly wanted that vulnerability to go away.

Because it hadn't been a wedding, not really. And this was a marriage only for the sake of the baby. Except even that got tangled and twisted around in her head.

Because he wasn't going to be the sweet, loving father that she'd had.

But still, you made the best choice possible for the baby. You protected the publishing company. You're making sure there are no ugly custody battles.

It was true. She had protected herself and the child in the best way she could think to. And there was no point second-guessing it now.

"I'll just go to my jail cell, then," she said.

"I thought you were intent on making it clear you were here of your own free will?"

Their eyes caught and held, and she found it difficult to breathe.

Why was it so complicated? It should be very simple. Simply put, he was the most aggravating man she had ever known. He was borderline heartless. And yet all of that was tangled around that relationship they'd spent six months having over text. The fact that she was having a difficult time joining that up with the man in front of her.

But what she did feel?

It was the heat. In spite of everything.

She really did need a reprieve.

"Well. You can have all my things brought to me later."

"You and I will have dinner together. And discuss the future."

"Oh, good. More edicts."

"You only see it as an edict because you are in fact buying into the narrative that you're a prisoner. You chose this."

"Yes. Shocking. I chose not to be in a fight with a billionaire over custody."

"You may not have liked your array of choices, but you did have them."

She hated him then, most of all because he was right.

Because she knew well enough that this was just life. A series of choices you didn't always want to make.

"Well, I'll see if I'm hungry."

"It wasn't a request."

"And my response didn't contain a stutter."

She turned away, glad to have grabbed a small part of her own back as she found the near hidden staircase in the penthouse and took the steps two a time, ascending to the third floor. She needed a shower, or maybe a scenic bath, and some rest. She needed to try to come to grips with everything that had just happened.

Three months. Three months she had sat there, feeling broken over what had happened. And today everything had exploded.

Thunder and lightning and doom, doom, doom.

And yet again, she wished that she had someone to talk to.

But her safe space had transformed into a villain.

And if she was going to be angry about one thing forever, it was going to be that.

CHAPTER NINE

CHRISTOS POURED HIMSELF WHISKEY as he waited for dinner to be served.

He had sent Sylvie a text to let her know that she could meet him at a specific time, and she hadn't responded.

But the time came and went, and she didn't appear.

The table was set, and it was beautiful in his opinion. She should've come downstairs wearing something lovely. He could have watched her enjoy her food and...

He supposed today had been...difficult for her. But it was really no different for him. She had her pregnancy confirmed, and it meant that both of their lives were going to change. She had no right to act as if she was the only person who was impacted by the event.

Yes, she had to marry him, but he had married her.

It was...

It was the same.

He thought of how she had looked, vulnerable as she had asked about the sonogram, and him looking at her. As if he disgusted her.

He had not disgusted her that night they'd been together at The Luxe. No. She had been aroused by him. And he by her.

She had wanted him then.

She had texted him and told him all of her fears.

And you stopped. Before you knew who it was. You cut her off.

He had done that. But it had been in a bid to preserve his way of being. He had recognized whatever he was feeling for her was... It was an anomaly, and he could not allow it. That seemed reasonable to him.

It was reasonable.

He found himself setting his whiskey down on the table, abandoning dinner and walking out of the room.

He found himself compelled to walk up the stairs. Toward her.

Perhaps she would be angry. Maybe she would shout at him and tell him to leave.

He paused at the door and raised his hand to knock, even as he chided himself of the ridiculousness of having to knock to enter a room in his own home.

He did, though. To prove a level of civility even to his own self.

But it was firm. Decisive.

"Go away, Christos."

"Sylvie," he said. "I wish to speak to you."

"And I don't wish to speak to you."

He growled, and reached into his pocket and pulled out his phone.

Baby: Don't be like this.

Kid: Like what?

Baby: Petulant.

Kid: It isn't petulant to need some time alone after the day that I've had. And it isn't like I'm going to get any emotional support from you.

Baby: I'm sorry. I'm sorry that you feel this way.

It was easier to type it than it was to say it. He didn't even really know how to think it.

Baby: I know that everything changed for you today. I felt that it must be the same for you as it was for me, but I recognize that it isn't. You are…pregnant. This is perhaps scary?

He heard footsteps, and then the door opened slightly.

He looked up from his phone, at her. "Are you trying to be human?"

"I'm trying to talk to you. The way that we did. Because we did one time."

"And then you stopped."

He didn't want to explain that.

"I didn't see anywhere for it to go."

"Well. Fate intervened and laughed at you."

He couldn't argue with that.

"Yes, it did."

She was barefoot now, wearing a matching pajama set with leopards on them. She looked soft, sexy.

He found himself wondering what it would be like to kiss her, knowing that it was Sylvie.

It had been a gut punch back when it had happened in the dark; it would be something entirely different now. He knew it.

There was a feeling at the center of his chest, the one that he had identified far too recently as being something that seemed to affect the ice in his core. Sylvie. It was Sylvie's fault. And she was looking up at him with an expression on her face so much like longing. He wasn't sure for what. For things to be easier? Simpler?

For...

"That night," he said. "We never spoke of it."

"Because you wouldn't speak of it."

"I have never... I have never experienced anything like it."

"Then, why did you leave my text unresponded-to? Why did you treat me like I didn't matter?"

"No one matters in my life," he said. "You have to understand that. I am a man who fashioned himself into an island. And there is no place in my life for...whatever that was."

"But now here I am."

"Yes. But it's different now. Because I know who you are."

"Does that make it different?"

"Yes. It changes things."

"Help me. Tell me what it changes."

"It changes everything. Because it must. Can't you understand that?"

"No. I can't, Christos. I can't understand it."

"It is just different. It was a dream before, again. You weren't real. You were...something that existed only on my phone, and I made a mistake... I made a mistake."

"But it wouldn't be the same now."

"Of course it wouldn't."

"Prove it," she said, stepping forward, tilting her stubborn chin upward. Her green eyes sparkled with rage, and he could barely breathe. He had no idea what was happening to him. The fire that was building inside of him...it shouldn't exist. It should not be like this. Not for him. Not for Christos Onassis, a man who had learned long ago that need was the enemy. That other people were a scam. He should not feel drawn toward her. He should not burn for her.

But she was...she was Sylvie Jones. And she was his wife. His *wife*.

His.

He growled, and he wrapped his arm around her waist, drawing her heart against the firm wall of his body. "You said that you could hurt yourself, flinging your body at me. Is this what you want?"

"I think it's what you want. And you won't admit it."

"Do you want it any less than I want it? I think not."

"Christos..."

"You want me," he said. "Tell me that you do."

"I want you, and I hate it, dammit. What I wanted was for you to be a different man. What I wanted was for you to be...a pleasant-looking man with glasses. That curated bugs in a museum. I didn't want you to be you. But here we are. And I can neither control it nor stop it. But I won't have you standing there pretending that you can. That you are somehow above it. When I'm not. Because that simply isn't fair."

He loved her like this and hated it in equal measure.

Because it made him feel things. And he didn't have the patience for that. He didn't have the capacity for it. This alchemy between them was something he was never supposed to know. Never supposed to experience. It was anathema to him in many ways. And yet he was addicted to it.

He had been correct when he had compared it to illicit substances.

He was at the end of his rope now, and that never happened. He never felt these things. Not for anyone or anything. And yet as she looked up at him with those green eyes sparkling, he felt something shifted inside of him. He felt himself begin to bend.

And so instead of suffering that indignity, he lowered his head and let his mouth crash down on hers.

He claimed her. In the bright light, he claimed her.

For one second he thought that she was going to push against him, and that he would have to let her go. But as she brought her hands up, she didn't push him away. Instead, she gripped his shirt, drew him to her.

"Christos," she whispered against his mouth.

He growled. She was a drug.

Her saying his name…it was everything.

It was like these two distinct pieces had come together, clicked into place. Like they fit together in a unique way that he had never foreseen.

That woman in the hotel room. The woman in his texts. Sylvie Jones.

They were the same. How had he ever missed that?

When he had felt the stirring urge to bend Sylvie over his desk, how had he ever been ignorant enough to believe that it was a free-floating desire? Disconnected from everything?

Of course it was because of her.

Because the woman in his phone was the one that made him act out of character.

She was the one that got under his skin.

She was the one who made him like this.

He couldn't bear it. It was awful, horrendous. Beautiful beyond belief. A bright, glimmering thing that he had never even expected to see, let alone touch. And so he kissed her.

He kissed her and pushed her back into the bedroom, his hands waited at her hips as he held her fast to his body, let her feel exactly what she did to him.

"I need you," he growled against her mouth.

She whimpered.

"Tell me," he commanded. "Tell me that you need me."

He gripped her chin and forced her to look up at him, making her meet his gaze.

"I need you," she said, her voice soft.

"My name," he said. He didn't let her look away. "Say it."

"I don't…"

"Do not turn me into your soft boy fantasy. Do not close your eyes and imagine that you are with a man who doesn't even exist. You want *me*. All that time, you wanted me. Admit it, Sylvie. That boy would never entice you. If you were a virgin, it's because I was the one that you craved and you couldn't admit it to yourself."

"Why do you have to be like this?"

"You want me like this," he said, and he wasn't sure why it mattered. Only that it did. "You want me like this, Sylvie. Because I am the only one that you want. Tell me," he said. "Tell me that you want me."

"I wouldn't. I wouldn't if…"

"I am what you crave. You want the darkness. You want the difficulty."

He said it maybe because he hoped it was true, more than he could prove that it was. He said it, because he needed to believe it. Because he needed to believe that there was one thing, maybe only one thing about him that was redeemable in any way. A part of him that Sylvie wanted.

And why that should matter he could not say. Why it should be important he didn't know.

He felt like he was drowning with her. And he resented it, he also couldn't control it. So if he was going to feel this, if it was going to be this way, then he would have her surrender. He would have her admit it.

He would have his triumph.

"Tell me that you want me," he said, sliding his thumb over her bottom lip. "Or I'll leave."

Then she reached out, her hand cupping him, her thumb sliding over his hardened length. "You won't," she said. "You won't walk away because you want it too badly. You've broken one of the most important rules in business, Christos. You've shown your hand. Or rather your..." She looked down.

"Have it your way," he said, beginning to move away.

"Christos," she said, reaching out toward him, nearly reflexively.

"I knew it. I knew that you would not allow me to walk away from you. Because you are hungry for me. Now, tell me what I want to hear. Say my name, Sylvie. Say it. Say it in anger if you need to, but I will have you screaming it in pleasure later."

"I want you," she said, her gaze meeting his, her eyes filled with anger. "Christos."

He growled in triumph and walked her back toward the bed. The windows were open, the view of New York City pristine.

It was one-way glass, and no one could see in. But of course Sylvie wouldn't know that, and she cast a slightly worried glance toward the view.

"We didn't even see each other the first time," he said. "I would not be opposed to the entire city watching this time."

"I..."

But he could see the color mounting in her cheeks. She liked that idea. But he would not lie to her. "No one can see in."

Her eyes cast down just slightly. "Oh. But you quite liked the idea of being watched."

She tilted her chin upward. "Maybe I just like the idea of everyone knowing that ruthless Christos Onassis is not quite so hard when he's with me."

He lowered his head, pressed his forehead against hers. "Oh, I am very hard."

He enjoyed the satisfaction then of watching her light up like a beacon.

"You know what I mean."

"Tell me. Tell me exactly what you mean."

"You soften for me. Even if you didn't know it was me. We...we had real conversation those nights."

"What did they matter?"

He asked that question, mostly for himself. "This is what matters. This is what's real. Feelings, words that you can type into a phone, what does that matter?"

Yes. It didn't matter. He knew that. It wasn't real, and it never had been. A video game. That was what it had been.

"This," he said, leaning in and tracing her lower lip with the tip of his tongue. "This is what's real."

She shivered beneath his touch, and then he claimed her mouth again, harder, deeper.

And as he kissed her, his desire built, and as his desire built, he made a vow inside of himself. He would make her understand.

He would make her feel the same intensity that he did. He would make sure she knew that this was the only thing that mattered.

You're having a baby. She is your wife.

It didn't matter. He had married her for the baby. But quite apart from that there was...

This need. Desire. Everything else was an illusion. Their prior relationship was an illusion. But this...this was something he could hold. He could touch her. He could taste her. He could have her.

And so he claimed her mouth, over and over again. He

kissed down the tender side of her neck, made her shiver. Made her tremble.

"I didn't know you could be such a very good girl," he whispered.

He felt her quake. Not the same sort of shiver as before, but felt how close she was to orgasm with those words.

"Is that what you like? Do you like being told what a good girl you are? How you are perfection? Exactly what I want. Exactly what I need. Sylvie, you are the most glorious of creatures. I could not ask for more. I could not ask for better."

She buried her face in his neck, and he heard a muffled cry on her lips.

"Is that all it takes?"

She met his gaze. "You're a bastard, do you know that? How can you be so—"

"I might be a bastard. But I'm a bastard that you want."

She grabbed hold of his face, stretched up on her toes and kissed him. And she poured all of her frustration into it. And then when they parted, it was like when she looked at him she saw straight down into his soul.

"I want you," she said. "I have wanted you from before I really knew what it meant. And I was desperate to fantasize about a man who wasn't you. So desperate to feel something for the nice man who showed me compassion in my texts. But you're right. I always wanted you. I always wanted what you had. That ruthlessness. I always wanted to know what it would be like to feel it… For you to touch me. For your hands to be all over me. I always wondered."

He felt a shudder not unlike the one he had just felt in her body go through his own. How was she doing that? How was she zeroing in on his weakness? On his vulnerability.

This aching, desperate need to be…

To be wanted.

Even thinking it made him feel small. Weak. Ridiculous. And yet, he craved it so much he could not silence her. He couldn't tell her to stop. He wanted to hear it. Wanted to hear those words flowing endlessly from her lips.

That she had always wanted him. That there was something in him that she saw...

There is nothing in you.

He pushed that away, and he consumed her. Stripped her naked so that he could finally see her beautiful body.

She was glorious. More than he had ever imagined that she could be.

Her nipples, rosy and tight. Begging for his mouth.

Her curves a revelation.

That strawberry-gold thatch between her thighs, pushing his lust to extremes.

If he would've seen her that first night...

He would've walked away. This would never have happened.

He didn't believe in fate. He didn't believe that there was any larger, guiding force in the universe. If there were, life wouldn't be so brutal. Some people wouldn't be chosen to live, while others died. You chose. You either found the hardness inside of yourself to push through whatever life gave you, or you didn't.

But she made him want to believe. And something bigger. Because how was it possible that she was here, and they were having a baby?

He was having a baby.

Christos Onassis, a man whose heart had never beaten for anything half as soft as another human being, was going to be a father.

He gritted his teeth, pushed that thought away as he lowered his head and sucked one nipple deep into his mouth.

As he tortured her in the way that she had been torturing him.

Her words had nearly sent him to heaven. Or perhaps hell. It could've easily been hell.

He kissed his way down her body, brought his mouth between her legs and began to eat her.

He gripped her hips and looked up so that she could not pretend it wasn't him. And he was only all too aware that it was her.

"Christos…"

He growled. "Yes. My name."

"Christos," she cried out.

And he felt her come apart in his arms. Felt her reach her peak.

He kissed his way back up her body, lifted her up and set her on the bed.

She began to tear at his clothes. He relished this. This animalistic desire. He didn't think another woman had ever wanted him, not like this. Not in this personal way. This felt like it could only be about him.

And it was a high that he wanted to keep on chasing.

When she had him stripped completely bare, it was her turn to growl as she reversed their positions, bringing herself over the top of him, sitting astride his body as she moved her hands down his chest.

From his position lying on his back, he gazed up at her, looking his fill. At her round, generous breasts, her slim waist, her stomach. Which was now slightly rounded. With his child.

He moved his hands upward, spanning her waist, to the undersides of her breasts.

She arched her head backward, that red hair wild.

He had, on occasion, thought of her as unkempt. But he had been wrong.

She was fierce, ferocious and untamed. Everything he could ever want in a woman.

She would survive, he thought.

She would be the one who would live. Who would battle against all odds.

A warrior who would fight, just as he did.

She was his match.

He positioned her over him, guiding his hardened length into her body. She gasped as he slid in, inch by inch, and he gritted his teeth to stop himself from reaching his peak then and there. She was so tight. So perfect.

She began to move, her hips undulating as she found a rhythm that tormented them both.

And he felt...undone. Unraveled in a way he never had before.

Her nails dug into his shoulders, her mouth dropped open, a perfect circle as she made whimpering noises of pleasure.

It was like that night, but it was new.

It was a revelation.

Because it wasn't a confusing thing now, that it had been Sylvie all along. Of course it was.

Of course.

It had to be.

She began to tremble, her whole body shaking, and when she came, she squeezed around him, tight, and pushed him over the edge.

He gripped her hips, his fingers digging hard into her as he shouted out his pleasure.

And it was like he was floating. Not in the air, not on the sea. It was like he had entered another space and time.

Christos was always connected with his body.

With everything that was happening around him. He never had the luxury of losing himself, and in fact, had never believed that it was possible.

But for suspended moments of time, the only thing was her. The only thing was them.

They were in a space created entirely for them. It was safe. And it was perfect.

It was like she had cast some sort of spell around him, one of protection, or maybe just an enchantment, but he, who felt like he had seen everything, known everything, suddenly felt as if he had never known anything at all.

And when the moment subsided, when he was brought back to reality, he felt something cold and hard double down in his chest. Expand there.

This wasn't real. More than that, it wasn't sustainable.

He was living in some kind of fantasy world. Still.

Finding out who she was, seeing her, it had done nothing to bring him back to reality.

He was a fool.

Yes, she was his wife. But she was having his baby, and logic was of the utmost importance here.

Keeping his mind sharp, his instincts honed, was essential.

He pulled away from her, sitting on the edge of the bed, pushing his hands through his hair.

"Christos…"

He knew better than to let an adversary see him in weakness.

But she was not his adversary. Not exactly.

It was complicated. He did not quite know what to make of it. He did not quite know what to do with it.

"Come to dinner," he said, standing, finding his legs unsteady.

He would have to collect his clothes. They could not go to dinner naked.

He looked at her, and her glowing skin, her bright eyes. That unruly hair. He wished that they could go to dinner naked. And part of him wondered why people didn't. Why they didn't just do whatever they liked. Why they didn't simply follow their animal instincts.

Because it leads to dark places.

He had never minded the dark. That was the thing. He had been thrust into it against his will. And he had decided that he could make quite a happy home there.

"Are you all right?"

She moved as if she was going to touch him, and he pulled away.

"I am well," he said. "I need dinner."

"Do you get hangry, Christos?"

He frowned. The gentle teasing and her tone were…odd. It was the kind of thing she might have said to him over text before she knew who he was. But not as Sylvie. And not to him.

"No," he said. "But it is dinnertime."

"I don't know, I think that you seem a little bit hangry."

"I do not get…angry when I am hungry." He realized that his thunderous tone seemed to make that a lie. "I am used to going without food. I do not like it. I wouldn't choose it. But I spent a substantial part of my childhood hungry. If I did not learn how to adapt and cope with that, then I would be dead."

She looked stricken by that.

"What?" he asked.

"I didn't know that you were…that you went without."

"Did you assume that I came from money?"

"Most very rich people do. And honestly, there isn't a lot about your personal life online. I know. I've googled you."

"By design, there isn't a lot about me online."

He dressed quickly.

"You know, most people don't have control over that."

"I'm a ghost," he said. "Onassis isn't even my surname. I chose a new one."

"What?"

"Why would I keep my bastard of a father's last name? Why would I carry on his legacy? I won't. Our child, he will carry my name. And it will be my legacy. His. Not any of my ancestors before him. They will die out. As they deserve."

He realized that he had said more to her just now than he ever had to anyone. About his past. About his feelings. The way that she looked at him… Did she not realize he was not some soft child? Who got fractious when he didn't eat? He had been deprived of food and water for days at a time. He had been worked to exhaustion often.

He was not…he was not insubstantial, and he was not someone to be teased.

"Let's go eat," she said softly.

She was being nice to him, and he didn't like it. It had been nice a few moments before when they'd been having sex. He didn't find it necessary now.

It felt like his chest was being split in two, and he didn't like it.

When they walked into the dining room, dinner was set out in a glorious array.

"It is probably not at its optimum temperature," he said.

"Christos, I wish that you would talk to me. You've suddenly gone very formal and very stiff."

"This is just how I am. You're used to seeing me in business meetings."

"And in text messages. And in bed."

"It's different. It was different."

"Why was it different?"

"It just was," he said.

He sat down at the head of the table, and he began to dish himself some chicken and vegetables. "I must leave town tomorrow."

He hadn't realized that he was going to say that until the words came out of his mouth.

"You...you're leaving?"

"Yes," he said.

"Since when?"

"It has always been planned," he lied. Easily. Smoothly. "It just didn't come up today."

"I have... I have work to do."

"Yes," he said. "I wouldn't expect you to come with me."

He didn't want her to. He wanted to get away from her, away from this. As soon as possible.

"Well. You were telling the truth, then. We really won't see each other all that much."

"No."

She froze, her eyes making very purposeful contact with his. "I won't share you with other women."

He hadn't even thought about other women. Not one time. "I won't share you with other men."

"As long as we are agreed. If we are having sex, then there is no one else."

"Satisfactory."

"Thanks, Spock. I really appreciate it."

Spock. He did get that joke. He didn't think it was funny, though. Mostly because he didn't see that there was anything wrong with being logical. It made the world work a whole lot better than acting out of your own selfish interests. Than following your own feelings.

Isn't that what you're doing?

No. He was being logical. He was leaving because he needed distance. Because he needed to be...himself. She made him feel not himself, and it stood to reason that he ought to get some time on his own.

It didn't matter what she thought. It didn't matter...

He wasn't acting from feelings. He didn't do that. He wouldn't even know how.

You're a liar. You feel plenty.

Anger. Vengeance. Yes, that was true.

But anything else...

Joy. Maybe joy is what you felt upstairs.

"I may be gone for quite some time," he said.

"Well. I guess my life will go back to normal, then."

He smiled. "I suppose it will."

CHAPTER TEN

EXCEPT NOTHING FELT NORMAL. She missed him, which was the strangest thing. Rattling around his house, which had nothing personal in it, she missed him.

In a fit of rebellion, she began to decorate. Adding bright pops of color, ridiculous, decorative artwork. She made an eclectic wall with decorative plates and framed photographs of possums and raccoons. Frankly, she thought it looked amazing with pink decorative frames and the stark neutral palette of his penthouse. He would hate it. She didn't care. He wasn't here.

If she was going to be the one primarily living in the penthouse, then she should be the one who got to decide how it was decorated. Not that she got any real joy or satisfaction out of that.

She had spent so many years without him.

Except...he always felt like a factor.

And then, for a while there, she really had thought she loved him.

Don't you?

No. That didn't make any sense. She wasn't going to indulge that part of herself. That part of herself that really *wanted* to confuse sex and love. He was the first one to say that what had happened between them wasn't real. So why she couldn't fully grasp that...

She really couldn't understand.

She really, genuinely couldn't.

She worked. She threw herself into it. Things were strange around the office, the rumors about her and Christos were mostly true, that was the problem. She was married to him. She was having his baby.

A couple of the women that she considered herself work friends with cornered her at lunch one day.

"How did you not tell anybody that you were banging the guy who was trying to buy the company?"

"I…didn't know that I was."

"What?"

She really didn't see the point in lying about how they had gotten together, so she didn't.

"You honestly met a guy for sex that you had never seen. Not even one picture of."

"Not even one."

"What if you hadn't been attracted to him?"

She rolled her eyes. "Well, it was dark."

"I mean you would've known if it was—" Elizabeth held up her pinky finger and looked at it solemnly.

It took Sylvie a moment, but the moment she realized what her friend was saying, she nearly choked on her salad. "Well. Thankfully for all involved it wasn't."

"Good to know," she said.

She felt better after that lunch, and she vowed to make more time for actual friendships.

She had been hiding for way too long.

She also realized that she couldn't keep avoiding her mother.

Christos was interesting, because while people were interested in him in a mythic fashion, his personal life wasn't much talked about online.

There were no rumors about them.

Christos was the villain of the media industry, and he was really only mentioned in context with the obscene profits that he made or things that he did that other people saw as ruthless. But there was nothing about his personal life.

Of course, if she wasn't embroiled in his personal life, she would've been convinced that he didn't have one.

She did not invite her mother to lunch. She wasn't that foolish. Coffee, so her mother could have water with lemon or some other ridiculous beverage that would allow her to perform her hard-won thinness as Sylvie drank a breve.

But this way, it would be over quickly.

Her mother was late, and they sat out on the patio, all the better for her to have her photo taken, because while Christos didn't deal in that sort of publicity, her mother did.

"I just wanted to let you know," Sylvie said, "I got married."

Her mother was frozen for almost a full minute. It would've been funny, except it was actually disconcerting to see her mother shocked.

She always acted like she was unbothered and several steps ahead of Sylvie. Or that like anything Sylvie said was deeply uninteresting. She didn't manage it this time.

"Really?"

"Yes. Really." She took a deep breath. "Christos Onassis."

Her mother's blue eyes rounded in shock. "And you didn't have a wedding?"

"No," Sylvie said, somehow completely unsurprised that that was her mother's biggest concern.

"Sylvie, it would've been fantastic business for you."

"I don't really care about business, Mom. I'm trying to survive this very strange left turn that my life has taken."

"It is not a strange left turn to marry a billionaire. It's perhaps the smartest thing you've ever done."

"I'm pregnant."

And just then her mother looked delighted, and Sylvie was entirely certain it had nothing to do with finding out she was going to be a grandmother.

"Oh, Sylvie. You trapped him. You really are a very, very smart girl."

"I did not trap him," she said. "If anything, he trapped me. He demanded that I marry him. He held the publishing company hostage…"

"Sylvie," her mother said, scolding. "There's no other choice when it comes to a billionaire. You marry him. How is your prenup?"

"Expansive, don't worry. He's very thorough."

"I would imagine. There are rumors that he is completely ruthless."

She took a sip of her water and tried to smile. "All true."

"I'm so *proud* of you."

And Sylvie, who had never expected to hear those words, ever, felt her stomach turn over. Her mother was proud of her. For doing something that Sylvie had not done, not really. She thought that Sylvie had schemed and trapped herself a rich man.

She was proud of her because…she had unprotected sex. With the "right" man—meaning a rich one. She didn't care if Sylvie was happy, she didn't care if her marriage to Christos was good. She didn't even care, really, that she was going to be a grandmother.

Had Sylvie ever really wanted her mother to be proud of her? When the end result was this…

Nothing that she did really mattered. She hadn't understood that. Not before.

All of the good things she did. All of the hard work. It just didn't matter.

It just didn't. She was lonely. Her mother didn't care. She had been strong-armed, and all of this her mother didn't care about.

She cared about the publishing company, and she had done anything she could to save it, and it wasn't that her mother found clever at all.

"Why did you marry Dad?" Sylvie asked.

"I loved him," her mother said, simply.

Sylvie sat there and looked across the table at her mother. Her long blond hair was artfully styled into curls that were designed to seem effortless. Her makeup was natural. It made her glow, made her seem youthful. She wore deceptively simple cuts of very expensive fabric.

Her father had never been that. That effortless chic, that simple elegance. Not even close.

"You really loved him?"

"Yes, Sylvie."

"Then, why didn't you stay married to him?"

She looked down. "Because I realized that as much as I loved him, for me a certain lifestyle was more important. I loved it more. And he could never be what I wanted him to be, and it didn't seem fair to keep on living with the man, to keep on being disappointed with him when it wasn't actually his fault."

Sylvie didn't know what to say to that. It was bizarrely one of the more rational responses her mother could've ever given. And Sylvie hadn't expected rational. Sylvie didn't know what she had expected at all.

"So you loved him, but not more than…"

"Not more than this. Than traveling, having lunches."

"That seems shallow," Sylvie said.

Her mother looked down. "I understand that you think that, Sylvie. But I guess I've never understood why people insisted on struggling. Why keep toiling at that wretched publishing company when you could simply… You could have money. You could enjoy living. Life doesn't need to be an uphill battle."

"So you married richer men than my father, divorced them when they didn't make you happy—"

"And now I'm happy. With myself. And if you play your cards right, you can do the same with Christos Onassis. That's what I want for you."

"That's not what you want for me. You want me to be you. Maybe because you want to feel like the choices that you made were… That's it, isn't it? You want to feel like you mattered in raising me. You want me to look more like you. You want me to want to be like you. But I don't. I want to be like Dad. He made something out of that publishing company. He was there for me. He raised me. He influenced me. That's what I'm doing this for. And I'm going to have something to give to my child. It won't just be my husband's money. And I get it. Christos is rich enough that our child will always have a place to stay, a place to eat. But I… I'm going to give them something to care about. Something other than themselves. I think everyone needs that. Otherwise, I think you're just destined to never actually be all that happy."

Sylvie stood up. Maybe that wasn't fair. Her mom had been honest with her. What had she expected to hear? That she loved Sylvie more than anything? Her actions proved that she didn't.

There was no point being upset.

It was just hard not to be. Especially now that she was having her own baby.

Especially now that she had proven she would do anything for them.

Did you? Or did you do it for you? Are you really that different than your mother? It's just that you want the publishing house. And you want your baby to care about the publishing house.

She stopped then. "No," she said. "I'm not going to make my child care about the publishing house. They're going to be whoever they want to be. And I'm going to be proud of them. Whoever that is."

She didn't know if her mother really heard that. She didn't know if she really cared. But as Sylvie left the café, she felt something take root inside of her.

She was going to be better than her mother.

In a meaningful way. Not just by being the opposite. Not just by trying to show her child her work ethic and passion for her job. Because it was possible her child wouldn't feel those things. No. She was going to be different than her mother by loving the child she had. Not wishing for a different one altogether.

Right as she got back home her cell phone rang.

"Hi, this is Noelle, the nurse who was at your ultrasound."

"Oh, hi," Sylvie said. "I promise you I'm fine."

"I believe you. And I hope you're doing well."

"I am," she said, looking around the empty penthouse, and all the changes she'd made. She still felt a hollow place inside of her when she thought of Christos. "I am."

"The doctor was wondering if you wanted a follow-up ultrasound to determine the baby's gender."

"Oh. I... Yes. That would be great."

"We can come by tomorrow."

"Yes. That would be perfect."

After establishing a time she got off the phone with Noelle. And she stared at her phone. She hadn't heard from Christos at all. Not in nearly two months.

She pulled up a text bubble.

Kid: Getting an ultrasound to determine gender tomorrow. Do you want to know?

There was no response. She went into the kitchen and began to rifle around in the fridge.

Her phone buzzed.

Baby: Yes.

Kid: Should I wait for you to come back?

There was a pause.

Baby: No.

Kid: Are you ever coming back?

Baby: Of course I am. Do not be dramatic.

Kid: Oh, I'm sorry, is my two months long abandonment meant to feel normal?

Baby: You don't even like me.

Kid: Do you care?

Baby: I don't want you to be unhappy.

She stared at those words. She had a feeling that they were a large admission.

Kid: You said that you don't have any friends. Why is that? Because you're a very powerful man. And you're charismatic, and I have a feeling that you could command the attention of any room that you wanted to. I've seen you do it. So why don't you have friends?

Baby: An interesting question. Because I have found that it's better to live life without connection.

Kid: You said something to me when I told you about the baby. About how people can die of loneliness.

Staring at the phone, she went and sat down on his couch. It mirrored the times that they had talked before. But this time, she could picture him.

And she had the very sudden, visceral realization that the man she had been talking to all this time wasn't alive. He was Christos.

A part of him that he didn't seem to be able to show in person, but he was very real.

It made her feel a strange longing in her chest.

This was what she had been longing for over the past two months. This connection.

Today, talking to her mother, she had realized something about herself, and somehow, that had moved enough stuff out of the way for her to finally see this. Finally understand it.

She missed him.

It had been so awful, so shocking to find out that the man of her dreams was Christos, because some part of her had known it would only break her heart.

She wished she knew why.

Why it was so...intense with him? And why he was just so hard to reach?

Baby: My mother died when I was very young. It changed my entire life.

Kid: I'm sorry.

Baby: It changed my father. It turned him into something that I didn't recognize.

Kid: And you were lonely.

Baby: Yes. I learned that I could be entirely free of that feeling, of that suffering, if I simply expected to be alone.

Kid: That's awful.

Baby: It worked very well. For a while. What made you text me that first time?

She frowned.

Kid: I guess I'm like you. I spent a lot of time feeling apart. School was strange for me. I got sent to a boarding school because it was what my mother wanted. Something prestigious. But everybody there was raised in that life, and I wasn't. I was an odd one out. Then my father decided he wanted me to come home, so I changed schools and I had trouble making friends there too. It isn't that I have none, it's just that I've always felt like I was sitting somewhere in between two worlds.

Baby: That isn't really the same.

Kid: It's not, I guess. But I understand what you mean. That feeling that you could die of loneliness. I made the publishing company into something that I could love. But still, that night, when I decided to text to make sure the person whose phone it was could contact me... I guess I just wanted to reach out.

She paused for a moment.

Kid: Why did you respond?

His answer was slow to come.

Baby: I have spent a great many years coming to terms with my life. With who I am in this life. But there are nights, I believe they are called the dark nights of the soul? There are nights like that. Still very dark. And it seems like it won't end. It was one of those nights. I just wanted to reach out to somebody. But there was no one. I was lonely most of my life through no fault of my own. And now, I have fashioned for myself an entire life where I am lonely by design. And that is fine. Mostly. But then, there is a wave of despair and you want to reach out for a hand and you realize there is no hand.

Her throat went tight, tears pushed at the backs of her eyes.
This was the same man. The one that she had talked to. The one that she had connected with.
He was there. It had all made perfect sense before she had known that he was Christos.

And then, because of the way Christos presented himself to the world, because of what she assumed about Christos, she had thought that it would be impossible to love him.

She had thought that it would be impossible for this to be real because she assumed that the man she saw in all those meetings, the one she had seen at publishing parties over the years, he was what was real.

No. It was the man who wrote to her. That was the most real, deep part of him. But for some reason he felt desperate to hide it when he was with her.

Kid: Why did you leave after we slept together?

Baby: I had planned to leave.

Kid: That's a lie. I know it is.

Baby: I don't know what you make me feel. The words started to come in fast. I don't understand it. You ignited part of me before I had ever seen you. I cannot for the life of me understand what it is.

Kid: Human connection?

Baby: I never asked for it.

Kid: You did. When you texted me that first time, that's what you were asking for.

He hadn't known that it would become sexual. She had a feeling that he was even now trying to distance himself from it by telling himself that it had been. But she knew that it wasn't. She knew that what he'd said first, what he had said just now about loneliness. Isolation. Darkness, that was the truth. He had reached out for a hand, and she had taken it.

Baby: Well, I don't like it. I want to go back to before. I want to go back to who I was before.

Kid: Before you felt something?

Baby: I don't even know what to call it.

Love. That word burned at the center of her chest. Was it possible? Did she love Christos Onassis? Had she always? It would make sense. It would make sense that she loved Christos Onassis, because from the moment she had first seen him she had been enraptured by him. From the moment she had first met him, he had made her feel things that were great and terrible and conflicting. They hadn't been sexual, not initially, but over the years she had begun to recognize it as attraction.

And she had thought that the soft, emotional connection tempered by arousing virtual sex had been something entirely separate from Christos, but it hadn't been. Because nothing could ever be wholly separate from Christos.

She loved him.

He was the hard, complicated, difficult man that she had known for years. And he was this wounded, insightful, caring man who had texted her for six months, who had gotten her through the trauma that he was causing.

She laughed. Because she really had no choice.

Kid: I want you to come back for the ultrasound.

Baby: I have work.

He was retreating. He was retreating because he felt like he had to, and she wished that she understood why.

Baby: If I were there, I would kiss you.

Kid: No. You don't get to do that. We had virtual sex because we didn't know who each other was. But now we do. If you want that connection with me, then you need to be with me. You don't get to leave me alone. And you don't get to distract from a serious conversation by trying to engage me that way.

Baby: I thought wives were supposed to make a man happy.

Kid: You clearly haven't been paying attention to pop culture.

Baby: I already told you I didn't.

True. He had. She had asked him if he had ever seen a Christmas movie, and he'd said he hadn't. It was implied that he didn't watch much of anything.

Kid: Christos, I'm trying to reach a hand out.

Baby: I have work. And once I'm finished I will be back.

And she felt like she had been dismissed. She also felt like she didn't have to take this.
Christos had a private plane, she knew that. But it was probably where he was.

Of course, there were whole Reddit threads devoted to following the private jets of the wealthy. And with a quick search, she found tracking on Christos's.

She laughed. He was in London. Great. Easy. He had offices there. She was sure that he had a residence nearby. And then she realized, she was his wife.

She contacted his personal assistant at his office in New York. "I want to go see my husband. Can we arrange a flight?"

She had that done within minutes. And then she contacted Noelle, her nurse and ally.

"Would you be interested in doing the ultrasound in London?"

CHAPTER ELEVEN

CHRISTOS COULDN'T STOP THINKING about the conversation he'd had with Sylvie last night. And he was trying to focus on a new acquisition. Which he could have done from anywhere in the world, but he was doing it from London.

Coward.

He saw it in his head like a text bubble from Sylvie.

He growled. She didn't know anything.

Because you won't tell me.

Another text bubble in his mind.

He loosened his tie as he walked into his London penthouse. And was shocked to see Sylvie standing at the center of the room, her hand resting on her stomach. It took him thirty seconds to notice that the doctor and the nurse were present as well.

"I brought the ultrasound to you," she said.

"I told you—"

"You tell me a lot of things. You told me that we were getting married. You told me that I had to get a DNA test for the baby. You told me that I had to get an ultrasound to determine whether or not the pregnancy was viable. And now I'm telling you that I want you at this ultrasound to see our child. I don't want to report back to you. I don't want you to distance yourself."

"I'm not distancing myself," he said. That would imply that he had any hope of being close even if he wanted to be.

Sylvie made direct eye contact with him and lay down on the table, lifting up her top and rolling down her pants.

"What happened to not wanting me to see?"

"That ship has sailed. Even if it's been a while."

It had been a while. He did his best not to let his eyes wander over her curves. Over all the changes that had taken place in her body. Her fuller breasts, her rounded stomach. He did his best not to stare at her. But it was nearly impossible. She was so beautiful. Had she always been?

She reminded him of a forest nymph. Her hair was wild, and she looked almost sinfully beautiful with her rounded pregnancy curves.

Or maybe it was the defiance. Maybe that was the biggest thing that grabbed hold of him and held him steady. That kept him in thrall.

She had shown up here when he had refused to come to her.

When had something like that ever happened? The only time a person had ever come to find him it had been to beg for something from him. But she wasn't doing that. She was making him bear witness. To this. To this thing that they were in together. The thing that he had been trying to deny.

The ultrasound tech squirted gel onto her stomach and began the process. The heartbeat was strong in the room. And he felt it echoing inside of him. Beating almost in rhythm with his own.

His child. A son or a daughter that had been created in the center of his passion with Sylvie.

He felt like he couldn't breathe.

And yet that heart beat on. Like it was his own.

He looked at Sylvie, trying to determine if she felt the same thing. He saw tears shimmering in her eyes.

And then she smiled. "This is what I was waiting for. This is what I was waiting to feel. I'm so… I'm so happy."

A tear spilled down her cheek, and right then he felt like a boy with his nose pressed up against the glass window, something uncompromising separating him from being entirely in this moment.

What exactly did she feel? How did he find a way to feel it too?

And at the same time, he wanted to turn and run away from it. He wanted to get on his plane again and fly somewhere else. He didn't want to stand there witnessing it, watching it. He would've preferred that she texted to him.

He would've preferred that he could have some distance. *Distance*.

That word again.

His whole life was distance.

But Sylvie wasn't allowing him to maintain it.

"What has kept you from feeling it?" he asked, his throat so tight the words were nearly strangled.

"It's been overwhelming. I was grappling with the idea that the person that I thought you were didn't exist. He does, though."

He had no idea what that meant. He had no idea what it meant, and he felt as if he had been stabbed clean through the chest.

But he wasn't going to ask. Not there in front of the doctor. Not there in front of that nurse that hated him. Openly. She was glaring at him even now.

"It's a boy," the doctor said.

A son. He was having a son.

And he had an instant, visceral image of himself as a

small boy. Looking up at his father. And his father staring back down at him with eyes black as coal. Nothing behind them.

And then he saw himself again, sitting in his office chair, and staring down at his father, now a withered old man. Prostrate on his knees begging for the kind of mercy that had never been shown to Christos.

"And now you know how it feels to be powerless."

Panic raged through him. Like all the years of fear he hadn't allowed himself to feel had suddenly come to rest on his shoulders.

He didn't know what to do. He didn't know who he was. He didn't know how to be a father.

He didn't even know how to be a son. He knew how to cause pain. He knew how to win.

He knew how to destroy.

How was he supposed to raise a child? How was he supposed to find tenderness in his hands? In his heart.

He couldn't breathe.

The room was tilting sideways, and he had no idea what was happening to him. "I think I'm having a heart attack," he said.

Sylvie pushed herself up off the bed. The doctor looked over at him. But it was the nurse who crossed the room and put a stethoscope on his chest.

"You're having a panic attack," she said.

"I am not," he said, wrenching his tie free, and tearing the top two buttons off his shirt. "I've never panicked in my life."

"You're panicking now," she said.

Sylvie sat up, pushing her shirt down in place and swinging her legs off of the table. "Christos, what's wrong?"

"Nothing," he growled. "Except maybe I can get an EKG, since I might be dying."

Sylvie looked at the nurse. "He's not dying, is he?"

"We can always double-check. But in my experience men like him live regrettably long lives."

Sylvie ignored the poisonous words, but they hit Christos squarely as intended. *Men like him.*

She knew that he was a bad man. That was why she hated him.

She had seen the way that he had treated Sylvie. And for that reason, she held him in disdain.

Perhaps he should have disdain for himself.

And he was going to be a father.

"You're not the first man to have a total and complete freak-out because you're having a son," she said. "But it's preferable to the men who break things because they're having a daughter and they're just angry that it isn't a son to carry on their family name."

Family name.

He didn't even have a family name. He had a name he had chosen for himself. A name that had come to mean… What? It was synonymous now with the ruthless way that he conducted business.

With his media empire. But what did it really mean? Would his son want to burn his name to the ground too? Just as Christos had done?

"Thank you," she said. "You can take the private plane back whenever you want. And in the meantime, you can enjoy the city."

His breathing seemed to be calming down, and he was outraged because it meant that perhaps the angry nurse was correct.

He had panicked.

An overflow of an emotion he had never allowed himself to feel. He didn't know what to make of that. He didn't understand it.

"I didn't expect to find you here," he said to Sylvie.

"I understand that," she said. "Is that why… Is that why this is so…"

"Nothing is too much for me," he said. "I have seen terrible things, Sylvie, and I have never once felt anything like that. If I die in my sleep it is on your head."

He walked away from her, moving into the kitchen so that he could pour himself some whiskey. He knew that she couldn't have a drink. He didn't care.

He braced his hands on the counter and looked down. He held himself there like that, trying to find himself. His breath.

Who he was.

"Christos, if you don't tell me what's going on, then I can't help you."

"What makes you think you can help me? You weren't there. Not for any other part of my life before this. You never have been. What makes you think that you could do something for me? We are having a son."

"Yes. We are. Does that make you happy?"

"I don't know how to be a father. How will I…"

And he realized exactly the abyss he was staring into. The horrible realization that the last thing he wanted was to raise a child who might turn out like him.

He was his own nightmare.

He was the monster in the shadows. Not his father. Not any of the men who had abused and mistreated him during his years as a trafficked laborer.

He had become the darkness.

And he couldn't bear the idea of a boy modeling himself

after him. Of him becoming the man that a woman like that nurse would look at with disdain.

The world could not contain more men like him. Because he was…

"I'm not a good man, Sylvie."

"That isn't true."

"Would you want our child to be like me?"

She looked at him for a long moment, and then she stepped forward, put her hand on his face. "I don't want our child to be traumatized. And I have a very strong feeling that whatever this is, whatever you are, it's connected to something that happened to you."

"How do I raise him? I need you," he said. "You were right. I am the dysfunctional parent. I-I can offer him nothing but money. Nothing."

"You can love him, Christos. I went and saw my mother. And she said that she was proud of me for getting pregnant with your baby. She thinks that I trapped you."

"That's ridiculous."

"I know. But it hit me then that my mother just doesn't understand me. She will never be proud of me. Not of who I am. Because nothing that I am means anything to her. She doesn't care about the same things I care about. She doesn't want the same things that I want. I'm not good enough for her because we just…we exist in two totally different spheres. And she doesn't know how to care about someone who doesn't reinforce her own values. If she could have just loved me, that would've changed a lot of things for me. I didn't need her to be a perfect example. I just needed her to…care."

"What if I don't even know how to do that?"

"If you didn't care you wouldn't have reacted that way."

"I still think it might've been a medical event."

"I don't think it was."

"You don't know that."

She looked around, her expression tacitly unconcerned. As if she didn't believe at all he was on the verge of death. "I hope you have a place for me to sleep here."

He frowned. "Are you staying?"

"Well, I'm certainly not flying back to New York tonight."

She stared up at him, and she had that look on her face. She was being particularly stubborn. He found himself wanting to lean toward her. He found himself wanting to get closer.

And so he took a step away.

"It's okay. I'll manage to find a room myself."

"Don't be ridiculous," he said. But he didn't move.

So she leaned in. She closed the distance between them. And she kissed him on the mouth.

CHAPTER TWELVE

Sylvie was drowning in him.

Maybe she shouldn't kiss him. Maybe she should punish him for the way that he had treated her for the last two months. He had abandoned her. Perhaps she should be angry. Perhaps she should hold it against him. Perhaps she should be spiteful and vindictive and make him miserable for the way he had treated her.

But the way that he had looked when they had found out they were having a son...

It made her want to cry.

He was terrified. And she kept reminding herself that he was the man she had been texting all those months.

He was.

Christos was hurting. He was broken.

He had revealed a little bit more to himself before she had decided to come. Before she had decided that she had to be the one to come for him, and today, even without him giving details about his life, she had learned more about him by watching his response to finding out he was having a boy.

He didn't think he was a good man.

He wasn't arrogant, not really. He didn't like himself.

I like you.

She poured that truth into the kiss. It was a sweeter kiss than any they had shared before.

It didn't have the same desperation.

And yet it was still intense.

Maybe even more so for it.

She angled her head, deepening the connection.

She bracketed his face with her hands, pulled him down to her as she parted her lips for him. As she encouraged him to take it deep. To slide his tongue against hers. She had missed him. She had missed him so much.

I love you.

She liked him. She loved him.

Because of all the things that he had told her about himself. Because of the way he had been there for her before.

She had to find a way to let that man escape. To break him out from behind the brick wall.

It isn't that simple. Because the fact is that he's both.

That stark truth made her feel out of her depth. Why had she realized that before she had gotten on a plane?

Because yes. That man who had connected with her was real. But so was this one. Equally. The one that had had a panic attack when he'd found out he was having a boy. The one that had no idea what to do with the strength of those emotions. With the fear and self-loathing that coursed through him. The one that didn't even know what to call a longing for connection. The one that didn't know what to call what he felt for her.

He was real. And he was damaged.

And she had to find a way to reach him. She had to.

Because she had spent a lot of years lonely. She had never known real connection until he had answered her text.

It had to be something they could bring into the real world. It had to be something they could create here. She was desperate for it. Not just because he was the father of her child. Because he gave her something. Because he completed something inside of her. Because he was the first person that she wanted to talk to when she woke up and the last person she wanted to talk to when she went to bed. Because it was that way, and it had been for almost a year now.

Because she had been devastated when they'd slept together, and he had cut off contact.

Because she had felt like the sun had finally come out from behind the clouds when she had started to talk to him in the first place.

Because he had changed her life. Completely and fundamentally.

She wanted to change his. She wanted to do something big enough, meaningful enough, that it would make him into someone better. Because her relationship with him had taught her something. She had learned that she needed to reach out to people. That she needed more connections.

She had found a way to talk out some of her more complicated feelings.

And she had learned that she was far more interested in sex and sensuality than she thought before. He helped her explore, and even though anyone reading the transcript of their encounters might find them cringe or embarrassing, she had learned new things about herself.

What had she done for him?

She wanted to give him what he needed. The sad thing was, she simply didn't know.

And she couldn't figure out how to learn.

So she kissed him. Because she knew how to do that. Because she knew how to connect with him here.

"I'm here," she said. "I'm kissing you. Because I'm here." She put her hand to his chest, she felt his heart beating hard.

Like it was going to beat right out of his chest.

"I'm here," she repeated.

He growled and backed her up against the wall. Flattening her against the hard surface. He moved his palms up her forearms, pinned her hands flat against the wall, held her fast. He poured his own desperation into the kiss, and she swallowed it down.

She began to finish the work he had started, taking his shirt off. Oh, how she loved the look of his body. How she loved touching him.

He was here. He was real. This was real. She moved her hands down his muscular chest, his stomach. She undid his belt with shaking fingers. And then she pushed his pants down his lean hips, exposing his length to her hungry gaze.

She curled her fingers around him. They had talked about this. She had promised to do this to him.

And now he was in front of her. She could see him.

She could finally take exactly what she wanted. She sank down to her knees in front of him. And she leaned in, darting her tongue out, slicking it over his arousal.

Then she took him into her mouth, looking up at him as she did. As he had done to her the last time they were together.

Watch me. Watch me give this to you.

It was like he heard her, because he was watching. Because he was giving himself over to this, and never taking his eyes off her.

She swallowed him down, luxuriated in the taste of him. The feel of him. She moved her hand down between her thighs and began to stroke herself as she continued to pleasure him.

His hand went back to grip her hair, and he pulled hard, drawing her head away. "Careful," he said.

"Are you afraid to lose control?"

"You don't want me to lose control."

She lowered her head again and took him in deep, keeping her eyes locked on his.

He growled, but he didn't pull her away again. She kept on pleasuring him. Pushing him until he was shaking.

And when she finally pushed him over that edge, she swallowed him down.

He was breathing raggedly. He pulled her to her feet. "You are...extraordinary."

He looked truly undone. He looked truly at a loss. And she relished that.

Because he was at a loss for her. Because he was undone for her.

He picked her up, cradling her in his arms.

"I'm too heavy," she said, even as he made a mockery of the statement by carrying her easily out of the room.

She clung to him. And he brought her into the bedroom, laying her down on the bed.

"Surely you can't do anything yet."

He growled again, completely feral now, and he stripped her of her shirt. Her bra. Her panties. Everything.

Then he forced her thighs apart and lowered his head between her thighs. She wrapped her arm around the back of his head, pushing her fingers through his hair as he pleasured her.

As he took her to the heights, he brought her crashing back down. He tortured her, over and over again. But this time she could see him. It was like that first night, but now she knew who it was.

Now she really knew what it meant to love him. With all of his difficulties. With all of his hard angles and lines.

But the inconvenient truth was that the man who had captured her body and soul was Christos Onassis.

She didn't know the details about who he was. She didn't

have his entire life story. But she knew that she loved him. And that they had time to get to know each other. That she had time to help him change. He was her husband.

It was that thought that pushed her over the edge.

Breathing hard, he moved up and kissed her on the mouth. Turning her onto her side, with her rear pressed snugly against him. She could feel that he was hard again. He positioned himself at her slick entrance and entered her from behind, holding her with his arm wrapped around her midsection, his hand on her belly as he moved inside of her. Deep and sure.

She began to tremble. She began to shake apart.

He took her slowly. Thoroughly. Until they were both out of breath. Until they were both at the end of themselves.

And when it was done, she lay with him, listening to his harsh breath in her ear.

She could feel him withdraw. She could feel him putting distance between them.

She reached out and grabbed his arm. "Don't."

But he got up anyway. He left. And she realized that he had carried her into a room she could stay in, not into his.

She lay there, staring at the ceiling, tears sliding down her cheek.

She didn't know what she was going to do with that man.

But she did know that she loved him.

She didn't know if there was anything to learn from her parents' marriage. From the mistakes they had made. Her father in marrying a woman who was never going to love him as much she loved herself. And her mother in not being able to recognize who she was.

Were they the same? Had she fallen in love with a man who could never love her back with the same intensity?

No. Christos had intensity.

It was real. In fact, it was so terrifying that he couldn't face it. That was the real issue. It wasn't that he felt nothing. It was that he felt everything.

She had chased him down. She had come here. And she wasn't going to stop.

She picked her phone up.

Kid: I wish you would talk to me.

She wasn't sure if he would respond. Her heart beat in her throat while she waited.

Baby: I don't know how.

Kid: Only because you never talked to anybody. You already told me you don't have any friends. You don't have any practice with it. Maybe that's what this has been all along. Let's practice. You can tell me. Anything.

She wondered if she'd pushed him too hard. If she'd overplayed her hand.

Baby: I've never told my story to anyone.

Kid: It's important. If it's what you think is going to stand between you and your own child, then it's important.

If it's what you think is going to stand between you and me. She didn't type that.

Baby: I told you when my mother died everything fell apart. It was worse than you can imagine. When my mother died my father lost himself entirely. He fell into a gambling addiction. He was drinking. He was deeply in debt, and he could not care for me. He heard about a man buying boys.

Her hand came up to her mouth. And she watched in horror as he continued to type.

Baby: For hard labor. They took us to different places, had us work in fields, in factories. The factories were the worst. Hot and inhumane. People died. Children. Working long hours. And there was no one to ask after them. No one to investigate their deaths. I don't even know where their bodies went. But not me. I didn't let it kill me. I didn't let the long hours kill me.

There was a long pause.

Baby: I didn't let the loneliness kill me.

A sob rose in her chest, and holding her phone close, she got out of the bed. She walked out of her bedroom. She wasn't dressed. She didn't care. She walked through the halls. She didn't know where anything was in this house. She pushed open one door and found an empty room. Then another.

When she arrived at the end of the hall, she saw light filtering beneath that last door.

She opened it, and there he was, sitting in a chair by the fireplace. "Christos," she said.

He turned to look at her, his eyes hollow.

"I wanted to be near you," she said. "We can talk in person."

"I don't know how to talk about this," he said.

"You've been through a really terrible thing."

"It was a long time ago. I survived it. But it did change me. And I don't think there's any way to change back. Even if I wanted to."

"I think you do want to. Otherwise none of this would have affected you the way that it did."

She moved to where he was sitting, and she slid onto his lap. He was fully dressed now. She was still naked. She looped her arms around his neck, and she made eye contact with him. "Why do you think you can't change?"

"Because I know how dark it made me. I know it."

"How? You keep saying things like that. You won't explain it."

He closed his eyes and let his head fall back against the chair. "I'm sorry. I'm sorry but I don't know how to talk about it. I'm sorry, but I don't know how to do this. I don't know how. I can't even remember what it was like to love my mother. I don't remember her at all. I wasn't a small child. I was eleven when she died. I don't remember her. I don't remember before."

Her heart ached for him. He was so painfully sad.

"I had to get rid of every shred of pity inside of me. Because if I stopped and worried about the other boys… They were going to die anyway. I couldn't stop. If you stop, then you could get beaten. If you got beaten you are at a greater risk."

"How did you escape?" she asked.

"It was like gladiators. In the arena." He was silent for a long moment. "It was a particularly hot day. The machinery in the factory was loud. There was dust in the air. The door was left open. And I decided that I was going to run. I knew exactly where guards were stationed. Mostly, there weren't guards. Because at that point, they assumed that we were all broken. But not me. Because I didn't let it. I let it make me hard instead. And so when the boss came through, I attacked him. We fought, and he wrapped his hands around my throat."

He cleared his throat, his eyes intent on the amber liquid in his glass. "I pushed him. Into the equipment. I could hear him screaming as I ran, I didn't pause to look back. He might've died, so be it. You should know that. Because there were conveyor belts and gears, and many boys were lost to the cruelty of that machinery. So if he did... I want you to know that I'm not sorry."

She nodded, her throat feeling tight.

"Then I ran. Into nothing. The factory was in the middle of nowhere. It was in the Midwest. There was nothing, and nowhere to hide, for miles. I crawled on my belly until I was sure no one was coming after me. I ran as much as I could in the dark. At night. Finally, I found a town. I was able to get enough money washing dishes to buy a bus ticket. I ended up going to New York. I was seventeen."

"Christos..."

"I saved money. And saved it. I ended up investing in an app for short-form videos very early. We made a lot of money. I began to look for other media to put money into. Eventually it became RedMedia. And I would love to tell you that I didn't care what I did as long as it made money. As long as it allowed me to win. But the truth is I found something magical in it. In movies. TV shows. News. We were cut off from everything for so long. Knowledge is power. Whether it comes in the form of stories or headlines. I know because I was deprived of that knowledge for a very long time. It's part of killing your spirit. If there are no books for you to read, nothing for you to watch, your soul begins to get dry. They count on that. They wanted it." He nodded.

"I used it. But I've always been glad to make the thing that I feel counteracts it."

She moved her hands over his back. Soothing. Holding him.

"I don't think your soul is dry."

"How can you say that? After everything I've done to you?"

"Well, you need to learn how to use your soul, sometimes. But I have no doubt that it's there."

"What if I never learn to use it?"

"I think you want to. And I think that matters. I think it might matter most of all."

"How would you know?" He wasn't actually being rude. He was really asking.

"I suppose I don't know for sure. I don't know anything about this. I feel like you didn't totally believe me, but you're the only lover that I've ever had. So I can't say for sure whether or not we are on the right track. Whether or not this will work. I don't have experience to draw from."

"I've never been in a relationship. I've had sex. Obviously. But it's never meant anything. No one has ever stayed with me. No one has ever come for me. I used to dream about my father realizing that he had done the wrong thing by selling me. I used to dream of him coming to find me. Saying that he loved me. Saying he was going to take me away from it." He got a faraway look in his eye.

And she felt a tear roll down her cheek.

"I'm so sorry. I'm so sorry that you were failed by the person who should've taken care of you."

"It's okay. I need you to hear the rest of this. Because I need you to understand who I am. I need you to understand… My father did come for me. Five years ago. He came to me because he was destitute. His gambling debts sky-high. Selling his son didn't pay his bills for very long. I don't know what else he'd done in the intervening years to try and feed his habits. I don't care. But he recognized me. When I achieved my success. He came all the way from Greece to throw himself at my mercy. Like I was a king. Like I was a god."

"And what happened?"

"I made him beg. I made him weep. And then I gave him his money, and I sent him away. But only after I got to watch him wiggle and struggle like a mouse in a trap. Only after I got to enjoy exerting the power I had over him. Only then."

She heard it then. The hardness. The ice. "I don't want my son to look at me that way. I don't want him to be like me."

"We will never let our child suffer the way that you did. We can start there."

She felt a sharp, stark pain in her chest, and she didn't know what to do with it. There was a coldness in him that was frightening. But she didn't believe that he would ever hurt their child. She also wanted to believe—so badly—that she was going to be able to reach him. That she was going to be able to connect with him. But it was terrifying. Terrifying to believe that she might not.

Maybe he was right. Maybe everything that had happened to him had made him into something other than a man. A gladiator. One that was still fighting for his life every single day.

Maybe there was no coming back from that.

She shook her head and buried her face in his neck. She didn't want to live in that world. Where a boy could be sold into hard labor to pay his father's debts and not be able to come back from it. Where he would pay for the sins of his father over and over again for the rest of his life. Where he would pay more than his father ever would.

She couldn't believe it. Because she was having a child with this man.

"You do care about things," she whispered.

"Not the right ones."

"But you do care. It's not all ice. Or you wouldn't have enjoyed that."

She clung to that. It was, oddly, something that gave her hope.

"But I was able to give you the publishing company back because I simply didn't care about it. Do you know, you must learn to hold the thing tightly. And as far as I can tell, loving someone is the act of hanging on to them so nothing can ever tear them from you. I… I don't even think I would want to do that if I could."

"But what about our child?"

He looked absolutely filled with sorrow. "I don't know. I don't know how I'm ever going to… I don't know how I'm ever going to be the right thing for him."

"We have to try. Both of us. I didn't go through what you did. Being hurt by my parents, it wasn't the same as the way you were hurt by your father. My father didn't mean to hurt me. But he loved the publishing company so much, and he made it very clear that the way to his heart was through the company. Through my interest in it. Not in a bad way. It was just what he loved to talk about. It was what he loved most of all, and I could never compete with it. And then there was my mother. Her preoccupation with herself. I have a career that I love, and I have to make sure that I don't put it before our child. Maybe we can just both learn."

"The things that you want to learn are good things. It will certainly make our child happier. But you would never destroy him."

"Neither will you."

She rested her hand flat on his chest. "Trust yourself."

"The problem is that I know myself."

"Come to bed with me."

"Sylvie, I—"

"Come to bed with me, Christos. Spend the night with me. If we're going to try this, then we need to. You can't stay hiding away from me. You can't hide away from your child. You can't run when it gets hard. You can't revert to texting me like a teenager when it's hard to talk."

She felt him nod nearly imperceptibly.

Then she stood up from his lap and held out her hand. She led him back to the bedroom, and then it was her turn to hold him. Until his breathing began to deepen. Until it became even.

And once she was certain he was asleep she brushed her lips over his temple. Then she buried her face in her pillow and she wept.

For the boy he had been. And for the man he had become.

No one had ever loved Christos, and it wasn't fair.

She wanted to love him. With the ferocity he should've always had love, but it was terrifying. Because she might end up in love alone.

People die of loneliness.

She clung to him.

Until her breathing matched his.

CHAPTER THIRTEEN

WHEN CHRISTOS WOKE UP in the morning, he was holding Sylvie. And then the previous day came flooding back to him. The panic attack. The sex. His text confessional, and then their conversation in his study.

But she was still there. Lying next to him.

She wasn't gone. She had come after him.

Her eyes fluttered open, and she looked at him. "Don't get out of bed," she said.

"Maybe I want coffee."

"You look like you're ready to run away," she said, far too cheerfully.

He scowled. "I'm not."

"I think we should watch Christmas movies."

He deepened the scowl. "It isn't Christmas."

"You said you've never seen them."

His chest ached. "I lied. Let's get coffee."

"Wait a second," she said, grabbing hold of his arm. He let her hold onto him, lifted her up out of the bed as he stood. She squealed and ended up clinging to him, her arms around his bicep, her legs curling up around his calf.

He gazed down at her, a strange sort of wonder filling his chest. Was this…intimacy? This sort of playful activity when two people were naked. Her looking up at him like there was something special about him. Like there was something good in him.

"You have to explain your life," she said, still hanging onto him as he began to walk out of the room.

"No, I don't."

"You do."

"It's not interesting."

"I think you're fascinating."

He looked down at her, pushed her hair out of her face and bent down, kissing her lightly on the mouth. "You are a fool."

She wrinkled her nose. "I already know that."

He bent down and plucked her up from where she clung to him, held her to his chest, carrying her down the stairs and into the kitchen, where he set her down on a barstool as he went to make coffee. She squeaked. "That's cold."

"You should have thought of that before you picked a fight while you were naked."

She didn't seem at all embarrassed to be naked in front of him. That felt like progress of a kind. He just wasn't sure exactly what the progress was.

He didn't have a name for it.

"Why did you lie about Christmas movies?" She tented her fingers in front of her face.

"Because it's sad. Like everything else. I watched a few. I told you... When I got away, I became quite obsessed with media. The Internet. Smartphones. Movies. TV. And Christmas movies... They're such an interesting lie, I find. This massive cultural delusion that everyone engages in once a year. The people around you are stressed and angry about the additional work, and there's this propaganda machine saying that Christmas is happy. But it's about family."

She propped her chin up on her elbows and stared at him while he touched the button on his automatic espresso machine to make a double shot for an Americano.

"I don't know. I always find that the best Christmas movies have a little bit of darkness to them. I think *It's a Wonderful Life*, for example, is really all about how difficult that time of year can be. But it's family that kind of pulls you back from the brink."

"Maybe I never understood because my family was never that for me." He swallowed hard. "Watching families…"

She nodded. "I get that. So many sweet, nurturing mother characters. And plenty of workaholic father characters which, frankly, did resemble my father a little bit, though he was always much nicer when he was around than those men were ever portrayed as. But I didn't have that nurturing other parent as a counterbalance. I loved my father, don't get me wrong. But you know, since I'm about to have a child of my own I've been thinking a lot about what I want to do differently."

He poured his espresso shot into a mug, and then turned to his hot water and added some to the coffee. "The worst part is that I liked them. The worst part is that I knew they weren't true. Not in any capacity. But still. When I watched them I would almost feel something."

She was looking at him like he was sad again.

"Let's watch Christmas movies," she said. "Because we're having a family. Because there is nothing stopping us from having beautiful Christmases, Christos. If we both want our family to look different than the ones that raised us, it can."

"Can it? I'm…*me*. You love Jones & Abbott, which is fine, but…"

"I've already been thinking about that. I love my job. I don't think being a mother requires that I lose an integral part of myself. I'll always be a happier person if I'm able to spend time on the things that I'm passionate about. But I don't need to make the publisher my child's life too. And I don't need for them to be a certain thing, or to be a certain way. And I think the major thing is that over the last few months I've realized that when you have a family it brings balance to your life. Because the publisher felt like my baby. It felt like if something happened to it then my life would be over. But now it feels like my life is bigger. That's only a good thing. I can care about more than one thing. I've been working on that, actually."

"Tell me about that."

He passed her the coffee he had made. And began to make another.

"Cream?" she asked.

He opened the fridge and took out a carton of half-and-half, then set it on the counter in front of her. She put in a generous amount and handed it back to him.

"I started trying to make more friends at work. I told them the real story of what happened between us."

"You actually told them about our text relationship?"

"Yes. And the anonymous in-the-dark sex."

"I'm not sure that I want friends if that's what it entails."

She waved a hand. "Don't worry. I spoke of you in flattering terms."

"Is it flattering if they're true?" he asked.

He was not insecure when it came to sex. Especially not the sex between the two of them. It was the only place he was certain he did everything right.

She laughed, while he finished making himself an Americano.

"Let's go back to bed," she said.

"Go back to bed?"

"Yes. I think that we should lie in bed and watch Christmas movies today."

"I don't do leisure time."

"I know. But I think you should. We're having a baby together. We got married. And I don't think it's reasonable to think that the two of us aren't going to have a relationship."

He realized that what she was saying was true. He just wasn't entirely certain about what to do with it.

"Agreed."

"And that means we're going to have to practice this. Being in a relationship. So that we can practice being a family."

Family.

Again, it was something that threatened to overtake the frozen feeling in his chest.

"Okay. I will try leisure time."

Which was exactly what they did. They went back to bed and played Christmas movies back to back. He watched her cry at each and every one.

He couldn't remember ever being so close to human emotion.

To another person feeling things so deeply.

It did things to him. But then, everything about her did.

Everything about her ignited something inside of him.

He wasn't used to burning. Not like this.

But if there was one thing he recognized about his response to finding out he was having a son it was that he needed to change.

And he had a feeling the only way he was going to accomplish that was silly.

For the first time in his life he was going to have to trust another person.

He couldn't use his phone. He couldn't distance himself in any way.

Sylvie was his wife.

And in order to create the right kind of life for his child, he was going to have to figure out what that meant.

CHAPTER FOURTEEN

THEY SPENT A week in London, and then they went back to New York. When they walked in, Christos had an expression of naked shock on his handsome face.

"You have hung raccoons on my wall."

She laughed. Because she had genuinely forgotten that he didn't know about that. "They aren't all raccoons. That's a possum."

"You say that as if it makes it better."

"Well, I thought it was stark. It needs a little bit of whimsy."

He looked at her, his expression stormy. "I disagree."

"I don't care."

She stretched up on her toes and kissed him on the lips, and he softened.

She loved him so much. She knew that he wasn't in a space to hear about how much she loved him. But that was okay. She didn't need him to hear about it. Not just yet. They were learning what it meant to be together. Marrying together the years that they had known each other, getting rid of some of the assumptions they had made. Engaging with some of the assumptions that turned out to be true.

Sifting through the relationship they'd had virtually, and figuring out what it looked like to be together in real life.

Also, they were expecting a child.

It was a lot.

She didn't need to push him. Not anymore than everything in life was already doing it.

They went to work and talked about their jobs at the end of the day over dinner.

On the weekends, she made him go grocery shopping with her.

"I have a service for this," he said, adjusting a black baseball cap on his head.

He was doing a sort of low-key, incognito thing. Which she thought was hilarious because a six-foot-four stunningly attractive Greek man was never going to be as undercover as he might like to be.

She thought shopping with him was hilarious, too.

"I admit," he said, pushing a cart through the produce section, "I have not actually gone to look at food and grocery stores myself since I could afford to buy it. It makes me consider what I might actually want."

"Food is supposed to be enjoyable."

"It's for survival."

"Christos," she said, moving around to the front of the cart and stopping it. "You're allowed to just enjoy things. You're allowed to like things. And to do them just because they bring you pleasure." She looked left and right. "You know, things other than sex."

He seemed to consider that.

They walked home carrying their reusable bags, and she wanted to hold his hand but didn't. They weren't quite at the stage where they engaged in casual contact. Not like that. They hauled all their purchases into the private elevator, and he sat and watched while she made dinner. She ended up grateful for her apron, which kept food off her stomach, which was rounding more and more and becoming more of a nuisance.

"I'll cook for you another night. Although, I don't know how to make anything good."

"What do you mean?"

"The time of my life when I was actually shopping for myself, cooking for myself, it was very basic. A lot of hot dogs. Canned chili."

"Well, does any of it make you feel nostalgic?"

"I'm not sure about that."

"I'd eat it, if you ever wanted to share that part of your life with me. It must have been happy in some ways."

He frowned. "It was. I was on my own, but I had the ability to control my life."

"You're really very amazing," she said, dishing pasta onto plates for the two of them. "Very few people could have come out of what you experienced half so functional."

He laughed, and it sounded vaguely bitter. "I don't know that I would say I am *functional*."

"You're a billionaire," she said, smiling at him across the table.

"Ah, right," he said. "I am."

"We're going to have to buy a house," she said. "I was raised in the city, and I know that it can be a happy enough experience. But that isn't what I want for a child."

"And why is that?"

She shrugged. "There was always something missing. I don't know if it was grass. Not that we can't go to the park. Maybe it wasn't a place so much as a feeling. Family. But we are going to be a family, aren't we, Christos?"

He leaned forward and cupped her chin. "I have promised this, *agape*."

She smiled. She couldn't help herself. He had promised,

her difficult, hard man. And she knew he didn't give promises easily. "I know. And I trust you."

His nostrils flared slightly, the look in his eyes bordering on feral. "You trust me," he said, his voice rough.

"Yes," she said. "With everything. Don't you know? I was never with another man before you because I felt so insecure about myself. I didn't feel beautiful. I didn't feel like I had anything to offer. My mother ground me down into nothing. It might seem foolish to you, but—"

"It doesn't seem foolish. The absence of a mother in my life ruined me. And no, yours was not absent in quite the same way, but it still leaves scars."

"Yes," she whispered. He understood her. That feeling was... This was why she was so drawn to him. It was why she had been so drawn to him over text. And sometimes she found she had a barrier with him in person much of the time, even though this time with him had been idyllic.

But she had given him a part of herself in those conversations that she had never given to anyone, and then she had given him her body.

Trust.

Electric desire shivered over her skin.

She thought back to all those text conversations. They had been edgy. They had promised each other things in those texts that she had never thought she would do in person.

And yet with him everything felt possible. Necessary. Like she wanted to prove this. Like she wanted to test the desire between them and the bonds of trust that they were building.

She closed the distance between them, placing her hands on his chest. "I want you," she said.

"Sylvie," he said, his voice deep. "You do not have to give me sex. You are tired."

"I'm not giving you sex, Christos. I want to show you what trusting you means." She leaned in, her lips pressed to his. "Have you ever had a relationship like this?"

"No," he said, reaching up to grip her wrist, holding her steady. "I have never had a relationship."

"In some ways, you're a virgin," she said.

He chuckled. "Well, I wouldn't say that."

"Have you ever had a woman who trusted you enough to let her do whatever you wanted? Didn't you once say that you would spank me?"

The heat in his eyes flared, and desire mounted within her.

"Yes," he said, holding her chin in his hand. "I did say that I would spank you for being bad."

"You haven't done it."

He stoked her face, his dark eyes almost black. "Because you've been my good girl. Why does a good girl want to be treated like she's bad?"

As ever, his affirmation of her aroused her and warmed her all at once. Made her feel so good. So special. Made her feel like she was enough, which nothing and no one ever had before.

"I *am* your good girl," she said.

"Yes, you are. So good," he said, his voice strained.

"I just want you to make me feel. And I want to show you. I want to show you how much I trust you."

"I believe you."

"Has *anyone* ever trusted you?"

"Only you."

"Mine," he ground out.

Suddenly, she found herself being put over his knee. The movement was fluid. He moved his large hand over her back, down around her ass. "No," he said. "A woman has never trusted me with this."

"I didn't think so," she said. "But I would."

Desire roared through her. She enjoyed this. Pushing the edge of pain and pleasure. Just skirting it. It made her feel reckless and wild. While she was safe with him.

He raised his hand and brought it down on her backside.

She gasped, the glorious sting radiating between her thighs turning her on.

He brought his hand down on her backside again. And again.

She shivered, need racing through her.

He was bigger than her. He could cause harm if he wanted to, but that wasn't what this was. It was a demonstration of his care, of how she wanted him. All the ways she wanted him. And the way she trusted him to always only make her feel good, no matter what he did.

She was slick and wet and ready for him. She needed him more than she needed to breathe.

He stripped her lovely summer dress away from her body and brought her down to the floor next to the table.

He kissed his way over her skin. Lingering on her pregnant belly. *"Mine,"* he said.

Primal. Perfect. And when he claimed her she cried out, the sensation of him filling her, taking her, everything she needed. Everything she wanted.

This was family. Their connection. And yet it was more than that. But there were no words typed or spoken that could give more to this moment than him being inside her could.

"Christos. Baby." She said both names. Because she knew who he was. She knew he was hers.

He thrust deep within her, and she gripped his shoulders,

her nails digging into his skin. She wrapped her legs around his lean hips and tried to keep tempo with his movements.

And when they both reached their peak they fell together, shattering, and clinging to one another in the aftermath.

She wanted to freeze time. To stop here.

Because right now, they were happy. Right now, she had him.

She trusted him. But the world was a terrible place, and it had left him with terrible scars.

And she worried about what the future might hold. So she just wanted it all to stop. Because right now, everything was perfect.

But she knew that time would march on.

CHAPTER FIFTEEN

THE WEATHER BEGAN to turn hot, and it was mere weeks before her due date, summer in the sweltering city. She was starting to feel ungainly. Unattractive, even though Christos seemed to find her beautiful no matter what.

And she realized something abruptly as she got into the elevator that would take her home after a long day at work. She didn't feel insecure anymore. Not about her value, not about her looks.

That conversation with her mother had changed so many things.

The realization that she just wasn't what her mother wanted. And that she didn't want to be.

Coupled with the way Christos treated her: like she was special.

He treated her like everything she did was amazing.

She supposed it wasn't really fair. Because in many ways he was like a child. It didn't take a lot to amaze him. It made her feel guilty, actually. Because the act of making him dinner was like handing him gold for his hoard. He didn't say anything, but the fire always burned in his dark eyes. She started to realize how little had ever been done for him.

Basic care seemed to be his love language because he had been denied so much.

They didn't talk about feelings, but she could see them, burning brightly inside of him.

He was home when she arrived. In the kitchen, wearing an apron.

"Christos," she said. "Are you cooking?"

"Yes. Chili dogs, so I hope that it is okay with you."

Her stomach growled. "Yes. It is. That actually sounds amazing. Of course, I'll be hungry again an hour later, but then I get to choose something else to eat. It's a win-win."

They ate dinner, and then, he drew her a bath. Not too warm, but just enough. She sank down into the water, and he reached down and lifted up her foot, massaging the sore spots, working her swollen ankles.

She groaned. "I'm really not the woman you married."

"But you are," he said. "Do you know, it's such an interesting thing, because I was fascinated with you starting… maybe five years ago. That was probably when I began to notice you. You were always so opinionated."

"I wouldn't have thought you noticed me at all," she said, the wind pushed out of her lungs.

"I did. I told you that."

"Yes. You told me about your very crude sexual fantasy. But I didn't think—"

"No. I noticed more than that. I thought you seemed very bright. A worthy opponent."

"Why did you go after the publishing company so hard?"

He looked down. "I chose it as a target. And I have never known how to back down from a battle. I wanted to acquire it, and I was willing to wait all that time to do it."

"It was about the win, not about the company specifically."

"Correct." His voice got rough. "I've been fighting for so long. I don't know how to lose. Even if…even if there are no stakes. Because everything feels like it has high stakes. It just…it still does."

She pulled her foot from his grasp and turned so that she

was leaning against the lip of the tub. She lifted her hand and touched his face. "It doesn't here."

"Sylvie," he said his voice rough. "I don't believe in fate. I don't believe in mysterious forces at work in the universe. I've never believed in much of anything except my own grit. My own will to survive."

"Who could blame you?"

"But why did you find my phone? Why did I drop my phone? I have never done that. Not once in all my life. How could that happen?"

"I believe in fate," she said, holding his gaze, willing him to see just how she felt about him. Exactly how much she loved him. "And I believe I was supposed to find that phone. Something compelled me, something outside of myself, to send that text message so that you can get in touch with me."

"Because you wanted me," he said.

"I did," she whispered. "I hated myself for it, but I wanted you."

"And you still do. Even knowing me, you still do."

He was so hungry for that. How could he not be? This man who had been sold for a pittance by his father. He would always be that boy. She could see that, clearly, painfully. He would always be that boy who hadn't been loved enough.

She wanted him to feel how much she cared. She wrapped her arms around his neck and she kissed him, kissed him deep and long. He lifted her out of the tub, pressing her wet body against his fully clothed chest.

"You're being ridiculous," she said.

"All of it," he said, pushing his hands through her hair. "It's all like magic. And I don't believe in magic. But I believe in you, Sylvie Jones. You have given me something that I never imagined possible. I want… I need… I have always…" He kissed her, crushing her up against him.

He walked her into the bedroom. And just stood her in front of the mirror, his large frame behind her. "Look at you," he said, tilting her chin up. The first thing she saw was how her body had changed. All of her flaws. Her breasts were bigger, her stomach distended, with silvery stretch marks moving across it. She looked tired.

"You're a goddess," he said. "There is nothing that can compare."

And suddenly she realized that she wasn't the only one engaging in acts of healing.

He was doing the same to her.

Yes, she had just thought about all the ways he had changed her. The ways that he had helped her see her own beauty. But there was something deeper about this. Something different.

"I wanted you then. I wanted you when you were an obstinate, angry woman yelling at me on the top floor of your publishing house. I wanted you when you were a soothing voice in my phone. I want you now. Like this. How were you made for me in all these different ways? I will never understand it. Because I shouldn't be here. I shouldn't be standing here with you. I should be on an island in Greece. I should be six feet in the ground. Lost forever like so many of the other boys sold into that life. I should have become the same manner of monster as the man I fought in the end. I shouldn't be here standing with you, but I am. We did not find each other at those publishing parties. We didn't find each other in a boardroom. It took me losing my phone."

It seemed like he was having a revelation. Like something was shifting inside of him.

He bent down and kissed her neck, his hand moving up to cup her breast, cover it. "Sylvie," he whispered.

"I have wanted this for a long time."

He bent her forward at the waist, and she gasped, grasping the edge of the vanity. She saw him behind her, looking intense. He undid his belt and freed himself.

She shivered with need.

If he could show her like this, then she would take it like this. If this was how he was going to show her the feelings that existed inside of him, then she wanted it.

She was desperate for him. Always.

They had found ways to speak over the phone. And they had found a way to speak with their bodies. Someday, maybe he would be able to speak everything with words.

But until then...

He moved his hands over her breasts, then slid one down between her thighs. He began to tease her. Torment her. He tilted her hips back farther, and the blunt head of his arousal pressed against her slick entrance. He slid inside, deep. She gasped, and he gripped her hair as he began to thrust inside of her.

She loved this about him. That he maintained his intensity. That he hadn't stopped seeing her as a woman, as his lover, even as she took such an obvious maternal shape.

He revered her, enough to want her.

And she adored him for it.

He wrapped his arm around her midsection, supporting her stomach as he thrust deep. And then with his free hand he slapped her rear, and she yelped, the pleasurable sting sending lightning strikes across her skin.

"Oh, yes," he said. "I have wanted this."

This thing between them was a storm.

It was always intense when they were together. But this was something more.

Everything that wasn't spoken, everything left unsaid was burning between them like a wildfire.

And she realized then that this was where she was a gladiator. Fighting for him.

This was where they did battle. She was doing battle for his heart and soul. To show him that he could open up.

Because she believed that Christos had a deep and endless capacity for love.

It was the kind of man he was.

If he wasn't, then she wouldn't be in love with him.

So many people thought he was cold.

She had for the longest time.

But it was because everything inside of him was too great and too terrible for him to control, and that was what scared him.

So she unleashed her own wildness. And when they reached their peak, she cried out her pleasure.

He held her against him, his body protective over hers as his breathing returned to normal. She could feel his heart beating hard against her back.

He leaned down and bit her shoulder. "Mine," he said.

And he might as well have said *love*, because she knew for him it was all the same.

She turned to him and cupped his face. "Yours."

She wanted more from him. She wanted everything. But what they had was wonderful. And nobody had ever said that life was going to be perfect.

After all, her mother had said that she loved her father. But it hadn't been real.

Not the kind of love she wanted.

This... She wanted this. Whatever they called it.

So she let her husband carry her to bed. And she listened to him breathing until they both fell asleep.

CHAPTER SIXTEEN

CHRISTOS WAS AWAKENED from sleep by the sound of Sylvie being sick in the bathroom.

He stood up and crossed the room, pushing the door open.

She was down on her knees in front of the toilet.

"Oh, don't," she said. "It's awful. I have indigestion."

"You're unwell?"

"Yes," she said, standing and flushing the toilet, then grabbing her stomach. "I feel awful."

"It's not labor, is it?"

"No. I'm not due for three more weeks. And it's very common for women having their first baby to—" She stopped and doubled over. She was breathing hard. "I'm so dizzy. My vision is all blurry."

"We need to go to the doctor."

"No, we don't. I just have a bug or something."

"We need to get to a hospital," he said. He walked over to her and tilted her face up. "You look…"

Panic tore through him. He had seen people close to death before. He could see it in her eyes right now. "It is an emergency. We are leaving now."

She was in a nightgown, but they would only put her in a hospital gown when they arrived at the hospital. He pulled on a pair of pants, put on a shirt, only to avoid being arrested for indecency, and he took her hand and began to lead her out into the elevator.

"Christos…"

"Listen to me," he said. "I don't know what's wrong, but I know when something is serious. We have to go to the hospital."

Panic tore through him. He had to stay present for her. He had to.

Sylvie…

The past few months had been ideal. He felt like he was… happy.

He had never been happy. Not in his memory. She took care of him and she… She was perfect and lovely. She was so much more than he deserved. If he lost her…

He couldn't even think about it. He walked her into the front seat of his car, and they drove off into the night. Only belatedly did he think that he should have perhaps called an ambulance. He wove through traffic, grateful that it was the middle of the night so that it was somewhat diminished.

They pulled up to the hospital, and he left his car running as he went around to the passenger side. She was looking more pale, more fragile.

He unbuckled her and lifted her out of the car, carrying her in through the front. "My wife," he said as soon as he walked into the reception area. "She's pregnant, she… Something is wrong."

"Come in here," a woman in scrubs said, bringing them into a small room. "We'll take her vitals." She listened to Sylvie's heart and frowned, and then she got out a blood pressure cuff. "How many weeks?"

"I… Thirty-seven," he said.

Sylvie smiled. "You knew."

"Of course I know," he said. Of course he did. Nothing else mattered. Nothing but this. Nothing but her. Nothing but that future that had left him so terrified that he couldn't breathe only four months earlier.

And now he was…

The nurse finished taking Sylvie's blood pressure, and suddenly her movements became urgent.

"Her blood pressure is too high," she said. "I suspect preeclampsia. We're going to send her back right away."

"What?"

"If it is preeclampsia, then we need to deliver. Tonight."

"What is that?"

Everything began to move far too quickly into slowly all at once.

There were so many people everywhere, the organized chaos making his head spin.

He had been right. She was dying.

"The only cure for preeclampsia," the doctor said to him only ten minutes later, "is delivery. We're going to prep her for a C-section. If you want to be present—"

"I'm not leaving her," he said.

"Then, we'll help you prepare too."

"Christos," Sylvie said, her eyes filling with tears. "Just make sure that the baby—"

"I care about you," he said.

"And thank you," she said. "The baby has to be safe. Our son…"

He had a flash then, of something he had forgotten. His mother in a hospital bed.

Just take care of Christos…

No. He didn't want to remember that. It hurt too bad. It was too much.

He didn't want to remember how much his mother had loved him. How much she had begged his father to care for him in a way that he hadn't.

He had let him down.

He had let them both down.

He pushed the past away. He didn't have time to think about it now. "Sylvie," he said, moving forward, putting his hand on her face, "I'm not leaving you."

They gave him scrubs to wear. And he looked around the room and saw that he looked like everyone else in it. All the money, all the hardness in all the world hadn't protected him from this.

He had no status in here. He had nothing. Nothing but hope in a fate he didn't believe in. Nothing but prayers sent out to a divine force he had confidently stated wasn't there, wasn't listening.

There were heart monitors. On Sylvie. On the baby. And he could see them. His own heart moving in time with the lines on the machine.

Their three hearts beating together.

He moved to stand next to Sylvie's head. Getting down on his knees and cradling her face. He pressed his cheek to hers, and he listened. He breathed with her. His heart beat with hers.

He had survived all this time. All these years.

This was what he had always wanted to avoid.

Because he suddenly realized his survival meant nothing without her. If she wasn't here, then he didn't want to be here.

He would trade places with her.

He, who had protected his own life at all costs…

He squeezed his eyes shut and felt a tear slide down his cheek. He had not wept since he was a boy.

"I would trade places with you," he said. "I wish I could take this from you."

She didn't speak. And terror froze him.

Everything went quickly.

He could hear metal instruments. Was only half listening to the instructions the doctor was giving. And then, he heard it. A baby crying.

He stood slowly and looked as his son was brought into the world.

"I want to see him," Sylvie whispered.

"Let her see him," Christos said.

They brought the baby around, swaddled tightly in a blanket. And suddenly, he was being handed this small, delicate creature who was screaming and crying for a mother that was in danger.

And he was his father.

And all of a sudden he saw himself clearly.

He had always thought of himself as a gladiator.

The important thing to know about a gladiator was that a gladiator was a prisoner. Forced to fight for the entertainment of others.

He had freed himself, but he still thought of himself as a captive. He was still fighting.

He had not been living.

He had been engaging in bloody, pointless battles all these years because it was all he knew.

But standing there holding his tiny infant son, looking down at his wife, he understood something.

He had to walk out of the arena.

He would lay down his life for theirs. He would fight for them. But he would not fight just to prove he could survive. Not anymore.

His father had been a man fighting for his own survival. It made you small and mean and selfish. But Christos… Christos loved Sylvie more than he loved his own life.

He loved this child more than his own life.

He would never abandon them. He would live for them. He would not live just to survive.

He knelt down and placed the baby next to Sylvie's face. "There he is, my love," he said. "*Agape*, there is our son."

Sylvie looked up at him, her eyes filling with tears. "He's beautiful."

"Of course he is," he said. "You're his mother."

After that, Sylvie was stitched up and brought into a recovery room. Her vitals were being monitored closely, but everything seemed to be returning to normal. The delivery really had done its job.

She was sleeping peacefully, and he was pleased that there were machines ensuring that she was all right. He sat in a rocking chair near the bed holding their son, rocking him back and forth. And then he remembered.

His mother.

She had protected him. She had loved him.

And it was like a wall of ice inside of him began to melt as he looked down at his son. It was like looking at a child of his own had suddenly brought it all back. This was how his mother had felt about him. Because even if she was dying, she had thought only of him.

Just like Sylvie had done. Like she had begged for them to take care of the baby, not her.

He looked down at his son, and he understood that love.

He had never wanted to remember it because he hadn't wanted to miss it. But even now, as grief overwhelmed him, as a tear slid down his face, he was filled with a great hopeful joy.

Because suddenly he could feel everything. And yes, there was pain. Yes, there was sadness. But there was so much hope.

He placed their son in his basinet, and he moved to Sylvie's bedside. He knelt there, holding her hand. "I love you," he said. "And I think it was fate that brought us together. Something bigger than the both of us. I think, Sylvie Jones, you might have been why I survived."

Her eyes fluttered open. "You're flattering me," she said.

"No. I remembered something," he said.

"What?"

"My mother. She begged my father to take care of me. But he didn't. Sylvie, I believe my mother sent you to me. Because I survived all of those years, but until you, I hadn't lived. And you have taken care of me... You have no idea how much."

"Christos," she whispered. "My love. I love you so much. I have... I didn't want to chase you away by saying it."

That broke his heart. Because it would have. It would've chased him away. He had been too afraid. But...

"I would've come back. I would have. For the same reason I answered the text that first time. I didn't just need a hand to hold, Sylvie. I needed yours." He squeezed her hand.

"And I needed yours."

The baby whimpered in his bed. And Christos moved to pick him up. And for some reason, he moved his finger toward his son's tiny hand, and the boy curled his perfect fingers around it. Christos stopped, and he found himself weeping again, because apparently after thirty years of denying himself, he did nothing but weep now.

"I needed your hand," he said. "And I will be his. And I will be yours. I promise it. We didn't make vows when we got married. But I will make them to you now. Until now I lived for myself. And now I live for you."

"What should we name him?" she asked, looking up at him.

"Apollo," he said. "In the Greek pantheon, he was considered the god of healing. And I can think of nothing more fitting."

Sylvie smiled. "Apollo Onassis. He has your name. Because you started something new with it. And now we're continuing it. Together."

He kissed her on the forehead. And after a while, he could no longer keep his eyes open. He dozed in the chair for a time. And then his phone buzzed.

He picked it up and saw that he had a text.

Kid: I love you. I love you. I love you. I love you.

He smiled. And then he turned to her. "I love you too."

EPILOGUE

Kid: Your son is causing mayhem.

Baby: Impossible. It must be your son doing that.

CHRISTOS CAME DOWN the stairs and into the living room of the home he and Sylvie had shared for the past five years, his daughter on his hip, her chubby hand clutching the front of his shirt.

His six-year-old son Apollo was sitting nicely with a coloring book. While his four-year-old son Aries was causing what could only be described as *havoc*.

He looked at his daughter, Athena. "You would never do such a thing, would you, *agape*?"

"She absolutely will when she is more mobile."

Sylvie was looking at all three children with indulgence. Then she looked up at him. The same love was there. And yet there was more.

Christos had never known happiness like this. He hadn't even believed it existed. He had spent all of his life believing that love in any real or lasting form was a myth. He had told himself that, perhaps so he would not die of loneliness.

He looked around the room, at his wife, his children. He had not felt a moment of loneliness in more than six years.

It had been such a large part of him that he couldn't imagine himself without it. A protective cloak that he wore.

And now, he didn't need it anymore. He let the sun warm his skin and Sylvie's love warm his heart. He let the weight of his children in his arms ground him, remind him of why he lived.

That was the trouble with survival as a be-all and end-all. It stole the concept of what it meant to truly live. But he had found it with Sylvie. He had found it through love.

"It's time for bed, tiny monsters," he said.

He took his children upstairs, gave them a bath, tucked them into their beds.

He stood in the doorway with Sylvie by his side. He luxuriated in the warmth of this moment.

"I was right, you know," he said as he closed the door to his son's bedroom.

"Oh, were you?" She looked up at him with skeptical eyes. "About what this time, my lord?"

"If you're going to be sarcastic, then I won't tell you."

"No, please, Christos, I am dying to know all the ways in which you are correct."

"It was the right thing for you to marry me."

She paused, there in the hallway of their glorious old home. The one they had bought because of the yard.

It was very different to their life in the city. It was not a symbol of success or all the financial battles he had won.

It was a symbol of happiness. Of love.

It was the sort of safety he had only ever experienced for a small part of his childhood.

And now he got to live it, every day.

"It was," she said. "You're right."

He smiled to himself as they walked to their bedroom.

He began to get undressed as Sylvie went into the bathroom. Putting various creams on her face he always maintained she did not need. But he thought they smelled nice, and they made her happy.

His phone buzzed on his nightstand.

Kid: If you were here I would kiss you.

Instantly, desire roared through his veins. This was a game they continued to play.

They had played it at various hotels across the world, in fact. Occasional anonymous meetings. Sexual chats on their phones.

This was still part of who they were.

"You could just kiss me," he called from the bedroom.

Sylvie walked in, wearing a translucent night gown that he hadn't seen before.

She had only grown more beautiful over the years. Each child had added to her lovely figure, just as the years had added more gray to his hair. They only loved each other all the more.

He only wanted her all the more.

"Baby," she said, "I think you should kiss me."

"I believe I will." He crossed the space between them and pulled his wife into his arms. And he kissed her. With all of the need and desire pent up inside of him. There was a time when texting was the only way he could reach her. But not now. Now he could have her whenever he chose, touch her, kiss her, love her.

He had been one thing for so long.

In this life, he was many things.

Sylvie's husband, a father. He still owned a business. Sylvie was his wife, a mother, the CEO of a publishing company.

But together they would always be Kid and Baby. They would always have this connection. The very first thing that brought them together. That hand that Sylvie had reached out to him.

A lost phone had become a whole world.

Christos had never believed in fate.

He did now. For it had taken him in the palm of its hand and had saved him for this.

For her.

"Come now," he said. "Let's go to bed."

* * * * *

Did you fall in love with After-Hours Heir*?*
Then you're sure to enjoy these other
passion-fueled stories
by Millie Adams!

Greek's Forbidden Temptation
Her Impossible Boss's Baby
Italian's Christmas Acquisition
Billionaire's Bride Bargain
His Highness's Diamond Decree

Available now!

MILLS & BOON®

Coming next month

THE HEIR AFFAIR
Heidi Rice

'Poppy,' he shouted.

The girl's head whipped around, responding to her name. Joy exploded in Xander's chest, as the need shocked him. Those eyes, that face. It was her. But as she turned toward him, depositing the tray back on the bar with a clash of glasses, his greedy gaze swept down her figure.

His steps faltered. And he blinked, exhilaration turning to shock, then confusion, then another blast of hunger. A compact bulge distended her apron where he had once been able to span her flat, narrow waist with a single hand.

He reached her at last, but it felt as if he were walking through waist-high water now as he tried to make sense of all the warring reactions going off inside his head.

But then his gaze snagged on her belly again—and the only question that mattered broke from his dry lips.

'Is it mine?' he demanded.

Flags of color slashed across her cheeks, but all he heard in her tone was the sting of regret when she whispered, 'Yes.'

Continue reading

THE HEIR AFFAIR
Heidi Rice

Available next month
millsandboon.co.uk

Copyright ©2025 Heidi Rice

COMING SOON!

We really hope you enjoyed reading this book.
If you're looking for more romance
be sure to head to the shops when
new books are available on

Thursday 28th August

To see which titles are coming soon, please visit
millsandboon.co.uk/nextmonth

MILLS & BOON

FOUR BRAND NEW BOOKS FROM
MILLS & BOON MODERN

The same great stories you love, a stylish new look!

OUT NOW

Eight Modern stories published every month, find them all at:

millsandboon.co.uk

afterglow BOOKS

Afterglow Books is a trend-led, trope-filled list of books with diverse, authentic and relatable characters, a wide array of voices and representations, plus real world trials and tribulations. Featuring all the tropes you could possibly want (think small-town settings, fake relationships, grumpy vs sunshine, enemies to lovers) and all with a generous dose of spice in every story.

♪ @millsandboonuk
◉ @millsandboonuk
afterglowbooks.co.uk
#AfterglowBooks

For all the latest book news, exclusive content and giveaways scan the QR code below to sign up to the Afterglow newsletter:

SCAN ME

afterglow BOOKS

THE CODE FOR LOVE

Her perfect plan has a gorgeous glitch...

NEW YORK TIMES BESTSELLING AUTHOR
ANNE MARSH

✈ International

⛅ Grumpy/sunshine

🎭 Fake dating

OUT NOW

To discover more visit:
Afterglowbooks.co.uk

LET'S TALK
Romance

For exclusive extracts, competitions and special offers, find us online:

- **f** MillsandBoon
- **X** @MillsandBoon
- **◉** @MillsandBoonUK
- **♪** @MillsandBoonUK

Get in touch on 01413 063 232

For all the latest titles coming soon, visit
millsandboon.co.uk/nextmonth

OUT NOW!

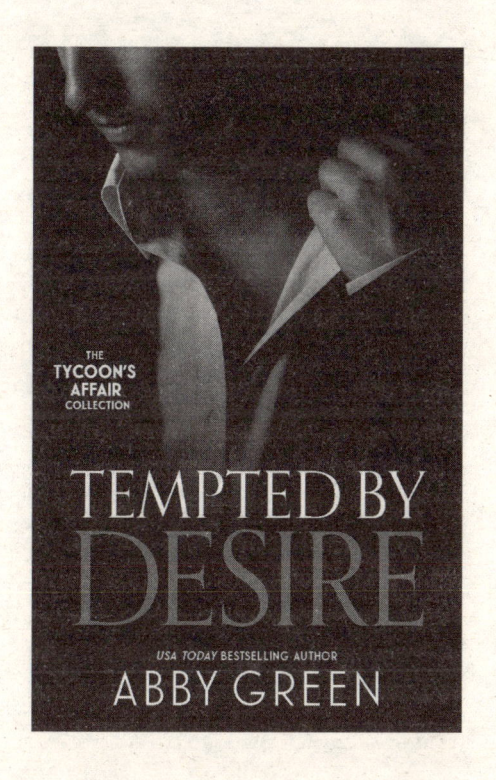

THE TYCOON'S AFFAIR COLLECTION

TEMPTED BY DESIRE

USA TODAY BESTSELLING AUTHOR
ABBY GREEN

Available at
millsandboon.co.uk

MILLS & BOON

OUT NOW!

A DARK ROMANCE SERIES

Thorns of Revenge

TARYN LEIGH TAYLOR · ABBY GREEN · JACKIE ASHENDEN

Available at
millsandboon.co.uk

MILLS & BOON